I0676321

Redeemed: Book 2 of The Crest Ridge Trilogy

The Crest Ridge Trilogy, Volume 2

PD Norris

Published by PD Norris, 2025.

REDEEMED: BOOK 2 OF THE CREST RIDGE TRILOGY

First edition. June 21, 2025.

Copyright © 2025 PD Norris.

ISBN: 979-8992133349

Written by PD Norris.

Table of Contents

Chapter 1

Marcus never thought owning his own auto shop would feel so lonely. On most days, the place was alive with the clatter of tools, the hiss of air compressors, and the hum of engines being brought back to life. It was work that made sense to him. He enjoyed using his hands to fix things. Cars didn't judge and didn't ask questions he didn't want to answer. But when the shop closed, and the noise faded, the silence crept in. That's when the past came knocking.

Tonight was one of those nights. He sat at his workbench, staring at a carburetor he didn't need to fix. The shop smelled of motor oil and sweat, but it was better than going home to his empty apartment. He wiped his grease-stained hand across his jaw, lost in thought.

The hum of the overhead light buzzed like a distant warning, a reminder that silence wasn't always peaceful. His fingers hovered over his tools, twitching with the muscle memory of repairs he'd done a hundred times before. But there was no urgency tonight. No customer waiting, no deadline pressing down on him. Just the ache in his chest and the questions he couldn't answer.

He leaned back on the stool and looked at the shelves lined with spare parts and half-finished projects. Everything in here had a purpose—unlike him lately. The radio in the corner crackled with static before settling on a slow blues tune, and for a moment, he closed his eyes to let the music fill the empty corners of his mind.

But then the memory returned. Her voice. That final time the family saw her leave for a date and never came back. Niyah. Her name was in his heart and he carried it everywhere. He couldn't outrun what had happened and couldn't change what he did. After closing up his auto shop, he'd return to his modest apartment on the edge of Crest Ridge. He took a long shower to wash away the grease and grime, and sat on his couch with a cold beer.

The living room was only lit by the orange glow of a streetlamp filtering through the blinds. He kicked his feet up on the worn coffee table, still dressed in sweatpants and a threadbare T-shirt, the steam from the shower already fading off his skin.

He flipped through the channels absently. He wasn't really watching, just needed something to fill the silence. The beer tasted bitter, but it was cold, and that was enough. He leaned back and rested his head against the cushions as his mind drifted between exhaustion and the low hum of loneliness that never really left. The old clock on the wall ticked louder than it should have. Somewhere outside, a dog barked. He thought about calling someone, but couldn't think of a single person who wouldn't pick up out of obligation rather than want.

Eventually, the TV screen went dark and timed out from inactivity. The room fell into a hush that pressed against his ears. The sharp trill of his phone pierced the quietness of the night. Marcus groaned as he fumbled for it on the nightstand. The clock glowed an unforgiving **2:47 a.m.** in the darkness. *Who could be calling at this hour?*

He answered without checking the caller ID.

"Marcus? It's Myia." Her voice was strained, and she sounded like she had bad news.

"What's wrong?" He sat up, already bracing for her answer.

"It's Jordan. He's been arrested. They're saying he robbed a store."

"What? That doesn't make any sense. Where is he?"

"At the police department. They called me because his phone was dead. Marcus... they're saying it was armed robbery."

The words hit him like a punch to the gut. *Jordan? Armed robbery? No way.* "I'm on my way."

Driving to the police station felt unreal, like a nightmare. Lost in thought, Crest Ridge's streets became a meaningless streak as he sped past. *Jordan? Robbing a store? It didn't add up. Sure, his brother had a wild streak, but he wasn't a criminal.* Marcus had worked hard to keep him out of trouble and to give him a chance.

He pulled into the parking lot, slammed the door shut, and strode toward the entrance. The police station was eerily quiet at this hour as he looked around the parking lot. He pushed open the heavy glass doors and walked in. At the front desk, a tired-looking officer barely glanced up.

"I'm here for Jordan Carter," Marcus said.

The officer sighed and flipped through some papers. "He's in holding. Are you family?"

"I'm his brother."

The officer stood and gestured for him to follow. They walked down a narrow hallway lined with holding cells. Marcus's pulse quickened when he saw Jordan slouched on a bench behind the bars, his head down, shoulders tense.

"J," he called out as he gripped the cold metal bars.

He looked up with his bloodshot eyes. A fresh bruise marred his cheek, and his knuckles were raw, as if he'd been in a fight.

"Marcus..." Jordan's voice was barely above a whisper. He sounded exhausted.

"What the hell happened?"

"I didn't do it." he said trembling. "I swear I didn't."

"Then what are you doing in here?"

"It's a long story."

Marcus turned to the officer. "What's he being charged with?"

"Armed robbery," the officer said flatly. "Corner Mart on Third Street. Witnesses say he was there with two others. Surveillance footage puts him at the scene."

"That's impossible. He wouldn't—"

"Tell it to the judge."

"Can I speak to him alone?"

"You can talk to him for five minutes," the officer said before walking away.

Marcus waited until they were alone before leaning closer to the bars. "Why didn't you call Mom?"

"She's been through enough. You know that."

"That's not an answer," he pressed.

"She had that health scare a few months ago. Her blood pressure's still high. You think I wanted to dump this on her? She doesn't need the stress."

"She's going to find out. You know that, right? What do you think is going to happen when she does?"

"I was trying to protect her, okay? I didn't want to be the reason..." He trailed off.

"Look, let me figure out what's going on. But you need to be honest with me. Everything, J. If I'm going to help you, I need the truth."

"Okay. I'll tell you everything. Just... get me out of here. Please."

"Time's up. Let's go."

Marcus didn't speak as he walked out of the interview room. He made his way to the front of the station, where a rookie officer sat behind a desk, bored and barely looking up from his paperwork. Marcus gave him Jordan's full name and the file number, and the officer grunted in acknowledgment before disappearing into the back to check with the sergeant on duty.

As the minutes stretched, Marcus ran a hand down his face and exhaled slowly. He'd told Myia he'd stay out of this kind of mess. But this wasn't just any case. It was Jordan. Family. And family didn't get abandoned when things got hard.

He glanced at the station door, then at the hallway behind him, as if either might offer a sign of what he was supposed to do next. Answers were coming. He just hoped they weren't worse than the questions.

Marcus leaned against the wall in the station's lobby and waited for the officer to return. He was trying to piece together what Jordan might have gotten himself into. He knew his little brother wasn't an innocent man, but he couldn't believe he was capable of something like this. There had to be more to the story. Robbery didn't sound like him, but then again, he wasn't exactly predictable.

When the officer returned, Marcus straightened. "Can I see the security footage?"

"Not unless you're his lawyer," the officer replied.

"Then I'll find another way."

"Also," the officer added as he read the file, "there's a gun linked to it. We ran fingerprints, and your brother's came back as a match."

The words hit him like a punch to the gut. "Fingerprints?"

"Yeah. The clerk said the suspect pulled it during the robbery. It was recovered a few blocks away."

"He doesn't even own a gun."

"Maybe not," the officer said with a shrug. "But his prints don't lie."

Marcus stood still, jaw tight, heart pounding. Jordan was reckless sometimes, but a stickup? A gun? That wasn't him. It

He forced his tone calm. "Where was the weapon found?"

"Alley off Langston and Fifth."

"Cameras?"

The officer rubbed the back of his neck. "We're checking. But with half the streetlights out and the clerk too rattled to give a full description, this might come down to forensics. And right now, the prints point to your brother."

Marcus didn't answer. Didn't argue. Just turned and walked off. He knew the system. Knew how easy it was to become a name on a list, a number on a docket.

Back at the shop, Marcus pulled out his laptop and started digging. Third Street wasn't far from here. It was close enough that

Jordan might have passed by. But robbing the place? Using a gun? He needed proof.

Myia walked in. "Did you see him? What did he say?"

"He says he didn't do it."

"Of course, he's going to say that. Marcus, what if he really did—"

"No," he snapped. "Not Jordan. I know him. There's something off about this."

"And what are you going to do? Play detective again? You know where that led last time."

Her words stung, but he didn't flinch. He couldn't let his brother go down for something he didn't do. Whatever it took, he'd find the truth.

"I'll figure this out," he said firmly. "I'm not letting him go through this alone."

"Just... be careful, Marcus. For once."

He leaned back in his chair. He didn't know where the truth ended and the lies began, but he was going to find out. Jordan's life depended on it.

Behind him, she gathered her coat. "If you're going to do this, at least let me know what you find. Don't shut me out again."

He gave her a slight nod, not trusting himself to say more. The last time he'd chased the truth, it had nearly destroyed him. But this time, someone else's future was on the line. As she walked away, he pulled out his phone and texted Tyson,

I need you to dig into this for me. Corner Mart robbery, Third Street. Anything you can find.

On it. You okay?

Marcus paused, then responded.

Not really.

He leaned back in his chair and rubbed his temples. He didn't know where the truth ended and the lies began, but he was going to find out. Jordan's life was on the line. He went to the notes app and began a new list.

Step one: Retrace Jordan's timeline.

Step two: Find the missing piece.

Chapter 2

The following evening, the family gathered at Zara's apartment. Myia, arms crossed, paced the small living room; Tyson, slouched in the corner, listened intently, earbuds around his neck. It was obvious Zara was worried as she put down the sweet tea. "I just don't understand how this happened," she whispered. "Jordan's never been... violent."

"He's not violent," Marcus insisted, standing by the window, hands in his pockets.

"The police disagree," snapped Myia. "What about the fingerprints on the gun?Can you explain that?"

"I don't know yet," he admitted. "But I'm going to find out."

"I'm sorry, but you don't just end up in the middle of a robbery by accident. Maybe he got himself into something he shouldn't have, and now we're all supposed to pretend he's innocent?"

"Hey, that's not fair, Myia," Tyson said, interrupting.

"It's not about being fair," she shot back. "It's about facing reality."

Marcus stepped forward and spoke in a commanding tone. "He didn't do this. I don't know how his prints got on that gun, but I know my brother. He's not a thief, and he's not a criminal."

"Knowing someone doesn't mean they can't surprise you. People change, Marcus. Sometimes not for the better."

"Seriously?" Tyson snapped. "He's your cousin. You're supposed to have his back."

"And you're supposed to use your brain," Myia retorted. "This isn't about loyalty; it's about facts. And the facts don't look good for Jordan."

Marcus intervened. "Enough. Both of you."

The tension crackled in the room as silence settled. He turned to Myia with a steely expression. "You're right. This isn't about loyalty. It's about finding the truth. And the truth is, he's being set up."

"Set up?" she scoffed. "By who? For what?"

"I don't know yet," he answered. "But I'm going to figure it out. I'm not asking you to believe me. I'm asking you to trust that I'm not going to let this go."

Zara finally voiced her thoughts for the first time since the argument began. "I believe you. How can we help?"

"Just... don't give up on him yet. I need to talk to Jordan again, dig into that gun, and figure out who the hell is really behind this. But the last thing he needs is to feel like his family's already written him off."

Myia folded her arms again, opting to keep her thoughts to herself. Tyson nodded firmly at Marcus. "I'm with you," he said. "Whatever you need."

He smiled faintly. "Thanks, Ty."

Myia followed Marcus to the door as he was leaving later on. She paused briefly before she spoke. "I don't want to believe Jordan could do something like this. But what if you're wrong?"

"Then I'll deal with it. But until I know for sure, I'm not turning my back on him."

"Just... be careful, okay? You've got your own ghosts. Don't let this drag you down too."

He nodded and stepped out into the cool night air. The door clicked shut behind him, sealing the tension inside. He climbed into his truck and pulled away from the curb. He didn't have a plan yet. Only instincts and a whole lot of questions, but he had to start somewhere.

On his drive back to the shop, Marcus replayed her words in his head. head. His own ghosts had never really left him, but he'd learned to live with them. It seemed, at that moment, that they were returning for more. He was determined to help find out the truth. He thought to himself, *"What kind of brother is he if he couldn't save Jordan?"*

The house was quieter after Marcus left. Near the window, Myia watched the dark street from her armchair as Tyson scrolled on his phone. Zara was in the kitchen washing dishes that were already clean.

"You didn't have to come at him like that," Tyson said, breaking the silence.

Myia didn't turn around. "He needs to hear the truth. You all do."

"And what truth is that? That you're too busy judging Jordan to actually help him?"

She turned to face her younger brother. "Don't start with me, Ty. This isn't about judging Jordan. It's about being realistic. If his prints are on that gun, that's not some coincidence."

"And you're so quick to believe that, huh? What, you think Marcus just taught him how to be a criminal or something?"

Myia froze for a moment. She hadn't wanted to say it out loud, but the thought had been nagging at her ever since she heard the news.

"Marcus has always been protective of Jordan," she said slowly, choosing her words carefully. "Sometimes too protective. And after everything that happened..."

"What are you trying to say?"

"You know exactly what I'm saying," she said quietly.

Tyson stood up. "You've got no right. None, to be throwing that at him. He's done nothing but try to move on. And Jordan? He doesn't even know what really happened back then."

With a raised eyebrow, Myia's suspicion flared. "Doesn't he?"

Tyson's silence was answer enough.

"You've always been good at deflecting," she continued. "But you can't sit there and tell me you've never wondered if Marcus had something to do with... what happened to Malik."

"Stop it," Tyson snapped, raising his voice. "You don't know anything about what happened. You weren't there."

"And neither were you," she shot back. "But I know enough. I remember how he responded to me when the news article came out. And I know how you and Jordan were both suddenly so loyal to him, like you owed him something."

Tyson remained silent. His eyes were fixed on the floor, the weight of old memories pressing down like lead. She watched him, arms folded, waiting for a response.

Finally, she said gently. "You think protecting him is the same as protecting the truth, but it's not. And if you're not willing to say it, I will. Something happened back then, and it's still affecting everything now. We can't keep pretending it didn't."

"It's not that simple," he replied. "If it were, maybe we wouldn't all be standing here wondering who to trust."

Zara stepped into the room, wiping her hands on a dish towel. "That's enough, both of you," she said firmly. "This family doesn't need more division."

"Division?" Myia laughed bitterly. "There's been division ever since my mom was killed. We just don't talk about it because no one wants to upset the peace."

"Myia, we all lost her. Not just you. And Marcus... he's been carrying his own guilt for years. Whether it's deserved or not, I don't know. But dragging it up now, when Jordan's in trouble, isn't going to help anyone."

"I'm not trying to make things worse. I'm trying to understand why this family is so determined to protect secrets instead of facing the truth."

Tyson yelled. "You want the truth? Fine. The truth is, Marcus would die for this family. He's been through hell, and he still shows up for us every single time. You don't have to trust him, but don't act like he hasn't earned the benefit of the doubt."

She was taken back with her brother's outburst. "I'm not saying he hasn't. But maybe it's time we stop expecting him to carry the weight for everyone else. Maybe it's time we all start telling the truth, even if it hurts."

Zara agreed. "Then let's start now. No more half-truths. No more silence. Whatever's coming, we face it together. As a family."

Myia looked back out the window and wondered if she could trust Marcus. But the shadows of the past loomed too large, and she couldn't shake the feeling that they were all still paying for secrets no one was willing to confess. As the night wore on, she found herself alone, staring at an old photo of the family. Her mother Niyah was front and center with her bright smile lighting up the frame. Marcus stood off to the side, looking serious even back then.

"What are you hiding?" she whispered, tracing her mother's face in the photo. "And how much longer are we all going to pay for it?"

Her gaze stayed fixed on the photo. She traced her thumb over her mother's smile like it could bring her back or unlock the answers that had stayed buried for too long. She thought about the night the police told her that they found her mother's body. The way the words hadn't made sense at first, how the air had been knocked from her lungs. The chaos that followed, the cold stares, the half-finished sentences. And then the silence. Deafening, deliberate silence. As if speaking about it might unravel everything they'd tried so hard to hold together.

And then there was the memorial. The way her cousins had suddenly "had to run an errand" just before the service. She remembered watching them slip away, whispering behind closed doors, avoiding her eyes when they returned. At the time, she'd told herself it was nothing. But now? Now she wasn't so sure. She knew they were keeping a secret from her. She wondered if that secret was what was surfacing, slowly, dangerously, spilling into their lives one lie at a time, poisoning trust, rewriting memories, turning family into strangers.

She placed the photo back on the shelf with trembling fingers. Her shoulders shook as the tears came, soft and sudden, years of grief cracking through her like a dam finally giving way. They had all moved on. All except her.

Chapter 3

Janelle had always prided herself on her intuition. It wasn't just a mother's instinct. It was an unshakable connection she felt with her children. For two days now, something had felt... wrong. It started with silence. Jordan always called or texted, even if it was just to check in. But this time, there was nothing. She'd sent messages—simple ones at first: *"How's it going?"* Then more urgent: *"Is everything okay?"* The lack of response gnawed at her.

A quiet panic began to build by the second evening. She tried to make sense of it. *Maybe he's busy. Maybe his phone died. He'll call tomorrow.* But the ache in her chest wouldn't go away. Now sitting at the kitchen table sipping on some chamomile tea, her uneasiness reached a boiling point. She reached for her phone and dialed his number. One ring... two rings... then it went straight to voicemail.

"It's your mom," she said, trying to keep her voice steady. "I haven't heard from you in a couple of days. Call me back as soon as you get this, okay? Love you."

She placed the phone down and watched it, as if willing it to ring. The unexpected buzz of the phone made her grab it quickly. But it turned out to be Marcus.

"Marcus," she called out, her voice hurried and strained. "Have you heard from your brother? I've been trying to reach him."

There was a pause on the other end. "Ma..."

Her heart sank at the tone in his voice. "What is it? Is he okay?"

"He's... he's not hurt," Marcus said carefully.

"Then what's going on?" she demanded, her voice trembling.

"Jordan's been arrested," he admitted. "It happened two nights ago."

"Arrested?" she echoed, disbelief and fear mingling in her voice. "For what?"

"Armed robbery," he said quietly.

Her knees went weak. She gripped the edge of the table and lowered herself into a chair. "No... no, that's not possible. He wouldn't—he couldn't do something like that."

"I don't think he did. But the police found a gun with his fingerprints on it."

"Fingerprints? How? He doesn't own a gun!"

"I don't know, Ma. But I'm going to figure it out. I promise you that."

"Why didn't he call me? Why didn't he tell me?"

"He didn't want to worry you. After your health scare..."

"I'm his mother. I should have been the first person he called."

"I know," he said softly. "But you know him. He thought he was protecting you."

The tears spilled over as she covered her mouth to muffle a sob. "This is my worst nightmare. My baby... in jail, accused of something so terrible. What do we do, Marcus?"

"We fight. I'm already on it. I've got a lawyer looking into it, and I'm going to do my own digging. I'll clear his name, Ma. You just have to trust me."

"I can't lose him. Not like I lost Niyah."

"You won't. I promise you. Whatever it takes, I'm going to bring him home."

"I know you will. But you need to keep me in the loop. No more secrets."

"I won't keep anything from you," Marcus said in a steady voice. "Not this time."

"Let me know the moment you hear anything,"

"I will. I'll check in tomorrow. Maybe sooner if the lawyer gets back to me."

"Okay. Be careful, Marcus."

"You too, Ma."

After the call ended, Janelle sat in silence, staring at her phone. She replayed Marcus's words in her mind, but they did little to calm her. She looked out the window at the street where Jordan used to play ball with his cousins. It made her heart heavy with memories and fear.

"I know my son didn't do this," she whispered. "And I'll do whatever it takes to get him out."

She looked toward the kitchen where Darren was sitting with the morning paper. He sipped his coffee, blissfully unaware of the storm about to hit. Taking a deep breath, she walked in and stood by the counter. "Darren, we need to talk."

Her tone made him lower the paper immediately. "What's wrong?"

"It's Jordan," she said, her voice trembling. "He's been arrested."

Darren's brow furrowed as he set down his mug. "Arrested? For what?"

"Armed robbery."

He stared at her, stunned. "That doesn't make any sense. He wouldn't do something like that."

"I know," she said as she sat down across from him. "I just got off the phone with Marcus and he doesn't think he did it either. But the police found a gun with his fingerprints on it."

"How is that even possible? He doesn't have a gun."

"I don't know," Janelle admitted. "But Marcus said he's going to find out. He's trying to prove Jordan's innocence."

"There's got to be more to this. Jordan wouldn't throw his life away like that. Not after everything he's worked for."

"I keep telling myself the same thing, but the evidence, at least what little I've been told, doesn't look good."

"Have you seen him?"

"Not yet. But I know in my heart he didn't do it. I believe him, Darren. I have to."

"Alright. First thing we do is find out exactly what the police have. Evidence, witness statements, everything. If Marcus is already looking into it, we double that effort. Jordan's not going down for something he didn't do. Not on our watch."

"Thank you. I just... I didn't know how to tell you. I didn't want to believe it myself."

"We're going to get through this," he said firmly. "We're going to bring our boy home."

"We will. But we need to stay calm. Panicking isn't going to help him."

"I'm going to call Dad. He needs to know."

A short while later, she was in the den on the phone. On the other end, her father's deep voice was heard.

"Hey, my sweet girl. Everything alright?"

A tearful "No, Dad," escaped her lips. "It's Jordan. He's been arrested."

There was a pause, and then her father's tone grew sharp. "Arrested? What for?"

"Armed robbery."

"That doesn't sound like him. There's got to be a mistake."

"That's what we think too," she said. "But the police found a gun with his fingerprints on it. Dad, I don't know what to do. I feel so helpless."

Her father's sigh crackled through the phone line. "You listen to me, Janey. Jordan's a good boy. We both know that. If Marcus is digging, then he'll find the truth. But you've got to stay strong. For Jordan and for yourself."

"I'm trying. It's just... hard. Everything feels like it's falling apart."

"You're not alone, sweetheart. We'll get through this together. And if Jordan says he didn't do this, and I believe he didn't, we'll prove it."

Janelle found comfort in the sound of her father's voice. "Thank you. I just... I keep thinking about the look on his face when he was little. When he was scared."

"He's still your boy," her father said gently. "No matter how old he gets. No matter how big the world tries to make him feel, he's still your son. And he still needs you."

"I know," she whispered. "And I want to be strong for him. I just hate feeling like I'm standing on the outside of it all."

"You won't be for long," he assured her. "You get involved. You ask questions. You stay close. That's how you fight for him."

There was a pause before he spoke again. "Have you spoken to a lawyer yet?"

"Marcus said he know one," she replied. "But I haven't talked to them myself."

"You need to. Make sure they're doing everything they can for Jordan. And tell Marcus, if he needs backup, I'm here."

"Thank you, Dad."

"Always. You call me if you need anything, alright? Anything."

"I will."

After they hung up, she sat back and stared at the family photos on the wall. One of them showed a younger Jordan, grinning with a basketball in his hands. He had sweat on his brow and pride in his eyes smiling as the sun was setting behind him. It had him looking like the world was his for the taking. She reached out and lightly touched the frame as her fingers trembled. So much had changed since that moment, but one thing hadn't. Her love for him. Her belief in him. She brushed away the tears in her eyes. "I won't let them take you away," she whispered. "Not without a fight."

Chapter 4

Marcus leaned against his truck as he watched the small convenience store. The bright yellow "Open 24 Hours" sign flickered in the afternoon sun. This was where it had all gone down. The place Jordan supposedly robbed at gunpoint. He inhaled deeply before entering; the bell chimed as he stepped inside. The counter clerk, a thin man nearing 40, was glued to his phone. Marcus looked around slowly. Chips, soda, and cheap souvenirs crammed the small store's shelves.

"Can I help you?"

Marcus said, "Yeah," as he walked toward the counter. "I heard about the robbery the other night. That's wild. You okay?"

"It wasn't that big a deal. Didn't even have a chance to get scared."

"Really? Someone points a gun at you, and you're not scared?"

"I've seen worse. Plus, it all happened so fast. Dude came in, waved the gun around, took the cash, and bolted. Wasn't like in the movies or anything."

"Right," Marcus said, leaning casually against the counter. "So, the guy, they say it was my brother, what did he look like?"

"Tall, dark, skinny. Hoodie, mask. Looked like half the guys that come in here after dark."

He frowned. The description was vague. Too vague. "You're sure it was him?"

The clerk gave him a sideways look. "Cops seemed sure enough. They got him, didn't they?"

"Yeah, they did," he said. "But that doesn't mean he did it."

The man shrugged again, clearly uninterested in the small talk. "Cops got their guy. Not really my problem, you know?"

He held back his frustration. "Mind if I look around a bit?"

The clerk waved a hand dismissively. "Knock yourself out."

Marcus walked the aisles slowly taking everything in. The place seemed ordinary, nothing stood out. But there was something about the clerk's attitude that bothered him. He was too calm and too indifferent for someone who'd been robbed at gunpoint just days ago.

He made his way to the security camera mounted in the corner and glanced back at the counter. "That camera working when it happened?"

"Yeah," the clerk said, not looking up.

"Mind if I see the footage?"

The clerk finally looked up, narrowing his eyes. "Why?"

Marcus shrugged. "Just curious. Figured it'd clear things up."

The clerk nodded toward a small office in the back. "Knock yourself out. It's all on the system."

Marcus sat scrolling through the footage in his cramped office. According to the video's timestamp, the crime took place just after 2 am. He watched as a figure in a dark hoodie entered the store, moved straight to the counter, and waved a gun. However, as he reviewed the footage, a detail caught his eye. There was barely a reaction from the clerk. No flinch, no panic. His movements were almost robotic as he opened the register and gave over the cash.

"Too calm."

He replayed it again. This time he focused on the suspected robber. The figure moved quickly but without any urgency, like they were going through the motions. He leaned closer. There was something about the way the clerk handed over the cash, like he'd done it before. Then he noticed something else. The robber never pointed the gun directly at the clerk. It was waved around. More for show than as a real threat.

"This doesn't feel right."

Using a USB drive he had, he copied the footage and left the office. The clerk gave him a cursory glance as he returned.

"I appreciate you letting me see the footage," Marcus said with a strained smile.

"No problem," the clerk responded and went back to being on his phone.

Suspicion weighed heavily on Marcus as he exited the store. Something about this robbery didn't add up, and he had a feeling the clerk wasn't as innocent as he seemed. Sliding into his truck, Marcus started the engine and glanced back at the store. "You know more than you're saying," he said.

The engine idled as he stared at the small USB drive in his hand. The footage he had copied from the store was starting to itch at his mind. Something was off, but he couldn't put his finger on it. His next stop needed to be someone trustworthy who could analyze and make sense of it. A technician, maybe. Someone capable of analyzing each frame and providing him with answers. Only one person came to his mind: Rick.

Rick Harris was an old friend from high school. In town, he ran a small tech repair shop, fixing all sorts of devices from phones to computers, and he had an uncanny ability to spot problems others missed. If anyone was going to find something the cops missed in that footage, it would be Rick.

Marcus started the truck and headed toward Rick's shop. His thoughts kept going to Jordan's arrest. His brother didn't belong in this mess. He just couldn't. But the more he dug, the clearer it became that this wasn't just a random mistake. There was something intentional about all of it.

As he pulled into the parking lot, he saw the "Open" sign on the door. Despite its worn appearance, the small building was one of the few businesses in Crest Ridge that had never closed. Jogging up the steps, he pushed open the door, causing the bell to chime. At the counter, Rick was working on a laptop as his curly hair kept falling into his eyes. He looked up as Marcus entered.

"Well, well, if it isn't the one and only Marcus," he said with a smirk. "What's up, man?"

"I need your help," he held up the USB drive. "Got something I need you to look at."

Rick raised an eyebrow, but his interest piqued as he handed him the drive. "This doesn't look like your typical file. What is it?"

"Surveillance footage of a crime that my brother was arrested for. I don't think he did it, but something about it's bothering me. I need you to take a look and see if you can find anything unusual."

With a nod, Rick inserted the USB drive into his laptop and began typing furiously. The video showed up on the screen. He was silent for a short while before pausing it.

"Something doesn't seem right here," he pointed at the screen. "You see this?"

Marcus stared at the screen. The robber was standing at the counter holding a gun. The clerk appeared completely unfazed.

"Yeah," Marcus said, "What about it?"

Rick fast-forwarded the footage to the part where the clerk handed over the money. "Look at the clerk's eyes. He's not even looking at the robber. He's looking down like he's counting the money or something. But that's not the weird part."

"Then what is?"

With a few clicks, Rick zoomed in on the footage. He froze it right when the clerk's face was most visible. "The clerk isn't scared. He doesn't even look worried. He's almost... bored."

"You think he knows the robber?"

"I'm thinking the clerk might've been in on it," he replied as he clicked through a few more frames. "Look at his hands. They never tremble, and when he opens the register, it's like muscle memory. This isn't the first time he's done something like this."

"So, what are you saying?"

"I'm saying this isn't a robbery. Not the way it's being portrayed. This is a setup."

"A setup?" Marcus repeated. "You think my brother's being framed?"

"I don't know for sure, but this footage says the clerk was playing his part in a much bigger game. And if your brother's fingerprints were on the gun, then maybe someone planted them there. They knew exactly what they were doing."

Marcus felt his head spin as the realization hit. Jordan hadn't done this. Someone had set him up, and the evidence was pointing straight to a conspiracy.

"Are you able to run this footage through a more advanced filter?" Marcus asked with urgency. "Anything unusual—facial features, hand movements, whatever—anything that stands out, I need to know."

Rick was already opening a new program on his laptop. "I'll have it ready in a few hours. But you need to be careful. Whoever's behind this is good at covering their tracks. This isn't some amateur job."

"I don't care. I'm not letting them take my brother down without a fight."

"You sure you're ready for what you might find?"

"I have to be."

Rick gave a slow nod and got to work. His screen was beginning to fill with distorted surveillance footage, lines of code, and enhancement software. Marcus didn't want to stick around. The waiting would only eat at him. He paced for a while, circling the block, then drove aimlessly through Crest Ridge's quieter streets. The ones with boarded windows and cracked pavement. The places that never seemed to change, no matter how hard folks tried.

He stopped at the diner they used to hit up after late shifts, just long enough to grab a stale coffee and ignore the side-eyes from a table of officers. The rumors were probably already spreading. By the time he made it back to the garage, night had dropped like a curtain. The overhead lights buzzed inside, but Marcus didn't go in.

He stayed in the truck, arms resting on the wheel, the empty lot lit by a single flickering light overhead.

Hours later, Marcus sat in his truck bracing himself for whatever truth was coming next. His mind was racing. *Who could have framed Jordan? And why?* He needed to get to the bottom of it. The phone rang, cutting through his thoughts.

"Marcus," Rick's voice crackled through. "I ran the footage through some filters. There's something you need to see."

"What is it?"

"I found the clerk's reflection in the register glass. He's not facing the robber. He's facing someone else. And it looks like the guy he's looking at is handing him something. A bag, maybe. A note. I can't tell for sure, but it's not the robber."

"You're sure?"

"Positive. I isolated the frame and enhanced the reflection. I'm sending you the stills now. You need to take a closer look. Something's definitely off here."

A buzz lit up Marcus's phone. He opened the message, and his breath caught in his throat as he studied the images. In it, he could just make out the shadowy figure of a second person standing behind the counter. It was too blurry to identify, but the way the clerk was interacting with them didn't look like the typical robbery at all.

"Thanks, Rick," Marcus said, his voice tight. "I owe you one."

"No problem. Just be careful, man. Whoever's involved, they're not playing games."

Marcus ended the call and stared out through the windshield. If the clerk wasn't afraid, if he was talking to someone, then this whole setup ran deeper than he thought. His brother wasn't just a convenient scapegoat. He was a target. This wasn't just about clearing his brother's name. This was about exposing whoever was behind this, and he wasn't going to stop until he found out the truth. And whoever they were, they'd just become Marcus's next lead.

Chapter 5

Frustrated, Marcus gripped the wheel tightly as he drove through Crest Ridge, lost in thought. Every lead he followed seemed to circle back to the same dead end. Jordan's arrest was already a grim shadow hanging over his family, and he wasn't going to let his brother rot in a jail cell without doing everything in his power to clear his name.

However, he hadn't yet contacted Jordan's friends. He knew most of them, but his brother had always kept a tight circle. They'd been close growing up, but since his brother's arrest he hadn't heard a peep from any of them. They all seemed to have vanished. His only shot at getting answers was to find them, ask the questions no one else was asking, and hope for something, anything, that would help him prove Jordan wasn't guilty.

He pulled up to the first house on his list: Desmond's place. Desmond had been Jordan's best friend since high school, and if anyone knew something, it would be him. He had been skeptical. Desmond had always seemed more like a follower than a leader, but he'd known Jordan long enough to be part of the story.

A sharp rap echoed as Marcus knocked on the door. A few moments passed before the door creaked open, revealing Desmond, disheveled, in the doorway. A flash of surprise widened his eyes before he composed himself.

"Marcus," Desmond greeted, his voice tight. "What's up?"

"I need to talk to you," he stated bluntly. "About Jordan."

Desmond shifted nervously from foot to foot, looking around. "What about him?"

"C'mon, man. Don't play dumb. I know you were close. You're one of the last people who saw him before he got arrested. I need to know what happened."

Desmond quickly looked over his shoulder, his eyes darting toward the house, as if searching for a way out. He swept his hand through his short Afro.

"I don't know what you're talking about. Jordan's in jail, and it's not like we can change that now."

"D—" he started, only to be interrupted by a woman's voice as the door behind Desmond creaked open.

"Des, who's at the door?"

It was his girlfriend, Kelsey. With her arms crossed and a cautious look, she emerged from behind him.

Marcus briefly looked at her before refocusing on Desmond. "I need to talk to you both. About the robbery. I'm trying to figure out who set my brother up."

Her gaze darted between both men as she pursed her lips. "Now's not the time for this," she said in a voice that was more forceful than Marcus expected. "You're just making things worse."

Desmond shifted uncomfortably, his eyes darting nervously between the two of them. "She's right. I don't know what to tell you. We all heard about what happened. But I didn't see anything. None of us did."

Marcus was starting to lose his patience. "D, don't lie to me. You were close with my brother. I know that you know something. If you don't tell me, then how am I supposed to clear his name?"

Desmond waited a long time before stepping aside to let Marcus in. Kelsey watched him cautiously as he walked towards the living room, yet he didn't care. He needed answers.

"I don't know anything," Desmond mumbled as he dropped into a chair. "The last time I saw J was the night before he got arrested. He came over, we talked, and just hanged out. I had no idea anything was planned."

Marcus stared at him. "He didn't say anything? Nothing about the robbery?"

"No. He didn't even seem nervous. I figured if he planned something, he'd tell me about it. But..." He trailed off, clearly uncomfortable.

Kelsey's voice softened as she spoke. "He's right. If he wanted to say something, he would've. But he didn't. It's over."

"You don't get it. If I don't find something that proves Jordan didn't do it, he's going to rot in that cell. Do you want that?"

"Look, I'm not saying I don't want to help, but I'm not gonna get dragged into this. I didn't see anything. You think if I knew something, I'd just keep quiet?"

"You know something, D. You're just too scared to say it. What aren't you telling me?"

Desmond glanced at Kelsey, then back at him. For a moment, Marcus feared he might crack. Instead, he shook his head and answered in a low, flat tone. "I don't know, okay? You're barking up the wrong tree."

Kelsey stood and walked over to the door. "I think it's time for you to go. He's told you everything he knows. You're wasting your time here."

Marcus glared at them both. "If you're hiding something, I will know. If I find out that you're involved somehow, then you better watch your back because I'll be coming back to kick your ass. If you care about your friend, then now is the time to come clean. All of you. Because I'll do whatever it takes to get him out of there."

Desmond's jaw tightened, but he didn't say a word. Kelsey kept her hand on the door and opened it wider.

"We get it," she said coolly. "You're angry. But threatening people won't get you the truth any faster."

"This isn't about threats. It's about loyalty. If you ever gave a damn about my brother, then help me. If not, then get out of my way."

He turned and stormed out of the house, slamming the door shut behind him.

Inside, Desmond said. "He's right, you know."

Kelsey looked over at him, startled. "What are you saying?"

He didn't answer. He just stared at the floor, as guilt crept into his eyes.

Marcus exhaled sharply before stopping to lean against his truck. His mind was spinning, but one thing was clear. Desmond was hiding something. And whatever it was, it mattered. He pulled out his phone and typed a quick message to Tyson:

Keep an eye on Desmond. He knows more than he's saying.

Marcus slid into the driver's seat and started the engine. He needed to talk to more of Jordan's friends. He needed to dig deeper. Because whatever was going on, it was a lot bigger than just a simple robbery. The truth was close. He could feel it. And he wasn't about to let fear, loyalty, or secrets stand in his way.

Chapter 6

His next stop was Carlos's apartment. Carlos and Jordan had been friends since middle school. Marcus remembered him as the quiet type, always quick to help but never one to get involved in anything that smelled fishy. But he also knew that Carlos was loyal, perhaps to a fault. He might be the one person who could tell him what had really gone down, or at least point him in the right direction.

Marcus pulled into the parking lot of the apartment complex and parked. Stepping from his truck, the evening's cool breeze did little to alleviate the simmering frustration he felt. He had to get answers, no matter what it took. The building appeared old. He went up the stairs to apartment 2B. Carlos, wearing a worn hoodie and sweatpants, answered the door after a firm knock.

"Marcus?" His face registered surprise, but it quickly shifted to a guarded expression. "What's up?"

"I need to talk to you," he said not waiting for an invitation. Stepping past Carlos, he entered the apartment. It was obvious he wasn't expecting guests, but Marcus didn't care about pleasantries. He needed answers.

Shutting the door, Carlos rubbed the back of his neck. "About what? Look, I don't really have time for—"

"It's about Jordan," he interrupted. "I know you know something. You've been avoiding me, Myia... Everyone. What's going on, man?"

He flinched at the mention of her name, and for a brief moment, Marcus thought he saw something flash in his eyes. Guilt, maybe? But it was gone too quickly to be sure. Carlos dropped into an old chair in the corner of the room, and he stood in the center of the small space waiting for him to speak.

"I don't know what you want me to say, man," he stated, avoiding eye contact. "I haven't talked to him in a while. He's been doing his own thing."

"Don't lie to me," Marcus snapped. "The robbery. You were there, weren't you?"

At the mention of the robbery, Carlos visibly tensed. It was a reaction that Marcus noticed. The way his fingers held onto the chair's armrests.

"I wasn't there. And neither was Jordan, okay? I don't know who's trying to set him up, but it wasn't us."

"Then why did you all go silent when he got arrested? You didn't come forward to help. What the hell is going on?"

He stood up suddenly and raised hid hands in a defensive gesture. "I'm not gonna get involved. You don't know what's at stake. People are involved in things you don't understand."

"What are you talking about?"

Carlos's eyes darted toward the door as if expecting someone to be lurking outside. He lowered his voice to a whisper. "It's bigger than just a robbery, okay? There's stuff going on behind the scenes . Stuff that we shouldn't be messing with. You think we're just gonna waltz in and try to fix everything?"

"What stuff? What do you mean by 'bigger?'"

With wide, fearful eyes, Carlos shook his head violently. "I can't tell you that. I can't. You have no idea what you're getting yourself into. If you keep digging, people are gonna notice. And then it's gonna be too late to do anything about it."

Overwhelmed by a pounding pulse, Marcus strained to comprehend his words. Someone was involved, someone powerful, and it had to be connected to the robbery. But if Carlos was afraid to talk, it meant the situation was worse than he had imagined. There were forces at play and his brother had somehow gotten tangled up in them.

"Look," Marcus said as he tried to steady his voice, "You're gonna tell me who's behind this. You're gonna help me prove Jordan didn't do it. Otherwise, I'll go to Myia and tell her that you're keeping a secret from her. You know she hates it when someone keeps something from her."

At the mention of her name , guilt was all over his face. "Don't do that," he said quickly. "She doesn't need to be part of this."

"Then talk to me. Because right now, you're protecting someone who's willing to let my brother rot for something he didn't do."

"Alright," he whispered. "I'll tell you. But you need to understand, once you're in, there's no way out. Not for you, not for me, not for anyone. The people behind this... They don't play fair."

Marcus's stomach sank. He knew he was getting closer to the truth, but the feeling in the pit of his stomach told him this was about to get even darker.

Carlos's eyes darted toward the window, as if expecting someone to be watching. "They call it The Circuit," he said, barely above a whisper. "It's not just one crew. It's a network. Dealers, smugglers, even people in law enforcement. Everything flows through them. Drugs, weapons, intel... and people."

"What do I need to know?"

"Jordan didn't rob that store. But someone he was involved with did... and they framed him for it."

"You can't just drop something like that and stop talking. If you don't tell me everything, Jordan could go down for something he didn't do. Do you understand that?"

"I told you. It's not that simple. These people... they don't just ruin lives. They end them."

"You think I'm scared of some nameless, faceless 'network'? I've already buried one family member. I'm not letting it happen again. So tell me. Who's pulling the strings?"

Carlos finally met Marcus's eyes. He saw the depth of fear behind them. It wasn't the fear of getting caught. It was the fear of being hunted. Whatever Carlos knew, it was dangerous enough to keep him locked in a state of constant anxiety.

"I can't say names," he whispered. "But I can tell you this. It's not just about money. It's not just about power. It's about control. They get their hooks into people, and once they do, you're theirs. Jordan didn't know what he was getting into. None of us did."

"Hooks?" Marcus repeated. "You're not making any sense, man. Was my brother working with these people? Did they make him do something?"

"Not directly. He... he was just in the wrong place at the wrong time. But that doesn't matter to them. They needed someone to take the fall for the robbery. Someone expendable."

Marcus's stomach churned. Jordan, expendable? His little brother wasn't perfect, but he didn't deserve to be treated like a pawn in someone's twisted game. "Why him? Why Jordan?"

"Because he's clean. No record, no priors. He's the perfect scapegoat. The kind of guy who looks guilty enough to the cops but not connected enough to fight back."

Marcus felt a surge of anger rising in his chest. Whoever these people were, they'd underestimated his family. He wasn't about to let them get away with destroying his brother's life.

"So what's the play?" Marcus asked, his voice calm despite the storm raging inside him. "What do they get out of this?"

Carlos began speaking in a low voice as though the walls had ears. "The robbery was just a cover. It wasn't about the money. It was about the shipment."

"Shipment? What shipment? "What the hell are you talking about?"

"The store," he continued, "it's a front. They were moving something through there. I don't know what, but whatever it was, it was valuable enough to risk everything. The robbery was staged to cover up that shipment going missing."

"And Jordan just happened to get caught up in this? You're telling me he had nothing to do with it?"

"He was just there to get a snack. Wrong time, wrong place. But now he's tied up in it, and those people don't leave loose ends. If you keep digging, they'll come for you too."

"Let them try."

"You don't get it, man. They don't try. They succeed."

Marcus turned toward the door as his began racing with his next steps. He couldn't let fear paralyze him. Not when Jordan's freedom was on the line. He'd seen what guilt and loss could do to a family, and he refused to let it consume them again.

"Carlos," he paused at the door, "if you think of anything else, you call me. You owe me that much."

He didn't respond, but the haunted look in his eyes said enough. As Marcus stepped out into the night, he felt the cold weight of dread settling in his chest. This was bigger than he'd thought. And whoever these people were, they'd made one mistake. They'd underestimated him.

Chapter 7

Marcus sat in his truck outside the Crest Ridge Police Department. His mind replayed everything Carlos had said the night before. The shipment. The scapegoat. The people pulling the strings. Nothing added up, and every lead seemed to raise more questions than answers.

But he wasn't about to give up. He'd reached out to an old contact, a cop named Jeff Tanner who had been a regular at his shop for years. He had always been a straight shooter, and Marcus hoped he'd be willing to bend a few rules for the sake of justice. As he entered the precinct, Tanner was already waiting for him near the front desk.

"Hey man," he said as he shook his hand. "You got here fast. What's so urgent?"

Marcus looked around the bustling station and lowered his voice. "It's about my brother. He's being railroaded for that armed robbery, and I need your help."

"You know I can't interfere with an active investigation."

"I'm not asking you to interfere," he said quickly. "Just... give me a little insight. Something's not right about this case, and I need to know what I'm up against."

Tanner sighed and looked at the officers moving around. "Alright. Come with me."

He led Marcus to a small office in the back and shut the door behind them. He wasted no time.

"They found a gun at the scene. Jordan's fingerprints are on it, but I know for a fact it's not his. He's never even owned a gun."

Tanner leaned against the desk. "You're sure about that?"

"Absolutely. He's no angel, but he's not the kind of guy who'd carry a gun, let alone use one in a robbery. There's gotta be more to it."

"Alright. Let me see what I can find."

He opened a laptop and typed rapidly, pulling up a series of files. Marcus watched as he navigated the police database, his eyes scanning the screen with practiced precision. After a few tense moments, Tanner froze, his expression darkening.

"What is it?"

Tanner moved behind the desk and powered on the terminal.

"You didn't hear this from me," he said as he typed in his credentials and pulled up the case file. "I'm risking a lot just letting you be in here while this is open."

"Understood. And I wouldn't ask if this wasn't life or death."

Tanner scrolled through the file in silence for a moment before frowning. "Huh."

"What?"

"There's a line in the evidence log that doesn't match the initial report." He turned the screen slightly. "See here? The clerk's original statement didn't mention a gun being visible at all. He said the guy kept his hand in his pocket. He assumed it was a weapon. But then two days later, suddenly, a gun shows up in the dumpster behind the store, clean except for one set of prints."

"Jordan's."

"Exactly." Tanner shook his head. "And here's the kicker. The chain of custody on the weapon? It was logged by a temp officer, someone brought in just for that day. No one on our regular team even touched it."

Marcus's blood went cold. "So the gun was planted."

Tanner didn't answer directly. He just looked at him. "I'll keep digging, but you need to be careful. If someone's going to these lengths to set him up, they're not working alone. And they've got access."

Marcus stood slowly, every nerve in his body on high alert. "Thanks, man. You have no idea what this means."

"Just don't make me regret this."

"I won't," he said, already halfway out the door. "But someone else will."

Just as Marcus reached for the doorknob, Tanner's voice stopped him.

"Wait. One more thing."

He turned. Tanner's eyes were glued to the screen, tension etching deeper lines into his face. "The gun," he said slowly, "it's been flagged in our system before. Ballistics matched it to a string of crimes over the past two years—robberies, assaults, even a couple of homicides."

"What kind of crimes?"

"Hits on small businesses, stash houses, low-profile but high-stakes jobs. And they all have one thing in common. They're connected to a local gang called the Vultures ."

Marcus felt his stomach drop. "The Vultures ? They're still around?"

"Unfortunately," Tanner said grimly. They're not just operating out in the open anymore. They've started covering their tracks, using scapegoats, staying one step ahead. This—" he gestured to the screen "—this smells like their work."

"And Jordan's just the latest fall guy," Marcus said, the weight of it hitting him like a brick. "Damn."

Marcus stared at the screen, his mind racing. If the gun belonged to the gang, then there was no way Jordan was involved. His brother wasn't the type to get tangled up with gangs.

"Why would they leave a gun like that at the scene?"

"Could've been intentional. Could've been sloppy. Either way, it's a big red flag."

"This is it. This is the proof I need to clear Jordan's name. If the gun's tied to them , then it's not his."

"Hold on," Tanner said, raising a hand. "It's not that simple. The fingerprints are still a problem. Even if the gun isn't his, we'll need to explain how his prints got on it."

Marcus nodded slowly, the pieces of the puzzle starting to come together. "What about the store clerk? The footage? Something's not adding up. Maybe someone planted the gun and made sure his prints were on it."

Tanner looked skeptical but didn't dismiss the idea outright. "It's possible, but proving that will be tough. They aren't exactly known for leaving witnesses."

Marcus's jaw tightened. "Then I'll find another way. Someone knows the truth, and I'm not stopping until I get it."

"Be careful. If they are involved, then you're not just going up against street thugs. You're dealing with people who've got connections, resources... maybe even someone on the inside."

"Then I need to dig deeper. And fast."

Tanner locked eyes with him. "Just don't get yourself killed in the process."

"I'll keep that in mind," Marcus said, standing up. "Thanks, Jeff. I owe you one."

As Marcus left the station, the weight of the discovery settled heavily on his shoulders. The Vultures had always been a ruthless gang, and now they were tied to the robbery that had landed Jordan behind bars. But he wasn't afraid of them. He'd faced worse and come out stronger. If the Vultures thought they could frame his brother and get away with it, they had another thing coming. This wasn't just about clearing Jordan's name anymore. It was about taking on a group that thought they were untouchable. And Marcus was determined to prove them wrong.

He climbed into his truck and stared at the city lights as his mind raced. Every instinct screamed that this went deeper than a gang hit. The way the evidence had fallen into place too neatly, the silence from people who normally ran their mouths. Someone was orchestrating this from the shadows. He knew what came next. He'd have to track down old contacts, dig through dangerous dirt, and get closer to the Vultures than anyone ever should. But if that's what it took to save his brother, so be it. He started the engine, eyes narrowing with focus. Time to hunt.

Chapter 8

Marcus sat in his truck as he thought about his next move. Confronting the Vultures head-on was out of the question for now. He needed more intel. Something that could expose their connection to the robbery and the gun without putting himself in the crosshairs prematurely.

One name came to mind: Trevion "Trey" Cain. He had been a low-level member of the gang back in the day but had got out without getting buried. Marcus had fixed his car a few times years ago, and while they weren't friends, there had always been a grudging respect between them. Trey wasn't exactly trustworthy, but he knew the gang's inner workings better than anyone. It was a long shot, but it was all Marcus had.

The sun was setting as Marcus pulled up outside a run-down bar on the outskirts of Crest Ridge. He scanned the vehicles until he spotted Trey's old black sedan parked crookedly near the back. Preparing himself, he entered the bar. The smell of stale beer and smoke hit him instantly, but he ignored it. He spotted him in a booth near the jukebox nursing a beer and scrolling through his phone.

"Trey," he said as he sat down across from him.

Startled, he looked up. "Carter. Been a while. What brings you here?"

"I need your help."

He snorted and took a swig of his beer. "Help? From me? Didn't think you were the type to ask for favors."

"This isn't about me. It's about my brother. Someone set him up, and I think the Vultures are involved.

The smirk left his face and was replaced by suspicion. "I don't mess with them anymore. You know that."

"I know. But you know how they operate. I need to know who might've been behind this. The gun they pinned on Jordan. Well it's tied to them."

He sighed and put his beer down. "You're playing a dangerous game. Even asking questions about them can get you killed."

"I don't care. They messed with my family, and I'm not letting it slide. If you know something, anything, it could save my brother."

He stared at him for a long moment then shook his head. "You don't get it, man. They aren't just some gang running the streets anymore. They've got connections now—money, power. They've got people on their payroll who can make problems disappear. Your brother... he's just a pawn in their game."

"Then tell me who's playing the game. Someone's pulling the strings, and I need to know who."

Trey looks around the bar as though he was checking for eavesdroppers. Finally, he leaned in. "There's a guy who goes by Rook. He's not officially a Vulture, but he works with them. Handles their... logistics, if you catch my drift. If that gun's tied to them, chances are it passed through him first."

"Where do I find him?"

He scribbled an address on a napkin. "This is where he hangs out sometimes. But listen, he's not the kind of guy you just walk up to and start questioning. He's paranoid as hell and dangerous to boot. If you're not careful, you'll end up in a ditch somewhere."

Marcus took the napkin, folded it carefully and slipped it into his pocket. "Thanks, man."

"One more thing. Just... be smart about this, alright? I don't want to see your name in the paper."

Marcus gave a nod as he rose to his feet. As he left the bar, the weight of his mission pressed down on him even harder. The name "Rook" was all he had now. A single thread in a web of deceit and danger. But he had no intention of stopping until he unraveled it completely. He didn't head to the address Trey had given him immediately. Charging into the lion's den without more information felt reckless. If Rook was as dangerous as he suggested, Marcus needed to know what he was walking into.

Back at his shop, Marcus shut the garage door and sat at his cluttered desk. He booted up his laptop and began digging for anything he could find. A quick search didn't yield much. Rook's real name didn't seem to be listed anywhere, and official records were sparse. But he had another idea.

A half-hour later, he was on the phone with Sam, an old friend who worked for a local towing company. Sam had a knack for finding out certain information and for keeping his mouth shut.

"I need a favor," Marcus said casually.

"Sure thing," he replied, the sound of clinking tools in the background. "What's up?"

"You ever heard of a guy called Rook? Supposedly works in logistics for... some people." Marcus avoided saying too much over the phone.

There was a pause, then Sam's voice came back, quieter this time. "Yeah, I've heard the name. Not someone you wanna mess with, though. Why are you asking?"

"He's tied to something my brother got caught up in. I need to know what he's about, where he operates, anything you can dig up."

"I can't promise much, but I'll ask around. Just... be careful. People like him? They don't play fair."

"I keep hearing that from people."

"That's because it's true. He doesn't just move crates and numbers. He moves silence. People who cross him disappear."

"Then I won't cross him. I just need leverage. Something I can use to make him talk, or to scare him into backing off."

Sam hesitated, the tool sounds gone now. "You're not gonna let this go, are you?"

"Would you if it were your brother?"

"...I'll see what I can find. But if I call you back and say drop it, you better think long and hard about what that means."

"Thanks, Sam. You're the best."

"Damn right I am."

Marcus slipped the phone into his jacket as he stared out at the empty street. The walls were closing in and now he had a name. Rook. Time to find out what kind of predator he really was.

The next day, Marcus decided to pay a visit to the pawnshop where the gun had been traced. It was a dingy place on the edge of Crest Ridge, the kind of shop where no one asked questions. The owner, an old man with a bald head and a permanent scowl, eyed Marcus warily as he approached the counter.

"Help you?"

"I'm looking for some info on a piece that came through here," he said as he leaned on the counter. "A nine-millimeter. Registered to the Vultures."

"I don't give out information about my sales."

Marcus pulled a wad of cash from his pocket and peeled off a couple of twenties. "I'm not asking for a receipt. Just a name or a description."

The man behind the counter eyed the bills, then Marcus, then the shop door. He snatched the cash and tucked it under the register like it never happened.

"You didn't hear it from me," he said. "Guy who brought it in was young. Mid-twenties, maybe. Shaved head, tattoo on his neck—vulture wings, black and red. Real twitchy. Looked like he hadn't slept in days."

Marcus leaned in. "Name?"

"A guy named Hector. He's a small-time dealer, but he's got connections. If the Vultures wanted a piece moved, they'd go through him."

"Where can I find him?" He asked.

The owner shrugged. "Last I heard, he hangs out at that pool hall on Jefferson. But be careful. He's not the friendly type."

"You got cameras in here?"

"Not ones that work."

"Of course not." Marcus straightened. "Thanks."

As he stepped outside, the pieces were falling into place. Vultures, Rook, and now a face. Half a ghost, half a warning. Marcus pulled out his phone and dialed Sam.

"We've got a lead."

The neon sign buzzed faintly above the door of Lucky Break. Inside, the air was thick with cigarette smoke, cheap cologne, and tension. Marcus spotted Hector near the back, lining up a shot like he didn't have a care in the world. Two other men leaned nearby, watching the game and sipping from plastic cups.

He approached slowly, shoulders squared, his face unreadable.

Hector didn't look up. "You lost, or just stupid?"

"I came to talk," Marcus said, planting himself near the table.

Hector straightened and chalked the end of his cue. "Then talk but make it quick. I don't like being interrupted during my game."

Marcus didn't flinch. "I'm looking into the gun that landed my brother in jail. Nine-millimeter. Traced back to a stash that came through you."

Hector's eyes finally met his, hard and cold. "I don't know what you think you're doing, but you're barking up the wrong damn tree."

"No, I'm not. I've got enough to tie the weapon to Rook. And I know he uses you to move inventory."

"You've been listening to the wrong people, man. You think you're the first one to come sniffing around here with a grudge and a theory? I don't owe you a damn thing."

Marcus took a step closer, his tone sharp. "You don't owe me, but you're gonna talk. You helped set my brother up, whether you meant to or not. He's sitting in a cell because of something you moved."

One of Hector's friends shifted, sensing the tension rising. Hector set the cue down slowly, cracking his knuckles. "You think walking in here, trying to throw weight around, is gonna scare me? I've been in this game too long to flinch at some angry brother with a savior complex."

"I'm not here to save anyone," Marcus said coolly. "I'm here to find the truth. And if I have to drag it out of you, I will."

Hector stepped forward until they were inches apart. "You don't know what you're poking at. This isn't about your brother. He's just collateral. The people I deal with? They make folks disappear for fun. You want to join him in a cell or a body bag? Because it can happen."

Marcus stared him down, unmoved. "Maybe. But you know what else? I've got nothing to lose. I already buried one family member. I'm not doing it again."

That made Hector pause. Just a flicker, a crack in the bravado. "You're pushing your luck."

"Maybe. But I think you've got a line you're scared to cross too. So here's what's gonna happen. You're gonna tell me who gave the order to plant that gun. You're gonna help me clear my brother's name. Or next time I'm not coming in here alone and I won't be asking nicely."

Hector's jaw clenched. He looked around the pool hall, then back at Marcus. "Get the hell outta here."

"I'll be back," Marcus said, backing away slowly. "And you better think real hard about what side of this you want to be on."

As he turned and walked out, he could feel Hector's eyes burning into his back, but he also knew he'd shaken something loose. The tension in the pool hall had shifted, like the low hum of a storm brewing. He didn't get what he came for, not outright, but Hector's silence had cracked. Just enough.

Outside, Marcus pulled his hoodie tighter around his shoulders and kept walking, replaying every word of that conversation. Every pause. Every threat.

He stopped at the corner, pretending to check his phone while glancing back at Lucky Break. Sure enough, one of Hector's guys stepped out moments later, looking both ways before crossing the street and disappearing down an alley. Marcus didn't follow. He didn't need to. That reaction alone confirmed it. Hector knew more. And more importantly, he was scared.

Back at his shop, Marcus locked the door behind him and went straight to his office, where the pile of notes and scattered photos had grown into a wall of red string and half-solved riddles. The conspiracy was real. Jordan had stumbled into something far uglier than bad timing.

That night, as he sat in his shop, Marcus stared at the napkin with Rook's address and thought about the conversation he had with Hector. He knew he was walking a fine line between justice and danger, but he couldn't stop now. The truth was out there, and Marcus was determined to find it, even if it meant confronting the darkest parts of Crest Ridge.

Chapter 9

The next day, Marcus was tightening the bolts on a carburetor when his phone buzzed on the workbench. He wiped his hands on a rag and glanced at the screen. Sam.

He quickly answered. "Talk to me."

"You're not gonna like this."

He set the wrench down. "What did you find?"

"Rook's real name is Raymond Booker. He's been flying under the radar for years. He's not officially a Vulture, but he's deeply tied to their operations—moving weapons, laundering money, covering their tracks. He's their go-to guy when they don't want to get their hands dirty."

"And the gun?"

"That's the thing. I talked to someone who used to run with them. That nine-millimeter your brother supposedly used? It's part of a batch he had smuggled in last year. He uses Hector as a middleman to offload the extras to smaller players, but it's him pulling the strings. If that gun ended up in Jordan's hands, it wasn't by accident."

"So it's a setup."

"Looks that way, and it gets worse. Word is, he's been paranoid lately. He thinks someone's sniffing around his business. If he gets even a whiff that you're onto him, he'll make you disappear. This guy doesn't leave loose ends, Marcus. You've got to be smart about this."

"Then I better make sure he doesn't see me coming."

"Whatever you're thinking, just promise me you won't try to handle this alone."

"I can't promise that" Marcus said, grabbing the wrench again, "but I can promise I'll be ready."

Sam sighed on the other end. "Just don't get yourself killed."

Marcus hung up without replying. He had a name now. A network. And the first real link between Jordan and the frame job. If Rook had orchestrated the setup, then confronting him directly was a risk he couldn't take, not yet. He needed more leverage, something that could expose him without putting himself or Jordan in immediate danger.

That night he poured over everything he'd gathered so far; the notes, the addresses, the connections. But there was still a gap. Why Jordan? Out of all the people Rook could've framed, why his brother?

The answer lay with him, but Marcus wasn't ready to knock on his door just yet. First, he needed to tie the gun to him definitively. If Sam was right and Hector was the middleman, then Hector held the key to breaking this wide open.

But he wasn't talking. At least not willingly. And Marcus had pushed his luck just walking in there. One wrong move and he'd wind up in deeper trouble than he could dig out of. He needed someone who could slip through the cracks unnoticed, someone with eyes in places Marcus couldn't reach.

He shot Tyson a message:

Meet me at Ruby's. Same booth. Tonight.

The response came quick.

I'm in.

He spent the next few hours going over everything again, pacing in his shop like a caged animal. He could feel the walls closing in. Between the Vultures, the corrupt cops, and the secrets no one wanted to say out loud, the city was a maze of lies. But somewhere in it was a thread that would lead him straight to the truth. He just had to keep pulling.

Marcus pulled up to the diner just after dusk. Inside, Tyson sat in a corner booth, hunched over a stack of notes, his hoodie drawn up but his eyes alert. He slid into the seat across from him and didn't bother with small talk.

"You find anything?"

Tyson pushed the papers toward him. "Yeah. I talked to a few people who were with Jordan the night of the robbery. Not the tightest crew, but most of 'em are small-time. His boy Trey says they were all hanging out at Desmond's spot until around one. Jordan left early to grab snacks. Said he had a headache."

"That lines up with what he told Ma. But the store was hit at 2:15."

"Right. And here's the kicker. Someone swears they saw a black sedan pull up outside the store before it went down. Same car that's been linked to some illegal activity a few weeks back. I've got a partial plate, but it's not much."

Marcus sifted through the notes, scanning every name, time, and detail Tyson had scribbled. "What about his other friends? Anyone acting different since it happened?"

"Deon's gone quiet. Deleted his socials, hasn't been seen around. That's suspicious. He used to be loud as hell. I tried to get a word in, but he's ghosting everybody."

"Think he knows something?"

"Maybe. Or maybe he's scared. Either way, something about that night doesn't add up. And none of them mentioned seeing a gun on Jordan. Not once."

"I need to hear it from him. No more guessing, no more third-hand stories."

"You going to the jail?"

"Yeah," Marcus said, grabbing the notes and folding them into his jacket. "I need to look him in the eye and get the truth. Not just about what happened that night, but about who he's been hanging around. If there's something he's not telling me, I need to know now."

"You think he's hiding something?"

He stood up. "I think he's scared. And I think he's trying to protect someone. But he's not gonna protect anyone if he ends up doing time for a crime he didn't commit."

He clapped Tyson on the shoulder. "Thanks, man. I'll keep you posted."

"Just be careful in there. If he's scared, it's probably for a reason."

"I know. But I'm done dancing around the edges. If we're gonna take down whoever's behind this, I need to know exactly what Jordan saw, what he did, and who he's covering for."

He walked towards the door and left. Marcus slid into his truck, started the engine, and pulled out of the lot with one destination in mind: the Crest Ridge County Jail. One way or another, he was going to get the answers. It was time to talk to his brother.

Chapter 10

Marcus leaned against the cold metal chair in the visitors' room and crossed his arms as he studied his brother on the other side of the scratched Plexiglas. The younger man looked tired and worn, the weight of the past few days etched deeply into his face.

"You've got something to tell me?"

Jordan looked over his shoulder as if expecting someone to be listening. "Yeah. But you've gotta promise me something first."

"I'm not making promises until I know what you're about to say."

"I didn't rob that place. I swear to God."

"I already know that," Marcus said impatiently. "What I need is the whole story. No half-truths this time, J."

He stared at his brother for a long moment, then nodded. "Alright. Fine. I was there. At the store. Earlier that night."

Marcus's expression didn't change. "Go on."

"I was picking up some snacks, alright? It's not a big deal. I didn't think it was worth mentioning because I wasn't there when it happened."

"Jordan..." Marcus's tone was heavy with warning.

"I swear, I was in and out in five minutes. I didn't see anything weird or anyone suspicious. But when the cops started questioning me, I panicked. I thought if I told them I was there, they'd pin it on me. I mean, look where I am now!" He gestured to the prison walls around him.

Marcus felt his anger starting to rise. "So you lied."

"I didn't lie, I just—"

"You lied," he interrupted, "You kept this from me, from Mom, from everyone. Do you know how much harder you've made this?"

"I didn't know what to do, alright? I've never been in this kind of trouble before."

"What time were you there?"

"Like... I don't know, around 1:30?"

"The robbery happened at 2:15. You're telling me you left, and then someone else walked in and did the job?"

"That's exactly what I'm saying!" Jordan insisted. "I left before anything went down. I swear, Bro, I'm not lying."

Marcus studied him. His instincts were pulling him in two directions. Jordan's story sounded plausible, but the timing was tight. Too tight.

"Did you see anyone hanging around outside? Anyone watching the place?"

"No. I mean, maybe there were a couple of people in the parking lot, but I wasn't paying attention. I just grabbed my stuff and left."

"And the gun? How the hell does a gun tied to a gang end up in your possession?"

Jordan's eyes widened slightly, but he quickly covered it. "I don't know. I've never seen that gun before."

"You're sure?"

"I'm sure!" Jordan snapped, his voice rising.

Marcus leaned back. Jordan's reaction seemed genuine, but there was still something off. Something Jordan wasn't saying.

"I'm gonna figure this out. But if I find out you're still holding back..." He let the threat dangle in the air.

"I'm not," Jordan said quietly. "That's the truth."

Marcus nodded slowly, though doubt still lingered. He hung up the phone receiver and locked his eyes on Jordan's.

"For your sake, you better hope it is."

Jordan held Marcus's gaze, but there was a flicker of something behind his eyes. Guilt, maybe. Or fear. Either way, Marcus had seen it before. The look people wore when they were in over their heads but didn't know how to ask for help. As the guard came to escort Jordan back to his cell, neither of them said another word. Marcus watched his brother disappear through the door as tension coiled tight in his chest.

When he stepped out into the cold evening, he thought about the conversation. Jordan might be innocent, but he was tangled up in something dangerous. Something he didn't fully understand or couldn't bring himself to admit. And if Marcus didn't uncover the full truth soon, it wouldn't just be Jordan's freedom on the line. It could be his life.

He climbed into his truck and figured out his next move. He just knee that he wouldn't be about asking nicely. It would be about getting answers, one way or another. Marcus pulled out of the jail parking lot and headed across town. Jordan's eyes had told him what his mouth wouldn't. He was hiding something, but not out of guilt. Out of fear.

Marcus ended up back outside the convenience store. He let the engine idle as he watched customers come and go. Jordan's admission replayed in his mind. He'd been here at 1:30, just 45 minutes before the robbery. If Jordan's story was true, then someone else had planned this hit, and they'd done it fast.

Marcus got out and stepped inside, the door chime breaking the quiet hum of the cooler units. The cashier barely looked up. It a different one than last time. It was a young dude wearing earbuds and an oversized hoodie. There were only two other customers: a man choosing scratch-offs and a woman digging through her purse by the coffee machine.

He approached the counter and pulled out his wallet. "Hey, can I get twenty on pump three?"

The cashier lazily punched in the amount. "That it?"

Where's the guy that usually work this shift?"

"Quit last week. Said he was going out of town."

"Where to?"

"I dunno, man. He didn't exactly leave a forwarding address." The cashier shrugged, clearly uninterested.

Marcus scanned the store. Nothing seemed out of place. Same dusty candy shelves, same flickering lights, but there was a tension in the air, like a room that had just been emptied of secrets.

"You remember anything weird about the night of the robbery?" he pressed.

"Just that Reggie was real quiet after. Jumpy. Like he'd seen something he didn't want to talk about."

"If he comes back or you hear from him, you call this number." He slid a card across the counter. "Don't think. Just call."

The cashier took it with a hesitant nod. Marcus turned and walked out. He climbed into the driver's seat and pulled out his phone to call Sam.

"I got something," Marcus said when he picked up. "The clerk who worked that night has quit. Can you find out where he went or his address?"

There was a pause on the other end, followed by the sound of a keyboard tapping. "What's his name?"

"Reggie. That's all I got. Worked the night shift. The new cashier said he bounced right after the robbery."

Sam let out a low whistle. "Convenient timing."

"Exactly. I think he saw something, or maybe he was part of it. Either way, I need to find him."

"I'll check DMV records, utilities, anything I can dig up. If he's gone underground, it might take a minute."

"You've got until morning," he said as he started the engine. "If he's part of this mess, I'm not giving him time to disappear for good."

"I'll do my best. I'll be in touch."

Marcus ended the call. Every step forward brought him closer to the truth and deeper into something he might not be able to walk away from. Whoever was behind this was sloppy, but not sloppy enough to leave an obvious trail. He'd have to dig deeper, and he knew time was running out before Rook, or the cops, closed in.

Chapter 11

Marcus stepped into the cramped office of Jordan's court-appointed lawyer. Papers and case files were stacked haphazardly on every surface, and the man behind the desk looked as tired as the office felt.

"Mr. Miller?" Marcus asked, extending a hand.

The lawyer glanced up, adjusting his crooked glasses. "Yeah, that's me. And you are?"

"Marcus Carter. Jordan's brother."

Miller shook his hand briefly, then gestured for him to sit. "Alright. What can I do for you?"

"I'm here because my brother says he's innocent. I'm trying to help him, but I need to know what you've done to prepare his case."

Miller sighed, leaning back in his squeaky chair. "Look, Mr. Carter, I understand you're concerned about your brother. But the evidence isn't exactly in his favor."

"Evidence can be misleading. What's the plan? Have you looked into the security footage? Talked to the store clerk?"

The lawyer scratched the back of his neck, clearly uncomfortable. "The security footage places him at the scene—"

"Earlier in the day," Marcus interrupted.

"True," he admitted, "but that detail isn't helping much when his fingerprints are on the weapon."

"That gun isn't his!"

Miller sighed again, folding his hands on the desk. "I hear you. But proving that is going to be tough without resources or time. I've got a lot of cases on my plate, Mr. Carter. I can only do so much."

"So, what are you saying? That you're just going to let him go down for something he didn't do because you're 'busy'?"

"I'm saying that the justice system isn't always fair, and without hard evidence to counter what the prosecution has, my hands are tied. You want a miracle? Then bring me something solid. Witness testimony. Paper trail. Anything that proves Jordan didn't pull that trigger and that someone else did."

Marcus stood with frustration. "I didn't come here for excuses. I came for help."

"I'm giving you my help," Miller said. "But this isn't a movie, Mr. Carter. I don't have time to chase ghosts. You want to clear your brother's name? Then get me something I can actually use in court."

"Fine. I've got leads, but I need you to keep the pressure on the cops. They're not looking for anyone else because he's the easy target. Make them look harder."

"I'll see what I can do."

"That's not good enough. I'm not letting my brother rot in here because you're too overworked to care. If you won't fight for him, I will."

"Mr. Carter —"

But Marcus was already heading for the door. He paused, looking back at the public defender. "You're not just fighting for my brother. You're fighting for the truth. Don't forget that."

Marcus stormed out of the lawyer's office. The idea that Jordan's fate rested in the hands of someone so indifferent made his stomach churn. If Miller wouldn't fight for justice, he would have to do it himself.

Sitting in his truck, Marcus pulled out his phone and called Sam. His impatience grew with every ring.

"What's up?" Sam's voice crackled on the other end.

"I'm done waiting around," Marcus said, his voice low and steady. "We're digging deeper into Rook's crew. You got anything for me yet?"

"I found something. There was a black SUV in the parking lot at the same time Jordan was at the store. It's registered to a shell company that's tied to Rook. It's a common trick they use to stay under the radar."

"You know where it is now?"

"Not yet, but I've got a lead. He's been meeting at an old auto garage on the edge of town. Word is, it's where they stash their bigger scores before moving them."

"Send me the address. If he was there that night, and that SUV ties back to him, then we've got something real."

"I will. But don't do anything stupid, alright? If that garage is what people say it is, you're walking into a lion's den."

I hear you. I'm not going in yet. I just needed to know where to look."

"Good. Play it smart. You show up at the wrong time, you might not make it out."

"Look I'm not looking for a fight, I'm looking for the truth."

"Just don't go alone."

"I never do," Marcus said, already shifting the truck into gear. He ended the call and stared out at the road ahead. The closer he got to the truth, the more dangerous it became. Rook wasn't just some street-level operator. He was connected, insulated, and smart. But Marcus wasn't turning back. He wasn't heading to the garage just yet. Not without a plan. Not without backup. But he would go tonight.

Later that evening, he parked a few blocks away from the garage. The building was rundown and surrounded by a chain-link fence with razor wire along the top. A few dim lights illuminated the lot, where a couple of cars and a black SUV were parked. He slipped on a dark hoodie and gloves and kept to the shadows as he approached the perimeter. The rhythmic sound of tools clinking and low chatter echoed from inside the garage. He crouched behind a dumpster, observing the movements of the men guarding the area.

Two guys near the front door were smoking and laughing in a relaxed posture. Too relaxed. Marcus wondered if that was because they assumed no one would dare come after Rook's operation. As he studied them, his phone vibrated in his pocket. He pulled it out to see a text from Sam.

Be careful. Place is wired with cameras. Watch your back.

Marcus cursed under his breath and scanned the building more carefully. This time he spotted a few security cameras mounted along the roof line. He'd have to be quick and smart about this. He pulled out a small pair of binoculars and focused on the garage door and spotted a stack of crates inside. The labels on them were blurred from the distance, but they didn't look like car parts. *If those crates contained stolen goods or weapons, it would explain why Rook was so protective of the place.* He thought to himself.

He needed more than a hunch, he needed proof. If he could tie those crates or the SUV to the robbery, then he'd have leverage. Suddenly, he saw a new figure emerged from the garage. It had to be Rook. He was barking orders at the men outside while pointing at the SUV. Marcus strained to hear but couldn't make out the words over the distance.

The SUV's trunk popped open, and one of the men began unloading a few smaller boxes. Marcus's stomach sank. If they were moving the evidence, he might not have much time. He slipped back into the shadows. He needed to get closer, but not tonight. This wasn't the time to make a reckless move.

Back at his shop, Marcus spread out everything he knew on the table in his small office. Notes, timelines—all of it. He stared at the mess, his frustration boiling over. "What the hell are you into, Jordan?"

He grabbed his phone and called Sam.

"I need more," Marcus said the moment he picked up. "What's in those crates? And what's Rook planning?"

"I'll dig, but you gotta slow down, man. If he finds out you're sniffing around, it won't just be Jordan in danger."

Marcus leaned back in his chair. "I don't have time to slow down. If I don't figure this out, he's done."

"Alright. I'll see what I can find. Just... don't do anything stupid."

"I can't guarantee it." He said as he hung up. He'd come too far to turn back now. If the system wasn't going to help his brother, he'd take on the fight himself. Even if it meant walking straight into the lion's den.

Chapter 12

It's been a couple of weeks since Marcus was at the lawyer's office and he was nowhere closer now than he was then. He was at his shop elbow-deep in an oil change. He tightened the filter, wiped his hands on a rag, and reached for the wrench when his phone buzzed on the nearby tool cart. He wiped his fingers on his shirt and picked it up.

Tyson: Found him. Terrance. The guy who was with Jordan that night. He's been hanging around the corner store off Franklin and 12th. Mostly at night. Hoodie, loud, always looking over his shoulder. You'll know him when you see him.

Marcus's jaw tightened. Finally. He stared at the message for a second, the steady drip of oil tapping the pan beneath the car like a ticking clock. Then he grabbed the wrench, finished tightening the bolt with one swift motion, and slid out from under the car. He wiped his hands clean and texted back:

Marcus: Good. I'm heading there tonight.

As he tossed the rag aside and shut the hood, the tension in his chest shifted. This wasn't just another lead, this was a potential witness. And if Terrance was still around, he was going to make sure he talked.

That evening, Marcus was in his truck parked a distance from the corner store. His eyes were locked on Terrence loitering outside. For the past half hour, he had been pacing, checking his phone every few minutes, his behavior jittery and impatient.

Marcus's gut told him this wasn't a casual hangout. He watched as a sleek, dark sedan rolled up, its headlights briefly illuminating the street before cutting off. A man stepped out. He looked rough around the edges, but his clothes were too clean for someone who belonged in this part of town.

Terrence greeted him nervously with his hands shoved in his pockets. The two exchanged quick words before heading down an alleyway. Marcus's instincts screamed at him to follow, but he moved carefully, parking his truck farther down the block and slipping into the shadows on foot.

He crept down the alley keeping his steps light as he strained to catch their conversation. The faint sound of their voices grew clearer as he approached the back of an old laundromat. Marcus ducked behind a stack of broken pallets.

"...so he's still locked up, huh?" the man said, his voice low and gruff.

"Yeah," Terrence replied, his tone shaky. "But I don't know, man. His brother has been sniffing around. Asking questions."

Marcus froze when he heard that.

The other man cursed under his breath. "That ain't good. Rook ain't gonna like that."

"What should we do?"

"You don't do anything. Boss got it handled. Loose ends are gonna get cleaned up, one way or another."

"Alright. But I didn't say nothin' to him, I swear."

"You better not have," the man said sharply. "If you're lying, you'll be the next loose end."

Marcus felt a chill run down his spine. He inched back, careful not to make a sound as the two men wrapped up their conversation. The gruff man clapped Terrence on the shoulder before heading back toward the sedan.

Marcus ducked farther into the shadows as the car drove off, leaving Terrence standing there, visibly rattled. He stayed still until he saw him disappear down the street. When he got in his truck, Marcus thought about what was said and unsaid. Rook was aware of his digging, and worse, he was planning to "clean up loose ends."

His mind raced. *Did that mean Jordan? Terrence? Or even himself?*

He took a deep breath as he tried to calm down. This wasn't just about clearing Jordan's name anymore, it was about staying alive. If Rook was getting desperate enough to start eliminating threats, then he needed to be one step ahead. He grabbed his phone and dialed Sam.

"We've got a problem."

"What now?"

"Terrence met with one of Rook's guys. They're talking about cleaning up loose ends. I think Rook knows I'm onto him."

"That's not good, man. You need to lie low."

"Lie low?" Marcus snapped. "I can't. If I stop now, Jordan's as good as gone."

"Then you need to move smart. He's got eyes everywhere. If they're onto you, you're walking a fine line."

Marcus leaned his head against the steering wheel feeling exhaustion creep in. "I need to figure out who these loose ends are. If it's Jordan..."

"We'll figure it out. I'll see what I can dig up on Rook's plans. Just don't do anything reckless."

Marcus hung up. He couldn't stop now, not when things were escalating. But one thing was clear: the deeper he got, the more dangerous this game became.

The next day, Marcus spotted Terrence at a basketball court near their old neighborhood. Terrence was leaning against the chain-link fence, scrolling through his phone with a distant expression. He stepped out of his truck and made his way across the cracked pavement.

"Terrence," Marcus called, his tone even but firm.

Terrence stiffened, glancing up sharply. His eyes darted around, looking for an escape route. "Yo," he said, forcing a casual tone. "What's good?"

"Cut the act. We need to talk."

"Talk about what?"

"About you meeting with Rook's guy last night."

"I don't know what you're talking about."

"Don't play dumb with me. I heard everything. Loose ends, T. You know exactly what that means."

"Look, I didn't say nothin' to them, alright? I kept my mouth shut!"

"You didn't need to say anything," he snapped. "Just meeting with them puts you in deep. And now they're onto me. You wanna explain that?"

Terrence shifted uncomfortably. "Man, you don't get it. These dudes... they don't mess around. If they think you're a problem, you're done."

"Then why work with them? Why put your friend and my brother at risk?"

"I didn't mean for any of this to happen! I didn't know they were gonna frame him, alright? I thought it was just a job. Quick money, no strings. But now it's all messed up."

"Then help me fix it. Tell me what you know."

"I can't, man. If he finds out I talked to you, I'm dead. And you will be too."

Marcus grabbed him by the collar. "I don't care about his threats. My brother is sitting in jail for something he didn't do, and you're out here covering for the people who set him up. That ends now."

Terrence's eyes filled with fear, but he managed to choke out, "You're in over your head. You think you can take him down? He's got connections everywhere. Cops, lawyers, judges. He got them all in his pocket."

Marcus let go of Terrence, shoving him back a step. "I don't care how connected he is. I'll find a way to bring him down. But if you keep playing both sides, you'll get caught in the crossfire."

"I'm telling you, man. Just back off. This ain't your fight."

"It is now," he said firmly. "And if you're not with me, you're against me."

Terrence hesitated, then turned to leave. "You don't get it. These people don't leave loose ends. If you keep pushing, you're gonna end up just like Jordan or worse."

Marcus watched him go. Terrence was scared. That much was clear. But fear wasn't an excuse to let Jordan rot in jail. As he walked back to his truck, he thought to himself. If Rook's network ran deeper than he'd thought , he'd need more than determination to save his brother. He'd needed a plan.

Chapter 13

The buzz of the fluorescent lights overhead was the only sound in the shop besides the occasional creak of metal and the low hum of the space heater near Marcus's feet. He sat on a stool with his arms crossed. His eyes were glued to the screen of his laptop, watching the security footage for the third time that night. The footage had no sound, just grainy black-and-white images, but every frame felt like it held a secret just out of reach.

Jordan walked into the frame, hood up, hands in his pockets. He moved toward the back of the store, grabbed a drink from the cooler, then headed toward the counter. So far, everything checked out with what he'd said. There was no sign of panic, no urgency. Just a guy grabbing a drink. But Marcus wasn't looking for what was normal. He was hunting for what wasn't. He leaned in closer, tapping the spacebar to pause. Rewind. Play. Again.

In the background, a tall man wearing a dark jacket lingered near the snack aisle. His head was down, face half-obscured by the shelf. He never picked anything up. Just stood there for a few seconds. Then, oddly, seemed to vanish between frames. He paused the video, rewound it a few seconds, and hit play again. A few other customers moved about in the background, but nothing seemed unusual until Marcus noticed it. The transition between two frames seemed too smooth, almost unnaturally so. He slowed the playback speed and squinted at the screen.

"Gotcha," he muttered under his breath.

In the slowed footage, the timestamp jumped ahead by several seconds, but the movement on the screen didn't align. It was as if a portion of the footage had been erased and the gap patched over. Marcus ran his hand over his beard. Someone had edited the footage. But why? To incriminate Jordan? Or to hide something or someone else? Marcus grabbed his phone and dialed Sam.

"What now?" Sam answered impatiently.

"The footage was edited."

There was a pause. "Are you sure?"

"Positive. There's a jump in the timestamp. Someone messed with it."

"That means someone's trying to cover their tracks. Can you figure out who?"

"Not yet, but there's someone in the footage who doesn't sit right with me. A guy hanging near the aisles. I think he might be involved."

"You need the unedited footage."

"No kidding. I don't suppose you've got any contacts who could help me with that?"

"Maybe. I know someone who used to work in private security. She's good with this kind of thing, but she's not exactly cheap."

"Let me worry about that," Marcus said. "Set it up."

Sam exhaled sharply. "Alright. Her name's Claire Pierce. Used to handle digital forensics for a corporate firm before she went freelance. If anyone can recover or trace that footage, it's her."

Marcus grabbed a pen and scribbled the name down on the back of an old receipt. "How do I get in touch with her?"

"I'll send her your number and let her know you'll be calling. Just... don't piss her off. She doesn't work with people she doesn't trust."

"Got it," Marcus said. "And Sam? Thanks. I owe you."

"You owe me about five favors by now," Sam said dryly. "Don't make me cash in all of them at once."

Marcus hung up and leaned against the truck, staring at the sky as dusk settled over the city. One step closer. If Claire could get him that unedited footage, he might finally start pulling the thread that unraveled the whole damn thing.

He pulled out his phone and typed the number Sam had just sent. He hesitated for a second. He didn't know what kind of person she was, just that she was sharp and had a reputation for getting things done. That was enough. He hit dial.

After a few rings, a woman's voice answered, cool and guarded. "Claire."

"Hey, name's Marcus Carter. Sam gave me your number. Said you might be able to help me with some edited footage I'm trying to recover."

There was a pause. "That depends on the footage and the reason."

"It's from a convenience store robbery. My brother's being blamed for it, but things aren't adding up. I think the security feed was tampered with. I need someone who can spot what was changed and maybe recover what was lost."

Another pause, then, "Alright. Bring whatever you have. Tomorrow. Noon. Text me for the address."

"I will. Thanks."

She hung up without another word.

Marcus pocketed the phone and let out a breath. He was used to silence. This kind, though, the calm before the storm, was different.

The adrenaline that had been fueling him all day started to wear off as he drove home. The moment he stepped through the door, the weight of everything hit him at once. Jordan's visit. The footage. The Vultures. Rook. He tossed his jacket on the back of the couch and sat down heavily, letting his head fall back against the cushion. For the first time in weeks, sleep didn't feel like a luxury. It felt like a necessity. Tomorrow, he'd face Claire. And maybe, just maybe, the truth. But tonight, Marcus finally let himself rest.

The next evening, he leaned against the side of his truck, staring up at the dim porch light of the house in front of him. Claire was his last shot at making sense of the security footage. He had spent sleepless nights replaying the robbery's events in his head, trying to reconcile Jordan's story with the evidence stacked against him.

"Alright, Marcus," he muttered to himself. "Let's do this."

The door opened before he knocked. Claire, a tech-savvy woman with sharp eyes and a no-nonsense demeanor, leaned on the doorframe. Her cropped purple hair was as striking as the way she sized him up.

"You're Sam's guy?" she asked.

"That's me," Marcus replied.

"Come in. But don't touch anything," she said, stepping aside.

Her living room was a chaos of screens, wires, and parts of what Marcus assumed were old computers. The hum of machinery filled the air, along with the faint scent of burnt metal. She gestured to a cluttered coffee table.

"Sam says you've got tampered footage. Show me."

He handed over the USB drive. "Convenience store robbery. My brother's locked up because of it, but I know he's being set up."

Claire plugged the drive into her laptop and pulled up the footage. Her eyes narrowed as she navigated the video. "Hmm. Definitely some post-production magic here. These cuts are almost seamless, but whoever did this wasn't as clever as they thought."

She rewound and slowed the tape, pausing to point out a split-second glitch in the timestamp. "See that? This section's been doctored. Someone wanted to remove something or someone from the picture."

"Can you undo it?"

She smirked. "I can do better than that. If I can access the store's security system directly, I might be able to find the original footage and trace the tampering back to whoever did it."

"And if they covered their tracks?"

"Then we dig deeper. But first, I need to get into that system. And I'm not hacking into it remotely. It's too risky."

"I'll handle it. Just be ready to work when I call."

"You really think you can just waltz into the store and get access to their system?"

"I'll figure it out. This is my brother we're talking about."

The next morning, he walked into the convenience store. The manager looked up from behind the counter with a wary expression.

"Can I help you?" the man asked.

Marcus forced a polite smile. "Yeah, I'm about the robbery a few weeks ago."

"I already told the cops everything I know," the manager said, folding his arms.

"I'm not a cop. I'm the suspect's brother. And I'm not leaving until I get some answers."

The manager sighed. "Alright, but make it quick."

"I need access to your security system. There's something wrong with the footage, and I think it can prove my brother's innocence."

"I can't let you mess with that. It's against policy."

"I'm not asking you to mess with anything. Just let me and my tech expert take a look. If we're wrong, you never hear from us again. But if we're right, we can clear this up for everyone."

The manager glanced toward the back office, clearly weighing his options. "You know how much trouble I could get in if corporate finds out?"

"I know. But I also know what it's like watching your little brother get blamed for something he didn't do. I'm not here to break rules. I'm here to get answers. That footage was edited, and I think someone's using your system to cover their tracks."

The manager frowned, torn between caution and curiosity. Finally, he nodded. "Fine. But if anyone asks, I didn't know about this."

Marcus gave a tight nod. "You won't regret this."

He texted Claire to meet him there. A few minutes later, she walked in wearing a black hoodie and glasses, all business, and a messenger bag slung over one shoulder. Without a word, she followed him to the back room, eyes scanning everything with quiet intensity. She wasted no time setting up her laptop at the security console. The manager hovered nearby, clearly nervous.

"Relax," she said without looking up. "I've done this a hundred times."

Marcus watched as she worked. After a few tense minutes, Claire's face lit up.

"Got it," she said. "Here's the unedited footage."

The original video played, revealing a man in a dark jacket pulling a gun from his waistband. The timestamp matched the edited footage, but Jordan was nowhere to be seen.

"That's not my brother," he said, his voice heavy with relief and anger.

"Nope," Claire said. "But this guy's bad news. He's flashing gang colors. See the patch on his jacket?"

"I know that patch. It's tied to one of the local gangs."

Claire paused the video and turned to him. "This is proof, but it's not enough. You'll need more to convince the cops and to stay ahead of whoever tried to bury this."

"I'll find it," Marcus said. "Whoever's behind this messed with the wrong family."

Claire nodded as she copied the video to a flash drive. "This footage will help, but you need to be smart. Whoever doctored it has resources and they won't take kindly to someone pulling back the curtain."

Marcus stared at the frozen frame of the armed man on the screen. His face was partially obscured by the angle, but the gang patch was clear. "That's Iron Vultures," he said. "No doubt about it. That confirms the gun was planted and that Jordan was set up."

She handed him the flash drive. "You've got the first domino. Now knock the rest down."

He pocketed the drive and stood. "I will. I'm not backing off. Not until I've burned this whole thing to the ground."

As he stepped out of the back room into the cold night air, he also knew the clock was ticking. Whoever was behind this wasn't just ruthless. They were smart. And Marcus was going to have to be smarter.

Chapter 14

Rook sat alone in a back room of the building. The hum of the TV in the corner did little to break the suffocating silence in the room. The blinds were drawn tight, and the faint glow of a streetlight outside barely filtered through. A half-smoked cigarette dangled from his lips, ash falling unnoticed onto the table cluttered with papers, burner phones, and a handgun.

He had always prided himself on staying ahead of the game. A few favors here, a few threats there. It was how he kept control. But lately, something was off. Loose ends were coming apart faster than he could tie them up.

He took a long drag from the cigarette and exhaled slowly as he eyed the corner of the room where a stack of cash was shoved into a duffel bag. It was supposed to be easy. Set up the robbery, frame a convenient scapegoat, and walk away clean. But this no name guy had changed the game. His name alone was enough to make his jaw tighten. He hadn't thought much of Jordan's older brother until now. A mechanic, supposedly minding his own business, suddenly poking around where he didn't belong.

Rook rubbed a hand over his face, his fingers brushing against the scar running down his cheek. It was a souvenir from a fight years ago. That scar had taught him to always expect trouble, and Marcus was trouble. He grabbed one of the burner phones and dialed a number. It rang twice before someone picked up.

"What?" came a gruff voice.

"We've got a problem," Rook said.

"I'm listening."

"Jordan's brother. He's digging. Asking questions. Got a tech freak involved, too."

"You want me to handle it?"

"Not yet. I don't need bodies piling up unless it's necessary. But keep an eye on him. And let me know if he gets too close."

He hung up and leaned back in his chair. Marcus wasn't the only problem. The gang's leadership had been asking questions about the robbery, too. Small-time jobs weren't supposed to attract attention, but now the whole operation felt like it was teetering on the edge. He stood and moved to the window, peeling back a corner of the blinds. The street was empty, but it didn't ease the tightness in his chest. He'd been feeling watched lately, though he couldn't say if it was paranoia or something real.

He opened a drawer in the desk and pulled out a folded piece of paper. It was a list of names, scrawled in his own handwriting. Some were crossed out. Others weren't. Marcus's name was at the bottom, circled in red.

"Should've stayed in your garage, Mr. Mechanic."

A sudden knock at the door made him jump. His hand instinctively went to the gun on the table.

"Who is it?" he barked.

"It's me," a voice called back.

Rook relaxed slightly and opened the door to reveal Darius.

"We've got another problem," he stepped inside.

Rook slammed the door shut behind him. "What now?"

"Word on the street is Marcus isn't just asking questions. He's tailing people and even Hector's spooked. Said he showed up at the pool hall last week. Didn't like the way he was looking at him."

"He was supposed to back off after the footage. That lawyer was barely holding the case together. Now he's got something new."

"Maybe. Or maybe he's just desperate."

"No," Rook muttered, his eyes narrowing. "Desperate people make noise. That man is moving like he's got something real. Something dangerous."

He walked back to the desk and stared at the list. With a hard scrape of the pen, he drew a thick line through another name just above Marcus's.

"What do you want me to do?"

He didn't look up. "Follow him. I want to know where he goes, who he talks to, what he's planning. And if he gets close to anything that can hurt us..."

He finally looked at Darius with cold eyes. "You handle it."

He nodded once and slipped out the door, leaving Rook alone with the list and the slow realization that Marcus wasn't just a mechanic. He was a problem. One Rook couldn't afford to ignore.

One of the boys said they saw him near the docks last night."

Rook clenched his fists, his mind racing. The docks were one of their key spots. If Marcus had been there...

"Alright," Rook said, his voice calm but cold. "Here's what we're gonna do. Start rotating the drop spots. And find out exactly what Marcus knows. If he's talking to anyone else, I want names."

"And if he gets too close?" Terrence asked.

"Then we remind him why people don't mess with us."

Terrence nodded and left, leaving Rook alone with his thoughts. He poured himself a shot of whiskey and downed it in one gulp.

"Game's on, Marcus," he muttered. "Let's see how far you're willing to go."

Rook paced the length of the warehouse, his boots echoing against the concrete floor. The dim light from a single hanging bulb cast long shadows, making the space feel more like a den of secrets than a simple storage facility. Around him, his trusted men, what was left of them, stood in tense silence, waiting for his orders.

Terrence leaned against a stack of crates, arms crossed. "You really think he's gonna stop digging?"

"No," Rook said, stopping mid-step. "He's too stubborn. Family types always are. But we're not waiting around to find out how much he knows. Time to turn up the heat."

He pulled a folded map from his pocket and laid it flat on the crate, jabbing a finger at a section marked with a red X.

"This is where it went down," Rook said, pointing to the convenience store. "Marcus keeps sniffing around here, so we give him something to find."

"What kind of 'something'?" Terrence asked, raising an eyebrow.

"Something that'll bury him as deep as his brother."

He turned to another man in the group, a wiry figure nicknamed Razor. "You still got that stash of unregistered pieces?"

Razor nodded. "Yeah, tucked away. What do you need?"

"Plant one of them near the scene. Somewhere it'll look like Marcus dropped it. We make it look sloppy, like he panicked."

Terrence frowned. "That's risky. What if he doesn't take the bait?"

"He will," Rook said firmly. "People like Marcus think they're untouchable until they're not. He'll either fall for it or waste time trying to prove it's fake. Either way, we stay ahead."

Terrence exchanged a wary glance with Razor but didn't argue further.

Rook's expression darkened. "And if he doesn't back off, we escalate. I don't care what it takes—he's not ruining this for us."

Later that night, Razor crouched behind a dumpster in the alley near the convenience store. He wiped his fingerprints from the gun with a cloth, careful not to leave a trace. The alley smelled like rotting food and motor oil, and the dim glow of a nearby streetlight barely illuminated his work.

He placed the gun in a crumpled paper bag, tucking it just far enough into the shadows to make it look like someone tried to hide it in a hurry. Satisfied, he took a few steps back and surveyed the scene.

"Done," Razor muttered into his burner phone.

"Good," Rook's voice crackled through. "Now get out of there. And don't screw this up."

Rook hung up the phone and poured himself another drink. He allowed himself a rare moment of satisfaction. The plan was in motion, and soon Marcus would have too much heat on him to keep digging.

But deep down, a flicker of doubt gnawed at him. Marcus wasn't like the others who had come after him before. He was smart, relentless, and worst of all, he cared about his brother enough to risk everything.

Rook clenched his fist, the glass in his hand trembling. He couldn't afford to underestimate Marcus, not now.

"Time to see how far you're willing to go, Marcus," he muttered to himself, downing the drink in one swallow.

Chapter 15

Marcus sat at his desk in the office of his shop staring at the collection of notes, photos, and timelines he'd pinned to the corkboard. He had spent hours trying to piece together the truth, but something still didn't add up. The robbery felt staged. Too clean in some ways and too messy in others. The sound of a car pulling into the lot outside broke his concentration. He glanced out the window and saw a battered sedan he didn't recognize. A figure emerged. It was an Hispanic woman in her late thirties with a determined expression. She looked around briefly before stepping into the shop.

Marcus wiped his hands on a rag and met her at the door. "Can I help you?"

"You Marcus?" she asked, her voice steady but edged with urgency.

"That depends. Who's asking?"

She glanced over her shoulder nervously before answering. "Name's Olivia. I work for the store where... where the robbery happened."

"What are you doing here?"

"I heard you've been poking around, asking questions," Olivia said, stepping closer. "If you're trying to help your brother, you're not gonna get far looking at the obvious. There's more to this than you think."

He folded his arms. "And you're just here out of the kindness of your heart?"

She hesitated. "Let's just say I've got my reasons. I knew something was wrong that day. The way they pushed us out of the store after it happened. How quickly the tapes were handed over to the cops. None of it felt right."

"You're saying the store's in on it?"

"I'm saying it's possible," Olivia replied. "The owner, Mr. Patel, has been acting strange ever since. Tight-lipped. And when I asked to look at the footage myself, he got real defensive. He was on the phone telling someone that you asked to see the video, too."

"So he's watching me now?"

"Looks like it. You're rattling cages. And people are starting to notice."

"Why tell me all this? What do you really want?"

She looked away for a moment, then met his eyes. "Because Jordan isn't the only one who got screwed over. My cousin was arrested last year, same kind of deal. Supposed 'evidence' that didn't hold up, but it was too late by the time anyone looked closer. I didn't do anything then. I'm not making that mistake again."

"So what now?"

Olivia pulled a folded piece of paper from her jacket and handed it to him. "I wrote down the number I saw Mr. Patel call. I don't know who it belongs to, but if someone's pulling strings behind the scenes, it might lead you there."

"Thanks. But if you stick around, it's gonna get dangerous."

"I figured," she said. "But like I said... I've got my reasons."

"Alright. What do you know about the footage?"

She glanced around the shop. "Not here. Too risky. Meet me tonight at the diner on 4th. I'll tell you everything I can."

"Fine. I'll be there."

She nodded and turned to leave but stopped at the door. "One more thing," she said, looking back. "Be careful. Whoever's behind this... they don't play fair."

Marcus arrived at the diner early and took a seat in the corner where he could watch the entrance. Olivia showed up fifteen minutes later, clutching a small folder to her chest. She slid into the booth across from him and set the folder on the table.

"This is all I could get," she said. "Payroll records, and inventory logs I... borrowed."

Marcus opened the folder and flipped through the documents.

"I don't know who or why, but I'm betting it's tied to whoever set this whole thing up."

Marcus leaned back in his seat. The evidence was mounting, but it still wasn't enough to clear Jordan.

"Thanks for this," he said and closed the folder. "You just gave me a direction to dig."

"Just don't tell anyone it came from me," Olivia said, standing to leave. "And Marcus? Watch your back."

He watched her go. Whoever had set Jordan up had gone to great lengths to cover their tracks. But now, Marcus had a piece of the puzzle they hadn't counted on.

The engine rumbled low as Marcus pulled out of the parking lot and merged into traffic. Just a few blocks down, he spotted Terrance loitering near a liquor store glancing around like he was waiting, or watching, for someone.

He kept his distance from and coasted into a parking spot across the street with a clear view. He cut the lights and leaned slightly forward, watching through the windshield. A few minutes passed before a dark sedan pulled up. Terrance leaned into the passenger window, speaking to someone inside. Marcus couldn't make out faces, but the interaction was sharp; quick head turns, jerky hand gestures. Tense.

Then the passenger door opened and Terrance slid in. The sedan peeled away from the curb and merged back into traffic. Marcus started the engine. He kept his distance three cars back, careful not to draw attention. The sedan weaved through side streets and took a turn onto a narrow road lined with industrial buildings. Finally, it pulled up outside a run-down auto garage with a rusted sign and boarded windows. Marcus eased to a stop half a block down. The garage. The same place Sam had mentioned. The Vultures' rumored stash house.

He killed the engine and pulled out his phone, snapping a few photos of the car and the building. He spotted a security camera on the garage's side, barely operational, and ducked lower in his seat. The front door creaked open, and Terrance stepped out with another man; bigger, heavier, face hidden beneath a hood. They exchanged a few quiet words before disappearing into the shadows behind the building. Marcus's gut twisted. Something was going down, he just didn't know when or where. He didn't know what they were planning, but he knew one thing: he was officially in deeper than ever.

Still crouched low, he reached into the glove box and pulled out the small notebook where he'd been keeping track of names, places, and connections. With one last glance at the garage, he jotted down the time and address, then slipped it back in place. This was the break he'd been waiting for. And he wasn't about to let it slip away.

In the backroom of the warehouse, Rook sat at the desk pouring a drink. The faint smell of oil and decay clung to the air, mingling with the tension radiating from his every movement. A few of his men stood nearby, exchanging uneasy glances as their leader muttered under his breath.

He stopped mumbling to look at Terrence, who stood awkwardly by the door.

"You're sure?" He asked.

Terrence swallowed hard. "Yeah, I'm sure. Marcus was tailing me yesterday. He's digging too deep, man."

"Marcus," he repeated, as if testing the weight of the name. "I told you to keep a low profile. Now we've got him sniffing around."

"I didn't do anything to make him suspicious!" Terrence protested. "He's just... persistent. Keeps asking questions, following leads. It's like he won't stop."

Rook stepped closer, towering over the younger man. "Of course he won't stop. He's got something to prove. And you let him get too close."

Terrence flinched but didn't respond.

Rook turned to another man sitting in the corner, an older figure known only as Griggs. He was the fixer. The man who handled problems before they became disasters.

"What do we know about this Marcus?"

He lit a cigarette, taking his time to answer. "Mechanic. Local. Tied to that kid in lockup—Jordan. Brothers, I think. Word is he's sharp, doesn't back down easy."

"Great. A hero type."

"Hero or not, he's poking around in things he shouldn't. And if he keeps going, he'll find something he shouldn't."

"Then we make sure he doesn't."

Griggs exhaled a long plume of smoke. "We could scare him off. Pay him a visit, rough him up a bit."

"Too obvious. If he's as determined as you say, it'll just make him dig deeper. No, we need to be smarter. Let's give him something to chew on. A trail that leads him somewhere... inconvenient."

"What do you have in mind?"

"Terrence will be the bait."

Terrence's eyes widened. "What? No way! I'm not—"

"You've already let him get close, so now you're going to use that to our advantage. Feed him just enough information to keep him chasing his tail. And if he gets too close..." he trailed off, letting the implication hang in the air.

Terrence shifted uncomfortably, eyes flicking toward the warehouse door like he wanted to be anywhere else. "You want me to lie to him?"

"I want you to manage him," he said smoothly, swirling the amber liquid in his glass. "Tell him what he wants to hear. Just enough to feel like he's making progress. Keep him focused on the wrong leads."

Terrence hesitated, but Rook's stare left no room for argument. "Alright," he muttered. "I'll do it."

"Good. Make it convincing," he said grabbing a file from the desk. "The less time Marcus spends looking in the right direction, the more time we have to clean up the mess."

Terrence nodded and left without another word. Rook stared at the closed door deep in thought. His paranoia was growing by the minute, fueled by Marcus's relentless investigation. He couldn't afford loose ends. Not now, not when everything was so carefully orchestrated.

Pulling out his phone, he dialed a number.

"It's me," he said when the line connected. "We might have a problem. If this Marcus keeps pushing, I'll need you to take care of it."

The voice on the other end was cold and efficient. "Consider it done."

He hung up and stared at the glass. If Marcus wanted a fight, he was going to get one. But he intended to make sure he would live to regret it.

Chapter 16

The shop was Marcus's sanctuary, the place he always turned to when the world got too loud. Tonight, it felt heavier than usual because he felt the weight of everything he was carrying. He crouched beside the open hood of an old muscle car moving on autopilot as he tightened a bolt. The rhythmic clink of metal on metal helped him think or at least it usually did.

He heard the garage door creak open but didn't look up. Only a few people ever came here unannounced, and he could already guess who it was by the sound of the footsteps.

"You're working late," Myia said, her voice cutting through the hum of the fluorescent lights.

Marcus stayed focused on the engine. "Gotta keep busy."

"Busy? "She repeated as she walked closer. "That what we're calling it now?"

He sighed and placed the wrench on the workbench with a loud clang. "What do you want, Myia?"

She didn't answer right away. Instead, she watched him with a mix of frustration and concern.

"I want to know what the hell you're doing," she finally said.

"I'm doing what I have to do."

"That's not an answer," she said sharply. "You've been out there poking around, chasing gang members, sneaking into places you probably shouldn't be. You're acting like you're in some kind of action movie, and it's gonna get you killed."

He raised his voice. "You think I don't know the risks? You think I don't know how dangerous this is?"

"I think you don't care," she shot back. "You're so focused on saving Jordan that you're not thinking about what it's doing to you or the rest of us."

"That's my brother. He's sitting in jail for something he didn't do. What am I supposed to do, just sit back and hope the system gets it right?"

"No, but there's a difference between fighting for him and throwing yourself into a war you can't win."

"I can win this. I just need more time."

"And what if you're wrong? What if all this digging doesn't lead anywhere? What if you get yourself hurt or worse?"

"Then at least I'll know I didn't quit on him."

"This isn't just about him, is it?"

Marcus stiffened. "What are you talking about?"

"I think you're still trying to make up for everything that happened with my mom. You couldn't save her, so now you're trying to save him."

The words hit like a punch to the gut, but Marcus didn't flinch. He turned back to the car.

"This isn't about her," he said through gritted teeth.

"Isn't it? You're carrying that guilt around like it's your job. But this? This isn't how you fix it."

"You don't get it, Myia. You weren't there. You don't know what it's like to wake up every day and wonder if you could've done more."

She stared at him, stunned into silence.

"Jordan's my brother. If I lose him too, I won't be able to live with myself."

"I get that. I do. But I need to know that you're not gonna let this destroy you."

Marcus didn't respond right away. He leaned against the car and stared down at the engine as if it held the answers he couldn't find. Finally, he said, "I'm not trying to destroy anything. I'm trying to fix what's broken."

"And what if you can't?" Myia asked quietly.

Marcus looked up, meeting his cousin's eyes. "Then at least I'll know I didn't quit. That I did everything I could."

"Just... promise me you'll be careful, alright? I don't want to lose you too."

He gave a faint, tired smile. "I'll be fine. I've got this."

But as she turned to leave, the words felt hollow, even to Marcus. The garage grew quiet again, but the tension hung heavy in the air, refusing to dissipate. Their conversation had him wonder if he was fighting a battle he couldn't win.

The sound of their footsteps echoed in the quiet parking lot as Marcus followed her out of the shop. They had just finished talking. Well, Myia had mostly been warning him and telling him to back off. She tried to convince him to stop digging deeper into the mess surrounding the arrest. He hadn't said much in return, mostly because he knew his cousin was right. But he couldn't stop now.

"You need to think about this," she had urged. "This isn't just about him anymore. It's about you, too."

But Marcus had brushed off the warning. He had no choice but to keep going. He couldn't let his brother sit in jail for something he didn't do. Now, as they stepped out, he felt the weight of the words lingered in the air between them. He knew he wasn't wrong, but things had already started to spiral. And there was no turning back now. They reached the front of the shop when Myia stopped abruptly.

"What the hell?"

Marcus followed her gaze. His stomach dropped. Both of the front tires of his truck were slashed, flat against the pavement. The jagged cuts were deep, deliberate. It was an unmistakable message.

"Shit," Marcus cursed under his breath. He reached down to touch the rubber, his fingers brushing against the sharp edges of the slashes. He knew exactly what this was; A warning. A serious one.

"This is them, right? The people you've been messing with?"

He didn't answer immediately. He scanned the lot looking for anything out of place. The emptiness of the parking lot seemed to grow thicker, like something was lurking just out of sight. Then his gaze flicked to the windshield of his truck. There, tucked under the wiper, was a folded piece of paper. Without a word, he pulled it free and opened it. Myia stood beside him, watching closely. The note was brief, straight to the point. *"Drop it."*

She exhaled sharply. "See I told you. They're not playing around anymore. Who's next?"

Marcus balled his fists. He had expected something like this. Expected them to send a message, but the weight of it still hit hard.

"Doesn't matter," he muttered. "I'm not backing down."

She lightly touched his shoulder, a gesture that was more about holding him back than offering comfort. "You're not the only one who's at risk here. This isn't just your fight anymore."

"It's my fight because it's about Jordan. And I'm going to make sure that he gets out. Especially when I know he didn't do it."

"I get it, but this... this is bigger than just you and Jordan."

He put the note in his pocket. He felt his hands trembling, but it wasn't from fear. It was from the adrenaline that coursed through him.

"Well, they've made it personal now," he said, looking back at his truck. "And I don't back down when it's personal."

Myia didn't respond. She didn't have to. Marcus could feel the unspoken words as he saw her expression. He was on his own now. And maybe that's how it had always been. The warning had been clear. But he was just as clear: He wasn't going to stop.

Chapter 17

The sound of the cell door clanging shut echoed through Jordan's bones. He'd heard it a hundred times by now, but it never got any easier. Cold. Final. Like a judgment. He sat on the edge of the thin cot, his elbows resting on his knees, hands clasped tightly together. It was another long day in Crest Ridge County Jail, and he was running out of hope.

The worst part wasn't the confinement. It wasn't the food, if you could call it that, or the constant tension that hung in the air like smoke. It wasn't even the stares from other inmates who thought they could size him up because he wasn't loud or reckless. The worst part was the waiting. The silence before his next court date. The wondering. Not knowing how much longer he'd have to stay here for something he didn't do.

He closed his eyes and leaned back against the cinder block wall, letting his mind wander to the night everything went wrong. The flashing lights. The cuffs. The cold words from the arresting officer: "You're under arrest for armed robbery." It had been a blur after that. Even now, the details didn't make sense. He was at the store. He never denied that. He'd gone to grab some snacks and a soda before heading home. But he left before anything went down. He was sure of it.

So how the hell did his prints end up on the gun? He'd asked himself that question a thousand times. He replayed every moment of that night, trying to find the crack. The point where someone else might've stepped in to set him up. And each time, he came up short.

A voice from the hallway snapped him back to the present.

"Carter. You've got a visitor."

He stood, heart pounding. Maybe it was Marcus again. Maybe he had something, anything, to offer. A shred of good news. A new lead. Something to keep him from drowning in the waiting. He followed the guard down the sterile corridor to the visitor room and sat in the seat across the Plexiglas partition. But it wasn't Marcus.

It was Mr. Miller, his public defender. He placed a stack of papers on the table before lifting the phone to her ear.

"How are you holding up?"

"Like anyone does in here," he said when he picked up the receiver. "What's going on?"

"I've been reviewing your case. I submitted a request for the full surveillance footage from the convenience store, but the copy we received... it's edited."

His heart sank. "Edited? So, they're hiding something."

"It looks that way. Your brother's been doing a lot of digging. More than I can legally do on my own." He gave a small smirk. It was the closest thing to encouragement he'd seen in weeks. "I think he's onto something."

Jordan pressed his forehead to the glass for a moment, trying to let the words soak in. "I told him not to get involved."

"And yet he is. Deeply. Whatever you two have going on, he's not giving up on you."

Jordan let out a breath. A knot of emotion twisted in his chest. Guilt. Gratitude. Fear.

"He shouldn't have to do this," he said. "He's got a whole life out there."

"You didn't do this, son. I can see it in how you talk about that night. But we need more than words. We need proof. And your brother might be the only one out there willing to risk finding it."

"I think I know who could've set me up. But I can't prove it."

"Who?"

He hesitated. "A guy named Rook. I don't know him personally, but I heard his name a few times from Terrence. He's deep with the Iron Vultures."

"The gang?"

"Yeah. I think someone needed a fall guy, and I was close enough to make it work. I'd been hanging with Terrence that week, mostly at his girl's place. I told the cops that, but they didn't care."

Mr. Miller paused, tapping the end of his pen against the table. "Why are you just saying this now?"

Jordan shrugged stiffly. "Because nobody's listened before. Soon as I was picked up, they decided I was guilty. I told the first guy they sent me. He didn't even write it down."

"What exactly did Terrence say about this 'Rook'?"

"He'd get these calls. Step outside to take them. Came back in saying things like, 'Rook don't like loose ends,' or 'we gotta move fast—Rook said so.' Real twitchy, like something was coming down."

He scribbled a few notes. "And you think they planned something that week?"

Jordan nodded. "Yeah. It wasn't just random. I think whatever went down at that store, they already had it lined up. I was just... convenient."

"Do you think Terrence would testify?"

"He won't," Jordan said bitterly. "He's in deep too."

They sat in silence for a moment. Then Jordan added, "When you see Marcus again can you tell him to just be careful? These people don't play around. If Rook finds out he's looking into him, it won't just stop with threats."

"I'll pass it along."

Jordan returned to his cell with the same thoughts chasing him in circles. He leaned back against the wall, staring up at the flickering light above him. He was tired of the walls, the fear, and the helplessness. He thought about Marcus. Always the one with grease-stained hands and stubborn determination. He didn't know how to let things go. Once he had his teeth in something, he'd fight until there was nothing left to bite.

Jordan wished he could be like that. But he wasn't built that way. Not anymore. He remembered when he younger, how he tagged along at the garage. He would watch Marcus fix up old engines and make them run like new. There had been a kind of magic in it. In seeing something broken come back to life. He wondered if he still believed people could be fixed the same way. Because Jordan wasn't sure he could. Still, there was one thing he did believe in: his brother. And if Marcus said he'd find the truth, then there was still a way out of this.

He crossed the small cell and opened the notebook he'd started keeping since the arrest. It was mostly notes, little things he remembered about that night, or people he thought might be connected. He flipped to a blank page and started writing.

Terrence was nervous that day. Kept checking his phone. Said someone was gonna "make a move."

He left the store before I did. Said he had to meet someone. Didn't say who.

There was a black SUV parked outside. Never saw who was driving.

Clerk barely looked at me. Seemed... off.

He paused, tapping the pen against the page. Then, in block letters, he wrote:

FIND ROOK. FIND THE SUV. PROVE I WAS SET UP.

He tore the page out and folded it once, twice. Then he slid it between the pages of his Bible. It was the only thing the guards didn't mess with. It was a small act of defiance. Of hope. As he lay back on the cot, staring at the ceiling, Jordan let his thoughts drift toward freedom. Not just for himself, but for Marcus too. Because this fight, unfair and ugly as it was, had dragged them both into its center. And if they were going to survive it, they'd have to lean on each other harder than ever before.

Marcus sat in his truck, parked just down the street from the warehouse where Rook ran his operation. The building loomed in the distance, a dark monolith surrounded by chain-link fence and scattered junk. Even now, even after all that had happened, the place looked like nothing more than an old storage depot. But Marcus knew better.

Claire's footage was burning a hole in his pocket. It was proof that Jordan hadn't been the one holding the gun. But it wasn't enough. Not for the cops, not for a jury. Not when the system was already treating him like a suspect instead of a victim. He needed more. A name. A link. Something that would make it impossible to ignore the truth. And that something might be sitting inside the rusted metal building in front of him.

He exhaled, rubbed a hand over his jaw. He wasn't stupid. He knew this was a gamble, maybe even suicidal. Rook didn't play fair. But if the footage Claire pulled was any indication, he had something to hide. And Marcus planned on finding it. His phone rang in the passenger seat.

"You watching the warehouse?" Sam asked.

"I've been here thirty minutes. No one's gone in or out."

"You sure about that? Because I just got word that his people are onto you. They've seen you tailing Terrence."

"So what, they're spooked?"

"They're worse than spooked. They're planning something. I don't know what yet, but I can feel it in the way the chatter's gone quiet."

Marcus looked in the rearview mirror to see the road behind him. Nothing obvious. No headlights. No movement. Still, his pulse kicked up a notch.

"I'm not backing off," he said.

"I didn't expect you to," Sam replied. "Just... don't go in there alone. Not tonight."

Marcus hung up without promising anything. Across the street, the warehouse door creaked open. A man stepped out—tall, hood up, hands in his pockets. He lit a cigarette and leaned against the wall like he had all the time in the world.

Terrence.

Marcus cursed again, this time under his breath. He wasn't ready for a confrontation. Not here, not yet. But seeing him now, after everything the lawyer repeated told him, made his blood run hot. He picked up his phone and dialed Claire.

"I need another favor," he said when she answered. "You said you could track that SUV, right? The one linked to Rook's shell company?"

"I've been narrowing it down," she replied. "There's one that pings near the docks every few days. I thought it was a dead end. It's probably just storage runs."

"No. That's your target. Keep eyes on it. I want to know every time it moves."

"Got it. You think the gun's still in there?"

"I think if we find that SUV, we find the truth."

After hanging up, Marcus leaned back in his seat to take one more long look at the warehouse. Then, slowly, he put the truck in gear and backed away from the curb. This wasn't the time to go in blind. Not with the heat rising. He'd regroup, let Claire do her thing, and wait for the SUV to slip up. Because once it did, he would be there—ready to finish what someone else had started.

Chapter 18

Marcus was under the hood of a rusted-out Buick, grease coating his hands and the tang of motor oil clinging to the back of his throat, when his phone buzzed in his pocket. He wiped his hands on a rag, grabbed the phone, and saw Sam's name flashing on the screen.

"Talk to me," he said, stepping away from the car.

"I found him," Sam said, no preamble. His voice carried a mix of relief and urgency.

Marcus's heart kicked up. "Who?"

"Reggie. The store clerk. The one who disappeared right after the robbery."

Marcus straightened, already walking toward the garage exit. "Where?"

"Lakehaven. Some small gas station off Highway 6. I got a buddy down there who recognized his picture. He says he's been working the night shift for the past couple weeks."

"Lakehaven's three hours away."

"Yeah, but he's there. Using a fake last name, but it's him. My guy says he keeps his head down and doesn't talk much. But you can tell he's scared of something."

Marcus was already thinking about the quickest route out of town. "He saw something."

"That's my guess. And whatever it was, it was enough to make him run."

"I'll head out tonight."

"You sure that's smart? Word's out that you're stirring things up. If someone knows you're chasing Reggie—"

"I don't care," Marcus cut in. "If he knows anything, anything that clears Jordan, then I'm not waiting."

"Alright. I'll text you the address. And Marcus?"

"Yeah?"

"Be careful. If someone went through the trouble of finding and threatening him once, they might do it again."

"Let 'em try."

He ended the call and grabbed his keys from the hook by the door. The Buick could wait. Tonight, he was chasing answers.

The road to Lakehaven stretched long and quiet, the highway flanked by pine trees and the occasional broken-down billboard. Marcus drove with the windows down, letting the wind clear his thoughts. The address Sam had given him was scrawled on a notepad in the passenger seat—Eastside Gas & Go. It was a small fuel station on the other side of the town.

By the time he pulled into the cracked parking lot, the sky was an ink-blue canvas, the last hints of daylight bleeding into the horizon. The gas station stood under a flickering fluorescent sign, its buzzing neon letters fighting to stay lit. A couple of pumps stood idle, and inside, a single man stood behind the counter. Marcus killed the engine and stepped out.

The glass doors slid open with a mechanical hiss, and the air-conditioned chill greeted him. A few customers milled about, grabbing snacks or paying for gas, but his eyes zeroed in on the clerk behind the counter.

"Can I help you?" the clerk asked as Marcus stepped up to the counter. His tone was polite but cautious. His eyes flickered briefly to Marcus's face before darting away.

He pulled out his wallet and slid a twenty onto the counter. "Yeah, let me get this tea, and one of those protein bars." He nodded toward the rack near the register.

The clerk grabbed the items, his movements quick and slightly jittery. "That all?"

"For now," he replied casually. He took a slow breath to remind himself to ease into this.

The clerk handed him the change and the items. "Next customer."

Marcus stepped aside as the next person in line moved up. He cracked open the tea and took a sip. He looked around the store as he waited for the clerk to finish.

When the line cleared, he stepped back up to the counter. "You got a minute?"

The clerk looked at him warily. "For what?"

Marcus didn't say anything at first. Just looked at him. "Reggie."

"I—I go by Rick now," he said too quickly, voice tight.

"Yeah, I figured. But we both know who you are."

Reggie glanced around like he needed someone to swoop in to save him. No one did.

"I'm not here to make trouble," Marcus said. "I just want the truth. You were working the night of the robbery. You saw what happened."

"I already told the cops everything I know."

"Yeah, I'm sure you did," he replied , keeping his tone even. "But I'm not the cops. I'm just a brother trying to figure out why my kid brother is locked up for something he didn't do."

"Look, man, I don't want any trouble."

"Neither do I. I just need the truth."

The clerk hesitated, his fingers tapping nervously on the counter. Marcus noticed the subtle signs of unease. The way his eyes kept shifting, the tightness in his shoulders. This guy was hiding something.

"Look. I've seen the footage. You were calm. Too calm. Now, either you're used to getting robbed, or you knew something was going down."

Reggie licked his lips. "I don't know anything, man."

"That's not what I heard."

Reggie swallowed. His hand trembled slightly as he set the rag aside. "I left because I was scared, okay? After it happened, these guys came around asking questions. Not the cops. Different guys. They knew my name. My schedule."

"Who were they?"

"I don't know! One of them had this tattoo - a snake coiled around a skull. Said I should keep my mouth shut if I wanted to keep breathing."

"You saw who did it, didn't you? The guy who actually pulled the gun?"

"Yeah. It wasn't your brother. He came in earlier, bought snacks, talked on the phone. The guy who robbed us came later. Had a hood up, gloves, moved like he knew where the cameras were. Like he'd done it before."

"You recognize him?"

"No, but... he had this patch on his jacket. Same tattoo as that guy who threatened me."

Marcus felt his gut twist. That symbol matched the one Claire had pointed out in the footage.

"Why didn't you tell the cops?"

"I tried. I started writing a report, but then that guy showed up at my apartment. After that, I packed my stuff and ran."

"You need to come back. Talk to the police. Give a statement."

"No way. I'm not dying for this. I kept quiet, changed towns, and I'm still looking over my shoulder."

"You think running forever is safer than speaking up?" Marcus asked. "My brother is sitting in a cell for something he didn't do. You can fix that."

Reggie looked down. He didn't respond.

"You're scared. I get it. But if you don't come forward, they win. And the next time they do something like this, there won't be anyone left to say anything."

Reggie looked around the empty store, then leaned in closer. His voice dropped to a whisper. "You don't understand. These people... they don't mess around."

"Who?"

"I can't—"

"You can. And you will. Because if you're scared now, imagine how scared you'll be when they think you're the reason this all comes out."

"I didn't know what they were planning," he said finally, his voice barely audible. "But a guy came in a couple of days before the robbery. Told me to keep my mouth shut, no matter what happened. Said if I played along, I'd be fine."

"Who was he?"

"I don't know his name. But he's head of a crew that works for the Vultures. They call him Rook."

"And what did he want you to do?"

"Just act normal. Pretend I didn't see anything. Said if I even looked like I was gonna call the cops, it'd be the last thing I ever did."

"And you didn't think to tell the cops this after the fact?"

"You think they'd protect me? Guys like him have connections everywhere. Even in here." He gestured around the store.

"But you are the key to my brother getting out."

Reggie closed his eyes. Finally, he nodded. "Okay. But I want protection. Witness stuff. I'm not walking back into Crest Ridge unless someone's got my back."

"I'll talk to someone," Marcus promised. "Just get ready. This ends with the truth coming out."

As he turned to leave, Reggie called after him. "Hey."

Marcus looked back.

"I saw the security footage before they swapped it out. It was cleaner. Showed everything. The guy—they edited him out."

"I've seen the original. We'll get there. One step at a time."

He pushed the door open and stepped out into the night. Time to bring Reggie home.

Chapter 19

Marcus sat in his car outside the convenience store processing what Reggie had told him. Rook's name loomed in his mind, heavy and foreboding. A name like that didn't just come up by accident.

Reggie hadn't said much. Just enough to let Marcus know he was getting too close to something people wanted buried. Rook. The fixer. The shadow. The name that keeps coming up.

He glanced at his phone, debating his next move. If this man had eyes and ears everywhere, he knew he couldn't just charge into this recklessly. But waiting wasn't an option either. Not with Jordan stuck in jail, and the clock ticking on clearing his name. A text notification lit up his screen.

Sam: Got something. Meet me at the spot in tomorrow .

Sam had already proven to be a solid ally. If he'd found more intel, it could be the break Marcus needed. He fired off a quick reply and started the car.

The "spot" was an old auto salvage yard. It was a place that they had met a few times to exchange sensitive information. It was quiet and remote, with rusting car frames piled high and weeds growing between the cracked pavement.

Marcus pulled off the road and down the gravel path driving passed twisted heaps of metal and shattered windshields. The further he drove, the more the world seemed to drop away. No traffic. Just the sound of his tires crunching over broken stone.

Sam was leaning against his sedan when Marcus arrive. He straightened up as Marcus approached.

"Thought you might bail after the warning they gave you," he said half-jokingly, but with an edge of concern.

"Not a chance. What've you got?"

Sam opened the trunk of his car and pulled out a file folder, handing it over. "I made a few calls, dug around. Turns out Rook's been running a side hustle—smuggling stolen goods. Small-time stuff, but it's lucrative enough to keep him under the radar. And here's the kicker: he's been using the same crew that pulled the job at the store."

Marcus flipped through the papers in the folder. There were photos, documents, even a partial list of names connected to Rook's operation.

"This is good," Marcus nodded. "Real good. But it doesn't prove Jordan wasn't involved."

"That's the thing. One of the names on that list? Terrence. Your brother's friend."

Marcus froze. "Are you sure?"

"Positive. He's been working for Rook for a while now. Mostly low-level stuff like running errands and making deliveries. But enough to tie him to the gang."

"He's deeper in than you thought."

Marcus shut the folder. He felt a wave of betrayal roll through him. "Jordan didn't know. He wouldn't have—"

"—protected him?" Sam asked carefully.

Marcus shook his head. "No. Not if he knew Terrence was tied to any of this. Jordan doesn't play like that. He's always been about loyalty, but not blind loyalty."

Sam watched him closely. "Loyalty makes people overlook things. Especially when it's someone they've known since they were kids. Someone who's been there during the hard years."

Marcus looked away. He remembered the nights Terrence used to crash at their place after his mom got locked up. The basketball games in the driveway. The way he and Jordan used to talk like brothers.

"If he's working for Rook, that puts him real close to the wrong kind of people," Marcus muttered. "And that makes my brother vulnerable by association."

"Exactly. Rook's not sloppy. He builds his circle with people who can get close to targets without raising suspicion."

"That means Jordan might've been a target from the start."

"Or a useful pawn," Sam replied. "I'm not saying he did. But it explains how the gun ended up in his orbit. If his friend was involved in the job, and he was with him earlier that night, it wouldn't take much to plant it. Or set him up as the fall guy."

Marcus turned, pacing a few steps away before looking back at Sam. "Terrence has been feeding me half-truths this whole time. Playing both sides."

"Yeah," Sam said. "And if he knows you're getting close, he might be ready to make his next move. You need to be careful."

Marcus was already calculating his next step. He'd trusted Terrence, maybe not completely, but enough to give him the benefit of the doubt. Now that trust was a liability.

"I need to talk to him. Face to face."

"You sure that's a good idea?"

"No. But I'm not letting him disappear before I get some answers."

He tucked the folder under his arm and headed back toward his truck. "Keep digging. If you find anything else, I want to know."

I've got another lead, too," Sam added. "There's a warehouse on the south side of town. Rook's crew uses it to stash goods before they move them. If you're looking for hard evidence, that's where you'll find it."

"How sure are you?"

"Pretty damn sure. I cross-referenced some of the deliveries Rook's been linked to; dates, times, locations. They all circle back to that warehouse. It's off Canal and Sycamore. Real quiet part of town. No cameras. No nosy neighbors."

Marcus leaned against the hood of his truck. "That could be the break we need."

"Could be. Or it could be a trap. You go in alone, you better be ready for anything."

"I'm not going in guns blazing. I just want a look. If there's something in there that proves a frame up, something they didn't clean up, I'll find it."

"Be smart about it. And don't hang around too long. If Rook catches wind you're sniffing around his stash spot..."

"He'll make a move. Let him."

"Just don't get yourself killed, alright? I'll keep working and see what else I can dig up."

Marcus gave a tight nod. "Thanks, man. Keep your phone close."

This time, he wasn't just following leads. He was hunting for the truth. And if it lived in that warehouse, he was going to drag it out into the light.

Later that night, Marcus sat at his kitchen table, the folder spread out in front of him. He'd already memorized the address of the warehouse, but he wasn't about to rush in blind. He needed a plan. His phone buzzed, pulling him from his thoughts. It was Myia.

"Hey," Marcus answered.

"Where are you?" Her voice was tense.

"Home. Why?"

"Because I just got a call from Auntie. She's freaking out. Someone's been asking about you. She said they were gang members. They also came by the shop today."

Marcus's blood ran cold. "Did they do anything?"

"No, but they made it clear they're watching. She's scared, Marcus. She doesn't know what's going on, but she knows it's bad."

Marcus stood up, pacing the length of the kitchen, the phone pressed tightly to his ear. His eyes flicked to the folder on the table, the pages now feeling heavier with risk.

"Damn it," he muttered. "They're trying to rattle me."

"Well, it's working," she snapped. "I told you that this isn't just about you anymore. What if she get caught up in the crossfire?"

"She won't," he said quickly, though his heart was pounding. "I'll handle it."

"How? By storming into some warehouse in the middle of the night? You think you're invincible or something?"

"No," Marcus said. "I just know if I stop now, Jordan goes down for something he didn't do. And Rook keeps getting away with stuff like this."

There was a long silence on the other end of the line before she spoke again, softer this time. "Just... be careful. I'm serious. You're getting too close, and they know it."

"I know," Marcus said. "But I can't back off. Not now. Not with everything I've learned."

"You need help."

"I've got Sam. I've got leads. I just need one more piece to tie it all together."

Another pause.

"I don't like this," she finally said. "But I get it. Just promise me you'll check in every day. Even if it's just a text."

"I promise."

"Okay," she said, and he could hear the worry still clinging to her voice. "You know I love you, right?"

"I know. Love you too."

He pulled out his phone and opened his messages. A thread with Tyson hovered near the top. He tapped it and started typing.

MARCUS: *You good?*

It only took a minute for the typing dots to appear.

TYSON: *Yeah, just finished up at the shop. You?*

MARCUS: *Long story. I'll fill you in later. Listen—can you do me a favor?*

TYSON: *Always.*

MARCUS: Can you keep an eye on Mama's place for the next few days? Nelly said some people came by asking about me. Gang types. I don't want her caught up in any of this.

A longer pause this time. Then:

TYSON: Say less. I'll swing by tonight and park down the street. I'll keep watch.

Marcus let out a slow breath, his fingers tightening around the phone.

MARCUS: Thanks, man. I owe you.

TYSON: You don't owe me a damn thing. We family. Just find the truth and bring your brother home.

Marcus stared at those words for a long moment. Then he walked back to the table, sat down, and pulled a map of Crest Ridge from a drawer. He circled the warehouse address in red, just like he had with Rook's name earlier that week. If they were watching him now, fine. He'd give them something to watch.

Chapter 20

Lost in thought, Marcus leaned over the counter of his shop. Jordan's situation had turned into a tangled mess, with each clue dragging him deeper and deeper. What started as a fight to clear his brother's name had become something far more dangerous than he expected.

He tapped the edge of a spark plug box absently, his gaze fixed on the far wall but not really seeing it. His mind kept circling the same questions: Who was setting Jordan up? How deep did Rook's network really go? And what the hell was Terrence doing mixed up with all of it?

Normally, the routine of fixing cars helped him think. Metal made sense, unlike people. But not today. He reached for his phone and checked it again. No new messages. He'd texted Sam twice since the meeting at the salvage yard, and still nothing back.

A photo of Jordan was pinned to the bulletin board beside the counter. It was from a year ago. He was laughing as he stood beside the Camaro they'd rebuilt together. Marcus stared at it. He couldn't let his brother go down for something he didn't do. Not when he could feel how orchestrated all of this was.

He opened the folder again, flipping through pages of surveillance stills and notes. His own scribbles littered the margins: connections, addresses, fragments of conversations he couldn't forget. He paused on a printout with Terrence's name circled in red ink, just as the chime of the front door pulled him from his thoughts.

A short husky man entered with his face partially obscured by a baseball cap. He carried himself nonchalantly, yet there was something about him that instantly made Marcus uneasy.

"I'm looking for Marcus."

"Who wants to know?" he replied, straightening up.

Removing his cap, the man revealed a round face and a barely visible scar along his jaw. "Name's Darnell. Heard you've been poking around Rook's business."

"And you just decided to stroll in here and tell me that?"

"Let's just say I got a vested interest in what you're doing. I understand your investigation might be causing trouble, but you're right to be suspicious. His crew ain't as tight as they like to pretend."

"Why do you care?"

"Because I've been in your shoes before. I used to run with Malik Johnson. Yeah, *that* Malik. Trust me, what you think you know about him is just the beginning."

The mention of that name was like a punch to the gut. Memories of the family tragedy flooded Marcus' mind as he clenched his fists. "You're wasting your time if you think I care about that POS. He got his just desserts for what he did to my aunt," he said coldly.

"You should," he shot back. "Because his mess didn't die with him. He had ties to that crew. Deep ones. The same crew that's framing your brother."

Marcus felt a tightening in his chest but kept a calm exterior. "You've got a funny way of proving you're not just here to waste my time. Why don't you start talking?"

Darnell sighed and pulled out a crumpled envelope from his jacket and put it on the counter. Marcus opened it to find a stack of grainy photos.

"That's him with Rook and his right-hand man, Tony. They go way back. Malik wasn't just some random hothead; he was working angles for the gang before he went off the rails. And now, they're trying to clean up any loose ends that could tie them to him."

Marcus examined the pictures. "What's their angle now? Why frame Jordan?"

"He's an easy scapegoat. They've got heat on them from the cops, and they needed someone to pin their mess on. A kid with no solid alibi? Perfect target."

He pounded his fist on the counter. "Why are you telling me this? If you're so deep in their world, what's stopping you from turning me in?"

"Because Malik's choices ruined my life too. He dragged me into this mess, and by the time I realized what kind of people I was dealing with, it was too late. I'm out now, but I've been watching. You're the first person who's actually got the guts to fight back. So yeah, I'm helping. Not for you, but for me."

Marcus eyed him, trying to see if he was being truthful. He didn't trust Darnell, not entirely, but the photos added weight to his story.

"If you're lying to me..."

"I'm not," he interrupted. "And if you're smart, you'll use what I'm giving you to take him down before he comes for you or your brother. You're in deeper than you realize. Watch your back."

With that, he headed for the door.

"Wait," Marcus called after him. "Why now? Why come to me now?"

He paused as he opened the door. "Because I know what it's like to lose everything because of that crew. Don't let them take your brother too."

The door shut behind him, leaving Marcus alone with the photos and a gnawing sense of dread. The stakes had just gotten higher, and the shadows of Malik's past were closing in.

He sank into his chair and stared at the photos spread out on the counter. If what Darnell said was true, then Jordan's case wasn't just about a robbery. It was about unfinished business and the fallout from a storm Malik had set in motion long before his death. Gripping the edge of the counter, Marcus made a silent vow.

Whatever it took, he'd find the truth. Even if it meant facing ghosts he'd tried to bury.

Each photo was a breadcrumb and each face was a shadow from a past he'd worked hard to forget. But now they stared back at him, demanding answers. One showed Malik outside a rundown building he hadn't seen in years. Another captured Jordan laughing with a group he didn't recognize... except for one man in the corner, half-obscured by shadow. Rook.

He rubbed his jaw and exhaled slowly. The deeper he went, the more the lines blurred. This wasn't just about justice anymore. He gathered the photos and slipped them into a manila envelope. He didn't know exactly what he'd find, but he knew where to start.

Marcus sat in his truck outside the pool hall. The photos from earlier sat on the passenger seat. He'd spent a majority of the day studying them. Every detail, every face, and every connection. Now, he was here to test Darnell's claims.

Near the entrance, a couple of men stood around smoking and talking. He recognized one of them from the photos—Tony, Rook's right-hand man.

His heart pounded, but he forced himself to breathe steadily. He wasn't here to start a fight. He just needed to confirm what was told to him.

Sliding out of the truck, he adjusted his jacket and made his way across the lot. He kept his stride steady and his expression neutral, as if he belonged there. The two men stopped talking as he approached, their eyes narrowing.

"Who's this?" Tony asked roughly.

"Just looking to shoot a few games," he said, nodding toward the door.

He blocked his path. "Ain't seen you around here before. What's your name?"

Marcus glanced at the other man, who was already reaching for something in his waistband. A gun? A knife? Either way, he had to think fast.

"Name's Marcus," he said calmly. "I'm just here to ask a couple of questions."

"Questions, huh? You're either real brave or real stupid coming here with that."

He held up his hands. "Not looking for trouble. Just want to talk."

The other man, now visibly holding a knife, stepped closer. "You got about ten seconds to explain what you're really doing here, or we'll make sure you don't leave walking."

Though his pulse pounded, he didn't flinch. "I know Rook's been busy lately. And I know he's got something to do with the robbery they pinned on my brother."

The smirk left Tony's face, replaced with a chilling, threatening stare. "You're walking on thin ice, man. You don't want to be throwing accusations around like that."

"Maybe not. But I've got proof your boss is cleaning up after Malik's mess. And I'm guessing he doesn't want that getting out."

The mention of that name was like a switch flipping. A dark look crossed Tony's face as he seized Marcus by the jacket and slammed him against the wall.

"You don't say that name around here," he growled.

"Why not? Afraid of what people might find out? Afraid someone might finally put it all together?"

The knife-wielding man advanced, but Tony stopped him with a raised hand.

"You got guts, I'll give you that," he said as he pushed Marcus away. "But guts don't mean much when you're dealing with us. If I were you, I'd drop this before you end up like Malik."

He straightened his jacket and smirked. "Yeah, well... I'm not you."

Tony stared at him for a long moment before chuckling darkly. "You're either crazy or suicidal. Either way, this will be interesting."

Without another word, he turned and walked into the pool hall with the other man following close behind. Marcus stayed where he was as his heart pounded in his chest. He'd gotten what he came for, confirmation that Rook's crew was hiding something. But now, he was on their radar in a way he hadn't been before.

As he walked back to his truck, he spotted a small envelope tucked under his windshield wiper. He opened it, finding a single piece of paper with two words scrawled in black ink:

Back off.

Marcus crumpled the note in his fist.

"Not a chance," he muttered, climbing into his truck.

The deeper he dug, the more dangerous this game became. But he had come too far to stop now. If they believed a few threats would intimidate him, they were about discover just how mistaken they had been.

Chapter 21

Marcus was halfway through tuning up an old Chevy when the sound of hurried footsteps reached his ears. Straightening up, he wiped his hands on a rag, his muscles tensed at the sight of a shadow approaching the open bay door.

"Marcus," the figure called out, voice trembling.

He walked closer to the entrance. It took a moment for him to recognize the disheveled, bloodied figure. "Deon?"

Jordan's friend, Deon, entered the room in a state of disrepair, his clothes torn and his gait unsteady as he stumbled. His breathing was uneven, and one hand was pressed tightly to his side as if in pain.

"Help me," he said as he sat onto a stool near the workbench.

Marcus rushed forward, grabbing a clean towel to press against the wound. "What the hell happened to you?"

He winced as he held the towel. "They found me... Rook's guys. I think they were trying to send a message."

"You've been missing for weeks. Where have you been?"

"I've been hiding," he said, his voice cracking. "After the robbery... things got out of control. I didn't know who to trust. But they found me anyway."

"Why now? Why come to me?"

"Because you're the only one who might actually listen."

Marcus pulled up a stool. "Start from the beginning."

He took a shaky, uncertain breath. "That day at the store, Jordan didn't know what was happening. I swear to God, he didn't. We were supposed to meet up, but when I got there... something felt off. These guys were hanging around, watching the place."

"And you didn't go in?"

"I stayed back, but I saw them walk out. I recognized one of them—Tony. They were carrying a bag, and when they saw me..." He trailed off, shaking his head.

"What happened next?"

"They didn't say anything at first, just stared at me like I was a loose end. I took off, and I've been running ever since."

"Why didn't you come forward earlier?"

"Because I didn't think anyone would believe me. And when I realized they saw me... I got scared."

A car passed slowly down the street, headlights sweeping across the cracked sidewalk. Both men tensed until the vehicle disappeared around the corner.

"I've been laying low, trying to figure out what to do," Deon managed. "But you asking questions again... you're stirring up stuff they buried a long time ago."

"I'm not gonna let Jordan take the fall for something he didn't do."

Deon looked at him. "You remember Reggie?"

"Yeah. He worked the register that day."

"Word is someone mailed him a picture of his daughter. No note. Just the picture."

Marcus swore under his breath. "They're cleaning house."

"Exactly. Anyone who was there, anyone who might talk..."

Marcus stood and started pacing. "We've got to get ahead of this. Take it public. Names, times, everything."

"You think that'll stop them?"

"No. But it makes it harder for them to move in the dark."

"Doesn't matter. They're paranoid. And now that you're digging into it..."

"They're targeting me too," Marcus finished, "I already know."

"You've got their attention, man. And if you don't back off, they're going to come for you next."

"You think I don't know that? They've been watching the shop. One of them tried to follow me home yesterday. I circled the block three times just to lose him."

Deon slouched against the wall near the tool cabinet still holding the towel against his left side. Blood seeped through the fabric in lazy pulses. "They caught me outside my cousin's place. No warning. Just rolled up, tossed me in the back of a van, and worked me over like I owed them something."

"What did they say?"

"Didn't need to say much. One of them, pretty sure it was Tony, kept whispering your name between hits. Said you were 'getting curious.' Said next time they'd come for you directly."

Marcus's fists clenched. "That's a mistake."

"Don't act like you're invincible, man," he said sharply. "This isn't like it was back when we were just dealing with street-level guys. These people have money, cops, even lawyers in their pockets. They erased Jordan's name like he never existed. You really think they won't do worse to you?"

"That's exactly why I'm not backing down."

"Then you're crazier than I thought."

A distant thud echoed from outside. Maybe a dumpster lid slamming shut, maybe not. Both men froze for a second, instinctively glancing toward the garage door. Marcus walked over, eased it up a few inches, and peeked through the gap. Nothing. Just the empty alley lit by a flickering streetlamp.

"They're sending a message," he said as he lowered the door. "But I'm not just going to sit around and wait for them to clean up the rest of us. You said Tony. Anyone else?"

"Yeah. A new guy. Haven't seen him before, but he's dangerous. Quiet. Didn't say a word, just kept looking at me like I was already dead."

"Name?"

"Didn't catch it. But he's the one who cut me. Got in close without a sound."

Marcus looked over at the first aid kit on the shelf, grabbed some gauze and tape, and tossed it to him. "You need to lay low for a while."

"Already planning on it," he caught the supplies. "Somewhere they can't find me."

As he pulled the towel away to adjust the bandage, a fresh wave of pain crossed his face.

Marcus knelt beside him to secure the gauze. "Thanks for coming here. I mean it."

Deon shifted uncomfortably as he adjusted the towel on his side. "Look, I don't want any part of this anymore. I came to warn you because you're the only one who might actually stand a chance against them. But you've got to be careful, Marcus. These guys don't play around."

"I know."

"I need to lie low again. If they find out I talked to you..."

"They won't. But if you remember anything else, you come to me first."

"Be careful. You're in deeper than you think."

As Deon limped out of the shop and disappeared into the night, Marcus felt the weight of the situation settle heavier on his shoulders. He stood by the open bay door and stared out into the dark street. If Deon's story was true, and he had no reason to doubt it, it meant Jordan wasn't just caught up in a botched robbery. He was collateral in a far more dangerous game.

The faint sound of tires crunching gravel drew his attention. A car rolled slowly down the street with the headlights off. Marcus narrowed his eyes and stepped further into the shadows of the garage. His gut tightened as the vehicle paused near his shop, idling for just a moment before moving on.

"Rook's people," he muttered under his breath.

The hum of neon buzzed faintly through the cracked window as Rook leaned back in his chair, cigar smoke curling lazily above his head. His office in the back of the pool hall was small, cluttered, and always dim. Just the way he liked it. Out front, the crack of pool balls and low thrum of music masked most conversations. But in here, silence ruled. The burner phone on the desk buzzed twice. He didn't move at first, just glanced at the screen. No name. Just a number he recognized. He snatched it up, pressing it to his ear with a grunt.

"Talk."

A nervous voice answered. Young. Edgy. One of his runners. "It's me. We got a situation."

He took a slow drag from his cigar. "I'm listening."

"Deon showed up. At Marcus's place."

"Come again?"

"I saw him with my own eyes. Kid looked jumpy, like he'd seen a ghost. Wasn't there long, but he came out looking like he dropped a damn confession."

"He wasn't supposed to be in town. Last I heard, he ran scared."

"Yeah, well... he came back. And he ran straight to Marcus."

For a long beat, he didn't speak. The only sound was the quiet crackle of the cigar and the muffled chatter outside the office door.

"Keep eyes on both of them, "he said finally. His voice was low, measured. Dangerous. "I want to know everywhere Marcus goes. Everyone he talks to. And if Deon opens his mouth again—"

"You want me to handle it?"

Rook exhaled slowly, the smoke unfurling like a threat. "Not yet. But if Marcus keeps pushing... this time we don't let him walk away."

He ended the call and set the phone down. His gaze drifted toward the dusty window that overlooked the alley. A stray cat darted past a garbage can, and in the distance, a siren wailed faint and uninterested.

Rook leaned back in his chair as the worn leather creaked beneath him. His fingers drummed slowly against the desk, tapping out a rhythm of impatience. They'd already cleaned up the mess at the corner store. But Marcus? He wasn't letting go. And Deon—Deon had the kind of memory that got people killed.

He crushed the cigar into the ashtray, the ember hissing in protest.

"Let him dig," he muttered to himself. "Let him think he's onto something."

He reached into the bottom drawer of his desk and pulled out a faded folder. Inside: surveillance stills, transcripts, receipts. A list of names with some already crossed out. There were only a few left. Marcus's was at the top. He traced it with his finger, then shut the folder and slid it aside as footsteps approached the office. A knock.

He didn't look up. "Come in."

The door creaked open, letting in a sliver of hallway light. A young man stepped inside, eyes nervous, hands tucked into the pockets of his jacket.

"They moved him," he said quietly. "Deon's not at the address we had on him."

Rook's lips curled into a slow, cold smile. "Then we find where he ran to. And this time... we don't just scare him."

Chapter 22

Marcus's truck rumbled through the dark street. He glanced in his rearview mirror, his gut telling him something wasn't right. The road was empty and quiet, but something felt off. The hairs on the back of his neck stood up. He checked the side mirror. Nothing. He did it again. Still nothing. A sudden noise, tires screeching, pulled his attention to the front. A car appeared out of nowhere, tailing him closely, headlights blinding in his mirrors.

He swore under his breath. "Shit."

The car was too close; The headlights too bright. It had to be Rook's people, or worse, their hired muscle. He could see their reflection in the side mirror now, a dark sedan that matched the profile of the vehicles Rook's crew used. They were playing the long game now, trying to scare him into backing off.

His hands tightened on the wheel as the car sped up, pressing him further down the road. It was a game of intimidation, a warning. He would not back down, not now, not when he was this close. Marcus sped up, his truck roaring as he pushed the engine harder, trying to lose them in the winding streets. The sedan followed.

"Is that all you've got?" Marcus muttered under his breath.

The car behind him stayed on his tail, inches away, making the already tight streets feel even smaller. He darted through an intersection, barely making the turn. The sedan followed, closer now, and he could hear the tires squeal as they fought for traction.

He pushed harder on the gas, his truck roaring as it shot forward. The sedan was relentless, staying right there and matching his every move. Marcus took another sharp turn, this one harder, forcing the truck into a near spin. But he didn't lose the sedan. They were still right behind him. He looked ahead. The road was getting narrower and more residential. He couldn't outrun them forever. He needed a plan.

Marcus's eyes darted to the right. A narrow alley, just wide enough for his truck to fit. He made a split-second decision, throwing his truck to the right, scraping past the side of a parked car as he shot into the alleyway. The sedan skidded in behind him, but it wasn't built for tight corners. He grinned darkly, his pulse quickening. He was about to lose them.

The alley twisted and turned, but he held steady, knowing the truck could handle the sharp turns. He glanced back, seeing the sedan trying to follow but struggling to make the same tight turns. He floored it. He truck's engine growled as it picked up speed. The sedan didn't keep up. For a moment, Marcus felt a rush of satisfaction, but he couldn't let his guard down. The alleyway opened up into a dead-end.

He cursed and slammed on the brakes. The truck skidded to a stop, barely avoiding the concrete wall ahead. He was cornered. The sedan had caught up. Its headlights cut through the darkness like a predator closing in on its prey. Marcus shifted his truck into reverse, his heart pounding in his chest. He was boxed in, but he wasn't going down without a fight.

Before he could make another move, the sedan's engine roared, its lights flashing as it surged forward, headlights aimed straight at him. But he wasn't about to let them win. He threw the truck into drive and revved the engine, charging straight at the sedan. The car screeched to a halt just in time; the driver swerved out of the way as Marcus pushed forward, determined to make it out of the alley. The sedan was forced to veer off, the driver swearing as he lost ground.

Marcus wasted no time. He gunned the truck forward, barreling through the alley and onto the main street. He glanced behind him, seeing the sedan's headlights fading in the distance. His heart was racing, his hands still gripping the wheel. He finally let out a breath he didn't realize he'd been holding. That was too close.

He didn't slow down, though. He kept his foot on the pedal, driving straight to Sam's place, his mind spinning with the adrenaline still coursing through him. He didn't have time to waste. He needed answers, and no one—no one—was going to stop him now. He pulled into the parking lot of Sam's building, slamming his truck into park. He didn't even bother with the engine; he hopped out, locked the door, and marched toward the entrance. His mind was still reeling from the chase, but it was the anger now that kept him moving.

As he reached the door to the apartment, he knocked once, sharply. Sam answered quickly, taking one look at Marcus's face and stepped aside without a word.

"You were followed," Sam said, closing the door behind him.

"No shit."

Sam stayed quiet, watching him. "What happened?"

"They tried to run me down. Came out of nowhere. No plates. No hesitation." Marcus ran a hand over his face. "That wasn't a warning. That was a message."

Sam walked over to the window, pulling the curtain back just enough to peek outside. "You shouldn't have come here. If they're tracking you—"

"I'm not hiding," he snapped. "Not anymore. They came after Deon. They came after me. And I'm supposed to just sit around and wait for them to decide who's next?"

"Charging into this half-cocked is going to get you killed."

"Then they'll know I didn't go down quiet," he replied, pacing the living room. "They're making moves, Sam. Tight ones. Clean ones. Like they've done this a hundred times before."

"They have, that's what makes them dangerous."

Marcus stopped and turned to face him. "We need to go on offense. Not sit around watching footage and trading stories."

"Footage is exactly what's going to save us," Sam said as he walked over to his laptop and pressing a key. The video of the robbery lit up the screen. It was muted but clear. "While you were playing Fast N Furious, I was going over the video again. I think I recognize the guy in the background."

The two of them watched the footage again as the clips from the robbery played. Sam paused it, rewinding to a moment where the clerk had looked too calm. Then zoomed in on a man in the background. "This guy..." He pointed to the screen. "I've seen him before. He's been connected to local gang activity. His name's Jace. I'd bet my life on it."

Marcus squinted at the grainy image on the screen. The man Sam pointed at was barely in focus. Just a blurred face and a dark hoodie near the back shelves. But but there was something about his posture that stood out. He lingered instead of running like the rest of the customers.

"You sure?" Marcus asked, his voice quiet but sharp.

"Yeah," Sam said without hesitation. "He's not just a hanger-on, either. Jace does cleanup, intimidation, surveillance. Low on the food chain, but loyal. If he was there, it wasn't by accident."

Marcus stared at the screen for another beat. "So if he was inside during the robbery... and Tony's crew was outside?"

"That robbery wasn't random," Sam finished. "It was a setup. A distraction. Or a test run."

Chapter 23

The realization hit Marcus like a freight train. If Jace, a known associate of Rook's gang, had been involved in the robbery, then the conspiracy extended far beyond Jordan. This wasn't about a simple setup anymore. This was calculated, controlled, and deliberate.

Sam leaned back in his chair. "This proves something. Maybe not everything, but enough to shake things up."

"Shake things up?" he asked. His adrenaline from the chase still coursed through his veins, mixing with fresh frustration. "This isn't about shaking things up. This is about saving my brother from getting buried alive in this mess."

Sam raised his hands in a calming gesture. "I get it, man. I do. But you're up against a gang with reach. You saw how they tried to scare you off. They're not playing games."

"Neither am I."

He sighed and turned back to the screen. "Alright, so what are you gonna do? You've got the footage, and now you know one of Rook's men was involved. You can't exactly waltz into the cops with this and expect them to take it at face value."

"No, but I can use this to turn up the pressure. If he is tied to Rook, then we're looking at more than just a gang playing small-time games. They're protecting something, and I need to know what."

"You keep pushing, and they're going to stop sending warnings. They'll come straight for you. You've got to think this through."

"I am thinking. I think about Jordan sitting in that cell, scared out of his mind. I think about my family, who won't rest until this is over. So don't tell me to think it through—I'm already there."

"Alright. So what do you need from me?"

"We need to find him. If he's on the run or lying low, someone knows where he is. And if I get to him first, he's going to start talking."

"That's a risky play. If he's not talking, it's for a reason. He's not going to roll over just because you ask nicely."

"Then I won't ask nicely," Marcus said as he grabbed his jacket.

Sam stood and followed him to the door. "You're really doing this, huh?"

"I don't have a choice. This isn't just about justice anymore. It's about finding out how deep this goes and making damn sure it ends."

"You're walking into something bigger than either of us, man."

"I know," he said without looking back. "That's why I need to be the one to do it."

"Just don't forget what you're walking into. You're not the only one with something to lose now."

"That's exactly why I'm not backing down."

As he drove away, he was Every shadow felt like it held a threat, every passing car a potential tail. He wasn't naïve. The gang had made it clear they were watching. But fear wasn't part of his equation. Not anymore. He pulled up to a bar where he knew he could get some answers. The parking lot was half full, mostly trucks and beat-up sedans. Marcus cut the engine and sat for a second. Growing up in the community center, he had an idea of who he could ask. But since was a long time ago , he didn't know if the person would talk to him or if they were still loyal.

The bar was called *The Hollow*. It was a fitting name given the people it attracted; lowlifes, ex-cons, and men who drank their guilt down with cheap whiskey. A few heads turned as he walked in, but no one said anything. He looked around the room until he spotted a familiar figure slouched in the corner drinking. It was Emmett, one of Jace's closest associates.

Slowly, Marcus walked toward him. Looking up, Emmett's surprise turned to irritation.

With a slow drawl, he put down his drink and said, "Marcus. Didn't think I'd see you here."

"You didn't think you'd see me anywhere," he responded as he sat down across from him. "But here I am. And I need to find Jace."

Emmett laughed, though it lacked humor. "You've got guts showing up here, asking about Jace. You know he's got his own problems, right? Why drag yourself into them?"

"Because his problems are my problems. I know he's tied to the robbery. And I know he's scared out of his mind, just like you are."

"You don't know what you're talking about."

"I know enough. He is running because your boss got something to hide, and you're all tangled up in it. So, you can either tell me where he is, or I can start making life a lot harder for you."

"You're crazy, man. My people aren't just going to let you walk away from this."

"They're already on me. Slashed my tires. Left me a note. Tried to run me off the road. But I'm still standing. Now, where is he?"

"Look at you trying to sound so hard. I remember when I used to beat you and your brother in basketball," he laughed as he took a sip.

"If you remember that, then you should know how important my family is to me. Trust me, I wouldn't be here if I knew where to find him. He was there the night of the robbery. If I can talk to him, maybe he could help free Jordan."

Emmett put the bottle down and was silent. Marcus could see how conflicted he was.

"Ok. You didn't hear this from me. And if it comes back to me, you'll regret it. He's been crashing at that old warehouse by the docks. But if you go there, you better be ready for a fight. Jace doesn't trust anyone anymore."

Marcus stood and tossed a few bills on the table. "Thanks for the tip. And just a heads up? If you're smart, you'll stay out of this. Because once I'm done with your boss, there won't be anything left to fear."

Emmett watched him for a beat, the corner of his mouth twitching like he wanted to say something more, but he didn't. Just picked up his bottle and took another sip as he walked out.

The bar door creaked shut behind him, muffling the buzz of voices and clinking glasses. He headed straight for his truck, every step purposeful. The old warehouse by the docks. It wasn't much, but it was a lead.

He climbed into the driver's seat and started the truck. His mind was already turning over the possibilities. What kind of security Jace might have, who else might be holed up there, whether Rook had eyes on the place. Didn't matter because Jace had the answers. And he wasn't leaving without them.

The warehouse loomed in the distance as he approached, the faint sound of waves lapping against the docks in the background. He parked a block away and moved carefully toward the building. Every step brought him closer to answer and deeper into danger. He didn't know if it was a setup or not. As he got closer he noticed the faint glow of a single light inside. It confirmed someone was there. Marcus tightened his grip on the crowbar he'd brought. He wasn't just looking for Jace anymore. He was looking for the truth.

Chapter 24

Approaching the warehouse, Marcus crouched close to the wall. He continued to move silently so no sound was made on the pavement. Peering through the broken window, he saw someone nervously pacing by some crates. Same profile from the video, Jace.

He hadn't come here to hurt anyone. This wasn't about threats. But Jace had answers, and he wasn't leaving without them. Keeping low, he moved along the building's edge. A loose sheet of it groaned softly in the breeze, and Marcus froze, listening. No alarm. No shout. Just the restless shuffling from inside.

He found a side entrance; a warped door hanging slightly ajar. As he reached for it, a sudden clatter echoed inside. Something had shifted, a board kicked or a bulb rattling, but it was enough.

Whatever it was caused Jace to freeze mid-step. He quickly turned his head towards the noise. Marcus stood still with one hand on the doorknob.

"Who's there?" Jace called, his voice sharp and on edge.

He stepped into the light and raised his hands slightly to show he wasn't a threat. "Relax. My name is Marcus."

Jace quickly retreated, his hand instinctively going to his waistband. "Stay the hell back. I'm warning you."

"I'm not here to fight you. I just want to talk."

"You think I'm stupid? I know who you are. You're the one who's been asking questions. You're the one poking your nose where it doesn't belong."

"I'm poking because my brother doesn't belong in a jail cell. He didn't do this, and you know it."

His hand hovered near his waistband. "You don't know anything. You don't know what's going on here."

"Then tell me. You're running scared because Rook's got something big going on, something he doesn't want anyone to find out. And you're right in the middle of it, aren't you?"

Jace flinched at the name. He started looking around as though expecting an enforcer to materialize. "Man, you have no idea. This goes beyond typical gang activity. It's bigger than that. And if I tell you anything, I'm as good as dead."

"You're already in danger. You know I'm being watched and now so are you. He's not going to let you go. You think hiding out in this dump is going to save you? He'll find you. But if you help me, I can take him down."

Jace laughed bitterly. "You're insane if you think you can stop him. He's got connections everywhere. People who can make you disappear without a trace."

"Let him try. I've been through worse, and I'm still standing. But you? You're not going to make it out of this unless you talk to me."

Jace hesitated. He began to debate if it was worth it. Finally he lowered his hand from his waistband. "Alright. Fine. I'll tell you what I know. But once I do, we're done. You hear me? I'm gone."

"Fair enough. Start talking."

Jace dropped to a whisper. "The robbery? It wasn't just about the cash in the register. He had us do it because the store was a front. They were moving product through the back, high-end stuff. Guns, drugs, you name it."

"And Jordan? Where does he fit into this?"

"He wasn't supposed to be there. He just... showed up at the wrong time. We didn't think much of it at first, but then he got paranoid. Said we couldn't take any chances. That's why they framed him. To cover their tracks."

"And the footage? The clerk?"

"All bought and paid for. He made sure the tape was edited, and the clerk knew better than to cross him."

"You're coming with me. We're taking this to the cops."

Jace's eyes widened in panic. "Are you crazy? I told you, Rook will kill me!"

"Not if I stop him first. Now let's go."

But before they could move, a loud crash echoed from the back of the warehouse. Both men froze, their heads snapping toward the sound.

"Looks like you've got company," Jace whispered.

Marcus stepped in front of him. "Correction. We got company. Now stay behind me."

Two figures emerged, their faces obscured by the dim light. Marcus's heart pounded as one of them stepped forward, a cruel smile spreading across his face.

"Well, well," the man drawled. "Didn't expect to find both of you here. Makes things easier."

Jace recognized the voice before he saw the full face. The enforcer, Vaughn. The guy was built like a tank and twice as mean, with a reputation for handling problems that talked too much. The second man stayed silent, but his stance was unmistakable;armed, and ready.

Jace backed up instinctively, nearly tripping over a broken pallet. "Marcus..."

"Quiet," Marcus said staring at Vaughn. "Let me do the talking."

The guy took another step forward, hand resting casually near the inside of his jacket. "You've been busy, Mr. Mechanic. Real nosy. Following trails that should've stayed cold. And now you're dragging our buddy into your mess like a damn hero."

"You think threatening me is going to fix this? It's too late. We know everything. About the store. About the shipments. All of it."

Vaughn's smile faltered just a fraction. "That so?"

"So unless you're ready to kill both of us right here, I suggest you walk out that door and pray the evidence doesn't land in someone's inbox by morning."

"Speak for yourself. I don't want to die," Jace howled.

The second man started to approach, but Vaughn held out an arm to stop him.

"You always were too stubborn for your own good. Rook said to send a message. But now I'm thinking maybe we take you in alive. Let him deal with you himself."

"Try it. But I don't go down easy."

For a moment, no one moved. Then—chaos.

The second man lunged first, drawing a blade as he closed the distance between them. Marcus reacted on instinct, sidestepping and snatching up a crowbar. He swung it with everything he had, the metal connecting with the man's forearm with a sickening crunch. The knife clattered to the floor as the attacker cried out, staggering backward and clutching his arm.

Jace dove behind a stack of crates, his breaths coming in ragged gasps. "He's got a gun!" he shouted.

Marcus barely had time to react before Vaughn pulled a sleek black pistol from his jacket and fired. The shot echoed like a bomb going off, the bullet slamming into the concrete pillar inches from his head. Shards of stone sprayed across his face as he hit the ground and rolled behind cover.

"You've really stepped in it now!" Vaughn shouted, boots crunching as he advanced. "Rook gave me options, but I'm liking the one where you bleed out right here."

"You're gonna have to aim better than that," Marcus growled, wiping grit from his eyes.

Another gunshot rang out. Sparks flew as the bullet ricocheted off a steel support beam behind Marcus. He ducked lower and scanned the ground. Nothing but trash and broken pallets. He needed something to create distance.

"Check that crate. Find something I can throw!" he shouted

Jace fumbled with a lid, finally prying it open. He yanked out a dusty liquor bottle and tossed it toward Marcus. He caught it, pivoted, and hurled it like a fastball. It shattered at Vaughn's feet, glass exploding across the floor and making him stumble.

Marcus didn't wait. He charged. Vaughn recovered just in time to turn and raise his gun, but not fast enough. Marcus tackled him hard, driving his shoulder into his midsection. They crashed to the ground in a heap and the gun skidding across the floor with a loud clatter.

Fists flew. Vaughn was built like a tank, each punch landing like a hammer. Marcus grunted as a blow caught him in the ribs, another in the side of the face. He saw stars. But he held on, pushing through the pain. He picked up a pipe and brought it down hard across Vaughn's shoulder. He screamed, the sound feral and raw.

Marcus hit him again, this time catching the edge of his collarbone. Vaughn groaned and went still, his body going limp beneath Marcus's weight. The second man, wounded and bleeding, began limping toward the exit. Jace stood shakily, knife in hand, and stepped into his path.

"Don't move," he said, voice shaking but steady enough to matter.

The man paused. Blood dripped from his hand. His eyes flicked to the fallen Vaughn, to Marcus rising over him with the bloodied pipe, and finally to the open warehouse door. He bolted. Jace let him go.

The warehouse was still again, save for the sound of Vaughn moaning and spitting curses under his breath. Marcus stood over him, chest heaving. He wiped a smear of blood from his mouth and leaned in close. "Go back to your boss," he growled. "Tell him we're done hiding. And next time, I'm not letting you walk away."

Vaughn didn't answer. He just glared with pure hatred as Marcus kicked the gun across the floor.

"Come on," he said, turning to Jace. "We've got to go. Now. Backup's probably already on the way."

Jace nodded, lowering the knife and wiping his forehead with a trembling hand. "I—I didn't think they'd find me this fast."

"They were probably tailing me," Marcus said between gasps. "Which means we've got a window, but not a big one."

They moved fast, ducking out the side door and disappearing into the night. Marcus's ribs throbbed with each step, and Jace limped slightly, his nerves frayed to the core. Behind them, the warehouse loomed like a dead memory and still crawling with danger. As they reached the street, Marcus glanced back once more. This wasn't over. But tonight, they'd survived. And tomorrow? Tomorrow he'd take the fight to Rook.

Chapter 25

Sitting at the head of a cracked wooden table, Rook exhaled a long plume of cigar smoke. His eyes were fixed on the two men who had just returned from their failed mission at the warehouse.

"You're telling me," he said slowly, "that you not only didn't scare Marcus off, but you let him walk away?"

Vaughn shifted uneasily in his chair, his bruised ribs making every breath a struggle. "We tried, boss. He's tougher than we thought. Got the jump on us with that damn pipe."

Rook leaned forward, his gaze cold and unblinking. "Tougher than you thought? He is sticking his nose where it doesn't belong. And now, thanks to your incompetence, he's even more dangerous."

Khari, sitting next to Vaughn, spoke up, his voice shaky. "Boss, we didn't expect him to have backup. That kid with him wasn't supposed to be there."

"What kid? Y'all were supposed to make him understand that my business is my business."

"That young dude Jace. You know the one who's always jittery."

Rook slammed his fist on the table, making both men flinch. "I don't care who was there. Marcus is a problem, and problems need solutions. If we don't handle this, he'll mess up everything."

It wasn't a light chuckle or even something bitter. It was sharp, cracked open like a broken mirror, echoing off the walls with a pitch that didn't feel quite human. A maniacal laugh that started in his throat and spilled out with a wild, uncontrollable edge.

Both men shifted uncomfortably, eyes darting to each other. Each asking the other was there something they didn't know. Rook continued laughing, like he was in on a joke that hadn't yet landed.

"You don't get it," he said between gasps of laughter. "You said his little brother's locked up, didn't you?"

Vaughn nodded cautiously. "Yeah. His name is Jordan. Been in county for a couple months now."

Rook tapped the ash from his cigar. "Good. If Marcus won't back off, we'll remind him what happens when you dig too deep. Send a message. Go down to the jail. Talk to one of our guys on the inside."

Khari hesitated. "What kind of message?"

"Something that'll keep his brother awake at night. And make Marcus think twice before poking around where he doesn't belong."

Khari exchanged a look with Vaughn and looked back at Rook. "You sure that's the move? We stir up too much heat in the county, and the wrong people start asking questions."

Rook didn't even blink. His chair creaked slightly as he leaned back, drumming his fingers slowly on the edge of the table.

"Are you questioning my order or do I need to find someone else to complete the job that you couldn't."

Vaughn shifted beside Khari, but kept quiet. He knew not to question an order, especially when it's directly from the boss.

Khari replied nervously. "No one's questioning your order. Just... thinking long-term. We push too far and our people may get exposed."

Rook stood without a word and walked to the bar in the corner of the room.

"You think I haven't thought this through?" he asked as smoke curled up around his face. "You think I don't know how far we can push?"

"No disrespect," Khari said quickly. "It's just that he's already on edge. We pull his little brother into it, that might make him go reckless."

"That's the point."

Vaughn cracked his knuckles as a cruel grin spread across his face. "I know just the guy. He owes me a favor. He'll make sure Jordan gets the message, loud and clear."

"Good. Make sure it doesn't trace back to us. No names. No slips. Just pressure. Enough to rattle Mr. Mechanic. Make him sweat."

Khari nodded. "It'll get done."

"You'd better," Rook said, taking another drag from his cigar. "Because if he doesn't back off, you'll wish I was as forgiving as he is."

He didn't look at them as they turned to leave. His focus remained on the darkness beyond the glass.

"You want to play hero, Marcus, then you better be ready to lose something."

Jordan laid on the hard cot in his cell, staring up at the ceiling. Sleep had been elusive since his arrest. The constant noise, the flickering fluorescent light outside his cell, and the oppressive weight of his situation made every moment stretch endlessly.

He hadn't told anyone, but the worst part was the uncertainty. Marcus had promised to help, but what if he couldn't? What if this really was the end for him? The sound of approaching footsteps interrupted his thoughts. Two correctional officers stopped outside his cell.

"Carter," one of them said, unlocking the door. "You've got a visitor."

Jordan frowned. "At this hour?"

The officer didn't respond, just gestured for him to step out. He reluctantly complied, his heart pounding. Visitors at this time of night weren't normal. They led him to a small, dimly lit room with a single chair in the center. The officers pushed him inside and closed the door behind him.

"Sit," one of them ordered.

He sat, his nerves on edge. Moments later, the door opened again, and a man walked in. He was tall and lean with a shaved head and cold, calculating eyes. Jordan didn't recognize him, but something about the man's presence set off every alarm in his head.

The man didn't speak right away. He simply studied him like he was sizing him up for something Jordan wouldn't like. He moved with slow, deliberate steps that said he was in control and knew it.

"You don't know me," the man finally said. "But I know you. Jordan Carter. Little brother of the guy who's been making a lot of noise out there."

Jordan stiffened. "Who the hell are you?"

The man gave a humorless smile. "Doesn't matter. What matters is the message I'm here to deliver."

He stepped closer and leaned down until he was eye-level with Jordan. "Your brother thinks he's some kind of hero. Thinks he's going to bring down people he doesn't understand. And you? You're his soft spot."

"You threatening me?"

"I'm educating you," the man replied. "You see this place? It's full of people who owe favors. People who'd love to make your time here... unpleasant. All I have to do is say the word."

He straightened up and took a slow breath, like he wasn't in any rush. "So, here's what you're going to do. Next time you talk to your brother, if you get to talk to him that is, you tell him to stop. Drop it. Walk away. Or you'll pay the price for his curiosity."

"He's not gonna back down. You don't know him."

The man laughed softly. "No. But I'm about to. And trust me, he'll fold when it's your blood on the line."

He turned to leave, then paused with one hand on the door. "Sleep tight, Carter. You'll want the rest."

The door closed behind him with a sharp click. Jordan sat there, heart pounding, sweat beading on his forehead, and a sick feeling settling deep in his gut. This wasn't a threat. It was a promise.

Jordan sat frozen for a long minute after the door shut. The threat echoed louder than any voice. He wiped a trembling hand across his mouth, trying to pull himself together, but the fear still clung to him like a second skin.

Eventually, the door opened again, and the same officer stepped in. "Let's go."

He stood slowly. "Who was that guy?"

The officer didn't answer. Didn't even look at him.

Back in his cell, Jordan collapsed onto the edge of the cot. The concrete walls felt tighter now, the air heavier. He stared at the cracks in the ceiling, his mind racing. That man had made one thing painfully clear. This wasn't just about him anymore. It wasn't even about Marcus poking around. It was about power. Control. And these people weren't just trying to scare Marcus. They were going to use him to break his brother.

He had to warn him. He sprang to his feet and stepped to the bars.

"Hey!" he called down the corridor, voice sharp with urgency. "CO! I need to make a call!"

No response. Just the distant clang of metal echoing through the block.

He shouted again, louder this time. "I need my one call! Now!"

A guard strolled by, leisurely, like he had all the time in the world. He barely spared Jordan a glance. "It's after hours. Try again in the morning."

He slammed his fist against the bars with a loud clang that echoed like a shot. "It'll be too late by morning..."

The guard paused just long enough to smirk over his shoulder. "Oh well. Maybe next time."

Jordan's hands tightened around the cold metal. His breath came fast, the pressure building in his chest like a scream he couldn't let out. He paced the small cell like a caged animal, mind racing. They're going to go after him. He could feel it in his gut. Rook didn't make empty threats. And if they touched his brother...

"No, no, no." Jordan said to himself, running a hand over his buzzed head. He looked around wildly, searching for something, anything. An officer still on rounds, another inmate who might have a favor to trade. Nothing.

He stepped back to the bars, calling out again, voice hoarse. "Please! Just one call. It's not for me—it's about someone's life!"

Silence.

From down the row, a voice called out mockingly, "Welcome to county, rookie."

Another inmate laughed, a dry, broken sound. "They don't care 'til there's blood."

Jordan backed into the corner of his cell, heart pounding. He could practically hear the clock ticking in his head, every second lost dragging Marcus closer to something he wouldn't see coming. He leaned his head against the wall and closed his eyes. *I have to find a way. Before it's too late.* He had to get word to Marcus. If he couldn't warn him, he could walk straight into a trap.

Chapter 26

Marcus was still in his truck, parked a few blocks from the old warehouse near the docks. It was early morning. His eyes were heavy from a sleepless night, haunted by Jace's confession and the ambush that had nearly gone sideways. The deeper he dug, the more dangerous this got. His phone buzzed on the console. Unknown number. He stared at it for a second before answering. A robotic voice clicked through the speaker:

"You have a collect call from—Jordan Carter—an inmate at Crest Ridge County Detention Facility. Press 1 to accept the charges."

He hit 1 without hesitation. Static crackled, then—

"Marcus? You there?"

He sat up straight. "Jordan?"

"Yeah. It's me." His brother's voice was low, strained. "I had to call collect. They wouldn't let me use my own minutes this morning."

"That's fine. Talk to me. You okay?"

There was a pause. "Not really."

Marcus's hand clenched on the steering wheel. "What happened?"

"They pulled me out of my cell last night. Said I had a visitor. Late—way past normal hours. The guards didn't say a word, just walked me to one of those little side rooms. No windows. No cameras. Just a chair and some shadows."

"Who was it?"

"I don't know his name. Never seen him before. Tall. Dark. Bald. Cold eyes like a damn statue. Didn't raise his voice once, but every word felt like a threat."

"What did he say?"

"That you're asking too many questions. That if you don't back off, I'll be the one to suffer." Jordan's voice cracked, like he was trying to stay composed. "Said you were poking around where you shouldn't be."

"They know everything."

"Yeah. They said if I wanted to stay healthy, I should tell you to shut it down."

"Did they hurt you?"

"No. Not physically. But the message was clear. They don't want you finding out the truth."

A long silence hung between them.

"They've got people in here, Marcus. That guy wasn't bluffing. The guards didn't even look surprised. Like they knew. Like this happens all the time."

"They're trying to scare us."

"Well, it's working," Jordan whispered. "You don't understand what you're dealing with. Rook's not just some street boss. He's protected. I heard he's got a lot of people in his pocket including judges and cops. After last night, I believe he even got the guards here. You think this is about a robbery? That was just the smoke. The fire is bigger."

"I'm getting close. Too close. That's why they came for you."

"Exactly. So stop. Please. I'm not saying let them win. I'm saying think before you make a move. Because if you get taken off the board, I've got no one left out there fighting for me."

"I'm not letting this go. They framed you. They nearly killed Deon. Tried to run me off the road. And last night? They came for their own member Jace. If we don't stop this, it doesn't end. Ever."

"I get it. But promise me that don't do it alone. This thing's too big for one person."

"I've got help. Sam's still on it. Jace gave us a lead. We're going to blow this open."

"You think he will talk to the cops?"

"Hopefully. If I can keep him alive long enough."

Another click broke through the line.

"You have one minute remaining."

"I've got to go. Just... be smart, alright? I can handle myself in here, but if something happens to you..."

"I'm not going anywhere. Just hang in there. I'm going to fix this."

Jordan chuckled softly, humorless. "Yeah, well... fix it fast."

"This call will be disconnected in 30 seconds."

"I love you, man."

"You too. Stay safe, Marcus."

The line went dead.

Marcus dropped the phone into the passenger seat and stared out the windshield. He could still hear Jordan's voice. He was afraid. And for good reason. This wasn't just about clearing his brother's name anymore. This was about cleaning out the rot in Crest Ridge before it swallowed both of them whole.

Marcus banged on Sam's door just before 9 a.m. The inside of the apartment was a controlled mess: takeout boxes, cables, and computer screens glowing with lines of code and surveillance feeds. Sam opened the door half-asleep, his T-shirt inside out.

Marcus dropped the phone into the passenger seat and stared out the windshield. He could still hear Jordan's voice. He was afraid. And for good reason. This wasn't just about clearing his brother's name anymore. This was about cleaning out the rot in Crest Ridge before it swallowed both of them whole.

He banged on Sam's door just before 9 a.m. The inside of the apartment was a controlled mess: takeout boxes, cables, and computer screens glowing with lines of code and surveillance feeds. Sam opened the door half-asleep, his T-shirt inside out.

"Marcus?" he muttered, rubbing his eyes. "You know normal people knock like—once?"

"We don't have time for normal today," he said, pushing past him and heading straight for the desk. "I need eyes on Rook. Now."

Sam blinked, confused. "Okay, good morning to you too. What the hell happened?"

"He's making a move. He's going after Jordan."

Sam's face dropped. The sleep vanished instantly. "You serious?"

"I need everything you can get me; locations, known associates, traffic cams, back alley whispers. I don't care. If he sends anyone near my brother, I need to know before it happens." He paused, pacing in front of the screens. "Jordan's the leverage. Rook's trying to shake me off the trail."

"You got it. I've been watching some of his crew already—Khari, Vaughn, a couple others. They've been moving quiet the last few days, but that might've just been setup." He started typing, screens flickering as he pulled up footage and flagged patterns.

Marcus stood behind him, arms crossed, mind already running ahead. "He wants fear to do the work. But we're going to turn that around. Make him feel watched."

Sam nodded, a trace of a smirk on his face. "Let's show him what happens when someone thinks they can outmaneuver you."

They watched a camera feed that showed Khari getting into a black SUV just outside a corner deli.

"There," Marcus said, pointing. "Track that vehicle. Let's see where the pieces are moving. And Sam?"

He looked up.

"If they even breathe near my brother—" Marcus's voice dropped to a dangerous calm, "—we don't wait. We hit back."

"Understood," he said, the usual sarcasm drained from his tone. He knew Marcus meant it. Not in the reckless way, but in that precise, calculated kind of way that came right before someone disappeared off the map.

Sam's fingers flew across the keys, multiple windows opening in rapid succession. Surveillance feeds. Cell tower pings. DMV records. "That SUV Khari got into? Hit a plate read two hours ago near Adams and Third. Industrial lot. No cameras back there, but it's off Rook's usual routes."

"He's hiding something."

"Either that, or meeting someone he doesn't want connected to him," Sam said, tapping in a flag and cross-referencing recent burner activity. "And Vaughn's phone went dark right after midnight. That's not nothing."

Marcus stood still for a beat, hands resting on the back of a chair, muscles tense. He hadn't slept. He couldn't. His mind kept cycling through Jordan's voice, that flash of fear behind the bravado.

"You think they'd use Jordan as bait?" Sam asked, glancing at him.

"I know for a fact that they will."

"Wait—how?"

"He called me collect. Someone visited him last night. Tall guy. Shaved head. Probably one of Rook's muscles. Told him to warn me off."

"Jesus."

"They've got people inside the jail. Guards. Maybe even the warden. They moved Jordan to a camera-free room in the middle of the night and let a threat waltz right in."

Sam's eyes widened. "Damn. They're getting desperate."

"Desperate enough to make mistakes?"

Sam walked over to the table. "I've been doing some digging. I was going to give it to you later, but since you're here." He picks up a folder and gives it to Marcus. "Turns out, the robbery wasn't just a random hit. It was a setup. A cover for something bigger."

Marcus opened the folder. Photographs, handwritten notes, and a blueprint of the convenience store were spread across the pages.

"What's this?"

"There's a hidden room in the store. It's not on any official blueprints, but it's there. My contact says it's where Rook's been moving... product."

"Drugs?"

"Worse. Weapons. High-grade stuff. And the robbery? That was a distraction. They needed a cover story in case anyone came snooping around."

"So, they used Jordan as a scapegoat."

"Exactly. But there's more. Rook's getting paranoid because someone higher up the chain is breathing down his neck. He's not just running a local crew; he's part of something much bigger. If we can expose that connection, we can take him down."

Marcus sat down. This wasn't just about clearing Jordan's name anymore. It was about dismantling a dangerous network that had corrupted Crest Ridge from the inside out."

"What's the next move?"

"We need proof. Something solid. My contact says the hidden room is still in use, but it's heavily guarded. If we can get in there, find out what they're storing, and get out without being seen..."

"I'll do it."

"Are you crazy? This isn't some small-time job. You'll need backup."

"I don't have time to wait. My brother doesn't have time. If Rook's escalating, he's not going to stop until someone makes him."

"Fine. But if you're doing this, we do it smart. No more flying solo. We'll need a plan, equipment, and a way out in case things go south."

"Deal," Marcus said as he stood up.

"Wait," Sam called after him. "Where are you going?"

"To see Jordan," Marcus replied. "If I'm walking into this, I want him to know I'm not backing down."

Marcus left the apartment and got back into his truck, pulling out into traffic. His mind was on fire. This wasn't just street crime. This was organized corruption embedded deep in the city's bones. But he wasn't backing down. He was going to pull this thing out by the roots. Even if he had to tear the whole city apart to do it.

Chapter 27

Jordan was led into the visitor room. He looked extremely tired. When he saw Marcus on the other side of the glass, a mixture of relief and frustration crossed his features.

"You shouldn't be here," Jordan said through the phone.

"And you shouldn't be in there. I'm not stopping until you're out."

"They're serious, bro. These guys... they don't play around. I don't want you getting hurt because of me. And I don't want to get hurt because of you."

"Listen to me. You're my brother. I don't care how dangerous this gets. I'm not letting them pin this on you. You didn't do anything wrong."

"You don't know that for sure."

"Yes, I do. You told me you were at the store, but you left before anything happened. I believe you. Now I just need to prove it."

Jordan took a deep breath. His brother's faith was almost too much to bear. "Marcus... just be careful. Please."

"I will. Just hang in there, okay? I'll get you out of this."

Jordan nodded slowly. His eyes glistened just for a moment before he looked away. "Time's running out. Word's spreading in here. People are starting to think I'm a problem. Not just to the crew, but to whoever's protecting them. If I make one wrong move, I might not make it out of here at all."

"Then don't move wrong. Stay quiet, stay smart. Keep your head down until I come through. I've got Sam digging into the footage. Jace gave us enough to start tearing this whole thing apart."

Jordan gave a short, bitter laugh. "Jace? You really think he's gonna hold up under pressure?"

"He knows what's at stake. And trust me, after the other night, he's just as motivated to see Rook fall."

145

"I hope you're right. But you're fighting more than just a crew now. This thing, the whole operation, is woven into everything. The cops. The courts. The guards walking past my cell. You cut the wrong thread, the whole damn city might come crashing down on top of us."

"Then I'll make sure we're standing when it does."

A buzzer rang out, signaling the end of their time. Jordan slowly stood, reluctant to leave but knowing the rules. "Don't do anything stupid."

"No promises," Marcus said with a smirk. "But I'll see you soon."

He stayed in his seat, watching through the glass as he was led away. His brother's shoulders were tense, head down, as if bracing for a blow that hadn't landed yet. The steel door clanged shut behind him, and Marcus finally set the phone back into the cradle.

He stood and walked out of the visitor area, but the weight of the conversation lingered like smoke in his chest. The cold, sterile feel of the jail pressed in around him—white walls, flickering lights, guards who barely made eye contact. Every one of them could be bought. Jordan was right. This wasn't just about one setup or one gang anymore. It was bigger. Dirtier.

As he stepped outside, the afternoon sun hit his face, but it didn't warm him. Not today. He got in his truck and sat for a long minute with the engine idling. His phone rang in the cup holder. Sam.

He answered with a clipped, "Talk."

"You're not gonna like this. I ran Jace's tip through a few old police reports. That warehouse he mentioned? It used to be owned by a shell company. Guess who's on the paperwork as a silent investor?"

"Rook," he answered without hesitation.

"Bingo. And get this. The temporary officer who 'worked' that one day? He used to do off-duty security gigs for that same company."

"So this thing goes way beyond street-level muscle."

"It's an infrastructure. He's got his hands in business, the police, maybe even the courts. Your brother has a right to be scared."

"It's time we hit back. But smart. We need something hard to pin this to Rook. Not just talk. We need evidence."

"I'll keep digging. See what else I can pull from the shell company. Maybe there's a paper trail."

"I'm going back to the warehouse. There's gotta be something we missed."

"Don't go alone."

"I won't," Marcus lied, and hung up.

Back in the jail, Jordan sat on the edge of his cot, still replaying the conversation with Marcus. The visit had been short, tense. Marcus looked worn down but determined, that familiar fire burning behind his eyes. They didn't say everything out loud. They didn't have to. But he had seen it clearly: his brother wasn't backing down. Not this time.

He glanced toward the corridor, hearing the distant sound of doors clanging shut and the shuffle of inmates moving between blocks. The visit had stirred something in him, hope, but it didn't last long. Not when he saw what was waiting beneath his mattress.

A folded piece of paper.

He hadn't noticed it when the CO brought him back. Hadn't felt anyone near his cell. But there it was, tucked just out of sight. His stomach sank. He pulled it out slowly, hands already clammy, and unfolded the sheet. Thick, blocky letters. No signature. No date. Just a message meant to rattle his bones.

HE KEEPS DIGGING. HE DIES.

He stared at it a long time. The warmth from seeing his brother faded, replaced by something colder. Sharper. He crumpled the paper in his fist and walked to the bars. The guards were in shift change. This meant less eyes and more noise. But someone had gotten that message in. That meant the walls weren't just closing in; they were compromised.

He leaned his forehead against the bars and said to himself, "This doesn't stop him. It just proves he's getting close."

But that didn't mean he could sit idle. He moved back to the cot, sat down, and tried to steady his breath. He had to warn Marcus. Again. This wasn't about pushing forward carefully anymore. It was about surviving the fallout. A moment later, the block buzzer buzzed and a CO stepped into view.

"Hope you enjoyed family bonding, Carter. Might be a long time before you'll have visitors again." He laughed and walked away.

The front door creaked open as Marcus stepped inside. The familiar scent of lavender incense and simmering stew floated in the air. He shut the door quietly behind him.

"Marcus?" his mother called from the kitchen.

"Yeah, it's me."

She appeared in the doorway with a concerned look etched deep into her face. "You were at the jail again."

It wasn't a question. He nodded as he made his way into the living room. "Had to."

"How is he?" she asked softly.

"He's holding on," Marcus said. "Barely. But it's getting to him. Someone paid him a visit last night. One of Rook's guys, I'm sure."

She crossed her arms tightly. "God help us. What did they do?"

"Nothing physical. Just talked. But the way he described it... it was a warning. They wanted him rattled." He sat on the couch. "And it worked."

She came and sat beside him. "You still trying to build something for that lawyer?"

"Mr. Miller, yeah." Marcus let out a breath. "He said if I found anything useful, to bring it to him. I've been chasing leads for weeks, but it's not enough. I got this guy to talk, but we got interrupted before I could record or get him to back it up. Now he's vanished again."

"Think Miller will still help?"

"He said he would if I had something real. I just don't know if what I've got is enough. A scared guy's word and a hunch about a crooked clerk won't hold in court."

His mother leaned back and stared up at the ceiling. "Mr. Miller's a good man, but he's not a miracle worker. You need something solid, baby. Something that can't be explained away."

"I know. And I'm working on it. I just... I need more time."

"You need to be careful too. This isn't just about saving your brother. It's about keeping yourself alive long enough to do it."

"I know. I'm being smart about it. Mostly."

"*Mostly* isn't enough," she said, giving his knee a squeeze. Her eyes didn't leave his. "Get what you need, and bring it to him. But don't do anything reckless. I already have one son behind bars. I don't want to lose the other to a grave."

"I'll find something. I'll bring it to him. I promise. I just have to dig deeper."

She rose to her feet and brushed his shoulder gently. "Then eat something before you do. You look like hell."

He managed a soft chuckle. "Love you too, Ma."

"Always."

She turned and went back to the stove. She fixed him a big bowl of stew, like she already knew he wouldn't be here long. He followed her and sat at the table. He ate the stew so fast, she didn't know whether or not to fix some in a container. When he was finished, he tucked the phone into his pocket and headed for the door.

"Be safe," his mother said, not turning around.

"I will," he replied as he shut the door.

Chapter 28

Marcus found Myia sitting on the back porch at their grandmother's house, She had a book in her lap, but she lost in thought. Marcus hesitated for a moment before stepping onto the porch.

"Myia," he called, his tone sharp with frustration.

She looked up, startled by his voice. The book snapped shut as she set it aside. "What is it now?" she asked defensively.

He stepped closer. "We need to talk. About everything."

"If this is about Jordan again, I already told you—"

"It is," he interrupted. "But it's not just about him. It's about all of us. I need your help. Real help."

"What do you mean by 'real help'? You're already dragging me into this mess just by keeping me updated."

"That's not enough. I need you to step up. You're smart. You know how people think, how they react. I can't do this alone, not with the gang breathing down my neck and Jordan sitting in jail for something he didn't do."

With an unreadable expression, she stared at him. "You're asking me to put our entire family at risk."

"I'm asking you to care!" he snapped, overcome with frustration. "He's your cousin, too. He doesn't deserve to rot in jail while the real criminals walk free."

Matching his tone, she insisted, "I *do* care. But there's a line.. You're out there poking at people who won't hesitate to hurt you—or anyone close to you. Do you even realize what you're doing?"

"I know exactly what I'm doing. I'm fighting for my family because nobody else will. What are you doing? Sitting here, reading a book, pretending this doesn't affect you?"

"That's not fair, and you know it."

"Isn't it?" he challenged. "You've been keeping your distance ever since... well, ever since *everything*. You think I don't know you're still suspicious of me and Jordan because of what happened with Malik?"

Myia flinched at the mention of his name. Her eyes narrowed, but there was pain behind them. "Don't you dare say that!!"

"Why not?" Marcus pressed. "It's the elephant in the room, isn't it? He killed your mom!! You haven't trusted me since the news reported his death. But guess what? I'm the only one out here trying to make sure another innocent family member doesn't end up buried or locked away!"

Myia's eyes burned. Not just with anger, but with years of confusion and grief that others had prevented her from voicing.

"You want to talk about elephants in the room?" she said, each word deliberate. "Let's talk about how you disappeared during my mom's memorial. Didn't answer your phone. Didn't show your face until hours later looking like you'd seen a ghost."

Marcus opened his mouth, but she didn't let him speak.

"And let's talk about how you already knew Malik was dead before the news even said anything. You said 'Been Knew' like you knew where he was the whole time he was running. How, Marcus? Who told you? Why didn't you say anything sooner?"

His jaw tightened, but he said nothing.

She took a step closer, her eyes searching his face for something. Truth, regret, maybe a crack in the armor. "You want me to trust you? To believe you're doing this for Jordan and not to cover your own tracks? Then start telling the truth. All of it. Because until you do, I don't know whose side you're really on."

The silence that followed was heavy and unforgiving.

"Whatever happened that day... I know you're keeping something from me," she added, her voice quieter now but no less firm. "And if you really care about us then stop lying. Before it's too late."

Marcus felt the weight of her words like a punch to the gut. He looked at her and saw the mixture of fear, betrayal, and something worse: fading hope.

"Look" he started, his voice low. "I didn't mean to disappear during the memorial. I wasn't trying to be disrespectful. I just... I found out something. About Malik."

Her arms folded across her chest, guarded. "What did you find out that was so important it couldn't wait?"

He hesitated. "I can't say. Not yet."

"See?" she snapped, taking a step back. "That right there. That's the problem. You're always saying you're trying to protect people, but you never tell the full truth. You leave just enough out to keep everyone off balance."

"I'm trying to protect you, Myia."

"No. You're trying to protect yourself from the fallout."

Marcus closed his eyes briefly, collecting himself before he spoke. "That day...some guys came to us at telling us they knew where he was hiding. We left to make sure he was still there. When we arrived, he had already left and his body was near his last known location."

Myia's lips parted, stunned, but she didn't interrupt.

He continued. "We knew he was dead before the police ever said anything, because we saw the body. And I knew if I came back and told you then, while you were trying to mourn your mother, it would break you all over again."

Her eyes brimmed with tears, but she held them back. "So, you decided for me?"

"I decided *with you* in mind. You were already carrying too much."

The silence between them lingered, growing longer and more noticeable with each passing moment.

"Do you still think I had something to do with it?" he asked, voice rough.

Myia didn't answer immediately. Her gaze dropped to the ground, then back to his. "I don't know what to think. You keep shutting me out. You act like this burden is only yours to carry. But the more you hide, the harder it is to believe you."

"Because I'm not doing this recklessly. I've got a plan. I've got people helping me. But I can't do this without you."

"You don't get to guilt me into this."

"It's not guilt," he said. "It's reality. We're family. Whether or not you like it, we're in this together. You can either keep sitting on the sidelines, or you can help me make things right."

Myia's shoulders slumped as she let out a long, weary breath. For a moment, Marcus thought she might cave. But when she looked back at him, her eyes were steely.

"I'm sorry," she said. "I can't do it. I won't risk putting Tyson or myself in danger. You're on your own with this one."

His heart sank, but he masked it with a curt nod. "Fine. I'll handle it myself. Like I always do."

He turned and walked away. Behind him, Myia sat back down on the bench, staring at her book without opening it. Neither of them felt good about how the conversation ended, but neither was willing to give in.

Marcus didn't look back. If he did, he wasn't sure what he'd do—go back and apologize, yell again, or just stand there, waiting for her to say something else. Anything else. But the silence between them was thick, stubborn, and filled with years of things unsaid.

His boots crunched along the cracked sidewalk as he made his way to his truck. He didn't even bother starting it when he climbed in. Just sat there in an overbearing silence. Eventually, the pressure in his chest became too much. He got out and walked to the front porch. Everything felt dimmer, like even the day was tired of fighting. He leaned against the railing, trying to calm the storm brewing in his chest. Her voice echoed in his head—*If you really care, stop lying.* Over and over, like a loop he couldn't shut off.

He stared at the empty street in front of him, hoping that the quiet would somehow soothe the frustration coursing through his veins. But he wasn't alone. Tyson stepped out from the shadows of the driveway.

"I heard everything."

"How much did you hear?"

"Enough to know she's not helping. And enough to know you're gonna need someone to back you up."

Marcus didn't move at first. His eyes were still on the street, like maybe if he ignored him long enough, he'd disappear. But he didn't. Of course, he didn't. His quiet nature allowed him to give space when needed, but his loyalty was always apparent, as he'd readily provide help and backup even if never asked.

He finally turned to look at him. "This isn't your fight."

Tyson shrugged. "Maybe not. But I've been watching everything play out from the sidelines, and I'm tired of pretending like none of it touches me."

Marcus rubbed the back of his neck. "It's dangerous, Ty. This is more than what you're doing. This is actual involvement. These people don't bluff."

He didn't flinch. "You think I don't know that? I've been watching you spiral deeper into this mess, and yeah, I've kept my distance, but not because I'm scared. I just didn't know when to step in."

"You don't get to just dip your toe in and walk away when it gets hot. Once you're in, you're in."

"I'm already in," Tyson said quietly. "You think I can sit back and do nothing while you're out here getting jumped, followed, threatened? You're family. And I know I haven't said it, but I've got your back. Always.

Marcus looked at him with a torn expression. Part of him wanted to tell Tyson to go home, stay out of it, and stay safe. But another part was relieved. The kind of relief you feel when someone finally shows up when you didn't know how much you needed them.

He let out a slow breath. "Alright. But if you're doing this, you're doing it my way. No surprises. No stunts. We do this smart."

"Just tell me where to start."

Before he could respond, the door creaked open, and Myia stepped onto the porch. She crossed her arms with an expression a mixture of frustration and wariness.

"What are you doing out here?" she asked, her eyes darting between them.

Tyson didn't hesitate. "Talking to Marcus. Since you don't seem interested in helping, I figured someone should."

"Ty, don't start."

"No," he shot back. "Didn't you just yell at him for protecting you, but you're doing the same to me? I get a say on what I want to do. It's my life."

"You don't see the big picture? I'm doing it for you. Can't you see that?"

"You don't get to act like you're protecting everyone by sitting on the sidelines. He is out here risking everything to fix this, and all you're doing is making him feel worse."

"I'm not making him feel worse. I'm trying to stop him from getting himself killed. Do you have any idea what you're walking into?"

"I know exactly what I'm walking into. And I'm not afraid. You're the one who's too scared to do anything."

"That's not fair," she said, her voice breaking slightly. "You don't understand what's at stake. This isn't just about you or him. It's about the whole family. If something happens to either of you—"

"Something's already happening," Tyson interrupted. "Jordan's in jail for something he didn't do. We can't just sit around hoping it'll fix itself. If you won't help, fine. But don't stop me."

Myia stared at him with a mixture of anger and fear. She opened her mouth to respond but seemed to think better of it. Instead, she turned her attention to Marcus.

"And you're okay with this? You're okay with dragging *my* brother into this mess, too?"

"I didn't ask him to get involved," he said carefully. "But I'm not gonna stop him, either."

"Of course you're not. Because that's what you do, isn't it? You drag everyone else into your messes and hope it works out."

"I'm dragging myself into it," Tyson interjected, his voice cutting through the tension. "This isn't about him. This is about family. And if you can't see that, then maybe you're the one who needs to take a step back."

The words hung in the air. Myia stared, tears welling. For a moment, it seemed like she might argue, but she turned and walked back into the house, slamming the door behind her.

Marcus sighed. "That could've gone better."

"She'll come around. She just needs time."

"I hope so," Marcus said, eyeing the door. "Because if she doesn't, this is gonna get a lot harder."

"She doesn't have to understand. I'm with you, Marcus. Whatever it takes."

Marcus, feeling both grateful and uneasy, rested a comforting hand upon his cousin's shoulder. The road ahead was clearly dangerous, and the decision to bring Tyson increased the already considerable risks. But for now, he had an ally. And in this fight, that was all he could ask for.

Chapter 29

Marcus sat in his truck staring at the address scribbled on the paper in his hand. Sam had mentioned the name of a delivery driver who might have seen something the night of the robbery. It was a long shot, but he had learned to take what he could get. The address led him to a modest duplex that was tucked behind a row of old oak trees. He parked on the street and took a deep breath before stepping out. The worn path to the door spoke of someone who kept to himself.

He knocked twice. The sound echoed in the still afternoon air. For a moment, there was nothing. Then, the faint rustle of movement came from inside. A man peeked through the blinds before cautiously opening the door.

"Yeah?" the man asked warily.

"I'm looking for Kevin Rodgers," he said. "You're the delivery driver, right?"

His eyes narrowed, and his grip on the door tightened. "Who's asking?"

I'm Marcus. I'm trying to clear my brother's name. They accused my brother of robbery, and I think you may have seen something helpful.

He shook his head and stepped back. "I don't know anything about that. You've got the wrong guy."

Marcus quickly grabbed the door before he could shut it. "Look, I'm not here to cause trouble. I just need to know if you saw something that night. Please."

"I didn't see anything. I told the cops that already."

"Yeah, but did you tell them the truth?"

Nervously, he glanced over Marcus's shoulder. "You don't get it. I don't want any part of this. It's not worth it."

"What's not worth it? Please, if you saw something, anything, it could make a difference. My brother's life is on the line here."

He looked around like he was being watched. Finally, he stepped back and gestured for Marcus to come inside. The interior was sparse but tidy. A stack of pizza delivery bags sat in the corner, and the faint scent of grease lingered in the air. Kevin motioned to a chair but remained standing himself.

"Fine," he said, his voice low. "I saw a car. That's it."

"What kind of car?"

"It was a dark sedan. Black, I think. Tinted windows. It sped out of the parking lot just as I was pulling in to make a delivery."

"And you're sure it was the same night as the robbery?"

"Yeah. I remember because I heard the sirens not long after I dropped off the food."

"Did you see the driver? Or anything else that stood out?"

"No. It was dark, and they were gone before I could get a good look. But—" He hesitated, glancing at the floor.

"But what?"

Kevin sighed. "The way they drove off... it wasn't just fast. It was like they didn't care who saw them. Like they knew no one would talk."

"Why didn't you tell the cops this?"

"You think I want to end up in a ditch? People who pull that kind of stunt don't mess around. I've got a family to think about."

"I get that," Marcus said. "But if we don't stand up to them, they'll keep getting away with this. My brother didn't do this. He's innocent. And you might be the one who can help prove it."

Kevin looked torn. He kept looking towards to the window as if expecting someone to be watching. "I can't," he said finally, his voice barely above a whisper. "I'm sorry."

Marcus stood. "I know you're scared. But the longer you stay quiet, the more power they have. Think about that."

He didn't respond. Marcus sighed and turned to leave. As he reached the door, Kevin called out. "Wait."

Marcus turned around.

"I can't testify or anything,. But... I might've caught something on my dashcam. I didn't check it because I didn't want to get involved. But if it helps you, it's yours."

"That could be huge. Do you still have the footage?"

He nodded and went to the closet. After a quick search, he pulled out a small box and handed it to him. "Just... don't tell anyone where you got it. And don't come back here."

"You have my word. Thank you."

As Marcus stepped back into the fading daylight, he felt a flicker of hope. The dashcam footage might be the break he needed. He sat in his truck, staring at the small box in his hand. The weight of it seemed to grow heavier with every passing second. He'd just left Kevin's place. Even though he had given him the footage, there was an unsettling edge to the entire exchange. Marcus sensed there was something more. But right now, all that mattered was the footage. He just had to watch it. Then figure out who else already had.

He slid the box onto the passenger seat, started the engine, and drove to the shop. He had to know what was on that dashcam. The moment the footage played, it could change everything. He parked in the back and grabbed the box, making his way inside. He locked the door behind him and set the box on the counter.

"Alright, let's see what you've got," Marcus said to himself as he pulled the dashcam from its case. The box clicked open with a soft snap. Inside, the flash drive looked harmless. Ordinary. But his gut told him it wasn't. He plugged it into his laptop and waited. The screen lit up—folder. File. Timestamp. He clicked play.

For a moment, there was nothing but static. Then the footage played, and he leaned in closer. It showed routine footage of cars passing by and the humdrum of a quiet neighborhood. But as the footage advanced, something caught his eye.

The timestamp read just after two. The camera was aimed at the intersection closest to the robbery site, near the convenience store. A dark sedan, just as Kevin had described, appeared in the frame speeding down the street. The driver dimmed the headlights, almost as if trying to stay hidden. The sedan wasn't just fast. It was erratic, weaving between lanes as if the driver didn't care who saw them. He zoomed in on the license plate, but it was blurry. Whoever was driving knew how to keep a low profile.

Then, as the car passed, something else caught his attention. A figure, hunched down in the front passenger seat. The figure wasn't fully visible, but Marcus could make out the faint outline of a person who looked out of place. Whoever was in that car wasn't just a random passenger. There was something deliberate about their position in the vehicle.

Marcus rewound the footage and watched it again. This time, he slowed it down. The car passed more slowly, giving Marcus a better chance to catch any details. As it moved into the frame, something metallic flickered. It was hard to make out at first, but then he realized what it was: a gun. He couldn't believe what he was seeing. The driver was holding a gun out in the open, with no attempt to hide it and no fear of being seen. The realization hit him hard. This wasn't just a robbery gone wrong. This was something far more calculated and more dangerous.

Marcus slammed his hand against the desk in frustration. This wasn't what he'd expected. The gun was too obvious. It was too blatant. Whoever orchestrated the robbery wanted to make sure it was connected to something bigger—and they were confident they'd get away with it.

He rewound the footage one last time, pausing it just as the car sped away. The gunman had shifted slightly, giving Marcus a better view of their hands. Something about the way they moved looked familiar. The grip on the weapon wasn't like an amateur. It was too clean, too controlled.

There was something about that movement. Something he'd seen before. The way the hand held the gun was too reminiscent of someone he knew. *Could it be? Was it possible?* The more he thought about it, the more the answer seemed to sink in. The gunman wasn't just anyone. It was someone who had experience with firearms. Someone who knew what they were doing.

Marcus stood up suddenly, his chair scraping back against the floor. This could prove the gun was planted, but now to find out how his brother's fingerprints were on it. He had to follow this lead, had to dig deeper. But he wasn't sure if he was ready for what he might find. The door to the shop opened with a creak, and he froze. He hadn't expected anyone nor heard the bell. But when he turned, he saw a figure in the doorway.

"Tyson," Marcus said, a slight relief in his voice.

"Everything okay?" He asked as he walked in the office. His eyes immediately fell on the screen.

"I think I've found something," Marcus said, his fingers tapping the desk as he stared at the footage. "But it's not good."

He walked over and peered at the screen. "What is that?"

"A dark sedan," Marcus replied. "It was seen speeding away from the scene of the robbery. But I don't think this is just a robbery, Ty. I think there's a bigger operation at play here. And I think someone we know might be involved."

He frowned, studying the footage more closely. "That's not just any car, is it?"

"No. That's what I'm saying. It's too clean. Too deliberate. Someone set this up, Ty. Someone knew exactly what they were doing."

"Do you think this is connected to the gang?" Tyson asked, his voice tight.

Marcus hesitated for a moment before responding. "I don't know. But I can't shake the feeling that whoever's behind this has been planning it for a long time. And now they've got their sights on Jordan."

"Then let's make sure they don't get away with it."

"Something just doesn't feel right," Marcus said quietly. "They covered up the robbery was nothing. Now they've got people scared into silence. Kevin wouldn't even let me stay five minutes. Kept looking over his shoulder like someone was gonna bust in any second."

"You think he's in on it?"

"No. But I think someone's watching him. And if they are, it won't take much to trace this back to me."

Tyson didn't flinch. "Let them come."

Marcus looked at him. "This isn't a fight in the school yard, Ty. These people don't throw punches. They bury you."

"I'm not scared," Tyson said. "Not if it means protecting our family. Jordan's in jail for something he didn't do, and whoever did it is walking around free. That should scare them, not us."

"We're already in this, Ty. There's no turning back now."

The two stood in silence, the weight of what lay ahead settling in the air. The evidence was in front of them clear as day. And Marcus was more determined than ever to get to the bottom of it. Whoever was behind this had a dangerous plan in motion, and he would stop at nothing to make sure his brother wasn't framed for a crime he didn't commit. The game had just begun.

Chapter 30

It had been a long week, too long. Between tracking down leads, arguing with Myia, and trying to keep Tyson from diving in too deep, Marcus hadn't had a moment to breathe. Now, as the elevator doors opened and he stepped into the hallway of his apartment building, he felt a strange sensation crept over him.

Now, as the elevator doors slid open with a dull chime, a chill moved through him. Not exhaustion. Not nerves. Something else. The hallway stretched out ahead, dim and too quiet. The usual hum of a neighbor's TV was missing. No distant footsteps. No muffled arguments. Just silence and not the comforting kind that came with being home. This silence pressed in.

The overhead lights buzzed once, flickered, then steadied. The air felt colder than it should have. He stepped out, each bootstep echoing sharp against the floor. His instincts prickled. Something was off. He moved slowly as he scanned the corridor. Apartment 3B. Almost there.

Then he saw it.

His door was cracked open. Marcus froze mid-step. He'd locked it. He always locked it. His stomach dropped. He pushed the door the rest of the way open with one cautious hand. The apartment greeted him with silence, but not the silence he was used to. It was the kind that screamed. The kind that made every creak in the floorboards sound like a threat.

His eyes swept the space in an instant. The small living room was in disarray. His couch cushions were slashed open and the coffee table was flipped. Books from the shelves were scattered across the floor, pages torn and curling like dried leaves. The TV had been knocked face-down, and one of the framed photos of him and Jordan lay shattered in the corner.

Marcus stepped inside and scanned for movement. Nothing. Whoever had done this was long gone. He moved to the kitchen, gripping the edge of the counter for balance. Cabinets had been yanked open. Dishes smashed. Drawers dumped out onto the floor. But the fridge door... it was still closed. Almost untouched, like a final insult—*they'd taken his peace, not his food*.

He made his way down the hallway toward the bedroom. The damage there was no better. His mattress was flipped, clothes torn from the closet, drawers dumped out, and the ceiling light had been shattered. But it was what was written on the wall that stopped him cold.

Black spray paint. Jagged, angry letters. Four words.

STAY OUT OF IT.

He stared at the message. He was caught somewhere between fury and fear. They hadn't needed to harm him. This? This was enough. The message was clear.He backed out of the room, his body tense, pulse racing. His phone was already in his hand by the time he reached the hallway. It rang once. Twice.

"Marcus?" Sam's voice was low, alert.

"They were in my apartment." he kept his voice steady, but it came out tight. "They didn't take anything. Didn't need to."

"Wait—what?"

"They broke in. Wrecked everything. Didn't take a damn thing, just left a message."

"What did it say?"

He exhaled. "Stay out of it and it was spray painted it on the wall."

Sam cursed under his breath. "That's not just a warning."

"I know," Marcus said. "It's a promise."

"You okay?"

"Yeah. I wasn't home when it happened. But they wanted me to find it. They wanted me to know."

"You're lucky you weren't there, man."

Marcus walked back into the living room, stepping over the broken glass and overturned furniture. "That's the part that gets me. They could've waited. Could've ambushed me. But they didn't. This wasn't just about scaring me. It was about control."

"You should file a report."

"With who? The same cops half in Rook's pocket? No. This... this is confirmation. They're scared I'm getting close. That means I keep going."

"Just don't do anything stupid, alright?"

"Already too late for that."

There was a knock at the door. He spun around, adrenaline flaring, only to find Tyson standing there, wide-eyed.

"Damn," Tyson breathed. "They really did a number on your place."

Marcus ended the call and tucked his phone away. "How'd you know I was here?"

"Drove by, saw your car and the lights on. Figured you were still up." He stepped inside cautiously, surveying the wreckage. "This wasn't random. They were searching."

"I know."

Tyson bent down, picked up a lamp and stared toward the hallway. "What were they hoping to find?"

"I don't think they care about that," Marcus said. "This wasn't just about digging for something."

Tyson looked at him. "You think it was about sending a message?"

Marcus didn't answer right away. He led the way down the hall and motioned for Tyson to follow.

When they reached the bedroom, Tyson stopped cold in the doorway. His face shifted from shock to anger.

"They left it here?"

"Yeah," Marcus said grimly. "On the bedroom wall."

"They're not playing."

"No, they're not. But neither am I."

He walked to the window and looked out into the street below. Nothing unusual. No one watching, at least not visibly. But he knew better now. They'd gotten in and out without neighbors seeing a thing. That took coordination. Power. It reeked of Rook.

"So what's the move now?"

"Now? Now I clean this up. Then I figure out how to hit back."

"You sure you don't want to lie low a little?"

Marcus turned toward him, eyes sharp. "I did that once. After Malik. I kept my head down and hoped things would fix themselves. But they didn't. That silence? That cost us too much. I'm not repeating it."

"Then I'm here. Whatever you need."

"Grab a trash bag. Let's get to work."

The last bag hit the dumpster with a heavy thud. Marcus stood beside it, rubbing the grime from his hands onto his jeans. Tyson leaned against the wall nearby.

"Thanks, man," Marcus said quietly.

"You good?"

He didn't answer right away. He stared at the alley behind the building, empty and still, but his mind was still on the wall where those words had been sprayed.

"I will be," he said eventually.

"Call me if anything happens. No matter what time."

He waited until Tyson's car disappeared around the corner before heading back upstairs. The apartment looked cleaner now, but it didn't feel like home anymore. Something had been violated, something sacred. He sat down on the edge of his mattress, now flipped right side up, and took a breath.

Then he pulled out his phone and scrolled to Mom.

The line rang three times before she picked up. "Marcus? It's late. You alright?"

He closed his eyes for a moment. Her voice had that tired softness it always did after a long day. She sounded concerned, but not panicked yet. He hated that he was about to change that.

"Yeah, I'm alright. I just... needed to hear your voice."

"I know you didn't call to hear my voice this late."

He sat down on the edge of the bed, the mattress still creaking from where someone had torn through it earlier. His fingers gripped the phone tighter.

"I didn't want you to worry."

"I always worry. That's not new." Her voice stayed steady, but something in it shifted. She was more alert now. "Marcus, what's going on?"

"They broke into my apartment tonight." He kept his voice even, tried not to let the anger slip through. "Tore the place up. Left a message."

"What kind of message?"

"Spray painted it on my bedroom wall. Said, 'Stay out of it.'"

There was a sharp breath on the other end. "Oh my God..."

"I'm okay, Ma. I wasn't there when it happened. Neither was Tyson. No one was hurt."

"Tyson?" she repeated. "He was with you?"

"He's been helping me with... some of this. Don't worry, he didn't do anything reckless."

"You mean you did," she said. " I told you this isn't your fight."

"It is," he said quietly. "It's always been. Jordan didn't do what they're accusing him of, and I'm not just going to let him rot in there. I can't."

"And what if you end up next?" she snapped. "What if I lose both of you?"

Her voice cracked on the last word. Marcus felt it deep in his chest.

"I'm being smart about this. I've already talked to Mr. Miller. He told me if I could find anything useful, to bring it to him. I've been trying. I'm not out here playing hero, Ma, I'm just trying to fix what they broke."

There was silence for a long moment.

Finally, she asked, "And what exactly did you bring to that lawyer?"

"Nothing yet," he admitted. "But I'm getting there."

"I hate that you're in the middle of this. But I hate worse that Jordan's in jail, and we don't know who's really behind what happened."

"We're starting to. Piece by piece. I've just got to keep going."

"You're walking a thin line, baby," she murmured. "Just promise me you both be careful. Promise me you'll come home in one piece."

He closed his eyes again, the weight of her fear pressing down harder than anything written on his wall. "I promise."

She didn't say anything for a while. Then, softer: "You sound tired."

"I am."

"Well... go get some sleep. Try, at least. Call me tomorrow?"

"Yeah," he said. "Love you, Ma."

"I love you, too, baby. So much. Don't forget that."

He hung up and let the silence take over again. No more phone calls tonight. No more conversations. Just the quiet hum of the city pressing in from outside and the echo of his mother's voice clinging to the corners of the room. He sat there a long time, staring at nothing, letting the promise he made settle deep into his bones.

Chapter 31

Marcus sat in his shop after hours, the dim overhead light casting long shadows across the cluttered workbench. The events of the past month had been a whirlwind: the threats, the gang connections, Jordan's predicament, and now the chilling realization that someone powerful might be pulling the strings.

He stared at a notepad in front of him. It was covered in scribbles and lines that connected names, events, and places. It was starting to make sense. He was seeing a bigger picture emerge from the chaos. He called Sam. The phone rang twice before Sam's gruff voice answered. "Yeah?"

"It's me," he said. "You got a minute?"

"Always," his tone lighter than usual. "What's up?"

"I've been piecing things together. Something's not adding up about this whole mess."

"Welcome to the club."

"No, I mean, look. The gang's tied up in this, right? But they're not acting like they're just protecting themselves. It's like they're protecting someone else. Someone bigger."

There was a pause on the other end of the line. "What makes you think that?"

Marcus tapped his pen against the notepad. "Think about it. The way they've been moving and the resources they have. They're not just a bunch of street thugs. They've got connections. And then there's the way the cops have been handling Jordan's case. Half-assed, like they're not even trying to find the actual story."

"You think someone in law enforcement's involved?"

"I'm not saying all of them. But someone high up. Someone with enough pull to make evidence disappear and to make a gang like Rook's cover their tracks."

"That's a hell of an accusation."

Think about it. The edited footage. The clerk too scared to recant his statement. The delivery driver who practically sprinted away when I pushed him. And now the break-in? They're not just trying to scare me. They're trying to protect something, or someone."

Sam was quiet for a beat. "You think Rook's working with a cop?"

"I think Rook is answering to someone higher up. Someone who has the authority to shut things down. Maybe not a cop exactly. Could be someone in the DA's office. A detective. Hell, even a judge. But the connections are too tight, too protected. Someone's pulling the strings."

"That explains a lot. Remember how quickly Jordan got arraigned? And the bail was denied without even a hearing?"

"Exactly. That wasn't protocol. That was a move to make sure he stayed locked up where no one could talk to him."

"You realize if you're right, you're poking a hornet's nest. People like that don't play games. They'll shut you down any way they can."

"I don't care. My brother is innocent, and I'm not letting him rot in jail because some powerful asshole wants to cover their tracks."

Sam exhaled heavily. "Alright. So, what's the plan?"

"I start small. I'll talk to Kevin again. This time, I press harder. He knows more than he's saying. Then I look at the other clerks who work there. They might know something. And I want to find out who signed off on Jordan's arrest. Someone had to rubber-stamp it. Maybe Mr. Miller can help with that part."

"You better be careful, man. If you're right about this, you're poking a bear ten times bigger than you thought."

"I know. But I've already started this. I can't stop now. Not when we're this close to the truth."

"Alright. I have a contact in the department who owes me a favor. I'll see if they can dig into the court records and notice anything unusual with Jordan's case."

"See if they can also pull anything on Rook's gang. Arrests, investigations, anything. If someone's protecting them, there'll be gaps. Cases that went cold for no reason, evidence that disappeared."

"I'll see what I can do. But you owe me a case of beer for this."

"Deal. Thanks, man."

After hanging up, Marcus stared at the notepad again. He traced one line with his finger, connecting Rook's gang to a recent drug bust that mysteriously fell apart. It was a long shot, but it was something.

The next day, he followed up on another lead. He drove to a run-down corner near Edgewood, where a local drug dealer named Dre usually hung out. Word on the street was that he had been seen near the gang the night Jordan was arrested. No one had said it outright, but the gossip hinted he'd witnessed something he wasn't supposed to see.

Marcus pulled up near a faded barber shop that doubled as a hangout for him and a few of his guys. A group of guys leaned against a row of busted-up cars, their eyes following his every move. Dre stood among them, tall and lean, with a gold chain glinting against his hoodie and a cigarette hanging loosely from his lips. He took a breath and stepped out of his car.

Marcus approached slowly as he tried to look casual without seeming weak. Dre's eyes narrowed as he saw him coming.

"MC," he muttered as he exhaled a puff of smoke. "Didn't expect to see you out here."

They moved away from the front of the shop and into a narrow alley. The space was tight, cluttered with old crates and shards of broken glass that crunched beneath their boots. Dre kept his hands buried in his jacket pockets, shoulders tight, posture guarded.

"What you want?"

"I heard you were near the gang the night they arrested my brother," Marcus said. "Word is you saw something. Something you weren't supposed to."

Dre looked away. "You shouldn't be saying that out loud."

"Why? Because it's true? You've been looking over your shoulder ever since. Don't think I haven't noticed."

"Man, you have no idea what kind of fire you're playing with."

"Try me," Marcus shot back. "They already broke into my apartment. Left me a message to back off. I'm not backing off. Not until I clear my brother's name."

Dre's eyes darted around the alley before lowering his voice. "I didn't mean to see anything. I was just... in the wrong place."

"But you *did* see something," he pressed.

"Yeah. I saw Rook. And someone else. Someone I'd never seen before. He wasn't from the street. This dude wore an expensive suit and had an attitude like he ran the entire city."

"You remember what they were talking about?"

"He came into the store after the robbery. He talked to boss like they were old friends. I didn't catch his name, but he had this... presence. Like he owned the place."

"And you're sure he's tied to the cops?"

"I heard boss mention something about keeping the heat off their backs. The guy said he'll 'take care of it'. I didn't stick around to hear more."

"Did you catch a name?"

"Nah. But I know this; boss was listening to him. Like really listening. That guy wasn't street-level. He was something else."

"So there's someone higher up that's connected. That's why no one's talking."

"I shouldn't even be telling you this. But I ain't trying to get caught up in no murder case. I got my own problems."

"Then help me stop this. Give me something I can use."

Dre glanced around once more, then reached into his pocket and wrote something on a crumpled napkin. "There's a spot they go sometimes. Old warehouse near the railyard. I seen boss go in and out. If the big guy's real, he'll be there."

Marcus took it. "Thanks, man. You did the right thing."

"Nah. I just don't wanna be next."

As Marcus walked back to his car, heart racing, he knew this was a turning point. The corruption wasn't just deep. It was protected. But he wasn't going to stop now. Not when he was this close.

Chapter 32

Marcus navigated the winding streets of Crest Ridge, his mind a storm of restless thoughts. The napkin Dre had slipped him felt like it was burning a hole in his pocket. The address scrawled across it pointed to a warehouse, but going in blind felt reckless. He needed more than a hunch. He needed clarity. And there was one person who might have it: Detective Frank "Big Frank" Rivers. He was a retired cop with a reputation for being one of the few honest ones this town had left.

Frank used to volunteer at the local community center and helped Marcus and Jordan stay on track when they were younger. He wasn't the kind of man who looked the other way, even when it cost him. That made him a rare breed in Crest Ridge and the kind of person Marcus needed now more than ever.

The sun had dipped low, casting golden streaks across the cracked sidewalks as Marcus pulled into the driveway of a modest brick house. The place looked tired but well-kept, like its owner had stopped expecting visitors but still kept the porch swept out of habit. A faded basketball hoop hung above the garage, and the faint smell of barbecue wafted from somewhere down the block. It looked like a quiet life, far from the chaos Frank had once worked in. Marcus hoped the old man hadn't completely turned his back on it.

He knocked on the door, and a few seconds later, Frank opened it. He was taller and broader than Marcus remembered. His hair was still cut close to the scalp, but the beard had filled in with streaks of silver. Time had thickened his frame, but not dulled his edge. His eyes were sharp, same as always, like he could still spot a lie before it left your mouth.

"Well, if it ain't Mr. Carter," Frank said, voice gravelly with age but full of weight. He stepped aside. "You're still tall and stubborn as ever."

Marcus offered a small grin as he crossed the threshold. "And you're still watching people like they owe you the truth."

Frank shut the door behind him with a solid thud. "Most of 'em do."

Marcus followed him down the short hallway, the air inside tinged with the scent of old coffee and cedar. The house was quiet, except for the low hum of a ceiling fan overhead.

"You still drink that bitter mess you called coffee?" Marcus asked, trying to ease into the conversation.

He grunted. "Keeps the arteries confused. Want a cup?"

"I'll live longer without it."

He cracked a half-smile. "Soft."

They passed a wall lined with framed commendations, faded newspaper clippings, and a photo of Frank in uniform shaking hands with a former police chief, one of the few Marcus didn't outright distrust. Frank led him into the living room. The light was dim, but cozy. Familiar. A space lived in.

"You still working with that loud-mouthed cousin of yours?" Frank asked over his shoulder.

"Tyson? Loud-mouthed is generous. But yeah. He's in it deep whether I like it or not."

He shook his head. "Didn't fall far from the tree, I guess."

"I try," Marcus replied as he stepped into the living room. Family photos lined the mantel, and a well-worn recliner sat in front of a muted news channel. "Didn't think I'd be coming to you for cop advice, but here we are."

He motioned for him to sit. "If you're knocking on my door, I know it ain't for no barbecue recipe. What's going on?"

"It's about my brother."

"I heard he got locked up. Thought it didn't sit right."

"It doesn't. He's being set up, Frank. And I think the people behind it aren't just street-level."

Marcus hesitated, then laid it all out: the gang's involvement, the edited footage, the threats, and Dre's tip about someone powerful pulling the strings. Frank listened without interruption.

When he finished, Frank let out a low whistle. "Damn. You're not just sticking your nose into trouble, you're diving headfirst into a hornet's nest."

"You know something, don't you? About the department?"

"Yeah. I know a thing or two. Retired or not, you don't spend thirty years on the force without seeing how deep the rot goes."

"What kind of rot?"

Frank sat back in the recliner. "You ever hear of Jack Haynes?"

"The name sounds familiar."

"Should. He's the deputy chief now," he said. "Back when I was still on the force, Haynes was just a sergeant. He always had a knack for politics and staying out of trouble, even when things were difficult. Word was, he had ties to some shady folks, but nothing ever stuck. Guy's a ghost for paper trails."

"You think he's connected?" Marcus asked.

"I don't think, I know," he answered. "Back in the day, there were whispers about him running interference for some of the local crews. Evidence disappearing, cases getting dropped, witnesses suddenly changing their stories. But no one could prove a damn thing."

Marcus felt a chill run down his spine. "And no one called him out?"

Frank chuckled bitterly. "You kidding me? He had half the department under his control, and the other half was too scared to defy him. Guy's got friends in high places; city council, business owners, even a judge or two."

"What about now? If I can connect him to Rook, would anyone listen?"

"Not unless you've got a smoking gun. Haynes is untouchable. Even if you had witnesses, they'd either clam up or disappear before they could testify."

"So what the hell am I supposed to do? Just let them get away with it?"

Frank studied him for a moment, then got up and walked to a cabinet. He rummaged around and pulled out a dusty file folder and tossed it onto the coffee table.

"What's this?" Marcus asked, opening the folder.

"Old case files,. Stuff I kept when I retired. Call it insurance. You might recognize a few names of people Haynes was connected to back then. Might be worth looking into."

Marcus flipped through the files. There were reports, photos, even handwritten notes from Frank. It wasn't a smoking gun, but it was a start.

"Why are you giving me this?" He asked, looking up from the folder.

Frank met his gaze, steady and tired. "Because I'm done watching this town get eaten alive from the inside out. Guys like Haynes? They don't stop until someone makes them. And you—" he gave a dry chuckle, "—you're just stubborn enough to try."

"I won't let you down," he said. "Tyson's with me. And maybe one or two more if it comes to that."

Frank raised an eyebrow. "You sure that's wise? That kid thinks he's bulletproof."

He smirked faintly. "He's grown. Got his head on straighter than most these days."

Frank grunted, skeptical but not dismissive. "Let's just hope he's smart enough to duck when bullets start flying."

He gave a half-smile. "This... this could really help. You sure you're okay handing it over?"

"I didn't keep it this long just to let it rot in a drawer," Frank said. He leaned back in his chair. "Haynes had friends. Still does, probably. But most of 'em, like him, think they're untouchable. That's what makes 'em sloppy. That file? It's a map of their arrogance."

Marcus flipped to a page near the back of the folder, where a faded photo caught his eye. A younger Jack Haynes stood with his arm slung around a man he didn't recognize. He had broad-shouldered, clean-cut, and a confident smirk on his face. But it was the badge clipped to the man's belt that made Marcus sit up straighter.

"Who's this?" he asked, tapping the image.

Frank leaned in, squinting at the page. "That's Wilkes. Used to run narcotics back in the day. Sharp guy. Too sharp, maybe."

"What happened to him?"

"Transferred out after a bust went sideways. Official report blamed bad intel." Frank's tone darkened. "But off the record? Someone tipped off the gang before we even got close. Whole thing stank, but no one wanted to touch it."

Marcus kept his eyes on the photo. "And you think he's still active?"

He shrugged. "I don't know. But if Haynes is pulling strings the way you think, Wilkes wouldn't be far behind. Those two were tight. Always had each other's backs. Sometimes too much."

He leaned back, voice firm. "Follow the names, son. Cross-reference the bust dates. The arrests that went nowhere. You'll see where the cracks run."

Marcus nodded slowly. The pieces were there. He just had to connect them.

He closed the folder carefully, as if it were something sacred. "This means a lot. You didn't have to do this."

"I did. Because someone has to."

Frank stood, his joints cracking as he moved. "Keep your head low. And remember don't trust anybody too easily. The good ones in that department... they either left, retired, or stopped sticking their necks out a long time ago."

Marcus rose with him, folder tucked securely under one arm. "I'll be careful. And if I find anything, I'll come back."

"You'd better," he said, walking him to the door. "Because if you don't... I'll assume the worst."

Frank opened the screen door but didn't step out. "This thing you're chasing; it's deeper than one bad cop. You know that, right?"

"I know." Marcus met his eyes. "Doesn't change what needs to be done."

Frank gave a slow nod, then offered his hand. Marcus took it—firm, brief, understood.

"Watch your back, Carter."

"Always do," Marcus said.

He stepped out onto the porch, the door creaking shut behind him. The air was cooler now, the night settling in like a warning. Marcus stood for a second before heading to his car. He glanced back once at the house. Frank was still standing in the doorway, arms crossed, watching him leave. A silent promise passed between them.

As he drove home, his mind raced with possibilities. The new information was a lifeline, but it also raised more questions. *If Haynes was truly at the center of this, how deep did his influence run? And how far would he go to protect his empire?* When he got to his apartment, he sat in the car for a moment, staring at the folder. The weight of it felt almost unbearable, but he knew there was no turning back now.

Chapter 33

Marcus sat at his kitchen table with the file spread out in front of him. Pages of notes, faded photographs, and old police reports formed a patchwork of corruption and deceit. The names of gang members, business owners, and even community leaders leapt off the pages, their connections to Deputy Chief Jack Haynes glaringly obvious in hindsight. He felt a surge of frustration. The evidence was damning, but it wasn't enough to take to the police or a journalist. Not yet. He needed something current, something irrefutable.

His phone buzzed on the table. Marcus grabbed it without thinking—Tyson's name lit up the screen.

"Yo," he answered, rubbing at his eyes.

"You good?" Tyson's voice had an edge of concern. "You sounded off earlier."

"I'm fine," Marcus said, though his voice betrayed his exhaustion. "Just got some new info from Big Frank."

Tyson let out a low whistle. "Didn't think he was still taking visitors."

"He almost wasn't." Marcus glanced at the open file. "But he gave me a file full of stuff."

"What's in it?"

"Stuff from back in the day. Ties Haynes to Rook's crew. But it's old. I need something fresh to make it stick."

Tyson let out a low whistle. "You're really going after the deputy chief, huh?"

"I don't have a choice," Marcus said. "Jordan's sitting in a cell because of this mess. I can't let it slide."

There was a pause, then Tyson said, "What's your next move?"

"Not sure yet. Gotta figure out where he fits into Rook's operation now. If he's protecting them, there's gotta be a reason."

"Well, if you need backup..." Tyson left the offer hanging.

"I'll let you know," Marcus said, though he knew involving Tyson any further would put him at risk.

After hanging up, Marcus returned his focus to the file. One name kept standing out: Derrick Lowe. He was a mid-level enforcer for the gang back in the day. According to Frank's notes, he had been caught running guns but walked free after a deal mysteriously fell apart. If anyone knew the inner workings of Haynes' protection racket, it might be him.

The next morning, Marcus sat in his car outside a run-down bar on the east side of Crest Ridge. Derrick's name had surfaced in a handful of recent petty crime reports. They were nothing major, but frequent enough to suggest he was back in circulation. A bartender Tyson had leaned on confirmed Lowe was a regular here, usually mid-morning, always looking over his shoulder

Marcus adjusted his ball cap and glanced at himself in the rearview mirror. He looked rough. Unshaven, shadows under his eyes, jaw set. Good. It fit the scene. He looked rough, but it matched the environment. This wasn't the kind of place that welcomed clean cuts or quiet questions. The goal was to blend in, not stand out.

Inside, the bar smelled of stale beer and cheap cologne—a mix that clung to the walls like history no one wanted to remember. A dim haze hovered in the air, filtered through the weak light of flickering neon signs. The few patrons barely looked up, lost in their drinks or hushed conversations.

Marcus moved slow, keeping his head down but his eyes sharp. At the far end of the bar, hunched over a lowball glass of whiskey, sat Derrick Lowe. He was scrolling through his phone, shoulders tight, one knee bouncing beneath the barstool like he couldn't sit still.

He took the stool two seats down, giving him a wide enough angle to watch without drawing attention. He ordered a soda. There was no reason to cloud his focus. He studied Derrick's reflection in the bar mirror. He was waiting for something. Or someone. And Marcus had a feeling it wasn't just another drink.

He let a few minutes pass, just long enough not to seem deliberate. Then he slid off his stool and made his way down the bar.

Derrick didn't look up until he was already beside him.

"What's up, Lowe," he said, voice low and even.

Derrick stiffened. His hand froze over his phone, thumb mid-scroll. He turned slowly, eyes narrowing.

"You got the wrong guy."

Marcus smiled without humor. "No, I don't."

Derrick glanced around. The barflies too drunk to care and bartender nowhere in sight. He shifted on his stool, angling away like he might bolt.

"Relax," he said. "I'm not here to make a scene. Just talk."

"You're a cop?" Derrick asked, jaw tight.

"Do I look like a cop?"

Derrick gave him a long look. "You look like trouble."

Marcus leaned in just enough to drop his voice lower. "Depends on how you answer the next few questions."

Derrick eyed the door.

"You bolt," he said, "and I'll be at your mom's place before you finish running. Just sit. Listen."

That landed. Derrick stayed put, though his jaw clenched.

"I ain't got answers."

"Funny, because I heard you might know something about Deputy Chief Haynes.

"Don't know what you're talking about."

"Come on. We both know he didn't just help you out of the kindness of his heart. I'm not here to bust you. I just need to know what he's up to now."

Derrick glanced around the bar, his paranoia evident. "You got a death wish or something?"

"Maybe. But I'm not walking away from this. You know something, and I need you to tell me."

"Even if I did, why the hell would I tell you? You think I wanna end up in a ditch?"

"I think you're tired of looking over your shoulder," Marcus said, his voice low but steady. "And I think you know he's not invincible. We take him down, and you're free of him."

Derrick didn't answer right away. His eyes flicked toward the bartender, who had stopped pretending not to listen. He downed the rest of his whiskey in one long swallow, then stood abruptly.

"Come on," he muttered. "Not here."

Marcus tossed a few bills on the bar and followed him through a side door that opened into a narrow alley behind the building. The morning sun barely touched the concrete back here—just shadows, dumpster stink, and peeling paint.

Derrick lit a cigarette with hands so shaky that his lighter flicked twice before it caught. He inhaled deeply, then exhaled slow, trying to steady himself.

"I shouldn't even be talking to you," he said, eyes locked on the smoke curling from the tip. "Guys like me don't get second chances in Crest Ridge. We get bullets. Or silence."

Marcus didn't speak.

"You think I don't want out?" he asked bitterly. "You think I ain't tried?"

"I think you're still here. That says something."

Derrick let out a dry laugh. "You ever wake up with your heart pounding, and you don't know if it's guilt or fear? That's what it's like working for them. You can't sleep. Can't eat. You watch your back every time you step outside."

"You're not the only one who's tired of living like that."

Derrick glanced at him. "Yeah? Then you know the only way out's through the fire. No mercy. No deals. Once you cross 'em, you're either a witness or a body."

"I'm not looking to scare them," Marcus answered. "I'm looking to finish it."

Derrick flicked ash onto the concrete. "You really think taking down one cop is gonna fix this?"

"Not one cop. The right one."

Derrick stared at him for a long moment. Then he shook his head, took another drag, and exhaled slow.

"You don't get it, man. He ain't just covering for the gang. He's running it. Rook might call the shots on the street, but he pulls the strings. He's the reason they're untouchable."

"What's his angle?"

"Money, power, take your pick. You think all those deals that fell apart were accidents? Haynes makes sure the gang stays in business, and they kick back a cut. Keeps him living large and keeps the cops looking the other way."

"And Rook? What's his role?"

"He's just a glorified errand boy. He keeps the streets in line, but he answers to him. Always has."

"Thanks for the tip."

"Don't thank me. And don't come looking for me again. I don't want to know what happens next."

As Derrick disappeared into the shadows, Marcus stood there for a moment, the enormity of what he'd learned settling over him. Haynes wasn't just a corrupt cop. He was the mastermind behind everything. Taking him down wouldn't just free Jordan. It would tear down an empire. But first, he had to figure out how to do it without ending up in a ditch himself.

Marcus unlocked his phone and opened a message thread with Tyson. He hovered for a second, thumbs poised. This couldn't be a quick update or another rushed call. He needed to lay it out, face-to-face. No distractions. No room for misunderstanding.

He typed:

Need to meet. Today. Something big. You free this afternoon?

He hit send and slipped the phone into his pocket.

Across the street, a couple of teens laughed as they raced their bikes down the sidewalk, oblivious to the rot beneath their city. Marcus watched them disappear around the corner and wondered if they'd still be able to laugh when the truth came out.

His phone buzzed.

Bet. I'll swing by after three. You good?

Marcus stared at the message for a beat.

He typed:

Not sure. But I will be.

Tyson's car pulled up to the curb in a soft roll, music low and windows down. He leaned over the passenger seat as Marcus stepped out of his building.

"You look like you've been digging through graves," Tyson said.

"I have," Marcus muttered. "C'mon. Let's go upstairs."

Tyson gave him a look but didn't press. He could tell from Marcus's tone that whatever this was, it was serious.

They walked up in silence, their footsteps echoing in the stairwell. Inside the apartment, Marcus didn't bother with pleasantries. He headed straight for the kitchen table, where the folder from Frank still lay open in a chaotic spread of reports, notes, and photos.

He stood over it for a moment, gathering his thoughts. Tyson lingered near the door, watching him closely.

"Derrick Lowe," he began. "I met with him this morning."

Tyson raised an eyebrow. "That twitchy dude? Thought he fell off."

"He's back," he said as he flipped through the pages. "And scared. But he talked."

He pulled out the napkin with the warehouse address, then a photo of Haynes from Frank's file, and laid them side by side. "He confirmed it. Rook might be the face on the street, but Haynes is the one calling the shots."

Tyson let out a low whistle. "Haynes? As in, the Haynes?"

"Yeah. He's not just covering for the gang. He's running it."

"Damn."

Tyson leaned against the wall near the window with his arms crossed. He was deep in thought.

Marcus sat at the table, scribbling notes on a legal pad. His movements were quick but tight, like he was trying to stay one step ahead of something that was already catching up.

"They've got a warehouse over on Brentley," he said. "Derrick says it's a front. Big shipments, late-night deliveries, heavy security. If we can get eyes on it, maybe—"

"Maybe what?" Tyson interrupted. "Get a blurry photo of some guys moving crates?"

"Every piece counts."

Tyson shook his head and pushed off the wall. "Not when the board's rigged."

He walked over, picked up a photo from the folder. It was an old shot of Haynes in uniform, shaking hands with a state official, smiling like a man who'd already won.

"You really think evidence is gonna be enough? You hand that over and it disappears before the ink dries. Or worse you disappear."

"That's why we don't go through normal channels. We document everything. Build pressure. Make it too public to bury."

Tyson stared at him, searching for cracks in his confidence. There were some—tired eyes, the slight tremble in his hand—but Marcus's jaw was set, and the fire in his voice hadn't dimmed.

After a moment, Tyson sighed and dropped the photo back on the table.

"I've been thinking about what Derrick told you," he said. "If Haynes is really running things, how do you even plan to touch him? The man's got half the department in his pocket."

"I don't know yet, but I'm not stopping. If he's calling the shots, then he's the reason Jordan's in jail. He's the reason all this is happening."

"Yeah, but you're going up against someone who's untouchable."

"This ain't just some street gang. This is Crest Ridge's golden boy. You really think you can take him down?"

"I don't have a choice. If I back off now, what happens? Jordan rots in jail, Haynes keeps running his little empire, and everyone just looks the other way."

"Alright. Sounds like you need a good plan."

"I don't know yet. But I've got enough pieces to start figuring it out."

"You think there's something in here that'll bring Haynes down?"

"There's gotta be," Marcus said. "We just need to connect the dots."

"You sound real confident for someone who just had their apartment trashed," Tyson said.

Marcus shot him a look. "You think I don't know what's at stake here? This ain't about me being confident. It's about doing what's right."

Tyson leaned forward, his expression serious. "I get that. But don't act like you're invincible. These people don't play fair. You saw what they did to Jordan, and now they're coming for you. You gotta be smart about this."

"I am being smart," Marcus said, his voice rising. "But I'm not letting them scare me off. If we don't stand up to them, who will?"

Tyson opened his mouth to respond but stopped as the sound of a car pulling up outside caught both their attention. Marcus tensed and instinctively reached for the wrench on the table. A knock at the door followed. Tyson shot Marcus a wary glance, but he motioned for him to stay put.

He approached the door cautiously. He looked through the peephole and saw it was Sam. Marcus opened the door and let him in.

"Thought you'd be working late," Marcus said.

"Had to make a stop first," Sam said, holding up a thumb drive. "I've got something for you."

Tyson stood as Sam entered the room. "What is it?" Tyson asked.

Sam set the drive on the table. "I've been doing some digging. Found a few things that might help. Bank records, mostly. Payments from Rook's crew to a couple of cops. Nothing that screams Haynes yet, but it's a start."

Marcus picked up the drive, turning it over in his hand. "This is good. If we can tie the money to him, then that's all we need."

"Don't get too excited," Sam said, his tone cautious. "This ain't a smoking gun. It's breadcrumbs. And you're gonna need a hell of a lot more if you want to take down someone like him."

"I'll take breadcrumbs," Marcus said. "They'll lead somewhere."

"Look, I know you're set on doing this, but you need to be ready for what happens if you push too hard. These people don't just fight back. They wipe you out."

"I'm ready," Marcus said. "I've already come this far. No turning back now."

"You're stubborn, I'll give you that."

Hours later, Marcus sat alone at the kitchen table. Tyson had gone home. Sam was back to his usual tech work, promising to keep an ear to the ground. Now, it was just him and the mountain of evidence spread around him like a storm mid-surge. Reports. Names. Photos. Scrawled notes in his own handwriting that barely looked like his anymore.

But his mind wasn't on the papers. It was elsewhere. He could still hear his mom's voice trying to sound strong for him even as she begged him not to do anything reckless. He thought about Tyson's words, sharp with concern, and Sam's cautious warnings laced with logic and fear.

Then he thought about Jordan. Locked in a jail cell. Bruised. Beaten. But not broken. Still fighting to prove he didn't do what the world was convinced he did. This wasn't just about clearing a name anymore. It was about survival. His brother's, and maybe his own.

The stakes weren't just high. They were astronomical. One wrong move, one leak, one whispered tip to the wrong person, and it could all come crashing down. Not just the case. Not just the plan. Everything.

Marcus looked down at the small thumb drive resting in his palm. It had taken Sam days to decrypt, and when he finally did, he sent it with one line:

"This is what they're protecting."

Marcus swallowed the tight knot in his throat and plugged the drive into his laptop. The screen flickered. Then it was filled with spreadsheet after spreadsheet. Cryptic codes, bank transfers, offshore accounts, LLCs tied to shell companies and fake vendors. At first, it was just noise. But then the patterns started to emerge.

Each transaction was a thread. And the deeper he followed them, the more the web began to form. Shell companies tied to city contracts. Payouts disguised as construction expenses. Donations rerouted through fake nonprofits. And threaded through it all, Jack Haynes. Front and center.

Marcus leaned in, scrolling faster now. Sweat beaded at his brow. His heart thudded against his ribs, but it wasn't fear—it was clarity.

Proof. Finally. He sat back, exhaling a breath he hadn't realized he'd been holding.

"This ends with Haynes," he said aloud. "No matter what it takes."

Chapter 34

Tyson rolled out of the corner store with a bag of snacks under one arm and a pack of bottled water under the other. He tossed the groceries in the back seat and wiped sweat from his brow before climbing in. He barely noticed the black SUV parked across the street until he started the engine. Its tinted windows gave nothing away, but the engine revved just seconds after his did. He told himself it was nothing. Just coincidence.

But when he turned right onto Crestline Avenue, the SUV turned right too. When he switched lanes, so did they. And when he made an unnecessary loop through the pharmacy parking lot just to test his suspicion, the SUV glided slowly through the same route, two cars behind.

Tyson's grip on the wheel tightened. "Nah, man. Not today."

He pulled out his phone and dialed fast. Marcus answered on the second ring. "What's up?"

"I think I'm being followed. Been on my tail since I left the store."

"Where are you now?"

"Headed toward Midtown. I'm about to lose them in traffic."

"No. Don't go home. Don't go anywhere near your place."

"You think they know where I live?"

"If they're following you, they might already know too much."

Tyson muttered a curse and veered left, taking a side street that cut behind an old warehouse. "You want me to go to your spot?"

"No. We're probably both being watched now. Just head to the old train depot. You know the one by the underpass?"

Tyson's pulse thudded in his ears as he swerved down the narrow back street. The SUV didn't follow immediately, but he wasn't naive enough to think he'd shaken them. Not yet.

"Yeah, I know it," he said, one eye on the rearview mirror. "You sure that's the move?"

"It's off grid. No cameras. No traffic. We can figure out next steps there," Marcus replied. "Just don't lead them straight in."

"Copy that."

Tyson hung up and dropped the phone onto the passenger seat. He turned again as he weaved through a neighborhood of boarded-up houses and crumbling sidewalks. The SUV reappeared two blocks back, creeping like a shadow.

"Persistent bastards," he said, checking his gas gauge. Half a tank. Enough to get creative.

He made a hard right, tires screeching against the pavement, then hit another left and gunned it through a yellow light. The SUV hesitated at the intersection. Tyson didn't look back. Not yet.

Up ahead, the tracks came into view—twisted steel half-sunk into broken concrete, lined with graffiti-tagged freight cars that hadn't moved in years. He cut the engine a block out, coasted into a narrow gravel path behind a rusted fence, and killed the headlights. Silence. He waited. Thirty seconds. A minute. Two. Nothing.

Tyson let out a slow breath, heart still hammering. He grabbed his phone again and texted Marcus:

Clear for now. You close?

Seconds later, the reply buzzed through:

Pulling up. Meet me behind the maintenance shed.

Tyson stepped out of the car. He moved low, fast, weaving between the derelict railcars until he spotted Marcus under the underpass, half in shadow.

"They peeled off a few blocks back. I circled for a while to be sure. But that wasn't some random tail. They were watching me."

"They're getting bold."

"This is payback. You stirred the hornet's nest. They know we're looking into Haynes."

"Yeah." Marcus rubbed the back of his neck. "I just didn't think they'd start coming for you."

"You think I care? I told you I was in. I knew what this meant."

"It's not just you. If they're tracking us, it's only a matter of time before they go after my mom. Or Myia. Or anyone we've talked to."

"You thinking about backing out?"

Marcus didn't answer right away. He sat down on the hood of his car and stared out toward the tracks.

"I keep thinking about what Frank said," he finally murmured. "That this thing is bigger than we know. That Haynes is connected to people who make people disappear. If I push too hard... what happens if my mom doesn't answer the phone one day? What if someone jumps Myia walking to her clinic? I've already brought too much heat down."

"You're not wrong. But ask yourself something: what happens if you stop? Think they'll just let it go? Let us walk away?"

Marcus closed his eyes.

"Jordan's still locked up for something he didn't do," Tyson continued. "You give up now, you leave him in there. You let Haynes win. You let them keep running this city like they own it."

"I'm not trying to be a hero. I just want my brother out."

"And we don't get him out unless we pull the whole house down. That's the truth."

"I'm scared, man."

"Me too. But I'd rather go down swinging than keep living in a city where people like Haynes decide who gets to breathe."

They sat in silence for a few minutes, the hum of distant traffic filling the air.

Marcus finally stood. "Alright. No more running errands alone. No one moves without backup. We stay low, we stay smart."

"Now you're talking like you got a crew."

"A broke crew with no weapons and barely a plan."

"But we got guts."

"And a folder full of dirt on the most powerful man in Crest Ridge," Marcus added.

"Let's go. We got more work to do. And next time they follow me, I'm leading them straight into a ditch."

They drove off in separate directions to avoid detection. The fear was still there, but so was the fire. The gang had made one mistake: They reminded Marcus what was really at stake. And now he wasn't just trying to save his brother. He was trying to save everyone Haynes had crushed.

Marcus sat in his car outside a run-down laundromat, heart still thudding from the conversation with Tyson. The street buzzed with normalcy—kids biking down sidewalks, someone blasting music from a passing car—but everything felt like it was hiding something now. Every corner, every shadow. He pulled out his phone and stared at the screen for a second before tapping Myia's name.

She picked up after the second ring. "Hey."

Her voice was soft, a little tired, maybe just getting off a long shift at the clinic. For a moment, he hesitated, not wanting to drag her deeper into this. But it was too late for hesitation now.

"Myia," he said, trying to sound calm, "you home?"

"Not yet. I'm walking to my car. What's going on?"

"Listen to me. I need you to be careful. Watch your surroundings. Don't go anywhere without checking who's around."

She stopped walking. He could hear it in the way her breathing paused. "Marcus... what happened?"

"There's been movement. Tyson was followed today. Probably the gang, or someone working for them. They're starting to close in."

"Do they know about me?"

"I don't know." His voice dropped. "That's what scares me. I don't think they've made a move on anyone else yet, but if they're following Tyson, they might know who we're close to. Who matters."

"You think they'd come after me to get to you?"

"I think they're capable of anything. And if they're feeling the pressure, they'll lash out."

She sighed heavily, and he could picture her standing next to her car. "Okay. I'll be careful. I'll switch up my route home, check for tails. I'll get Aiyden and we'll stay at my best friend's place tonight, just in case."

"Good," he said, feeling a small bit of tension ease. "Keep your phone on you. And if anything feels off, even a little, call me. Don't play it cool."

"Marcus..."

He could hear the hesitation in her voice.

"I'm sorry. I didn't want to drag you into this. I've tried to keep you away from it. But it's spreading."

"I know what you're doing," she said quietly. "Trying to fix everything. Trying to protect your brother. You don't have to apologize for that."

"I just... I can't lose anyone else."

There was a long pause. Then she said, "You're not going to. But you have to be careful too. Don't do something reckless trying to protect everyone else and end up gone yourself."

"Yeah. I hear you."

"I'll text you when I'm home. And I'll keep my eyes open."

"Thanks, Myia."

"Be safe, Marcus."

He ended the call and leaned back in his seat, staring at the cracked ceiling of the car. The war was getting closer to home. And now, even the people he loved were walking targets. If he wanted to finish this, he'd have to out think and out last everyone coming for him. And make damn sure no one else got hurt in the process.

Chapter 35

Marcus was busy putting in an engine of a Buick. A socket wrench clinked against the engine block as he tightened a bolt. For a moment, everything else faded. No corrupt cops, no hidden files, no looming threats. Just metal, muscle memory, and the steady satisfaction of getting something to work again. Then his phone rang.

He glanced at the screen, recognizing the Crest Ridge County Jail number instantly. His stomach twisted. He yanked off his gloves, grabbed the phone, and stepped out behind the shop where the noise of drills and engines wouldn't drown the call. He answered and then the robotic voice kicked in.

You have a collect call from an inmate at Crest Ridge County Jail... Do you accept the charges?

He pressed the number. The moment he heard his brother's voice, he knew something was wrong.

"Marcus," Jordan said, voice low, strained.

"What happened?"

"They roughed me up, man."

"What?"

"In the hallway," he continued. "Two of Rook's boys. Said it was a message. 'Tell your brother to back off before it gets worse.' Then they threw me into the wall."

Marcus swore under his breath and kicked at a loose bolt on the ground, sending it skittering across the concrete.

"They hit your face?"

"Just ribs, back of the head. I'll live. But it was meant to shake me."

"Did you tell the guards?"

Jordan gave a dry, humorless laugh. "You think they don't already know? One of them was standing right there. Just watched. Like it was entertainment."

"I swear to God, I'm gonna burn this whole thing down."

"No. That's what I called to say. I need you to stop, bro. Seriously. I thought maybe if you stayed quiet, they'd back off, but now? They're watching you. They want to hurt you."

"I don't care what they want. They think they can lay hands on my brother and I'll just sit back?"

"I'm not telling you because I want you to get angry," he said, his voice ragged. "I'm telling you because I want you to stay alive."

Marcus stopped pacing. He stared out at the street where cars passed, people walked by, all of them unaware how close the world around them was to collapse.

"I'm not stopping. But I promise you, I'll be smart. I'll move careful. I'm not letting what they did to you stand."

"They're serious. This ain't some game of cops and robbers. Haynes is untouchable. He's got dirt on everyone—politicians, cops, maybe even judges. And Rook? He'd kill you just to make a point."

"You think I don't know that? I've seen what they're capable of. I've been to too many funerals already."

Jordan's breathing was shallow through the line. "I'm just scared, man."

"I know. Me too."

There was a pause before Marcus added, "But mom didn't raise us to be the kind of men who walks away. We took beatings for each other back in the day. I won't leave you in here to rot for something you didn't do."

The silence stretched again.

Then Jordan asked, "What if you can't fix it?"

Marcus looked at his grease-stained hands. "Then I'll go down trying. But I'm not letting fear write our story."

"You better not get yourself killed."

"I won't. Not before I get you out."

Just then, one of the younger mechanics poked his head out the shop door. "Yo, Marcus! You good? The old lady with the Camry is back, says it's still squeaking!"

Marcus nodded at him but didn't respond right away. He turned slightly, still holding the phone close.

"You need to let the infirmary look at you."

"They already did. Told me to take some aspirin and walk it off."

"Yeah. Of course they did."

"I gotta go soon. Time's almost up."

"Call me tomorrow. And if you hear anything else, you tell me. No matter what."

"You'll be careful?"

"I'll be smart. But I'm not backing down."

"Then I guess we both better be ready."

The call ended with a click, and the quiet that followed was deafening.

Marcus slid the phone into his pocket and leaned back against the wall. His ribs ached from tension, and he felt like he hadn't taken a full breath in hours. He looked down at his hands again. The hands of a man trying to rebuild something. And right now, he wasn't just fixing cars. He was fighting for his brother's life.

Jordan's voice echoed in his head—hoarse, tired, afraid.

They roughed me up, Marcus... they said it was a message for you.

The call had been short, but the weight of it settled like a boulder on his chest. Jordan wasn't just scared. He was pleading. And that was something he couldn't ignore. He took a slow breath, then pulled up a contact and hit call. Jeff picked up on the third ring.

"I knew you were going to call sooner or later," Jeff said, voice low and cautious.

"Yeah, well. I wouldn't be calling unless it was important."

A pause. "Go on."

Marcus turned and leaned against the side of the shop. "Jordan called me earlier. Said he got jumped in the hallway by some of Rook's guys. Called it a message. Told me to back off."

Jeff sighed on the other end. "Damn. I heard something went down, but they didn't put names on the report. Just called it a 'minor inmate altercation.'"

"They roughed him up. And no one stopped it. One of the guards just watched."

Another pause. This one heavier.

"You think someone inside tipped 'em off?"

"I think it's worse than that. I think someone inside let it happen."

Jeff didn't argue.

"That's why I'm calling," Marcus said. "I need someone on the inside to keep an eye on him. Not officially. Just someone you trust. Someone who won't look the other way if they try it again."

He was quiet for a long time before responding.

"You know this could blow back on me."

"I do. But if it were your family, wouldn't you make the call?"

A beat.

"I'll make some calls," he finally said. "There's a guy named Ortiz—quiet, young, works nights. He's solid. Not part of the boys' club. I'll see if I can get him on Jordan's tier, or at least close by."

"Thanks, Jeff. I owe you."

"No, you don't. You're just doing what I wish more people would."

There was a long pause before he added, "Look... if you're digging into what I think you are, just watch your back. This thing runs deep."

"I figured that out the hard way."

Jeff's voice dropped lower. "And if you get something real, don't bring it to the department. Not yet. Too many ears in too many rooms. Bring it to me directly."

"Got it."

"Stay sharp," he said. "And Marcus?"

"Yeah?"

"Get your brother out before they find a reason to bury him."

Chapter 36

Marcus's morning started with a bad feeling. Not the kind he could name. Just a pressure in his chest, like something was out of place and hadn't shown itself yet. He tried to shake it off by focusing on the job in front of him: a Pontiac that needed more than just a new belt.

His hands moved with practiced precision, socket wrench clicking in steady rhythm, the shop alive with the whirr of tools and the distant thump of a radio playing old soul tracks. But the feeling wouldn't let go. And then the call came.

"Marcus?" Sam's voice on the other end was low, almost urgent.

"Yeah?" he responded, setting down a wrench and grabbing a rag to wipe his hands. "What's up?"

There was a pause. "It's the delivery driver. He's gone."

"Gone? What do you mean 'gone'?"

"Dead. Some kind of accident. Car flipped over into a ditch late last night. They're calling it a blowout."

For a second, Marcus couldn't speak. His mind raced, images flashing faster than he could control; skid marks on asphalt, twisted metal, blood.

"No. No way that's an accident. He just talked to me the other day. This isn't a coincidence."

"Yeah, I thought the same thing," Sam said. "But there's nothing to prove it wasn't an accident. At least, not yet."

"We both know it wasn't an accident. They're tying up loose ends. This is how they work."

"I know, man. I know. That man was scared. That's why he kept his mouth shut for so long. And the moment he agrees to talk, boom—car crash on Crest Ridge Parkway. No witnesses, no skid marks, just a fireball."

"Exactly," Marcus said, slamming a socket wrench down on the workbench. "They made it look like an accident so nobody would ask questions. And now he's gone. Another person we needed, gone."

The metallic clang echoed through the shop. Marcus leaned against the bench, gripping the edge as if he needed to steady himself..

"He gave us his dash cam. Even if it was just a little bit. A time, a place, who was around that night. It's still something we can build from."

"It's not enough. And now the only guy willing to put his name on it is dead. They're sending a message."

"To you," Marcus said darkly. "And probably to anyone else, once they start talking."

"They're paranoid," Sam replied. "That means they're scared."

Marcus shook his head. "Or confident enough to clean up in broad daylight."

Sam didn't argue with that.

"I should've moved faster. I should've warned him to stay low."

"We all should've. But he didn't want protection. Said he wanted you to leave him alone."

"Didn't matter. He was a target the moment he gave me the dash camera "

Sam exhaled. "Listen, man... you need to turn on the news."

"What?"

"Turn it on. Channel 4. They're already spinning it."

Marcus grabbed the remote a turned the small TV on the shelf to Channel 4. Static flashed, then resolved into the familiar face of the local anchor seated stiffly in front of a still image of the crash scene.

Sam's voice came through again, clipped with disbelief. "They're calling it mechanical failure. No foul play suspected."

On-screen, the reporter echoed the same language.

"Authorities believe the crash was caused by a tire blowout. Investigators found no initial signs of foul play."

Sam's voice crackled back in. "You'd think nobody in this town's ever heard of brakes being cut."

Marcus didn't answer right away. He just watched the wreckage footage loop again on the screen; twisted metal, caution tape, first responders standing around like it was routine. Like it wasn't a hit job dressed up to look like bad luck.

The crash footage faded from the TV screen, replaced by the anchor's polished smile and a smooth transition to the next story, some fluff piece about a local fundraiser. Like nothing had happened. Like a man hadn't just died for trying to do the right thing. He stared at the screen a second longer before switching it off.

"And just like that," he said bitterly, "he's a footnote."

Sam didn't answer right away. The line stayed quiet except for the faint hum of static between them.

"Not to us," Sam said. "We remember."

"Yeah, well..." he exhaled sharply. "Memory won't hold up in court."

"You still got the flash drive?"

Marcus's gaze drifted to the lockbox under his workbench. "Safe and sound."

A pause.

"You thinking what I'm thinking?" Sam asked.

"That now more than ever, we can't let it go."

"Exactly," Sam said. "They're panicking. They don't know how much we have. That's our advantage—for now."

Marcus nodded, then glanced toward the shop's side door. He could still see the ghost of Kevin's anxious face in his mind. How he fidgeted during their last conversation and how he kept looking like he knew he was being watched.

"He didn't deserve that."

"No," Sam agreed. "But if you stop now, he dies for nothing."

That landed hard. Marcus looked down at his grease-stained hands. They trembled slightly. Not from fear, but from rage boiling just under the surface.

"I won't stop. But we need to be smarter. Move in the dark, stay ahead of them."

"And watch your back."

"Especially that."

Marcus rubbed at the tension building behind his eyes. "We need to talk in person. Not like this. I don't trust it ."

"I was just thinking the same," Sam replied. "Walker's Diner. One hour."

"You sure?"

"Yeah. No cameras. No foot traffic. We can sit in the back and talk without worrying about who's listening."

"Alright. I'll be there."

An hour later, Marcus sat in a corner booth at Walker's Diner, a worn-down spot with cracked vinyl seats, buzzing light fixtures, and a jukebox that hadn't worked in years. It was the kind of place no one paid attention to, which made it perfect. The waitress poured his coffee and shuffled away without small talk. He didn't touch the mug. Just kept his eyes on the door.

At exactly seven past, Sam walked in and went straight to the booth when he saw Marcus. He slid a folded newspaper across the table. The headline glaring up at him:

"*Local Driver Dies in Tragic Accident.*"

Marcus stared at it for a long time. Kevin's name was buried halfway through the article. No mention of his recent run-ins with the law, no context. Just a paragraph about "brake failure" and how "he lost control near the curve." A few sentences to summarize a life. A warning. A threat.

"They want you scared. But if you back down now, they win."

"Then I guess they'll just have to come harder."

He was frustrated as he read the brief article. It painted a picture of bad luck. A worn tire, a late-night delivery, and a curve on the highway that the driver didn't make. But he wasn't buying it. He could almost hear the gang's invisible hands rewriting the narrative.

"He was the only one who could corroborate anything," Marcus said, folding the paper and tossing it back onto the table. "Now he's gone."

"And we're not exactly swimming in witnesses. You think they're coming after anyone else?"

"I don't know. But if they're this bold, nobody's safe. Not me, not you, not Tyson."

"You think they know we talked to him?"

"I'd bet my shop on it. They've got eyes everywhere. Probably knew the second I left his place."

The waitress came by with their food, setting plates down with a practiced efficiency. Marcus barely glanced at his burger, his appetite long gone. Sam poked at his fries, his unease radiating across the table.

"You still sitting on that flash drive?"

"Yeah."

"You don't have to, Marcus. You choose to."

"You don't understand—"

"I understand fine. That flash drive shows the robbery. The real version. Before it got edited and passed around as 'evidence.' It clears your brother. And it proves somebody inside the department tampered with the footage."

"I know exactly what's on it."

"Then what the hell are you waiting for? Get it to the lawyer. Let him tear this whole thing apart before the gang takes out everyone involved."

"You think I haven't thought about that? But if I give it to Miller now, it disappears."

"You don't trust your own lawyer?"

"I trust that Miller's trying. But he's up against a machine. You've seen how this town works. You know what Haynes can do. If someone tips him off, that drive ends up 'lost in transit.' That footage never sees a courtroom."

"So what's your plan? Just sit on it until Jordan rots in jail?"

"No. My plan is to get something else. Something that ties the whole operation to Haynes. So when I drop that drive, there's no dodging it. No way to twist the story. He goes down, and he takes the rest of them with him."

"You really think you'll find something bigger than that video?"

"I think I already have. The warehouse Derrick told me about. Frank's old case files. The payments traced through shell businesses. And Rook running scared every time someone says Haynes's name? It's all pointing in one direction."

"You need to move fast then. One person is already dead. A so-called accident, just when you were closing in on him. That wasn't coincidence. That was a message."

"I know."

"They're tying up loose ends. And you're walking around with a lit fuse in your pocket."

"I'm not giving it up yet. Not until I have a clear line from the footage to Haynes. I need to prove he ordered the edit. That he knew what really happened and buried it."

"You're playing a dangerous game."

"I don't care."

Sam sighed, leaning back in the booth. "You should. Listen, this ain't just about you, man. They're not gonna stop at scaring you. They've already shown they're willing to kill to keep their secrets."

"I know. But if we back off now, that's it. Jordan stays in jail, and these guys keep running the show. Someone's gotta stop them."

"And that someone's gotta be you? Because last I checked, you weren't wearing a cape."

"Never said I was a hero. Just a brother who's not willing to let his family go down for something they didn't do."

"Just give it to the lawyer. Let him use it before someone else ends up like Kevin."

"I can't."

"What do you mean, you can't?"

"I mean, if I hand it over now, without context, without backup—what do you think's gonna happen? You think Miller's gonna be able to protect it? That it won't just... disappear?"

Sam looked like he wanted to argue, but he had to agree. He knew Marcus wasn't wrong. "You think someone in the legal team's dirty?"

"I don't know who's dirty anymore. That's the problem. We give them the flash drive and it might just 'get misplaced.' Evidence vanishes all the time around here. If I don't have something to tie it all together, proof that Haynes is the one pulling the strings, then it's just more noise they'll bury."

"You think you've got time to wait? They're already cleaning up, Marcus. Kevin's gone. Next time, it's you. Or your family."

"I get it, I do. But I need something more solid. The flash drive is leverage right now. Once I hand it over, I lose that."

"And what if they find out you have it? That leverage you're holding turns into a damn target on your back."

"They already know I'm looking. But yeah, if they knew I had it, they'd come for me. Which is why I've got it stashed somewhere safe. Not at the shop. Not at home. No one's getting their hands on it unless I want them to."

"You're gambling, man. I hope you know that."

"I do."

"You planning on letting Miller in at all?"

"When I've got enough to burn Haynes and his whole little empire to the ground. Not a moment before."

"Alright. But don't wait too long. People like Haynes don't just protect themselves. They erase the trail behind them."

"That's why I'm still moving. Because I don't plan on being erased.

Chapter 37

Sam hadn't been able to shake the feeling all day. Ever since Kevin's death, "accident" or not, something in his gut told him they were all running out of time. He'd seen too many wrecks, too many so-called freak accidents during his years with Ridge County Towing. And this one had the stink of a cover-up.

It was after ten when Sam finally clocked out and made his way to the back lot, where a row of battered cars waited for insurance assessments and quiet investigations. He wasn't headed to the tow truck tonight, though. He was here to meet a guy who knew the undercurrent of Crest Ridge better than most: Raymond "Ray" Deeks. Former courthouse janitor, part-time fixer, full-time eavesdropper.

Ray was already there, leaning against the hood of a burnt-orange Buick with a thermos in one hand and a cigarette in the other. His eyes glinted in the dim security light, a crooked smile pulling at his lips when he spotted Sam.

"You came," Ray said, as if he hadn't been waiting nearly forty-five minutes.

Sam waved off the greeting. "Let's skip the pleasantries. You said you had something about Haynes?"

"You always were the impatient type."

"And you always liked to talk too much. Start talking. I've got someone in danger, and every second counts."

Ray tossed the cigarette. "Alright. You remember Judge Kessler?"

"The old man? Yeah. Retired early last year. Word was health issues."

"Not health. Blackmail."

Sam blinked. "What?"

Ray popped open the thermos, poured steaming coffee into the cap, and offered it to Sam, who ignored it.

"I cleaned the judge's office for years, man. Used to see things. Hear things. Kessler and Haynes? They weren't just passing each other in the halls. Haynes used to show up late, after hours. Sometimes with files, sometimes just to 'talk.'" He used air quotes with a smirk. "Then one day, Kessler's decisions started changing. He was dropping charges and giving lenient sentences for certain names. Gang names. Names tied to Haynes."

"You got proof?"

Ray looked around and tapped his coat pocket. "I got a photocopy of one of the memos Haynes left on his desk. Don't ask how I got it. Just know it matches the kind of info that'd make someone roll over if it went public."

He pulled out a folded envelope, worn and creased, and handed it to Sam. Inside was a photocopy of a typed memo on department letterhead, with Haynes' signature scrawled at the bottom. The message was vague but suggested upcoming "cooperation" and referenced a list of names tied to gang activity that needed "alternative legal resolutions." One of the names on the list: Raymond Booker.

Sam swore under his breath. "This is huge."

Ray nodded, sipping from his thermos again. "I think the judge got cold feet. He started talking about going public and setting the record straight before he passed."

"But he didn't."

"Nope. Two weeks later, he retires and moves out of state. Disappeared. No public statement, no interviews. Just... gone."

Sam stared at the memo. "You think he threatened him?"

"I think he had someone else do it. Cleaner. Less obvious. Maybe even made the judge think he was protecting his family. You know how these people operate."

Sam folded the memo and tucked it into his jacket. "You got anything else?"

Ray reached into his coat and pulled out a flash drive.

"This ain't mine. Came from someone else who was cleaning up old courthouse backups. Security cameras. This clip? You'll want to see it on your own time. Shows Haynes going in and out of the judge's office when no one else was around. Not illegal, maybe. But sketchy? Hell yes."

Sam took the flash drive carefully. "You're doing the right thing."

"I'm doing what keeps me up at night if I don't. And before you ask, no, I don't want in. I don't want updates. I gave you what I had. If anyone asks, we never talked."

"Fine. But if you remember anything else, you know where to find me."

As Sam watched him walk away, the memo and flash drive burning like lead in his pockets. Haynes had influence over a judge. That changed everything. It proved the corruption wasn't isolated. It was systemic. Deep. Dangerous.

A couple of days later, Sam's desk was cluttered with stacks of papers and half-empty coffee cups. He rubbed his temples and leaned back in his chair. The deeper they dug, the more tangled the web became. It wasn't just street-level corruption anymore. Something bigger was festering underneath it all. Something institutional.

One of his contacts rang his phone. "You said to let you know when the background check came back on Judge Langston?"

He sat up straight. "Yeah. You got it?"

"Sending it to your email now. There's something weird in there. Figured you'd want to see it yourself."

"Thanks."

He opened the file and skimmed through the summary. On the surface, Judge Theodore Langston had a spotless record. He was decorated for his service on the bench and known for his no-nonsense sentencing and public speeches about restoring community trust in the justice system. But he wasn't interested in what was on the surface. He skipped to the financial section and stopped cold.

Multiple large deposits had been made into a private trust fund under his wife's name. Each was just under the federal reporting threshold, spaced out over two years. The source was buried in a maze of shell companies, but he recognized one of them immediately: Whitestone Development Group.

It was the same front Haynes had funneled kickbacks through when he was still actively "cleaning up" the streets, before he got promoted and started outsourcing the dirty work to gangs.

"Son of a..." Sam muttered. He reached into a drawer and pulled out a folder that he'd been building with Marcus. Cross-referencing the entries, the timelines lined up. Just weeks after Jordan's arrest, Langston had quietly approved the sealing of evidence motions that helped keep several key details out of public record. Motions filed by prosecutors with clear connections to Haynes.

Sam didn't need a conspiracy board to see the connection now. Haynes wasn't just using his badge to protect the gang. He had people in robes doing his bidding too. He grabbed his phone and called Marcus.

"Yo," he answered sounding tired.

"It's me," Sam said. "You alone?"

"Yeah, finishing up at the garage. What's going on?"

"You remember Judge Langston? The one who handled your brother's arraignment?"

"Yeah, why?"

"Turns out he's been getting paid off. I just found deposits tied to a trust in his wife's name. The money trace back to Haynes's old shell company. Not only that, he helped bury evidence on multiple cases that would've pointed the heat toward Haynes."

"So tell me. This judge Langston, what exactly did he do?"

"Two weeks after Jordan was arrested, he sealed the surveillance footage from the store. Said it was for 'public safety reasons.' That's the same footage that was edited and what you have on the flash drive now."

"He helped cover up the doctored footage."

"Exactly. And not just that. he also denied a request from the defense to subpoena gang communications. Those messages would've shown they had a man inside the department tipping them off."

"He isn't just biased. He's an active player. And the only reason he's getting away with it is because no one's put all the pieces together before."

There was silence on the other end of the line.

"You're serious?"

"Dead serious. This goes deeper than we thought, man. It's not just Haynes and the street-level players anymore. He's got judges in his pocket. That explains why every official complaint, every suspicious case tied to him gets dismissed or sealed. They're rigging the system from the inside."

"So what do we do now? We've got the footage. We've got this on the judge. Is it enough?"

"It's close. But we still don't have that smoking gun tying him directly to the gang's current operations. What we have would make noise, but it could get buried in bureaucratic BS. We need to link him to something active. Something recent."

"What about the drop on South Ridge last week? The one that got pulled before it went down. That wasn't random. Haynes knew."

Sam shook his head. "No proof he was the leak. And even if he was, we can't trace the intel directly to him."

Marcus leaned back, exhaling hard through his nose. "Then we need someone who can."

"We're running low on sources," Sam said. "And lower on time."

"What if we stop thinking of him like a corrupt cop?"

"Continue."

"What if we start treating him like a kingpin with a badge?"

Sam's eyes narrowed slightly, considering. "You're saying build the case like he's running a criminal enterprise."

"He is. Only difference is, he uses a precinct instead of a corner crew. We've been trying to find the moment he slipped. But what if this was always the play? What if every bust he ordered, every case he buried, every patrol route he shifted... was part of keeping his operation clean and protected?"

Sam sat back. "If that's true..."

"He isn't just biased. He's an active player. And the only reason he's getting away with it is because no one's put all the pieces together before."

"Well, now we do."

"Once we get this last piece, proof Haynes is still coordinating with the gang, we go to the lawyer. We drop everything," Marcus said. "Flash drive. Financials. The whole thing."

"You sure about that?"

"No. But if we wait any longer, we're going to lose more people. And if they're already killing witnesses..."

"Then we're on borrowed time."

"We need to make a move. Even if it's small. Something to rattle them. Let them know we're not just watching, we're working."

"You sure you're thinking straight?" Sam asked. "Because this isn't just about evidence anymore. It's about survival. We kick the wrong hornet's nest, they'll come for you next."

"They already are," Marcus said quietly. "Just not loud enough to stop me yet."

"Before i forget, I got some more information from my contact right before I met you."

"What kind of information?"

"Bank statements. Wire transfers. Names that shouldn't be there. Judge Kessler's among them and he's not alone."

Sam went on to explain the connections: payouts made from shell corporations, deposits into personal accounts belonging to Judge Kessler and at least two other names Marcus recognized, Judge Elaine Merrin and Judge Tyron Briggs, both of whom had presided over high-profile cases connected to gang activity in the last five years.

"What the hell..." Marcus breathed.

"I'm sending you a copy. Look at the dates. They line up with case dismissals. Every single one of those judges tossed out charges or handed out wrist-slap sentences to known associates. And you're gonna love this. One of those transfers? Came just two days before Jordan's sentencing."

"No. You're telling me Haynes paid off a judge to make sure my brother went away?"

"I'm saying he made sure no one looked too closely. Maybe your brother was supposed to be a distraction. Maybe someone needed him out of the way."

Marcus opened the email and stared at the figures. Every line, every deposit, told the same story: the justice system in Crest Ridge wasn't just failing. It had been bought.

"This... this could blow the lid off everything."

"It could," Sam agreed. "But it also puts a target on your back the size of a damn billboard."

"I'm already a target," he snapped. "So is Jordan. You could be next if they know you are helping me."

Sam didn't argue. He just leaned back and rubbed his face with both hands. "You need a plan. And fast. You can't just drop this off at the lawyer's office and hope it sticks. You were right before. This could disappear if the wrong person catches wind."

Marcus's mind was racing, piecing it together like a puzzle made of broken glass. The flash drive, the memo, the statements. They had enough to force someone's hand. But who could they trust?

"The moment I can connect Haynes directly to these payments, or to someone he controls making them, it's over."

"There's a name I saw in the bank records. 'Manning Holdings.' They've got ties to Rook's construction front, and guess who approved a city grant for them last year?"

"Haynes."

"Bingo. It's a money funnel. They move cash through 'legit' channels so it's harder to trace. But now that we know where to look…"

"We build the case. Slowly. Carefully."

"Quietly," Sam added. "Because now we know they've got judges. What's next? A DA? Another cop?"

Marcus looked down at the bank statements again. Every number felt like a nail in someone's coffin. "They think they own this city," he said quietly. "But not for long."

.

Chapter 38

Marcus stood in the lobby of Miller & Hayes LLP, his hand clenched around the flash drive in his coat pocket. The receptionist barely glanced at him before motioning toward the double doors. "He's expecting you, Mr. Carter."

He gave a nod and walked down the hall. Mr. Miller's office loomed at the end. It was wood-paneled and too quiet. He knocked once before pushing the door open.

"Mr. Carter," Miller greeted as he rose from behind his desk. "I didn't expect to hear from you so soon. Find something useful?"

Marcus closed the door behind him and didn't sit. "You could say that."

Miller gestured to the chair across from him. "Have a seat."

"I'll stand."

"Alright. What's on your mind?"

Marcus pulled the flash drive from his coat and set it on the edge of the desk. He didn't let go of it. "This has the unedited footage of the robbery. Shows the whole thing. The setup, the real robbers, the cops who came in late. All of it."

Miller's eyes sharpened, the fake pleasantries fading. "Are you sure it's legit?"

"I wouldn't be standing here if it wasn't."

"You want me to review it?"

"No. Not yet."

"Why bring it to me if you're not ready to hand it over?"

"Because I need to know something first. Can I trust you?"

"You came to me for legal help. I've done my job."

"Have you? Because the way things are going, I don't know if handing this over is going to help Jordan or get him killed faster."

"You think I'd put him in danger?"

"I think a lot of things lately. Like how judges are getting paid off to look the other way. Like how witnesses are turning up dead. Like how someone on the inside is feeding Haynes information."

"Those are serious accusations."

"I've got proof. Bank statements. Wire transfers. A memo from a certain police chief, signed and dated. It's not just street-level corruption, Mr. Miller. It goes all the way up."

For the first time, Miller looked genuinely rattled. He didn't speak for a long moment.

Marcus pressed. "If I give you this flash drive and it ends up 'missing'... if someone gets tipped off... my brother dies in that cell."

"I've never mishandled evidence."

"But you've worked with these people for years. Some of them are probably your friends. Golf buddies. You telling me none of them ever made you feel like looking the other way?"

Miller stood up now. "You're right to be cautious. But you came to me because I don't play ball with them. That hasn't changed."

"Then prove it."

"What are you asking?"

"Help me build the case. Quietly. On my terms. You don't get the full drive yet. Just enough pieces to start putting pressure on the right people. Enough to scare someone into making a mistake."

"That's dangerous."

"So is doing nothing."

"If what you're saying is true... it won't be enough to expose corruption. Not unless we bring down the judges, the cops, the shell companies, all of it."

"I know. And I'm not walking away. But you need to understand that this isn't about one crooked cop anymore. It's about a whole damn system."

"You really think you can take them down?"

"No. But I can blow a hole big enough for someone else to."

"Alright. We do it your way. But you don't disappear on me. I need updates. Documents. Chain of custody."

"You'll get what you need when I have it." Marcus finally released the flash drive and set it fully on the desk. "That's the copy. Enough to start rattling cages without giving away the whole deck."

"You planning to scare someone into talking?"

"No." he turned to leave. "I'm planning to show them they're not untouchable."

As he reached the door, Miller called after him. "Mr. Carter."

He paused.

"I believe you. About the corruption. Just... be careful. There's a reason no one's stood up to it in over a decade."

"Yeah. And there's a reason I'm not waiting another one."

Then he stepped into the hallway and shut the door behind him with a soft click. He took the stairs down two at a time as he mind filled up with everything he couldn't afford to forget. Haynes. The files. The wreck. The fear in Sam's voice when they watched the news. But more than anything Jordan.

Marcus didn't even realize where he was going until he turned onto the familiar street. His mother's porch light was on, even though it was still early afternoon. She always said the extra light made the house feel safer, even if it didn't actually do anything. He parked at the curb, sat in the car for a moment, then made his way to the door. She opened it before he could knock.

"Figured you might show up," she said softly. "You want to come in?"

He followed her inside. The smell of baked cornbread still lingered faintly in the air. She poured him a glass of sweet tea without asking and sat down across from him at the kitchen table. He didn't drink it right away. Just stared at the condensation sliding down the glass.

"You talked to your brother recently?" she asked gently.

Marcus hesitated. "Not since the other day."

Her lips pressed together. "Is he eating?"

"Some. Said they roughed him up."

She closed her eyes, breathing in deep. "Lord, help that boy."

"I'm doing everything I can, Ma."

"I know you are. But I also know what this city does to people who push too hard."

Marcus looked at her, seeing the worry behind her words. She wasn't scolding him, she was scared. And that scared him more than anything.

"I went to the lawyer again today. Gave him something useful. Not everything. Just enough to start turning the screws."

"You think this is the way?"

"I have to believe it is. I can't just sit back and do nothing while they bury Jordan."

She reached across the table and took his hand.

"Look at you being Mr. Stubborn as always. I know it's for a good reason, but think about your safety and from the looks, yourself."

"I just don't want you or Jordan or anyone else getting caught in the crossfire."

"I've lived too long to be scared of cowards in uniforms or corner boys with guns," she said with a small smile. "You let me worry about me. You focus on bringing the truth to light and your brother home."

"I promise."

Just then, the sound of feet pounding down the hall echoed off the hardwood floors.

"Marcus!" came a familiar voice, pitched with excitement but deeper than it used to be.

Ellis burst into the room, all long limbs and growing confidence. At fourteen, he was smack in the middle of that awkward phase: part boy, part man, taller than anyone expected, and testing out his new height like it was a superpower.

Marcus turned, grinning as Ellis skidded to a stop near the table. "Dang, look at you. What are they feeding you at that school?"

Ellis stood up straighter, grinning. "I'm taller than you now. So I'm the big younger brother."

Marcus laughed, getting up to stand beside him. "You might be taller, but I still got you in the shoulders. And the hands. And pretty much everything else."

"Not for long," Ellis said, puffing out his chest. "Coach said I might hit six-two before the year's out."

Their mom looked over her shoulder from the stove. "As long as you hit those grades too, Mr. Six-Two."

Ellis ducked his head and said, "Yes, Ma'am" before flashing Marcus a quick smile. "You staying for dinner?"

"Wouldn't miss it," Marcus said.

As Ellis bounded toward the pantry, Marcus leaned back in his chair, letting the moment settle around him. His mother's music, the smell of food, his little brother bragging about being the "big" younger brother, this was what he was fighting for. All he needed was his middle brother there and it would be like old times.

Rook leaned against the hood of his SUV. He lit a cigarette and took a drag. Behind him, two younger guys, both muscle, and both jumpy, stood waiting for instructions. They were stealing glances at their phones like they'd rather be anywhere else. He didn't care. He enjoyed keeping people on edge. It reminded them of who was in charge.

The side door creaked open.

"Yo, boss," said a voice. "We got a problem."

He turned as Vaughn stepped into the lot, eyes darting like a rat sensing fire. He held a burner phone in his hand that was still lit up with a call history screen.

"What kind of problem?" He asked, exhaling a plume of smoke.

"That mechanic. He's been digging. And earlier today, he went to that lawyer—uh, Miller. The one who's been handling his brother's case."

His expression didn't change. He just took another drag, let the silence hang until Vaughn started squirming.

"Did he hand anything over?"

"That's the weird part. He brought nothing in, and he didn't come out with anything. But he stayed in there a while. It was long enough for it to not feel like some routine check-in."

"So, nothing?"

"Nothing in his hands. But the way he came out... he looked like a man with a plan."

Rook flicked ash onto the pavement. "How sure are you about that?"

"Pretty sure. My contact in the office saw the whole thing. He walked in frustrated, stayed about twenty minutes, and then walked out calm. You know that look."

"Yeah. Like he knows something we don't."

"He's moving different. Like he's got some intel."

"If he didn't hand Miller anything, it means either he's bluffing... or whatever he's holding onto, he still has. Either way, it's bad for us."

"You want me to send someone to check Miller's place?"

"No. Not yet. Too early to rattle the cage. If he gave something up, the lawyer probably already duplicated it. Press him, and we'll be dealing with the whole damn city in our business."

Vaughn nodded, shifting nervously.

"Put eyes on him. Not just where he goes. Who he talks to. Tell me if he meets up with anyone. And keep tabs on Miller too, from a distance. Nothing that looks like heat."

"And if he makes a move?"

Rook looked him dead in the eye. "Then we move faster."

He turned and slid into the SUV without another word; the engine rumbling to life as he pulled off into the dark.

Once the cars were out of sight, Vaughn sent a text.

"Keep watching Marcus. Quiet-like. He's about to play his hand."

Chapter 39

The next evening, the sun had barely set when Tyson pulled into the alley behind the garage. He gave a quick nod at Marcus at sitting st his desk, holding up a brown paper bag. "Brought food. Figured if we're gonna dive into this mess, we might as well not do it hungry."

Marcus gave a faint smile and moved aside to clear some space. "Appreciate it. Long day?"

"Yeah," Tyson said, setting the bag down. "Worked a double. But I've been thinking about your text about something I need to see, so let's get to it."

Marcus sat in front of his laptop, the flash drive already inserted. "This is it," he said. "The unedited version of the robbery footage. No audio cut, no blurred faces. Raw as it was before someone tried to bury it."

They sat in silence for the first few moments, watching the grainy footage of the gas station robbery. The time stamp in the corner ticked on steadily. It all looked the same—until it didn't.

"There," Marcus pointed. "Pause it."

Tyson squinted at the screen. "That's the delivery car."

They played the footage again, this time slower. From the shadows behind the gas station, a figure emerged wearing a suit, and a badge clipped to his belt. A second figure followed behind that was clearly armed. The two stood just outside the security camera's direct line of sight, but the flash of a face was unmistakable.

"Haynes," he said under his breath.

"And Rook," Marcus confirmed. "They were already there before the robbery even happened."

Tyson sat back, hands on his knees. "So they staged it. Set the whole thing up."

"Yeah. And Jordan walked right into it. He never had a chance." Marcus clicked over to another file on the drive. "But it gets worse."

He pulled up a folder marked "Transfer Logs." Inside were dozens of documents—payment records, wire transfers, surveillance reports. The digital trail wasn't just about the robbery. It was about everything.

"Look at this," Marcus said, scrolling through a series of PDFs. "Funds moved from shell accounts tied to the department's 'community outreach budget' and straight into private accounts. Judges. Officers. Even a local real estate developer."

Tyson's eyes widened. "They've been laundering money for years."

"Not just laundering," he said. "Controlling people. That robbery wasn't just about making my brother a scapegoat. It was a warning. A message to anyone who tried to talk."

As Jordan walked out of the store, two figures appeared from the shadows outside. One of them instantly recognizable to Marcus. They entered the store, their faces partially obscured by hoodies.

"Pause it," Tyson said sharply. "That's them, isn't it? Rook's guys."

Marcus nodded grimly, rewinding a few seconds to get a clearer view. "Yeah. And look at this" He pointed to the timestamp. "They showed up ten minutes after Jordan left."

The video continued, showing the two men confronting the clerk, who visibly tensed. One of them placed something on the counter. Marcus squinted.

"A gun."

"They forced him to do it."

The clerk, as shown in the footage, nervously eyed the door. The two men spoke to him briefly before leaving. The robbery didn't happen until several minutes later, when a third man, this time masked, entered, pulled a gun, and demanded cash.

"They set it up. They planted the gun, scared the clerk, and waited for Jordan to leave so they could frame him."

"And they covered it up."

Marcus clicked through the remaining files on the drive, hoping to find more. One file caught his attention. It wasn't footage from inside the store but from a parking lot camera behind the building. The timestamp placed it hours before the robbery. Two cars pulled into view, parking side by side.

"That's him," he said, pointing to the figure stepping out of one car.

Tyson squinted. "And that's Rook," he added, recognizing the gang leader's broad frame and signature leather jacket.

The two men stood by the cars, talking in low voices. At one point, he handed him what looked like an envelope, while Rook slid a duffle bag into the trunk of the detective's car.

Marcus paused the video and stared at the screen. "That's it. That's the link we needed. This is the proof he is working with the gang."

"The same cop who's supposed to be investigating this is in bed with gangs. No wonder Jordan got framed so quickly."

Marcus ejected the USB and turned to him. "This is it. This is the proof we need to clear Jordan. But we can't take this straight to the police. We both know Haynes will bury it."

"So what do we do?"

Marcus stared at the drive in his hand. "We leak it. Get it out there before they can silence us. If the public sees this, they'll have no choice but to act."

"And you think that'll stop them?"

"It's not about stopping them. It's about making sure they can't ignore the truth."

"Alright, man. Just...be careful. We're already walking a fine line."

"When have I ever played it safe?"

As Marcus packed up his laptop and the USB, his phone buzzed on the table. It was a text from his mother: *"Marcus, call me when you can. I have a bad feeling about all this. Please be safe."*

Chapter 40

The next morning, Marcus began his search. He spent hours searching local news sites for a reporter willing to take a risk on a crime and corruption story. Because powerful interests could easily influence them, he distrusted the larger outlets. He needed someone independent, someone hungry for the truth.

Finally, he came across a name: **Elena Chavez**, an investigative journalist who'd written several exposés on corruption in small-town police departments. Her articles were sharp, uncompromising, and full of detail. He picked up his phone and dialed the number listed on her website. It rang three times before a woman's voice answered.

"This is Elena," she said briskly.

"My name's Marcus. I have information about corruption in Crest Ridge. Evidence that ties him to a gang and to a wrongful arrest."

There was a pause. "What kind of evidence?"

"Unedited security footage. Financial records. A witness statement."

Another pause, longer this time. Then: "And why are you calling me? Why not take this to the police?"

The one who buried it is the same one I'm calling out. His name is Deputy Chief Haynes, and he's been working with a gang leader named Rook."

Elena's voice was cautious, but intrigued. "That's a big claim. And a dangerous one."

"I'm not asking you to take my word for it. I have the proof. But I can't sit on it any longer. If I don't get it out there, more people are going to get hurt or worse."

"Alright. Meet me at the Cornerstone Cafe tonight, 7 p.m. We'll talk."

"Thank you."

He hung up and immediately texted Tyson,

"Meeting's on. Tonight. Gotta be careful."

By 6:40, Marcus was already there tucked into a booth near the back with a black coffee growing cold in front of him. The Cornerstone was quiet at this hour, with only a few customers scattered across the room. Students with laptops, an older couple playing checkers, a lone barista humming along to an old soul track.

Tyson walked in five minutes later, wearing a hoodie pulled low over his brow. He didn't speak as he passed Marcus's table, but gave a small nod and settled at a table across the room with a clear view of the door. He ordered a bottle of water he wouldn't drink and kept his eyes moving. They didn't know if Elena would come alone or who might be watching.

She walked in at precisely 7 p.m., a slim woman in her forties with sharp eyes and a no-nonsense demeanor. She scanned the room, spotted him, and walked over to his booth.

"You must be Marcus," she said, sliding into the seat across from him.

"That's me. Thanks for meeting me."

She placed a small recorder on the table and folded her hands. "Alright, let's hear it."

He took a deep breath and began. He told her everything—from Jordan's arrest to the delivery driver's death, the break-in at his apartment, and finally, the footage that tied it all together.

She listened intently, asking pointed questions.

"And you're certain it's Haynes in the footage with the gang leader?"

"Positive. I've seen him around town. Same build, same car. It's him."

"This is explosive. If this checks out, it's not just a local scandal. It's a state-level one. But you know what that means, right? Once this goes public, your life is going to change. These people will not take it lying down."

"My life has already changed the moment my brother got arrested for something he didn't do. I don't care what happens to me. I just want my brother out and I want these people held accountable."

"Alright. Let me see the footage."

Marcus pulled out his laptop, inserted the USB, and opened the files. He played the footage for her, explaining each critical moment—the gang members planting the gun, Haynes's meeting with Rook, and the edited version that had been used to frame Jordan.

Elena's eyes stayed locked on the laptop screen, her brow furrowed as the last clip ended. The footage gradually chipped away at her neutral expression, leaving behind only a hard line of concern and resolve. She leaned back, crossing her arms tightly across her chest.

"This is damning," she hissed. "But it's also dangerous. You're going to need more than just me to make this stick."

Marcus didn't flinch, but he could feel the weight of the moment pressing into his chest.

"I can write the article," she continued, "release the footage. But that won't be enough. We'll need public pressure to force the department's hand."

He nodded slowly. "What do you suggest?"

She tapped her fingers against the table, thinking. "Find more witnesses. People who can corroborate what's in those videos. If we can't find them, we need to focus on the public. Social media. Protests. Noise. Anything to shine a light on this."

She looked up at him, eyes sharp. "If they think they can make this go away quietly, they'll try. We can't give them that option."

"Then we make it loud."

She was already pulling out a notepad from her bag. "I'll start drafting the article tonight. I'll need quotes, timelines, names. Anything you can give me that's solid."

"I'll get it to you by morning. And I'll try talking to a few more people, see who's willing to speak up."

"Good," she said. "We're not just exposing corruption here. We're exposing a system that let it thrive. That's going to rattle cages."

"Let them rattle."

Tyson walked up as the meeting wrapped, eyes still scanning the café like a sentry. "We good?"

Marcus nodded. "We're good."

He and Elena exchanged one last glance, a silent agreement forged between a reporter and a man with nothing left to lose. As Marcus left the café, he felt a strange mix of relief and apprehension. The wheels were in motion now, but the road ahead was uncertain, and dangerous.

Tyson fell into step beside him. "So? What did she say?"

"She's in. But she thinks we'll need more witnesses, or public support, to really make this stick."

"Well, that's something. You think we can trust her?"

"I don't know. But she's our best shot."

They reached his car, and as he unlocked the door, he noticed a piece of paper taped to the windshield with a single word scrawled across it in red ink:

"Enough."

He stared at it for a long moment, his mind racing. The message was clear, and so was his determination.

"They're scared," Tyson said quietly.

"Good," Marcus replied, crumpling the paper in his fist. "Because they should be."

Chapter 41

Marcus had another bad feeling that morning. He'd called and texted Tyson numerous times and had gotten no response. No read receipts. Just silence. He stared at his screen a moment longer before finally tapping the name he'd been avoiding.

The phone rang once. Twice. Then—

"What?"

Her voice was sharp, clipped, and immediately defensive.

"Myia, hey," he said, trying to keep his tone even. "Have you heard from Ty today?"

Silence crackled on the other end for half a second too long.

"No. Why?" she asked, guarded.

"I've been trying to reach him. Nothing. He was supposed to come by the shop. I figured maybe he saw or texted you."

"No," she snapped. "He didn't text me. He didn't stop by. And if you're just now realizing something's wrong, that says a lot."

"Look, I know you're upset—"

"Upset? I told you this would happen. I told you something like this was going to happen if you kept dragging him into this mess! But you didn't listen. You never do."

"Myia—"

"No! Don't 'Myia' me! He's my little brother! And now you're calling me like it's some surprise he's missing? Like you didn't know exactly how dangerous this was getting?"

"I didn't ask him to disappear. I told him to lie low. We've been careful—"

"Clearly not careful enough," she cut in. "I swear if something's happened to my brother ..."

"I'll find him," he said. The words came out like a vow. "I swear to you, I'll find him."

"You better," she hissed. "Because if you don't, if this turns into another funeral or headline, I don't care what noble thing you think you're doing. I'll never forgive you."

The line went dead. As he stared into the street, he slowly lowered his phone. He had to find Tyson. He drove off in his truck. His phone rang soon after he started, and he felt relieved when he saw "Ty" on the screen.

"Ty, you good? I've been trying to reach you all day."

But the voice on the other end wasn't Tyson's. It was unfamiliar. "He's with us, Carter. We warned you to stay out of it. But instead you go talk to a journalist. Guess you didn't listen."

"Who the hell is this? Where's Tyson?"

A faint sound of a struggle came through the line, followed by Tyson's voice. "Marcus! Don't—"

The line went dead.

Marcus pulled his truck over and stared at his phone. Panic rose in his chest, but he forced himself to think. He grabbed the phone and dialed Tyson's number again. It went straight to voicemail. He immediately put the truck in drive and got back on the road. As he drove, he called Elena.

"They've got my cousin."

"Who?"

"The gang. They just called me using his phone. They know I went to you. They're trying to shut me up."

"This is serious. You need to let me call the police..."

"No! They're part of the problem. Haynes would just tip them off. I'll handle it myself."

"Marcus..."

"I'll call you when I know more."

His first stop was Rook's territory. He parked a block away from the warehouse where he'd knew Rook would be. Steeling himself, he stepped out of the car and checked his surroundings before heading toward the building. As he approached, a young man loitering near the entrance spotted him. "Hey! You lost or something?"

Marcus squared his shoulders. "I need to talk to your boss."

The man laughed. "He doesn't take walk-ins."

"I'm not asking."

The man's smile faded. "You got a death wish, mechanic?"

"Tell him Marcus is here. He'll want to hear what I have to say."

The man sized him up, then disappeared inside. Minutes later, the door creaked open, and someone ushered him into a room. At a table, Rook casually cleaned his nails with a knife. He looked up with a sly grin on his face.

"Well, well, well. If it isn't the guy who's been a thorn in my side. We finally meet," he drawled.

"You've got my cousin," Marcus said, cutting to the chase.

Rook leaned back, feigning innocence. "Cousin? Can't say I know what you're talking about."

"Cut the crap. I know you took him. Where is he?"

"You've got guts, I'll give you that. But you've been sticking your nose where it doesn't belong, and now you're surprised there are consequences?"

"If you've hurt him—"

"Relax," he said, holding up a hand. "Your cousin's fine. For now. Whether he stays that way depends on you."

Rook gestured toward a seat for Marcus, but Marcus declined .

"You want him back? Here's the deal: drop the investigation. No more reporters, no more snooping around. You keep quiet, and your cousin walks away. Simple."

He couldn't back down now. Not with everything he'd uncovered. But Tyson's life was on the line.

"And if I don't?"

"If you don't," he said smoothly, "then your cousin doesn't walk anywhere. Might end up in a ditch like that delivery driver. Accidents happen all the time."

He leaned forward, voice dropping to something quieter, and far more menacing.

"And I know where your mama lives, too. That little house off Maple, right? She still drives to work early in the morning?"

Marcus didn't answer, but the flare in his eyes was answer enough.

"Would be a damn shame if something happened to her car."

He let the words hang in the air like poison, watching Marcus with that same cold calm. "This ain't just about your cousin anymore, mechanic. Keep pushing, and more people will get hurt."

The room fell silent as the weight of the threat hung in the air. Marcus forced himself to stay calm.

"I'll need proof he's alive," he said finally.

Rook smirked. "Fair enough."

He gave a subtle nod to one of the men standing by the wall. The guy disappeared through a door, and a few tense moments later, returned holding a phone. He handed it to him, who pressed a button and held it up on speaker.

Tyson's voice crackled through the line, strained and anxious. "Marcus, don't—"

The call ended abruptly. A sharp click, then silence.

Rook casually set the phone down on the table like they'd just finished a business call.

"Happy?" he asked, raising an eyebrow.

Marcus stared at the phone. It was enough to know his cousin was alive, for now, but not nearly enough to ease the weight pressing on his chest.

"I'll be in touch," Rook added. "Don't make me regret giving you that little favor."

Marcus left the warehouse. Every step away from that place felt heavier, like he was dragging a chain of consequences behind him. He knew Rook wouldn't keep Tyson alive indefinitely, not unless he gave them what they wanted. And even then, there were no guarantees. He jumped into his car, hands trembling as he slammed the door shut. He didn't bother starting the engine. He just pulled out his phone and called Sam. The line rang once before he picked up.

"They've got Ty," he said, his voice strained.

"What? When?"

"I don't know exactly. He hasn't answered my calls or texts all day. I went to the warehouse. Rook was there. He made it clear. Drop the investigation, or Tyson doesn't make it out."

"Jesus," Sam muttered. "Did they show proof?"

"Yeah. They had him speak briefly. He's alive for now."

Sam was quiet for a beat. "What do you need me to do?"

Marcus stared out through the windshield. "I don't know yet. But I can't back down. If I do, this keeps happening. To other people. To families. They threatened my mom, Sam. Said she might have an 'accident' on the way to work."

"They're making this personal now."

"It's always been personal," Marcus said grimly. "But now it's war."

"I'm with you. Whatever you need."

Marcus finally turned the key in the ignition. "Then help me find where they're keeping Tyson."

Chapter 42

After he left, Rook and his lieutenants discussed the next move. They moved Tyson to a dingy basement in an abandoned motel. A rotating crew of gang members kept watch, armed and ready. Rook sat at the head of the table. His usual smug demeanor was replaced with grim determination.

"Mechanic man is getting too close," he slammed his fist on the table. "He's got evidence, connections, and now the media sniffing around. If we don't shut him down, we're all going to burn."

"Why not just take him out?" Vaughn suggested nonchalantly.

Rook shot him a sharp glare. "If we take him out, it draws attention. The cops might be dirty, but a mechanic getting taken out after raising hell? That's too messy. We need to be smarter."

He lit a cigarette. "We send a message, loud and clear. Something that'll make him drop everything and run."

One of Rook's younger recruits, Jamal, spoke up hesitantly. "What about his shop? It's his pride and joy. If we torch it…"

He tapped the ash off his cigarette, a thin trail of smoke curling upward as he mulled it over. The room was dim, thick with the scent of sweat, smoke, and tension. A fan clacked in the corner, barely cutting through the stifling heat.

"Yeah," Rook said slowly, his smirk deepening. "His shop's more than just a job. It's his legacy. His business. If we hit that, it cuts deep. Sends a message without drawing too much heat."

Vaughn cracked his knuckles. "You want it blown up? Burned down?"

"Nothing flashy. No bodies. Just enough fire to make the news and destroy what matters most. A warning. We rattle his world, show him we can touch anything he loves, anytime."

Jamal shifted uneasily. "You sure he won't come back harder after that?"

Rook's eyes locked onto him, cold and calculating. "He might. But the goal isn't to destroy him. It's to break him. Fear does that better than bullets. He's got a cousin in our hands, a mom we know how to find, and his brother we can get to at anytime . Burn the shop, and he'll know the clock's ticking. He either folds or he loses everything."

The room fell silent. Then he nodded.

"Make it happen. Tonight."

Marcus spent the day driving around Crest Ridge, trying to piece together clues about Tyson's whereabouts. Exhausted and frustrated, he returned to the shop to find a small crowd gathered outside. Smoke billowed from the garage, flames licking at the edges of the building. His heart sank as he sprinted forward, shouting for the crowd to move back.

Firelight danced in the reflection of his eyes as he ran. The acrid stench of burning oil and charred rubber hit him like a punch to the gut. His lungs tightened. The heat was intense, radiating from the heart of the garage like a furnace gone mad. Someone tried to grab his arm to stop him from getting closer, but he shoved them off blindly.

"Call 911!" he yelled, though he could already hear the wail of sirens in the distance.

The flames had already devoured the front office and were now clawing their way into the bays, consuming the place that had been his sanctuary. His father's tool chest, characterized by faded stickers and a damaged drawer, was engulfed by the orange and black. The lift he'd rebuilt, the sign his mother painted when they first opened, the old posters on the walls, everything that told the story of his life, turned to ash in front of him.

Someone called his name, but it barely registered. He stood frozen, sweat pouring down his face, mouth dry. His fists clenched at his sides as the fire department arrived, hoses hissing and shouting orders. Firefighters pushed back the crowd, but him remained near the curb staring into the inferno.

Sam came jogging up minutes later, breathless and wide-eyed. "Marcus, what the hell?"

"They torched it," he said hoarsely. "They set it on fire."

He looked from Marcus to the flames. "Jesus. This was no warning. This is war."

Marcus didn't answer. His eyes stayed locked on the burning wreckage. Memories flickered with the flames: working late with his dad, Tyson cracking jokes while handing him wrenches, Ellis pretending to fix things beside him. Now it was all gone.

A firefighter stepped over. "We've got it contained, but the structure's pretty much a loss. I'm sorry."

He only nodded, barely hearing him.

Sam put a hand on his shoulder. "This was a message. You know that, right?"

Marcus exhaled, chest tight with rage and grief. "Yeah. I got it loud and clear." He turned his head. "But they just made the biggest mistake of their lives."

Behind him, the fire crackled, stubborn in its destruction. He stared in disbelief as the flames consumed the shop he'd worked so hard to build. The memories, the sweat, the years of effort, it was all turning to ash. He didn't move, didn't blink. The heat pressed against his face like a cruel hand, and the scent of burning metal mixed with oil and wood filled his nose. Everything inside him felt hollow. That garage wasn't just a building. It was his escape, his legacy, his purpose when everything else had fallen apart.

Sam stood beside him in silence. "I don't think they're leaving room for interpretation."

He didn't respond. A fireman passed by, shouting instructions to another. Hoses whipped across the pavement, spraying jets of water that hissed when they met the blaze. The growing crowd murmured, faces lit by the red and orange light. Some recording on their phones and others just staring like it was a show.

Marcus's fists clenched at his sides. "They're trying to break me."

Sam glanced sideways at him. "They think if they hit you hard enough, you'll fold. Make it personal enough, you'll back off."

"They're wrong. They're dead wrong."

Sam looked at him with cautious respect. "What now?"

"I find Ty. I get this story out. I burn every last one of them down before they get the chance to hurt anyone else."

The words came out through gritted teeth, but his chest still ached, the fire reflecting every piece of pain. He thought of his family and how close the gang had come already. They were circling like vultures, and this was more than just intimidation. This was war. He stepped back as another section of the roof collapsed with a crash, sparks flying skyward. A firefighter shouted, and the hoses redirected to keep the blaze from spreading.

Marcus ran a hand over his face, wiping sweat and ash from his brow. "This was supposed to be the backup plan. If everything else failed... this shop was the one thing I could always come back to."

Sam rested a hand on his shoulder. "We'll rebuild. But first, we survive this."

He nodded once, eyes still locked on the burning wreckage. Through the chaos, his phone buzzed in his pocket. He pulled it out, his stomach tightening when he saw the unknown number.

He answered. "What?"

Rook's voice was calm, almost mocking. "Hell of a sight, isn't it? Shame about your shop. Bet it had sentimental value."

"You son of a—"

"Careful," Rook interrupted. "You don't want me to lose my patience. This is just the beginning. You back off, and this all stops. Keep pushing, and next time, it won't be your shop."

"You think you can scare me?"

"I don't think, Mechanic. I know." There was a pause, then he added, "You've got till tomorrow to decide. Walk away, or watch what happens to what's left of your family."

The line went dead.

Meanwhile, back at the motel, the gang's next move was already underway. Tyson, bruised but defiant, sat in the corner of the basement, his wrists bound.

Vaughn stood over him, a cruel grin on his face. "You're lucky, kid. My boss got plans for you, or else we'd be having a lot more fun right now."

Tyson glared up at him, blood trickling from a cut above his eye. His wrists ached from the zip ties binding them behind the chair, but he kept his back straight and his chin lifted. "You think you scare me? My cousin's coming for me. And when he does, you'll regret this."

"Your cousin's a dead man walking. He just doesn't know it yet," Vaughn sneered. He crouched so low that they were eye to eye. "He should've stayed in his lane. Instead, he kicked the hornet's nest. Now everybody around him gonna get stung."

The door creaked open and Jamal stepped in. He looked uneasy, glancing from Vaughn to Tyson and then back again. "Boss wants us to call him again. Let him hear his cousin's voice and remind him what's at stake."

Vaughn stood and cracked his knuckles. "Right. Let's keep the pressure on."

Tyson smirked despite his pain, blood staining the corner of his mouth. "You really think a phone call's gonna stop him? You don't know my cousin."

Vaughn's face twitched, and then his hand moved fast, too fast to dodge. The slap cracked across Tyson's cheek and his head snapped sideways.

"We'll see how brave you are when he's six feet under," he said with a simmering fury. "Let's make the call."

Jamal looked at Tyson, then fished the burner phone from his pocket and dialed. Vaughn stepped back as he waited. Tyson slowly turned his head, breathing through the pain, his eye already swelling. But his spirit hadn't cracked. Not yet. Because he knew his cousin was out there and he didn't give up.

Chapter 43

Marcus sat alone at his kitchen table with the evidence spread out before him like the pieces of a puzzle. His laptop screen displayed the unedited footage showing gang members entering the convenience store minutes after Jordan left, as well as photos of Rook and Haynes meeting behind an abandoned warehouse. This was everything he had worked for. This was proof of Jordan's innocence and the gang's ties to law enforcement. But now, it wasn't just about clearing Jordan's name. Tyson's life hung in the balance.

Trading the evidence meant losing his leverage, possibly forever. But what choice did he have. The soft knock on the front door startled him. Marcus quickly closed his laptop and shoved the evidence into a folder before answering. He approached the door cautiously, peeking through the peephole. Standing on the other side was Sam. He opened the door and let him in without a word.

"I came as fast as I could," he said, brushing past him. "You okay?"

"No," Marcus said , closing the door behind him. "They've got Tyson. They torched the shop. I'm out of time."

Sam's eyes swept over the cluttered table. "So this is it? The whole case?"

Marcus nodded. "Everything we've collected. The robbery, the cops, the payoffs. It's all here. Enough to start a storm if I get it to the right people."

"And if you hand it over now," he said slowly, "Rook let him go?"

He sat down heavily, elbows on the table, head in his hands. "That's the deal. But once I give this up, I've got nothing left. No way to prove they're still out there pulling strings. No way to stop them from doing it again."

Sam leaned against the counter, arms folded. "You give it to them, you might save Tyson. But you're right. They'll disappear and bury every trace of this. And the next guy, the next family caught in the middle... they won't have a shot."

Marcus lifted his head, eyes bloodshot and tired. "But if I don't give it up—"

"They kill him," he finished quietly. "Or worse."

The words hung in the air like smoke, thick and impossible to ignore. Marcus sat frozen at the kitchen table. His fingers tapped restlessly against the wood.

"You know how this works. Rook doesn't return hostages out of the goodness of his heart. If you give him what he wants, he'll tie up loose ends the moment you're no longer useful."

"I know."

"Then why are you even considering it?"

Marcus looked up slowly, meeting Sam's eyes. "Because that's my family."

Sam's expression softened slightly. "And so are you, man. That's why I'm here. But you need to be smart. Giving him the flash drive just like that might save Tyson for a minute. But what happens after? What if they take both of you out? What if they find your mom?"

"You think I haven't thought about that every second since they took Ty?"

"I know you have." Sam's voice lowered. "But thinking and planning aren't the same thing."

Marcus stood abruptly and began to pace. His eyes bounced around the room as if trying to pin down an invisible thread of logic.

"I've got the video, Sam. The original footage from the robbery. Jordan leaving the store clear as day. Then Haynes' guys showing up minutes later. Rook's crew following close behind. I've got the warehouse photos. The payments to the judge. All of it. This could take down half the department."

"Then we release it. Now. While we still have the upper hand."

"And if we do and Tyson dies tomorrow because of it? You gonna tell Myia you backed that play?"

Silence.

Marcus exhaled through his nose, turning back toward the table. "I can't live with that. Not again."

Sam rose from his seat, crossing the room slowly. "So what's the plan? You stall them? Set up a fake handoff?"

"I give them just enough to make them think I'm playing ball. Something to buy time. Keep Tyson alive while we line everything else up. Backup copies, reporters on standby, trusted eyes on every move."

"You'll need someone watching your back."

"I was hoping you'd say that."

"You know I'm in. But even with both of us, this is dangerous. You're betting that Rook won't smell the setup."

"That's why we make it look real. A drop that's convincing. And while they're distracted, we work on getting Tyson out. Quietly."

Sam studied him for a moment. "These people don't play by the rules. You can't just hand over everything and hope they keep their word."

"I'm not hoping," he said firmly. "I'm planning."

Marcus spread a map of Crest Ridge across the table, pointing to an industrial park on the outskirts of town. "They want me to meet them here," he said. "Neutral ground, they called it. It's isolated enough that no one will hear anything if it goes south."

"And you're just gonna walk in there alone?"

"No," Marcus said, shaking his head. "I'm bringing backup."

"Who?"

"A pal name Rick. He's setting up a remote feed for the evidence. If anything happens to me, he'll send it straight to the media and every law enforcement agency in the state."

"That's smart. But what if they force you to prove you deleted it?"

"Then I'll bluff. They don't know how many copies I've made or where they're stored."

Sam wasn't convinced. "And if they call your bluff?"

"Then I'll do whatever it takes to protect Tyson.

As they finalized the plan, Marcus's phone buzzed on the table. The caller ID showed a blocked number. He picked up, his voice tense. "Yeah?"

Rook's voice came through the line. "Hope you're ready, mechanic. Clock's ticking."

"I've got what you want," he said. "You'll get it when I see my cousin safe and unharmed."

He chuckled darkly. "You're not in a position to make demands."

"Neither are you," Marcus shot back. "You want this evidence gone? You'll play by my rules. Tyson comes first."

There was a long pause on the other end before he finally said, "Fine. Tomorrow night. Eight o'clock. Don't be late."

The line went dead, leaving Marcus gripping the phone tightly. He stood in the silence that followed, the weight of Rook's words sinking deep into his chest. Tomorrow night. Eight o'clock. That was the deadline. The moment everything would come to a head.

He lowered the phone and exhaled slowly, forcing himself to stay calm. He couldn't afford panic. Not now. Tyson was still out there scared, hurt, maybe worse, and if Marcus screwed this up, he wouldn't get another chance. He turned and looked at the folder containing all the evidence that could bring down half of Crest Ridge's power players. It was enough to get people killed. It *had* gotten people killed.

He tucked the phone in his pocket, locked the evidence away, and moved with quiet determination toward his bedroom. He had a deal to prepare for and a cousin's life to save.

Marcus barely slept that night. Every time he closed his eyes, he saw Tyson tied up, hurt, or worse. He tried to focus on the plan, running through every possible scenario, but doubt crept in. *What if he failed? What if Tyson didn't make it out alive?* Just after midnight, he grabbed his phone and called his mother. Her voice was groggy but immediately concerned.

"Marcus? What's wrong?" she asked, already more awake than she sounded seconds ago.

He hesitated, swallowing the lump in his throat. "I didn't mean to wake you... I just... I needed to hear your voice."

There was a pause, then her tone softened. "You okay?"

Marcus sat on the edge of his bed. "No. Not really."

"Is it Jordan?" she asked gently.

"Ty," he said quietly. "They've got him, Ma. Some bad people. And they want me to trade what I've got to get him back."

A sharp inhale on the other end of the line. "Why didn't you call sooner?"

"I didn't want to scare you," he said. "But I needed to hear your voice tonight. I don't know how this is going to play out."

His mother was quiet for a moment, then he heard her moving around. Probably getting out of bed. "Listen to me," she said, her tone shifting into that steady, firm cadence he'd heard his whole life. "You are not alone in this. I raised you to fight smart, not scared. You're doing what you have to do for your family. But don't you go running into something blind, you hear me?"

"I'm not," Marcus said, though his voice lacked conviction. "I've got people. Sam, a reporter. We've got a plan, but it's risky."

She sighed, then asked quietly, "Do they know where I live?"

There was a long silence before he answered. "Yeah. They made sure I knew they did."

"I see." Her voice dropped lower. "Then you do what you have to do. But promise me something."

"Anything."

"Don't lose yourself in this. I've already got one son behind bars. I'm not burying another."

Marcus's throat tightened. "I promise."

"Good," she said. "Now go get some rest, baby. You'll need it. And Marcus?"

"Yeah?"

"You make sure Tyson comes home."

"I will." His voice cracked, but he meant it with everything he had. "I swear."

They ended the call, and he sat for a moment longer in the silence of his room. The darkness around him felt heavier than ever, but his mother's voice, steady and sure, gave him something solid to hold onto. He laid down, eyes open, heart steadying. Tomorrow, it all came down to this.

Chapter 44

The next evening, Marcus arrived at the industrial park early. The area was dark, lit only by a few flickering streetlights. He parked his truck a block away and walked the rest of the distance with a Manila envelope tucked under his arm. He could see Rook and his men waiting near a loading dock.

Marcus approached slowly. As he got closer, he saw Tyson sitting on the ground with his hands bound and a gag in his mouth. Two gang members stood on either side of him, guns in hand. He stopped just short of the loading dock and lifted his hands to show he wasn't carrying a weapon.

Rook stepped forward from the shadows with his trademark smirk. A cigarette dangled from his fingers, its ember flaring as he took a slow drag.

"Right on time," he said coolly. "You mechanics always so punctual?"

He didn't respond. His eyes stayed locked on Tyson, whose face was bruised but alive. The relief nearly buckled his knees, but he held firm.

"I came alone," Marcus said. "I held up my end. Let him go."

Rook laughed as he exhaled a puff of smoke. "That's not how this works, my friend. First, I see the goods. Then, you get your cousin back. Fair trade, isn't it?"

Marcus opened the envelope and pulled out the flash drive. He held it up, letting the light catch its metallic sheen.

"This is it," he said. "Everything you're so desperate to bury."

Rook nodded to one of his men, a stocky guy with tattoos creeping up his neck. The man stepped forward and reached for it.

But Marcus pulled his hand back, his tone sharp. "Not until my cousin's free."

The smirk faded from Rook's face as he made a motion with his hands. One of the men by Tyson began untying the ropes. He groaned; his movements sluggish as he tried to stand.

Marcus watched every motion, his eyes darting between Tyson and the gang members like a hawk. The moment Tyson was fully untied, he called out, "Let him walk. No one touches him."

One of the guards gave him a shove, but Tyson steadied himself and began limping toward Marcus.

"Come on, man," he urged under his breath, clenching the flash drive tighter.

Tyson came near and Marcus caught his arm, steadying him. He didn't let go. Partly to support his cousin, and partly because he wasn't ready to hand over the drive just yet.

"Now," Marcus said, raising the flash drive again, "he's free. You get this."

As the tattooed man reached for it, Marcus let it fall into his palm. But as the man turned back toward Rook, he sprang into action. He grabbed Tyson by the arm and shoved him toward the cover of a nearby container.

"Run!" He shouted.

The shout made the guy drop the USB. He bent down to pick it up as the others reacted instantly. One of them pulled a gun, but Marcus was already moving. He grabbed the flash drive and ran behind another container as a shot rang out, ricocheting off the metal.

"Get them!" Rook bellowed.

Marcus and Tyson weaved through the maze of containers, their breaths coming in ragged gasps as boots pounded the pavement behind them. The echo of shouts and gunfire turned the industrial park into a warzone of shadows and steel.

Tyson stumbled, still weak from captivity, and Marcus caught him before he hit the ground.

"Come on, Ty," he urged, dragging him back up. "Just a little farther!"

They ducked between two rusted dumpsters as another shot rang out, thudding into the side of a shipping container just inches from Marcus's head.

"We're not gonna make it to the truck," Tyson gasped. "They're too close!"

"Yes, you can," he snapped. "Keep moving!"

They reached a stack of pallets, crouching behind them to catch their breath. Marcus peeked around the edge, spotting two of Rook's men fanning out in search of them.

Tyson leaned against the pallets, his face slick with sweat. "You had a plan, right? Please tell me you had a plan."

Marcus gave a grim smile. "Always."

From his jacket pocket, he pulled out a remote trigger.

"What's that?" Tyson asked, his voice laced with both curiosity and fear.

"Insurance," Marcus replied. "I rigged one of those containers with a flashbang. When they get close, we're gonna give them a little surprise."

Tyson's eyes widened. "You're insane."

Marcus grinned. "Probably."

Footsteps grew louder as one of the gang members rounded the corner with his gun raised. Marcus waited, his finger hovering over the button. The man moved closer, his weapon scanning the shadows. Just as he stepped in front of the rigged container, he pressed the trigger. A deafening explosion of light and sound filled the air, sending the man sprawling to the ground. He grabbed Tyson's arm and pulled him toward the edge of the industrial park.

"Move!" he shouted.

The other gang members were disoriented by the flashbang. They cursed as they scrambled to regroup. Rook's voice cut through the chaos. "Find them! Now!"

They reached Marcus's truck , which was hidden behind a cluster of trees. He yanked open the passenger door, practically shoving Tyson inside before running to the driver's side. As he started the engine, the gang's SUV came into view, its headlights slicing through the darkness.

"They're coming!" Tyson yelled.

"I see them!" He floored the gas pedal and the truck's tires kicked up gravel as they sped away.

The SUV roared after them. Marcus swerved onto a narrow road and the truck bouncing as they hit a series of potholes.

"They're gaining on us!" Tyson shouted.

Marcus focused on the road ahead. "Not for long."

The SUV drew closer, its bumper nearly grazing the truck. One of the gang members leaned out of the window, a gun in hand.

"Hold on!" He yelled and turned the wheel sharply.

The truck veered off the road and went through a thicket of bushes and onto a dirt path. Branches slapped against the windshield as Marcus fought to keep control of the truck. The SUV barreled after them, headlights bouncing wildly over the uneven terrain.

"They're still with us!" Tyson shouted, twisting around in his seat to look.

"Not for long," Marcus said. He spotted a sharp drop-off, a dried-out drainage ditch, that ran along the woods. Without hesitating, he yanked the wheel left. The truck lurched and skidded toward the ditch.

"Marcus!" Tyson braced himself.

The truck slammed into the ditch and bounced violently, but Marcus kept his foot on the gas. The suspension groaned in protest, but they surged forward. Behind them, the SUV wasn't so lucky.

It tried to follow, but the heavier vehicle nosed into the ditch too fast—and bottomed out with a loud crunch of metal and a burst of sparks.

"They're stuck!" Tyson whooped, slamming his fist against the dashboard.

Marcus didn't slow down. He pushed the truck harder, barreling through the woods until they hit another service road. Only then did he allow himself a glance in the rearview mirror. No headlights. No sign of pursuit. For now. Breathing hard, he eased off the gas and looked over at Tyson. His cousin was battered, bruised, and bleeding, but alive.

"You good?"

Tyson nodded shakily. "I am now."

Marcus exhaled, still felling the adrenaline coursing through him. "We're not outta this yet. We need to get you somewhere safe. Then we blow this whole thing wide open."

"Damn right we do."

Marcus tightened his grip on the wheel and drove into the night, the stolen truth burning a hole in his pocket and the fire of what came next already lighting in his chest.

Chapter 45

The next morning Tyson sat at the kitchen table, still looking rough but better after a full night of rest. Marcus was pouring them coffee, relieved that he was able to save his cousin. But they knew it wasn't over. A firm knock sounded at his door and he exchanged a look with Tyson before heading over. He peered through the peephole. It was an older white man in a gray button-down shirt and slacks stood outside, flashing a badge at the door.

Marcus cracked it open, but keeping the chain on. "Yeah?"

"Detective Cole," the man said in a calm, even voice. "Internal Affairs. Mind if I come in?"

Marcus hesitated. Tyson stood now, alert. He slowly reached for the bat leaning against the counter. Marcus undid the chain but didn't step aside immediately. "You alone?"

Cole nodded. "Just here to talk."

Marcus let him in, staying close to the door just in case. Cole saw the exhaustion on the men faces. He didn't know the extent of the events that occurred.

"I heard you've had a hell of a week," Cole pulled a slim notepad from his jacket pocket. "I won't take much of your time."

"That's good, 'cause we're fresh outta patience," Tyson muttered under his breath.

Cole didn't react. He opened his notepad and flipped to a marked page. "I'm here because Officer Ortiz filed a report. He claims he witnessed other officers mistreating your brother, Jordan, inside the holding facility."

Marcus stiffened. "What kind of mistreatment?"

"Rough handling. Verbal threats. Trying to provoke him into a fight so they could stack more charges on him." Cole paused with a grim expression. "He also said he was warned to stay quiet or he'd be reassigned, or worse."

Marcus swore under his breath. Tyson slammed his palm against the table. "We knew it! We knew they were trying to break him."

Cole nodded. "And now that Ortiz has come forward, we have leverage to dig deeper. Problem is, his statement alone won't be enough. We'll need more. Patterns of behavior. Witnesses. Concrete proof."

Marcus was trying to hide his relief. They finally had a crack in the wall, but it wasn't enough yet.

As Cole tucked his notepad away, Tyson spoke up. "What about Haynes? Ain't he the one calling all the shots behind the scenes?"

Marcus tensed. Tyson realized his mistake a second too late.

Cole's head snapped up. His eyes sharpened, zeroing in. "Haynes?" he repeated slowly. "You saying he's involved?"

Marcus shot his cousin a warning look, then turned back to Cole. His gut churned. They'd worked too hard and risked too much, to get this far. He wasn't about to spill everything to the first badge that walked through the door.

"How do we know we can trust you?" Marcus asked bluntly.

Cole didn't flinch. "Because I'm not here on behalf of the department. I'm here because people like Haynes make a joke out of the badge I worked twenty years to honor."

It sounded good. But Marcus had been lied to before by men with practiced voices and clean smiles. He needed more.

He pulled out his phone and scrolled through his contacts and made a call. Frank picked up on the second ring.

"Marcus," His deep voice rumbled. "You good?"

"Got a guy here. IA detective. Name's Cole. Claims he's looking into Jordan's case...and Haynes."

He said, "Put him on."

Marcus held out the phone. "Big Frank wants a word."

Cole's brows rose slightly but he took the phone without protest. "Detective Cole."

They watched silently as Cole listened to whatever Frank was saying. They couldn't hear what was said but saw his face change.

"Yes, sir. Understood." He handed the phone back.

Marcus pressed the phone to his ear. "You can trust him. He's one of the few good ones left. But watch your back, kid. Haynes has friends in high places."

Marcus hung up. "All right. We'll talk."

Cole exhaled. "Start with Haynes."

Marcus nodded to Tyson, who pulled out an envelope from under a loose floorboard they'd hidden it in. Inside were copies of the flash drives Marcus hadn't handed over. Photos, notes, everything tying Haynes to corruption and the dirty money flowing through Crest Ridge.

Marcus laid it open on the table between them, standing guard over it as the detective leaned down to look. Cole flipped through every photo and printed email.

"Jesus," he muttered. "This...this could take down half the people sitting on the city council."

"That's the idea," Marcus said darkly.

Cole asked. "Can I take this?"

Marcus shook his head immediately and put everything back in the envelope. "No. You've seen it. That's enough for now."

"Smart. Don't let anything out of your hands until it's time."

Tyson, still buzzing with caffeine, asked, "So what happens now? You take what you know and make it stick?"

"Not yet. If we move too fast, they'll bury us. We need a little more. Then we go public. Press, oversight committees, the whole works."

Marcus crossed his arms. "And my brother?"

"We move him today. Ortiz is helping arrange it. New facility. No warning to the current staff. Fresh eyes."

He continued in a serious tone. "But once this starts rolling, Haynes and his crew will know the walls are closing in. You better be ready. He'll come at you harder than ever."

Tyson smirked. "Let him come."

"I'll be in touch. Keep your heads down and keep copies of everything."

He moved toward the door but paused with his hand on the knob.

"Marcus. Tyson. You're doing something most people wouldn't dare. Stay sharp. Stay alive."

Then he slipped out. They sat in silence for a long moment. Finally, Tyson let out a slow breath.

"You believe him?" he asked.

Marcus stared at the closed door. "I believe Frank. And that's good enough for now."

He picked up the envelope and held it like it weighed a thousand pounds. The war wasn't over. It was just getting started.

Chapter 46

The late afternoon sun dipped low over Crest Ridge as Detective Cole pulled up outside Marcus's shop. He saw the burned-out ruins which looked black scar against the street. Tyson spotted him first through the window.

"Here we go again," he said.

Marcus didn't say anything. He just opened the door and let Cole in. The detective didn't waste time His expression was serious. He already knew he wasn't about to get an easy conversation.

Tyson crossed his arms and leaned against the wall. Marcus stayed standing too, too restless to sit. The air was thick with unspoken tension.

"You got something for us, or is this another 'be patient' speech?" He said.

Cole sighed, "I'm not here to stall. Things are moving faster than we expected."

"Great. So we're just supposed to sit back and let them come after us?"

"No," Cole said firmly, his voice sharp enough to cut through the frustration hanging in the room. "But you need to be smart about this. If you take this evidence to the media like I know you're planning to, they'll discredit you. They'll destroy your reputation and come after anyone close to you."

Marcus asked. "Then what do you suggest?"

Cole stepped closer. "We need to bait them into making a mistake. Something that ties Haynes directly to the gang. If we can do that, we can take him and the gang leader down in one move."

Tyson narrowed his eyes. "Bait them? How, exactly? Pretty sure they're already paranoid enough to shoot first and ask questions later."

Cole pulled a folded sheet of paper from his jacket and tossed it onto the table between them.

"There's a meeting happening tomorrow night. I don't have all the details yet. The location's still being finalized, but I know that the both of them will be there. We heard that it's about tying up loose ends."

Marcus read the paper. It wasn't much. Just some notes and a few coded names.

"If you're willing to take a risk," he continued, "we can use the evidence you have to draw them out. Offer it to someone inside the gang, make them think you're desperate to cut a deal. If Haynes shows up to personally oversee it, that's our opening. We catch him dirty."

Tyson shook his head slowly. "Man, this sounds like suicide."

"It's dangerous. But it's cleaner than going public too soon and getting buried before you can even tell your story."

Marcus thought about it. His mind flashed to his mom, to Jordan still sitting behind bars, to the wreckage of everything he'd built.

"And if it goes wrong?"

Cole's mouth tightened into a thin line. "Then you better make sure that you're ready to run."

Tyson looked at Marcus. "Your call, fam."

He met his cousin's gaze, seeing the trust there and the fear he wasn't saying out loud. He turned back to Cole and in a steady voice said, "We're in. Tell us where and when."

"I'll get you the details by tomorrow morning."

As he headed toward the door, he stopped and looked back at them.

"Just remember, these people aren't afraid to get blood on their hands. Play this smart, or there's no second chance."

As the door clicked shut behind him, Marcus turned back to the cluttered table, his eyes falling on the USB drive and the envelope that had caused so much chaos. He took a deep breath, grabbed his laptop, and began typing with a quiet intensity.

Tyson sat across from him. "What are you doing now?"

"Making a copy," He replied without looking up. His fingers moved quickly, transferring the contents of the USB to another drive he'd pulled from a drawer.

"A copy?" Tyson repeated.

"Yeah. One copy stays with me. The other... it's in case things go south."

"What's that supposed to mean? What are you planning?"

Marcus closed the laptop with a soft click and looked Tyson in the eye. "It means if something happens to me, you'll know what to do."

Tyson shot to his feet, his voice rising. "You're seriously talking like you're not coming back from this! What the hell?"

Marcus stood as well, stepping around the desk to face his cousin. "I'm being realistic, Ty. These people aren't playing games. If I go to that meeting tomorrow, there's a good chance they'll try to take me out. I can't leave this to chance."

"You're not doing this alone. I'm not just gonna sit here and wait for something to happen to you."

"You have to. I need someone I can trust to follow through if things go wrong. That's you."

Marcus pulled a piece of paper from his pocket and scribbled a name and address on it. He handed it to Tyson, who stared at it, his brow furrowed.

"Elena Chavez?" Tyson read aloud, confused. "Who's that?"

"She's a reporter," Marcus explained. "Works for a major outlet. If anything happens to me, you take this USB to her. Don't go to the cops, don't go to anyone else. Just her."

"And you think she's just gonna blow the whistle on this whole thing? What if she doesn't believe you?"

"She will," Marcus said with conviction. "She's been digging into corruption for years. This is exactly the kind of story she's been waiting for. She'll run with it."

Tyson stared at the USB. "And what about Auntie? Myia? You're telling me to sit here and act like everything's fine while you're out risking your life?"

"That's exactly what I'm telling you. If you're here, you can keep them safe. If we all go down, there's no one left to protect them."

Tyson let out a frustrated sigh. "This is insane,. You're asking me to just watch you walk into a trap."

"I'm asking you to trust me," he said firmly. "I've got a plan. And if it doesn't work... then this is Plan B."

Tyson looked at Marcus with a worried expression. "You better not make me use this," he said, holding up the USB.

He managed a faint smile. "I'll do my best."

"Fine. But if this goes south, I'm coming after you. You hear me?"

"I'd expect nothing less."

Tyson shook his head, muttering under his breath as he headed for the door. Before he left, he said, "Just... be careful, man. We've already lost enough."

Marcus's smile faded as he nodded. "I know. I will."

As the door closed, Marcus let out a deep breath. The stakes had never been higher, and every move he made felt like walking a tightrope over a pit of fire.

He glanced at the USB drive in his hand.

"This ends tomorrow."

Chapter 47

Marcus crouched low in the shadows of an adjacent building, his breathing steady despite the adrenaline pumping through his veins. His phone, tucked securely in his jacket pocket, was already recording, a small red light blinking faintly to indicate it was capturing everything.

He could see the gang members gathering through a cracked window of an empty building. He could hear a faint hum of voices carried through the gaps in the worn walls. This was the meeting Detective Cole had told him about. The one where Haynes himself would be discussing plans that could prove just how deep the corruption ran in Crest Ridge.

Marcus adjusted his position as he inched closer to the open window. If he could get this on record, he'd have the proof he needed. Haynes's voice was unmistakable: smooth and cocky, laced with a confidence that came from years of skating above the law. His stomach churned as he listened.

"Let me be clear," Haynes said. "This Carter guy is becoming a problem. He's poking around where he doesn't belong, and it's only a matter of time before he stumbles onto something he shouldn't."

Vaughn spoke up. "We already tried scaring him off. The break-in didn't work, and taking the kid didn't shut him up either. What's the next move?"

Haynes sighed with irritation. "The next move is making sure he can't use whatever he's got. I've got someone looking into whether he's passed that USB drive to anyone else. If he has..." He let the threat hang in the air, his meaning clear.

Jamal asked, "Why not just take him out? We've done worse for less."

Haynes responded in a calculated tone. "It's not that simple. He has eyes on him now. We know he got a cop friend. How else would his brother get moved. And we know he talked to a journalist. We can't risk it blowing back on us. But we will make him wish he'd stayed out of it."

Marcus felt his anger bubble beneath the surface. He adjusted the phone slightly and angled it to catch Haynes's face through the dirty window. Every word was damning, every sentence proof that the man supposed to uphold the law was working hand-in-hand with criminals. He shifted his weight slightly and his knee pressed against a loose piece of metal. It let out a faint *clang*.

Inside, Haynes stopped mid-sentence, his sharp gaze snapping toward the window. "Did you hear that?"

Marcus held his breath and didn't move.

"Probably a stray cat or something," Jamal said with uncertainty.

"Check it out," Haynes ordered.

Marcus's heart pounded as he heard heavy footsteps approaching. He crouched lower, sliding back into the deeper shadows of the adjacent alley. His fingers tightened around the phone in his pocket, careful not to let it slip or make any noise.

Jamal stepped outside with a flashlight. "If it's a cat, it's a big one," he said with irritation.

Marcus remained still as the beam of light passed dangerously close to him. He counted each second and thought of his contingency plans.

"Anything?" Haynes called from inside.

"Nothing out here," Jamal replied, though he didn't sound convinced. He lingered for a moment longer before retreating back into the warehouse.

"See?" He said as he re-entered. "Probably just the wind."

Haynes didn't look convinced. His eyes flicked toward the window one last time before he sighed and continued. "Fine. Let's focus. The important thing is keeping this operation running smoothly. No more loose ends."

"What about the delivery driver?" another gang member asked.

Haynes smirked. "Taken care of. No witnesses, no problems. That's how it's done."

Marcus felt the weight of what he was hearing sinking in. They'd killed the delivery driver, just as he suspected, and now they were planning their next move. He'd heard enough. The phone had captured Haynes's face, his voice, and his damning words. Now, all he had to do was get out.

He inched away from the window, moving as quietly as possible. His muscles ached from tension, but he forced himself to stay slow and deliberate. One wrong move could give him away. Finally, he reached the corner of the building and saw his car parked just a few feet away. He looked back one last time to make sure he wasn't followed. Satisfied, he slipped into the driver's seat, started the engine, and drove off, the sound of gravel crunching beneath his tires the only indication he'd ever been there.

Marcus kept his grip tight on the steering wheel as he sped down the darkened back roads of Crest Ridge. Every few seconds, he checked the rearview mirror, half-expecting a pair of headlights to emerge from the night, chasing him down. But the road stayed empty. He closed his eyes for a second, inhaled through his nose, exhaled slowly through his mouth, trying to calm himself. He had what he needed, finally. Proof. The Deputy Police Chief, caught on audio and video, admitting to covering up a murder. No more speculation, no more theories. This was real.

He tapped his pocket where the phone rested, making sure it was still there. It buzzed slightly against his hand, a silent reminder of the weight he now carried. He didn't go straight home. Too risky. If anyone had spotted him lurking around, they'd go there. He took a long, looping route through the quieter streets. Only when he was sure he wasn't being tailed did he head toward Sam's.

He opened the door the moment Marcus pulled up.

"You got it?" he asked.

Marcus nodded as he walked inside. "I got everything. Haynes incriminated himself. Delivery driver, gang activity, the works."

Sam locked the door behind them, then pulled the shades down tight. "Good. Because once this gets out, they're gonna come hard."

Marcus set the phone on the table. "We need to back it up immediately. Two copies. One hidden, one for Cole."

Sam was already grabbing his laptop and cables. "On it."

As the files transferred, Marcus leaned back against the wall. He felt exhaustion finally catching up with him. His muscles still felt coiled, his mind running through every scenario, every way this could still go wrong.

When the backup was done, Sam handed him two flash drives.

"You're playing a dangerous game," Sam said quietly.

Marcus gave a tired half-smile. "Ain't no other kind in Crest Ridge."

Sam just shook his head. "Be careful, man."

Marcus nodded, slipping the phone back into his jacket. He couldn't afford to let his guard down. Not now, not ever. Tomorrow night would be the beginning of the end for Haynes, for Rook, for all of them. One way or another.

Chapter 48

The next morning, Marcus sat at his kitchen table . He opened his laptop and stared at the folder labeled "Evidence." Inside were videos, audio recordings, and photos. Everything he'd risked his life to gather. It was the truth, raw and unfiltered, and it was time for Crest Ridge to see it.

He tapped the trackpad and started an email draft. At the top, he'd written a list of recipients: Elena Chavez at *The Crest Ridge Sentinel* ; Mark Hargrove at the state news network; and a few other trusted journalists he'd researched.

The subject line read: *URGENT: Corruption in Crest Ridge PD and Criminal Syndicate Evidence.*

His fingers paused over the keyboard before he typed a brief but powerful message:

To all recipients,

The attached files contain undeniable proof of a criminal syndicate operating in Crest Ridge with the cooperation of a corrupt officer in the local police department, identified as Deputy Chief Haynes. I'm sharing this anonymously for my safety, but it's imperative this story is told. Lives are at stake, and the community deserves to know the truth.

—A Concerned Citizen

Marcus attached the files, ensuring the recordings from the warehouse meeting were highlighted. He clicked Send and watched it go from drafts to Sent. The ball was rolling now, and there was no turning back. By noon, the story was already gaining traction. Marcus smiled as his phone vibrated incessantly with notifications.

Bro, did you see the news?!

He hadn't watched the coverage yet, but the flurry of messages told him everything he needed to know. He turned on his TV to the local news. Elena Chavez's familiar face appeared on the screen, her tone urgent.

"We've just received a bombshell report implicating a Crest Ridge police officer and a notorious gang in an extensive corruption and criminal enterprise," she said. "The evidence includes video and audio recordings allegedly capturing Deputy Chief Haynes conspiring with gang members to cover up illegal activities, intimidate witnesses, and more. Viewer discretion is advised."

The broadcast cut to snippets of the footage Marcus had sent. There was Haynes, leaning against a table in a clear voice:

"...no witnesses, no problems," as he smirked cruelly.

The screen cut back to Elena.

"Authorities have yet to issue a formal statement, but sources tell us an internal affairs investigation is already underway. Community leaders are calling for immediate suspension and arrest of those implicated. We will continue to bring you updates as this story develops."

Marcus felt a mixture of grim satisfaction and steeled nerves running through him.

Tyson, who was watching the news with him, started laughing. "Man. You actually did it. You really set it off."

"It's not over yet. They're cornered. That's when people get dangerous."

As if on cue, his phone buzzed again. More messages, missed calls, people wanting confirmation, congratulations, or information. He ignored them all for now. There were bigger things to worry about.

Tyson sat down on the couch. "Fam, you're a legend."

"Legend don't mean much if they find us dead in a ditch."

Tyson's grin faltered slightly, the weight of the situation settling back over them.

"We still gotta finish this," Marcus said. "The press is one thing. But taking Haynes out of Crest Ridge for good? That's the endgame."

"Whatever you need, I'm in."

Marcus glanced over at the muted television again, where Elena Chavez's serious face filled the screen with a new update ticker scrolling below. Arrests were likely imminent. Pressure was mounting fast.

"Good," he said quietly. "Because we're about to light a fire they can't put out.

As they walked out of his apartment, the world outside felt different. Neighbors were gathered in small clusters, whispering and pointing at their phones.

A man he vaguely recognized from the neighborhood approached him, jogging slightly to catch up. "Did you hear about the news? They're saying there's proof the cops are in on it with the gangs."

"Yeah, I heard," he said.

The man shook his head, still wide-eyed. "Crazy, right? You think it's true?"

"It's on tape," Marcus replied simply, not offering any more details.

The man let out a low whistle. "Man, this town's worse than I thought. Used to be you just had to worry about the streets... now you gotta watch the badge too."

He just gave a small nod and kept walking, his mind already spinning ahead to everything still left to do. The man lingered for a moment longer before heading the other way.

Later that evening, Marcus sat on the couch. He was watching the updates when his phone buzzed. He froze when he saw the name.

He hesitated before answering.

"Hello?"

Her voice came sharp and furious through the line. "It was you, wasn't it?"

Marcus leaned forward. "Myia—"

"Don't 'Myia' me!" she snapped. "I know it was you who leaked that video. You think you're some kind of hero? You've made all of us a target!"

He closed his eyes, fighting to stay calm. "I did what I had to do. You think I wanted this?"

"I think you didn't think at all!" she said, her voice cracking with anger. "You've painted a bullseye on our backs! We have to live here!"

"I didn't do this for fame or attention. I did it to protect us! To clear Jordan's name! To stop them from hurting more people!"

She was quiet for a moment. Then, softer but still tense, she said, "And what happens when they come after us anyway? When they realize they can't get to you and go after the people you love instead?"

His voice dropped low, filled with pain. "Everything I've done... every risk I took... was for this family. I wasn't gonna let them bury my brother or scare us into silence anymore."

Myia said quietly, "You better hope you're right. Because if anything happens to Auntie... to Jordan..." She didn't finish the sentence. She didn't have to.

The line clicked dead. He kept hearing her words replaying over and over in his head. He didn't hear Tyson come in until he spoke.

"You good, fam?"

He looked up. Tyson was had a concerned look on his face.

He forced a tight smile. "Yeah. Fine."

"Man, don't lie. You're a terrible liar." He walked into the room, dropping onto the couch with a grunt. "That was my sis, wasn't it?"

He set the phone down on the coffee table.

"She's scared. Can't blame her for that."

"I know," he said quietly. "I just... I did all this to keep everyone safe. And now it feels like I've made everything worse."

"You didn't make this mess. They did. Haynes, Rook, all of them. You just finally shined a light on it. You think it was safer when everybody was too scared to fight back?"

Marcus didn't answer. He wasn't sure he could.

"Look, maybe it gets rough for a while. Maybe we gotta watch our backs. But at least now we know who we're fighting. And that's because of you, man."

Marcus looked at him and saw it all. The anger, pain, and loyalty in his cousin's face clear as day.

"Don't let her fear make you doubt yourself," Tyson said. "You did what needed to be done. You saved my cousin, your brother, and you saved me." He shrugged, smirking a little. "You're not just fixing cars anymore, fam. You're fixing this whole damn town."

Marcus felt a flicker of something deep in his chest, hope.

"Thanks, Ty," he said.

"Anytime. Now come on, man. If we're gonna survive this, you need to eat something. I ain't getting shot at on an empty stomach."

Marcus chuckled under his breath and followed him toward the kitchen. Tyson opened the fridge and pulled out two foil-wrapped plates.

"Leftovers from Auntie. I stopped my there yesterday. You're lucky I didn't finish these last night."

Marcus raised an eyebrow. "That supposed to be comforting or a warning?"

Tyson smirked and tossed a plate in the microwave. "Depends how fast you eat."

For a brief second, it felt like things used to be, two cousins talking mess in a kitchen, instead of mapping their moves against a corrupt system.

Then Marcus's phone rang. He walked over to pick it up and saw Elena's name. His smile faded. He hesitated before he answered.

"Hello?"

"Marcus," her voice was calm but probing. "I know it was you who sent the evidence."

"I don't know what you're talking about."

"You're the only person in this town who's been stirring things up lately, and this evidence has your fingerprints all over it. I just wanted to say... thank you."

"Don't thank me yet. This isn't over."

"True, but it's a start," she said. "This is going to rock Crest Ridge to its core. Are you prepared for the fallout?"

"I'm more worried about my family," he admitted.

Her tone softened. "I'll do what I can to protect your identity. But Marcus... the people you've exposed, they won't take this lying down. Be careful."

Meanwhile, across town, Haynes sat in his car.

"What the hell is this?" he barked.

Jamal responded nervously. "It's all over the news, man. Someone leaked everything. Videos , audio, the whole nine yards."

He slammed his hand against the steering wheel. "You think I don't know that?! Find out who did this, now!"

"Yes, sir. We're working on it."

Haynes ended the call and stared out the windshield. Whoever had done this was going to pay. He gritted his teeth, breathing heavily as he tried to think. Every plan he had carefully built was crumbling. The higher-ups wouldn't protect him now. Especially not with this much dirt out in the open.

His phone buzzed again. Another number, another desperate call. He ignored it. He needed to focus. One name kept flashing in his mind: Marcus. *That damn mechanic had been poking around for months.* He had dismissed him at first, but now, it all made too much sense. He pulled a crumpled pack of cigarettes from the glove compartment, lighting one with a shaky hand.

"You want a war?" he muttered under his breath. "Fine. You just declared one."

He snatched it up and dialed a number from memory. It rang once before the line picked up.

"Yeah?" came a gruff voice.

"It's me," Haynes said. He glanced around before continuing. "I need you to do something. Tonight."

"What's the job?"

"Marcus Carter. His mother's house. I want someone sitting outside. Watch everything. Who comes, who goes. Make sure he knows without knowing."

The man on the other end chuckled darkly. "You want subtle, huh?"

"For now," he snapped. "Sit on it for a couple of days. Keep the pressure on. If he so much as breathes wrong, I want to know about it."

"You got it."

Haynes hung up without another word. He leaned back against the seat, staring up at the concrete ceiling. His pulse was hammering in his ears, but he forced himself to breathe slow. This wasn't over. Not by a long shot. He'd lost the first round—but Marcus was about to find out just how far he was willing to go to protect himself.

Across the street, hidden behind a row of parked cars, a pair of eyes watched Haynes silently. They slipped back into the shadows and pulled out a burner phone.

"Yeah," the voice whispered. "It's him. He's losing it."

Chapter 49

The next morning, Crest Ridge felt different. Marcus stood on the cracked sidewalk outside his shop, watching the steady flow of cars and people. Normally, a Tuesday morning would've been slow, people dragging their feet on the way to work or school. But today, the city buzzed with energy.

Across the street, a group of people huddled outside a corner store with their faces glued to their phones. News vans patrolled up and down the main road like sharks circling prey. Reporters leaned out of their windows, barking questions at anyone who looked remotely important.

"Chaos," Tyson muttered beside him. "Straight-up chaos."

Marcus nodded grimly. The bomb had dropped, and there was no putting it back. Word had spread faster than he could have imagined. Deputy Chief Haynes wasn't just under suspicion anymore, he was practically radioactive.

Social media was flooded with posts from angry citizens. Parents demanded to know how deep the corruption ran. Business owners worried about their safety. Students organized a walkout at the local high school. And everywhere, there were whispers. *Who else was involved? Who could be trusted?* But amidst the noise and confusion, there was one thing Marcus hadn't expected, hope.

He turned as he heard the familiar rumble of a car engine. A moment later, Cole pulled up to the curb and stepped out, his face serious but not grim.

"We got movement," he flashed a slight smile. "Your brother's case is being reopened. Officially."

Marcus stared at him for a second, letting the words settle.

"You serious?" Tyson blurted out.

Cole nodded. "Serious as a heart attack. The footage that was leaked wasn't just the spark. It's a full-on fire now. They can't ignore it. The DA's office is scrambling. There's enough public pressure that they had no choice. Jordan's case is under review as we speak."

Marcus exhaled a shaky breath. Relief washed over him, tangled with anxiety. They weren't across the finish line yet, but it meant Jordan had a real shot.

"What's the catch?" he asked. "Because I know better than to think it would be that simple."

Cole's smile faded. "The catch is, Haynes is still out there. And he's desperate. He's going to try to clean up loose ends, any way he can."

"We're not running."

"I didn't expect you to." Cole glanced around and lowered his voice. "But you need to be ready. They'll look for ways to spin this, to make you and your family out to be criminals, liars, traitors. The next few days are going to be hell."

Across the street, another news van rolled up. Cameras swung in their direction like hungry vultures.

"Wonderful," Tyson muttered, walking back toward the shop.

Cole handed Marcus a folded piece of paper. "There's going to be a preliminary hearing in a few days. The DA's office wants to talk to you before then. They'll probably try to offer you some kind of deal to testify."

Marcus took the paper. "I'll be there."

Cole hesitated before stepping back toward his car. "You did the right thing, Marcus. Just...be ready. The storm's only just started."

With that, he climbed into his car and drove off.

"Bro," Tyson said after a minute. "You think Jordan knows yet?"

Marcus pulled out his phone and hesitated. There had been no calls from the jail yet. Part of him hoped he had already heard through the grapevine. Another part of him worried about what might happen to him inside now that Haynes's protection was collapsing.

"He'll call soon," Tyson said, trying to sound more confident than he looked.

Suddenly, his phone buzzed in his hand. Unknown number.

Marcus answered cautiously. "Hello?"

"Mr. Carter?" a brisk, professional voice said. "This is Assistant District Attorney Rachel Keene. I'm part of the team reviewing your brother's case."

"Yes. I'm listening."

"We'd like you to come downtown this afternoon to provide a formal statement regarding the evidence you submitted. It's critical for the motion we're filing to have Jordan's conviction vacated."

Vacated. Marcus's pulse quickened. That wasn't just a review. That was real.

"I'll be there," he said.

They exchanged details and ended the call. Tyson looked at him with raised eyebrows.

Marcus allowed himself the smallest of smiles. "They're filing to throw out Jordan's conviction."

Tyson whooped and jumped, clapping Marcus on the shoulder hard enough to nearly knock him off balance.

"Man, you did it!" He grinned. "We did it!"

Marcus shook his head. "Not yet. We got the door open. Now we have to walk through it."

"Then let's finish it."

Later that afternoon, as Marcus pulled out onto the main road toward the courthouse, he couldn't help but glance around, hyper aware of every car behind him. Every pedestrian on the sidewalk. Haynes wasn't finished with him. He could feel it like a weight pressing on his chest. But he wasn't afraid. Not anymore. The people of Crest Ridge were watching and so was the world. He was going to bring his brother home. And this time, they weren't going to bury the truth. No matter who tried.

Marcus parked a block away from the courthouse. He didn't trust being too visible right now. Tyson had wanted to come, but Marcus insisted he stay behind , just in case Haynes tried something while he was there. As he walked toward the courthouse, every nerve in his body was alert. He scanned the sidewalks, the doorways, even the rooftops, but saw no obvious threats. Still, he kept his head low, his hands tucked in his jacket pockets.

When he entered the building, he had to pass through security. The guards barely looked up as they waved him through. Inside, the halls echoed with footsteps and murmured conversations. News crews weren't allowed past the front steps, but he could feel their presence and the buzz of whispered speculation. He saw the way people looked sideways at him and quickly away.

Marcus followed the directions the assistant DA had given him: third floor, Room 312. As he climbed the stairs, he spotted a few familiar faces lingering near the courtrooms. Some avoided his gaze. Others watched him openly, their expressions a mixture of hostility and unease. He kept moving. When he reached Room 312, he found it already half full. Not a courtroom exactly, more like a conference room, but the mood inside was just as heavy.

At the head of the table sat Rachel Keene, a caramel woman in a dark blue suit with sharp eyes and a no-nonsense air. She stood when Marcus entered.

"Mr. Carter. Thank you for coming."

He nodded and stepped inside.

There were two other officials present, a man and a woman, that introduced themselves as part of the DA's internal review team. One of them started a recorder and laid a thick file on the table.

Rachel gestured for him to sit. "This is just a preliminary statement," she said. "We'll ask you some questions about the evidence you submitted and the circumstances around how it was obtained. Please answer truthfully and clearly. Understand?"

"Yeah," Marcus said, settling into the chair.

The questions started out basic; verifying his name, his relationship to Jordan, how he came into possession of the video recordings. Marcus stuck to the truth but was careful not to implicate anyone else unnecessarily.

Rachel folded her hands and asked. "Mr. Carter, did anyone threaten you or coerce you into gathering this evidence?"

"No," he said. "I did it because no one else would."

She nodded slightly, scribbling notes.

"Are you aware that by leaking this information publicly, you may have compromised parts of the official investigation?"

"I didn't leak anything. I gave some information to Jordan's lawyer proving his innocence. Apparently that didn't work since he's still there. Seems to me if it hadn't been leaked, we wouldn't be here right now."

Rachel exchanged a glance with one of her colleagues but said nothing. She turned the line of questioning toward Haynes next. She asked if he had ever interacted with him directly, or if he knew about his connections to the gang.

"I suspected something," he said carefully. "The way things went down the night my brother was arrested. The way evidence disappeared, the way witnesses changed their stories, it didn't add up."

She wrote more notes. At one point, Marcus glanced toward the door. A man in plain clothes with his arms crossed was staring at him. He recognized the face as one of the guys from a picture with Haynes. Not an official officer anymore, if rumors were true, but still loyal. Still dangerous. She noticed his sudden tension. She glanced toward the door, then back at him.

"You're safe in here," she said quietly.

"Sure, in here, but what about when I leave?"

After another half hour, they wrapped up the questions. Rachel stood and gathered the papers into a neat stack.

"We're moving forward with filing a motion to vacate Jordan's conviction based on your evidence," she said. "It's not a guarantee yet, but it's a strong case. We'll need you to testify at the hearing, possibly at future proceedings related to Haynes and the gang."

"I'll be there," he said firmly.

Rachel offered a small smile. "You're brave, Mr. Carter. Most people wouldn't have dared to do what you did."

Marcus didn't feel brave. He felt exhausted. But he nodded and rose to his feet. As he stepped out of the room, the man was gone. The hallway was empty except for a janitor pushing a cart. Still, he didn't relax. He moved quickly, cutting down a side stairwell instead of the main stairs, and kept his hand close to the pocket where he kept his phone.

Outside, the reporters were still camped near the steps, but Marcus slipped past them, keeping his head down. He didn't see the black sedan parked two streets over or the two men watching his every move.

Chapter 50

Marcus reached his truck and slid inside, locking the doors out of habit. As he pulled out into traffic, he caught a glimpse of the black sedan in the side mirror. It wasn't just parked anymore. It was moving, slowly, smoothly, merging into the flow of cars right behind him. His hands tightened on the wheel.

They're following me.

He took a left instead of heading straight home. The sedan followed. He turned right at the next light and slipped into a residential neighborhood with tight curves and narrow streets. Again, the sedan stayed with him, keeping a two-car distance.

He began to worry. He couldn't lead them back to Tyson or his mom. No way. If they were connected to Haynes, and he had no doubt they were, they wouldn't hesitate to hurt anyone he cared about. He pressed harder on the gas, weaving through side streets, trying to lose them. For a few blocks, it seemed like he had. The mirror showed nothing but empty road.

Just when he thought he was clear, the black sedan reappeared, cutting through an alley to intercept him. Marcus muttered a curse under his breath.

Alright, you wanna play? Let's play.

He spotted a gas station up ahead and quickly pulled in. He killed the engine, grabbed an old ball cap from the seat next to him, and tugged it low over his face. Then he climbed out and headed toward the store as he kept the sedan in his peripheral vision.

Sure enough, the black car eased into the lot and parked near the curb. The windows were tinted and too dark to see inside. He entered the gas station but didn't linger. He grabbed a pack of gum off a display and paid cash at the counter.

Two men had gotten out of the sedan. They stood near the pumps, pretending to be casual,but their stiff body language and the way their eyes tracked every move he made, told a different story.

He tucked the gum into his pocket and slipped around the side of the building, moving fast. The alley behind the gas station led into a cluster of small shops and abandoned lots. Places he knew better than almost anyone. Growing up, he'd biked every inch of this part of town.

He ducked between two dumpsters and sprinted across a narrow alleyway, cutting through the broken fence behind an old auto shop. The men saw him and ran behind him.

Marcus didn't stop. He vaulted over a fallen trash can, kept low, and darted through another alley that opened onto an overgrown lot. Ahead was an old drainage culvert, half-hidden by weeds and brambles. It was a tight fit, but he dropped to the ground and crawled inside just as the men rounded the corner.

He pressed himself against the damp concrete wall. The men skidded to a stop a few feet away, swearing under their breath.

"Where the hell did he go?" one of them hissed.

"I don't know. Spread out. He's gotta be close."

He stayed perfectly still, barely breathing as he listened to their footsteps move off in opposite directions. He waited five minutes before emerging, careful to stay low. He slipped through the tangle of weeds and backtracked toward the street where he'd parked. His truck was still there, thank God, but the sedan was gone, probably split up to circle the block.

Marcus didn't waste time. He fired up the engine and pulled away, taking back roads and side streets, doubling back twice to make sure he wasn't still being followed. When he was sure he'd shaken them, he headed toward a rundown trailer on a forgotten patch of land. He parked behind the trailer, hidden from the road, and sat there for a minute, catching his breath.

His phone buzzed. A message from Tyson: "Everything went good?"

Marcus stared at the screen, then typed back quickly: "Yeah. Close call. Laying low for a bit."

He leaned back in the seat. This wasn't over. If anything, the stakes had just gone through the roof. Haynes was getting desperate. Sending guys to follow him in broad daylight? That meant he was scared. Dangerous. He knew he couldn't keep dodging them forever. He had to hit them harder. Finish what he started.

His phone buzzed again, this time showing a different number: a correctional facility line.

He didn't even hesitate. As soon as the automated voice started, "You have a collect call from—" and Jordan's voice came through, he was already pressing the button to accept before the recording could even finish.

"Yeah, yeah, I accept," he said urgently anxious just to hear his brother.

"Marcus?" Jordan's voice came through, a little distorted but unmistakably his.

He couldn't help but smile, a genuine one this time. "I'm here, man. I'm here."

After everything, just hearing Jordan's voice alive, still fighting, it meant more than he could say.

Jordan sounded a little rough. "Man... it's good to hear you."

"Right back at you, bro." He leaned back against the headrest, the knot in his chest loosening just a little. "You holding up?"

"Trying to. But listen, I had to call. Something's different in here."

Marcus was instantly alert. "What's going on?"

Jordan lowered his voice like someone might be listening. "New guards. They posted up around my block real heavy. They ain't acting right, not like before. Watching me close. Like they're waiting for something."

"They're nervous. They know the game's changing."

"What do you mean?" He asked quickly.

Marcus, trying to keep his voice calm, "It's out, J. The evidence. Haynes, the gang, the dirty cops. It's all over the news. Elena Chavez ran it last night. People are pissed. They're reopening your case."

"You serious?" Jordan finally rasped.

"Dead serious. They can't sweep it under the rug now. Too many eyes on them."

Jordan laughed again, but this time it sounded almost disbelieving. "Man... I don't even know what to say."

"You don't gotta say nothing," he said. "Just stay smart. Stay safe. We're not done yet."

"I hear you," Jordan said, but there was a note of caution in his voice. "I want to believe it, bro. But I've been in here too long. Seen too much. They'll try something, I can feel it."

He hated how Jordan sounded. Beaten down by years of injustice, by fear he wasn't ready to shake yet. And he hated that Jordan had good reason to feel that way.

"They might try," Marcus replied. "But they're scared now. We flipped the board. Just gotta stay one step ahead."

"Thanks, man. For everything you've done. You didn't have to—"

"Stop," he interrupted. "You're my brother. That's it. That's the only reason I ever needed."

"Yeah, well... next time you wanna save my life, maybe find a way that don't make you a target too."

"No promises."

A voice in the background announced that they had one minute remaining on the call.

Jordan's tone grew serious again. "You be careful, man. They're not just coming for me anymore. They're coming for you too."

"I know." Marcus's voice was steel. "Let 'em come."

The line clicked and the call ended. He started the engine, and pulled out of the lot. One step closer. One more thing to protect. And this time, he wasn't letting them take anything else.

Chapter 51

What remained of the shop was little more than blackened rubble and twisted metal beams. The acrid smell of burnt rubber and scorched wood still clung stubbornly to the air. Marcus stood on what used to be the front steps, his boots crunching over charred debris as he surveyed the wreckage.

Tyson was already there, moving slowly through the ashes, poking at what little remained with a piece of scrap metal.

"This ain't a cleanup," he said, shaking his head. "This is a burial."

He didn't argue. It wasn't just damage. The fire had gutted the place. The office, the garage, the storage room, all gone.

"Could've been worse," Marcus said after a long moment. "We could've been inside when it happened."

Tyson gave a dry laugh, kicking aside a burnt tire. "Yeah, great silver lining there, fam."

Marcus crouched down and picked through a pile of melted tools, most of them beyond saving. They had insurance, but even so, rebuilding wouldn't be easy. It never was. He straightened as Sam's car pulled into the lot, kicking up a swirl of ash and dust. Sam hopped out, waving a phone in the air as he jogged over.

"You're not gonna believe this," he said with a wild look in his eyes. "It's happening. Rook got arrested this morning."

Marcus blinked. "What?"

"Serious, man. They got him trying to sneak outta town with fake plates and a duffel bag full of cash." Sam showed a video from a local news feed.

The footage was shaky but clear enough. Rook being led away in cuffs, his mouth running a mile a minute as reporters shouted questions. One of the cops shoved him into a squad car like tossing trash into a can.

Tyson let out a low whistle. "Bout time that piece of trash got what's coming."

"That's not it," Sam said, flipping to another headline. "Haynes resigned this morning. Effective immediately. Internal Affairs started sniffing around and boom. He's out."

Marcus absorbed the words slowly. Part of him had dreamed of this day, but he hadn't dared believe it would come so soon.

"What about the others?" he asked. "There's more."

Sam's expression grew serious. "That's the thing. Some folks are saying the conspiracy goes way deeper. They are just the faces they're willing to sacrifice. The real dirt's buried under the department."

Tyson kicked at a collapsed beam. "Great. So we burned down our lives just to cut the weeds. Roots still alive underneath."

Marcus just stared at the hollow shell of the shop. His mind wasn't on the shop anymore. It was on Jordan. It was on his mother. It was on everything still left to protect.

Sam shifted awkwardly. "Frank's sending some guys over to help clear out anything salvageable. Said it's the least he could do."

Marcus nodded. He wasn't good at accepting help, but right now, he didn't have much choice.

Around noon, a beat-up truck pulled into the lot, and Big Mike climbed out, two of his crew in tow. Without a word, they started hauling out the bigger chunks of debris, stacking them neatly at the curb. Marcus joined in, grateful for something physical to focus on.

They worked for hours under the punishing sun, clearing the worst of it. Every so often, passing cars would slow down, drivers craning their necks to stare at the wreckage. Word had spread about the corruption, the fire, and the arrests. Crest Ridge was buzzing like a kicked beehive. By late afternoon, they'd cleared enough space to see the ground again. Blackened , cracked, but still there. Tyson flopped down on a half-burned cinder block, wiping his forehead with a dirty rag.

"Well," he said, panting. "At least now we can see just how much you lost."

Marcus didn't answer right away. He stood at the edge of the lot, staring out at the city.

They hadn't lost. Not really. They were still breathing. Still fighting.

His phone buzzed in his pocket. He pulled it out and saw Detective Cole's name flashing on the screen.

He stepped away from the others before answering. "Yeah?"

Cole's voice was sharp. "Wanted to give you the heads up. Based on the evidence you handed over, the D.A. is filing more charges. Rook's going down hard. Haynes too, and maybe a few others."

"How many?"

"Six more officers under investigation. And three more gang associates." Cole's voice dropped lower. "You stirred up a hornet's nest, Marcus. They're scared. That's why you're feeling the heat."

Marcus looked over his shoulder at the remains of the shop. "They already burned me out once."

"Then be ready," Cole said. "Because they're not done yet."

The call ended, and Marcus lowered the phone slowly.

Across the lot, Tyson was tossing loose pieces of scrap metal into a growing pile. Sam was arguing with Big Mike about what parts might be salvageable. Normal noises. Normal movement. But none of this was normal anymore. Tyson caught the look on Marcus's face as he walked back over.

"What now?" Tyson asked, already bracing for bad news.

Marcus shook his head. "Cole says more arrests are coming."

"That's good, right?"

Marcus looked around at the ruins of the shop, the ashes still thick on the ground.

"It's a start," he said quietly.

Marcus had just finished dragging another scorched beam to the scrap pile when his phone buzzed again. He checked the screen: Mr. Miller.

He wiped his hands on his jeans before answering.

"Hello?"

"Mr. Carter." The lawyer's voice was tight, sharper than usual. "We have a problem."

Marcus stiffened. "What's going on?"

"My office was broken into last night." Miller paused, as if weighing how much to say. "Ransacked. Files overturned, computers wiped. Whoever did it wasn't looking for cash."

Marcus felt the familiar coil of tension in his gut. "You think it's connected to Haynes?"

"I don't think it. I know it." Miller's voice dropped lower. "Someone inside my office... someone I trusted... is helping him. I don't know who yet."

Marcus ran a hand over his face, pacing a slow circle in the dust.

"You're sure?" he asked.

"I'm sure." Miller exhaled heavily. "Certain files were targeted. Ones connected to Jordan's case, and the evidence you've been collecting. They knew exactly what to look for."

Marcus's mind raced. That explained how Haynes's people stayed one step ahead sometimes. They had eyes — even inside the places that were supposed to be safe.

"What about the copies?" Marcus asked.

"They didn't get everything." Miller's voice steadied a little. "I made backups outside the office, just in case. But it means from here on out... we have to assume they're watching everything."

Marcus cursed under his breath. "Is it safe for you to even stay there?"

"No," Miller said bluntly. "I'm relocating the essentials. Quietly. I've got a trusted courier bringing the backups to a secure location. I'll keep you updated."

There was a pause on the line. Then Miller added, "Marcus... be careful who you trust from now on. We're in deeper than I thought."

Marcus's throat tightened. He glanced toward Tyson, who was still sifting through debris, oblivious. Toward Sam and Big Mike arguing by the curb. People he trusted. People he hoped he could still trust.

"I got it," Marcus said. "Same goes for you."

Miller gave a grim chuckle. "Funny thing about the truth. Once it's out, it doesn't make you safe. It just makes you a bigger target."

The call ended, but Marcus stood there for a long time, the dead line still pressed against his ear. The truth was out, but the fallout had only just begun.

Somewhere out there, Haynes was either running or retaliating. And Marcus couldn't shake the feeling that both options would get someone killed. His phone buzzed again in his hand, jerking him from the thought. Unknown Number.

He almost let it go to voicemail, but instinct made him answer.

"Hello?" He answered, his voice guarded.

"Marcus, it's Elena," she said quickly. "What you sent... it's blowing up faster than we expected. But listen, things are moving fast on the police side too. I heard that Internal Affairs is scrambling, and there are rumors Haynes is trying to skip town."

"Not surprised. He knows the walls are closing in."

"There's more," she continued. Her voice dropped to a whisper. "I got a tip from one of my sources. They're saying there's another meeting planned for Friday night. Haynes and what's left of his crew. They're desperate."

"Where?"

"Old train yard off Marlowe Street at Midnight."

"You sure about this?"

"Positive," Elena said. "If you're going, please be careful. They're not gonna go down without a fight."

"I know," he said grimly. "Thanks for the heads-up."

"Marcus..." she hesitated. "After everything you've done, you don't have to keep putting yourself in danger. Let the system handle it."

"Yeah? The same system that let all this happen in the first place?"

There was silence on the other end, but she didn't argue.

"I'll be fine," Marcus said, ending the call.

He stared at the phone for a long moment before grabbing his keys. If Haynes was desperate, that made him dangerous. But he wasn't about to sit back and hope someone else finished what he started.

Chapter 52

Marcus sat at the kitchen table lost in thought. Yesterday had been long, filled with phone calls, cleanup, and brief moments of respite, but his mind kept returning to one nagging thing: his mother. After everything that had happened, he couldn't help but feel the weight of the situation bearing down on her as well.

He dialed her number, the phone ringing through, but it felt like an eternity before she answered.

"Hey, baby," she said. Her voice was calm, but there was an undercurrent there Marcus didn't miss. Something wasn't quite right.

"Hey, Ma." He leaned back against the headrest. "You doing okay?"

"I'm alright," she said, a little too quickly. "You been busy, huh?"

Marcus gave a soft chuckle. "Yeah, you could say that." He paused. "You saw the news?"

"Everybody saw the news. They finally exposed what you've been sayin' all along. About the police, the gangs. About Jordan."

Marcus swallowed hard. "They reopened his case, Ma. It's official. He's got a real shot now."

There was a beat of silence. He expected her to cry, to laugh, to praise God like she usually did when hope finally cracked through the mess. But instead, she was quiet.

"That's good," she said, but there wasn't much relief in it. "That's real good, Marcus. I'm proud of you for fighting for your brother."

He sensed it now. The reason for the tightness in her voice.

"What's wrong, Ma? I mean, after everything that's come out—"

"I'm fine," she interrupted quickly. "But there's been something odd lately." Her voice dropped to a quieter tone, and he could tell she was hesitating. "There's been a car parked outside my house for the past two nights."

Marcus straightened in his chair. "A car? What kind of car? Have you seen who's in it?"

"No," she replied. "I haven't seen anyone, but it's been there, parked across the street, just sitting. I haven't said anything, but it's making me uneasy. Not that I'm worried, mind you." She paused, then added, "But I'm just wondering why it's there."

His protective instinct flared to life, and before he could stop himself, he told her calmly, "If it's still there now, I'll head over right away."

His mother was silent for a long moment before she responded, her tone soft but resolute. "Marcus, I'm fine. I don't need you worrying about me. It's probably just someone waiting for someone else. Don't waste your time."

"I'll stop by tonight," he said. "When it's dark. I'll handle it."

"Don't be stubborn about this," she said, her voice gentle but firm. "I'm okay. You have enough on your plate."

"I know you think you can handle it yourself, but you've got me for a reason," he said. "Let me help."

She sighed, a long, tired sound that seemed to echo through the phone. "Fine. But promise me you won't go making a scene. I don't want you putting yourself in danger. You've done enough already."

"I'll be careful. Just stay inside, okay?" He said, his tone softening. He could hear the familiar concern in her voice, but that didn't stop him from feeling like he needed to go.

"I will. Just... be safe, son."

"I will," he repeated.

That night the drive to his mom's house felt too long, each minute stretching like a rubber band, taut and about to snap. Marcus could feel the unease in his gut growing the closer he got. His hands tightened on the steering wheel as his mind raced with images of his mother alone with some unknown threat outside her home.

He made the turn onto her street and his eyes were immediately drawn to the car parked across the street from his mother's house. It was a dark sedan and the driver was sitting there with the engine idling.

It was the same one he had noticed before. Same tinted windows. Same slow, steady hum. Marcus wasn't going to let them intimidate his family. He grabbed the tire iron he kept under the seat, slid out of the truck, and approached the sedan on foot. He made sure to stay low and out of the direct streetlights.

When he got closer to the car, he pulled out his phone and snapped a quick picture. He took a second one of the license plate. He crouched behind a parked truck to get a better look at the car. It was obvious now. This wasn't just some random person parked here. A feeling of cold dread spread through him.

A few minutes passed, but the car didn't move. The figure inside remained still, and Marcus felt his frustration mount. Whoever was sitting in that car had been there long enough to know something wasn't right. He needed to act fast. He couldn't risk his mom being exposed to whatever threat this was.

When he was only a few feet away, he veered sharply toward the driver's side door and banged the tire iron against the window. The figure inside jolted and fumbled for something in the front seat.

"Out of the car!" Marcus barked. "Now!"

The door cracked open, and a man stepped out slowly, with his hands raised. He recognized Khari immediately.

"You," Marcus pointed the tire iron toward his chest. "Why are you watching my mom's house?"

He smirked and shrugged like it wasn't a big deal. "Just keeping an eye on things."

"You think threatening her is gonna scare me off?" Marcus stepped closer. "Wrong."

Khari's smirk faltered. "Relax, man. It wasn't supposed to be personal. Just watching. Making sure you didn't get any more ideas about causing trouble."

Marcus felt rage bubble up in his chest. "You torched my shop. You hurt my cousin. You threatened my family." He tapped the tire iron against the guy's chest, just hard enough to make a point. "You're already out of chances."

He didn't move. "Look, I'm just following orders. Haynes said to keep tabs, that's all. Sit tight a couple days, nothing crazy."

"Where's he now?"

Khari didn't answer.

"Figures," Marcus said.

He weighed his options. Taking a swing at him would feel good, real good, but it wouldn't fix anything. What mattered was getting him gone and keeping his mom safe.

"You're gonna leave," he said as he stepped back. "You're gonna drive away, and you're gonna tell Haynes he's running out of people willing to do his dirty work."

Khari hesitated. "And if I don't?"

"You won't like what happens next."

For a few long seconds, neither one of them moved. Then, with a low curse, Khari climbed back into the sedan. The tires squealed slightly as he pulled away from the curb and drove away. Marcus stood there for a minute longer, breathing hard. He turned toward the house.

His mom's porch light was on. She was waiting for him inside, just like always. He loosened his grip on the tire iron and headed up the steps. He knocked lightly before letting himself in. Janelle was already standing in the hallway, arms crossed, and a worried look on her face.

"What happened?" she asked immediately.

Marcus set the tire iron down by the door and tried to force a small smile. "Handled it."

She gave him a look that said she wasn't buying it for a second. "Handled it how?"

He sighed and ran a hand over his face. "It was one of the guys from the warehouse. Same ones that jumped Tyson. Haynes sent him to keep tabs on you and to scare me. I made sure he left."

Her mouth tightened. "Watching me? Watching this house?" she repeated. "Marcus..."

"I know." His tone softened. He stepped closer, lowering his voice like he could protect her just with words. "I'm not gonna let anything happen to you, Ma. I promise."

"You shouldn't have to be out there fighting these people," she said, her voice thick. "You think just because you're grown now I don't still worry?"

"I know you do." Marcus reached for her hands, holding them gently. "But this... this isn't just about me. It's about Jordan too. They tried to bury him, Ma. Pretend he didn't matter. I couldn't let that happen."

Tears shone in her eyes, but she blinked them back stubbornly. "You're my son, Marcus. I can't lose you too."

"You won't." His voice was steady. "I'm being smart. Careful. I'm not out here looking to be some kind of hero. I'm just trying to fix what they broke."

She squeezed his hands tightly. "You're your father's son, you know that?"

"I'll take that as a compliment."

"It is. He never backed down from what was right either."

"I'll be around more," he promised. "Until this is done. You won't be alone."

"You better not be," she said, managing a smile that almost reached her eyes.

He helped her double-check the locks on the doors and windows. The two of them moving through the house in a quiet rhythm born from years of understanding each other without too many words.

Before he left that night, Marcus paused at the door and looked back at her.

"Love you, Ma."

She smiled softly, tired but proud. "Love you too, baby. Be careful."

He sat in his truck outside his mom's house for a few minutes, making sure everything stayed quiet. Satisfied, he pulled out his phone and shot Tyson a quick message:

Handled the watcher. Ma's okay. Staying close till this is over.

It only took a few seconds before Tyson responded.

Good. You need backup, you call me. I mean it.

Marcus shook his head, a small smirk pulling at his mouth despite everything. He tapped out a reply:

MARCUS:

Chill, my guy. Got it under control. But I'll let you know if I need you.

Another buzz almost immediately:

No "if." You WILL need me. Don't do something stupid alone.

Marcus leaned back in his seat, staring up at the stars peeking through the clouds. Family. They fought, argued, got on each other's nerves , but when it mattered, they showed up. He sent one last message before starting the engine:

Thanks, man. I got your back too.

Chapter 53

Marcus tossed a battered tarp off the last worktable in the burned-out remains of the shop, sending up a cloud of dust and ash. Tyson kicked at a charred board, his face tight with frustration.

"This place...man." He shook his head. "Feels like they're still winning."

Marcus wiped his hands on his jeans and looked at Tyson. "They're not," he said?. "Not if we finish what we started."

Tyson crossed his arms. "So what's the play, fam? 'Cause I'm telling you right now, they're getting desperate. If we don't move smart, they'll come at us harder than ever."

Marcus nodded. He'd been thinking the same thing ever since he confronted Khari at his mom's house. Enough was enough. No more hiding, no more waiting for Haynes to make the next move.

"I'm gonna do a live stream," Marcus said.

Tyson's eyebrows shot up. "A live stream? Like...right now?"

"Tomorrow night. At the train yard," Marcus said, already mentally walking through the plan. "Out in the open. Public enough that they can't make me disappear without it being obvious, but isolated enough that it's not chaos."

"So let me get this straight," Tyson said, crossing his arms. "You're not showing yourself at the yard. You're hiding. Streaming them while they meet."

"Exactly. No grand confrontation. No speeches. Just evidence. Raw, live, undeniable."

"You're sure about the location? What if they spot you?"

"Then make noise. Set off a distraction, something to draw them away. Then we scatter."

"Man, you really thought this through."

"Had to. After what they did to the shop, to Jordan...and now sitting outside my mom's place? Nah. This ends now. But smart. No hero moves."

Marcus parked his truck a block away from the train yard. This was the moment he planned to bring it all down. It had to explode into the open, unfiltered and undeniable. And the only way to do that was to go live.

Before stepping out, he opened his phone and started a live stream. The screen flashed for a moment before his face appeared, framed by the faint glow of the streetlights. The chat box at the bottom quickly began filling with viewers. He didn't say much, just enough to set the tone.

"This is Marcus Carter," he began. "Some of you are not aware but I am the guy who leaked the evidence about the gang and the cops. Tonight, I'm here to finish what I started. If you're watching this, it's because I need everyone to see what's really going on in Crest Ridge. No more threats. No more hiding. This ends tonight."

With that, he slipped the phone into his jacket pocket, the camera peeking out just enough to capture what was ahead. He moved silently as he approached the train yard. When he got nearer, he saw two cars pulling up at the same time. One was the familiar black sedan and the other was a silver sedan. He flattened himself against a wall, and let his phone record every second as Haynes stepped out of the silver sedan. He looked polished, his suit was immaculate, and his posture exuding authority. But Marcus knew the truth.

A SUV later arrived with some of Rook's gang emerged. He didn't recognize them, but their stance and demeanor made it clear they were dangerous. From his hiding spot, he could hear them, though their voices were faint. He crept closer, keeping his movements slow and deliberate.

"Things are getting out of hand," Haynes was saying. "That leak has people looking into places they shouldn't. Do you have any idea how hard it's been to keep the department off your back?"

"We've handled worse," the new gang leader replied gruffly. "The heat will blow over, just like it always does."

"Not this time," he snapped. "This guy, Carter, he's not backing down. And now he's got people thinking they can question me, question my authority."

Marcus's phone captured every word.

"You're the one who suggested keeping tabs on him," the gang leader replied. "Sending someone to his mom's house was your idea, not mine."

"That was a precaution," he shot back. "And it worked. He knows we're serious."

"Doesn't seem to be working if he's still digging into our business."

Marcus's breath caught in his throat. They were talking about his family like pawns in a game, and it made his blood boil. He adjusted the angle of his phone slightly. This time he wanted to make sure that the camera captured Haynes and the gang clearly. The chat on his live stream was blowing up, but he couldn't risk looking at it now. He could only imagine what people were saying. Shock, outrage, disbelief.

"What's the plan, then?"

"The plan is simple," Haynes said coldly. "Carter doesn't know how deep this goes. We keep applying pressure, and he'll back off. If he doesn't... well, accidents happen."

The gang leader smirked. "Just say the word."

Marcus knew he couldn't stay much longer. He'd gotten what he came for, and every second he stayed increased the risk of being caught. Slowly, he began to back away and moving toward the path that would lead him back to his truck.

His phone was still live capturing his every step. He was almost to safety when one of the gang members turned suddenly. He started looking near where he heard the sound.

"Did you hear that?"

Marcus stopped.

"Hear what?" another man asked.

"I thought I heard something," the first man said.

Marcus held his breath, pressing himself against the wall. His hand hovered near his pocket, ready to turn off the live stream if he had to.

"Probably just a rat," the gang leader said dismissively. "This place is crawling with them."

The man hesitated for a moment longer, then shrugged and turned back to the group. Marcus didn't wait. As soon as the coast was clear, he ran. By the time he reached his truck, he was trembling. Not with fear, but with adrenaline. He climbed into the driver's seat and saw that the live stream still running. He adjusted the camera to show his face.

"You saw it," he said, his voice steady despite the storm of emotions inside him. "You heard it. Your former deputy chief Jack Haynes is working with the gang. They've been threatening me, my family, and anyone else who gets in their way. But it ends now."

He paused, letting his words sink in.

"This isn't just about me. This is about Crest Ridge. This is about everyone who's ever been silenced, everyone who's ever been afraid to stand up to people like them. I'm not backing down, and I'm not letting them win."

He ended the live stream and sat in silence as he caught his breath. The world knew the truth now. There was no turning back.

Chapter 54

The next morning, the TV blared nonstop coverage of the livestream from the night before. Anchors speculating , experts weighing in, and politicians squirming under questions they couldn't dodge anymore. Marcus was on his couch, elbows on his knees, watching in silence. Tyson was too restless to sit.

"Bro, you really shook 'em up," he said. "They don't even know how deep this goes yet."

Marcus didn't answer right away. He was thinking about Jordan, about his mom, about Haynes and whatever moves he'd try next. Victory wasn't safe until the right people were behind bars. His phone buzzed against the coffee table, rattling loud in the heavy quiet. He snatched it up.

Mr. Miller.

He answered immediately. "Yeah?"

Miller's voice came through sharp but energized, almost like he couldn't believe the words he was about to say.

"Mr. Carter, listen carefully. I need you to get down to the courthouse this afternoon."

He stood up. "What's going on?"

"The DA's office reviewed the footage from last night , your livestream, along with the other evidence you collected. They're reopening Jordan's case officially. He's going to be released today."

Marcus couldn't believe it. He was feeling like the air had been knocked out of him. He turned to Tyson, but was only able to mouthed "Jordan's free."

"Say that again?" He said, coming closer, seeing the look on Marcus's face.

Instead, Marcus put the call on speakerphone.

"Can you repeat that for my cousin to hear? He's the one who's been helping me."

"Of course and great work young man. Jordan's release paperwork is being pushed through. The DA's office is making a public statement after lunch. I want you at the courthouse around one o'clock."

Marcus closed his eyes and exhaled. The weight of months of fear, guilt, and anger crashed into him all at once.

Jordan was coming home.

"Yeah," he said finally. "We'll be there."

Miller lowered his voice. "Marcus...you did good. But stay sharp. Haynes and whoever's left from his crew aren't gonna take this loss quietly."

"I know," he said. "We'll be ready."

They hung up. Tyson grabbed his shoulder, grinning wide.

"Man! My cousin's coming home!" he whooped, pulling him into a quick, hard hug before pulling back and punching the air. "I told you, fam! I told you we'd get him out!"

Marcus smiled, but it was a cautious smile. There was still a long road ahead. They hadn't seen the last of Haynes, not by a long shot. But today was for Jordan. For family. He grabbed his jacket, and looked back at the TV one more time where the news scrolled another headline:

"Corruption Scandal Shakes Crest Ridge: Officials Scramble as Public Demands Justice."

He turned the TV off. "Let's get ready. We got a stop to make first."

Tyson already knew where they were headed by the second turn.

"You sure you don't wanna call her first?" He asked.

Marcus shook his head. "Nah. Gotta tell her in person. After everything... she deserves that."

Tyson didn't argue. He just nodded and leaned back in the seat, tapping his fingers lightly against the door.

They pulled onto his mom's street a few minutes later. There was something in the air. They hadn't seen so many neighbors outside before the livestream, before the bombshell news reports. They knew something big was happening. Crest Ridge wasn't the same anymore, and maybe it never would be.

Marcus parked at the curb, cutting the engine. He sat there for a second, staring at his mom's house. It had always been a safe place, but now he wondered if it ever really had been, or if they'd just been lucky for a while.

"You good?" Tyson asked.

Marcus nodded once and pushed open the door. "Come on."

They walked up the short driveway together. Marcus raised his hand and knocked a rhythmic tap they all knew by heart.

A few seconds later, his mom opened the door. Her brown locs were tied up in a scarf, and she had a dish towel thrown over one shoulder, like she'd been in the middle of cleaning. But the moment she saw them, her face shifted, worry flickering deep in her eyes.

"Marcus? Tyson? Everything okay?"

He smiled. A real smile, the first one in what felt like forever.

"Better than okay, Ma," he said. "Jordan's case is being vacated. They're letting him go. Today."

For a second, she just stared at him, like her brain couldn't quite catch up. Then her hand flew up to cover her mouth, and her knees buckled slightly. Tyson reached out instinctively, steadying her.

She let out a shaky breath, her eyes shining. "Are you serious? Jordan's—" she broke off, her voice trembling. "He's coming home?"

"He's coming home, Ma. The DA's office is making a statement this afternoon. Miller just called."

Tears welled up in her eyes, and she pulled them both into a fierce hug. "My baby's coming home," she whispered. "Thank you. Thank you, God."

Tyson smiled too. "Told you we had a plan," he said.

She let them go finally, wiping her eyes with the corner of the dish towel. "I need a minute," she said, half-laughing, half-crying. "I gotta pull myself together. I can't meet my son lookin' like a mess."

Marcus chuckled under his breath. "You look fine, Ma."

She shook her head, still wiping at her cheeks. "No, no. Y'all go ahead. I'll meet you there."

"You sure?" He asked. "We can wait."

She waved him off, her hands trembling slightly but her voice firm. "Go. I need to change and grab something. I'll be right behind you."

Marcus hesitated for half a second longer, but he saw the determination in her eyes. The same fire he'd inherited. He nodded.

"Alright. We'll see you there."

She stepped forward and smoothed his jacket, like she used to when he was a kid getting ready for school. Then she turned to Tyson and did the same, swatting his hand away playfully when he tried to dodge it.

"You boys be careful," she said, her voice low and serious again. "You hear me?"

"We will," Marcus promised.

They walked back to the truck. Marcus glancing back once to see her standing there on the porch, her hand resting lightly on the doorframe, watching them.

"Man," Tyson said as they climbed in. "Feels like we're finally getting a win, huh?"

Marcus glanced at him and nodded. "Feels like it. Just hope it holds."

He started the engine and pulled away from the curb. The drive downtown was quick but tense. Tyson kept tapping his fingers against his knee as the restless energy poured off him. Marcus kept his focus locked on the road ahead.

The city looked different today. Or maybe he just saw it differently. People were gathered on sidewalks, huddled near corner stores and bus stops, their faces turned toward their phones. Some had little radios cradled to their ears. Whispers filled the air like static. Everyone was waiting, wondering what would happen next.

When they pulled up near the courthouse, Marcus slowed the truck. There was already a crowd gathering. Reporters with cameras, people holding up their phones, some even waving homemade signs. A low buzz of excitement and tension hung heavy in the air.

Tyson looked out the window.

"Looks like half the city showed up," he said.

Marcus parked a block away, not wanting to get boxed in by the growing crowd. They climbed out, and Tyson slapped him lightly on the back.

"You ready for this?"

Marcus adjusted his jacket, feeling the weight of everything settle on his shoulders. The fear, the hope, the anger, the relief. He thought about Jordan, about his mom, about all the nights they'd spent wondering if this day would ever come.

"Yeah," he said. His voice was steady. Sure. "Let's bring him home."

Chapter 55

As they pushed through the gathering crowd, the buzz of conversation swelled around them. Camera flashes lit up like small explosions. Reporters clustered near the courthouse steps, holding microphones and yelling rapid-fire questions into the thick, humid air.

"Is it true Jordan Carter is being released today?"

"Does this mean more arrests are coming?"

"Who leaked the footage? Was it someone inside the department?"

Marcus kept his head down. Tyson walked close beside him, scanning the faces around them, alert for any trouble. The last thing they needed was someone recognizing them and starting something before Jordan was even free. Still, some in the crowd seemed to notice. A few people nudged each other, whispering Marcus's name. He caught snatches of their conversation —

"That's the guy, right?"

"The one who took them down?"

"Yeah, that's him. Marcus Carter."

A woman holding a homemade sign caught his eye. In bold black letters it read:

Justice for Jordan. Justice for All.

She smiled at him, a small, tight smile, and nodded once. He nodded back. They reached the bottom of the courthouse steps just as Mr. Miller appeared at the top, With him was a few aides and a couple of other lawyers from his office. He spotted Marcus and Tyson immediately and motioned them closer with a quick wave. Marcus felt his mom's hand on his arm before he saw her.

"I'm here, baby," she said.

He turned and hugged her. She pulled back after a second, wiping at her eyes and straightening her shoulders like she was preparing for battle.

"No tears yet," she said, her mouth twitching into a small, proud smile. "We save that for when he walks out those doors."

Marcus smiled too.

"We're almost there, Ma," he said.

The doors to the courthouse creaked open. A hush fell over the crowd. It was the District Attorney himself . A tall, gray-haired man named Kenneth Lawson. His face was grim but resolute as he stepped up to the podium.

"Good afternoon. Over the past few weeks, my office has received substantial evidence indicating a deeply troubling pattern of corruption, misconduct, and criminal collusion involving members of the Crest Ridge Police Department and organized crime elements."

Murmurs rippled through the crowd. Lawson continued, laying out how Marcus's evidence, though he never mentioned him by name , had forced a full review of Jordan's case and several others. He emphasized that swift action was being taken to root out any additional corruption, and that more charges would be forthcoming.

Marcus barely heard the rest. His heart pounded in his ears when Lawson finally said:

"Effective immediately, Jordan Carter's conviction is vacated. He will be released today."

Behind him, two officers led Jordan through the doors. Marcus's heart nearly stopped. He was thinner than Marcus remembered. But his eyes, his eyes were clear. Awake. Still fighting. The crowd erupted into cheers. Some people clapped. Others shouted his name. A few wept openly.

Marcus barely registered any of it. All he could see was his brother free walking forward with slow, disbelieving steps. Jordan scanned the crowd until his eyes locked with Marcus's. For a moment, neither of them moved. The noise of the world faded into nothing. Then Jordan smiled.

Marcus was moving before he even realized it. He pushed through the final few feet separating them, and pulled his brother into a fierce hug. Jordan's arms wrapped around him just as tightly, the two of them holding on like they might never let go.

"You did it," Jordan whispered hoarsely into his ear. "You really did it."

Marcus pulled back just enough to look at him, both of them blinking hard fighting back tears.

"We did it," Marcus said. "You held on. You didn't let them break you."

Their mom joined them, pulling both of them into a messy, tearful embrace. Tyson hovered nearby, smiling wide and clapping Jordan on the back as soon as he got free.

"You scared the hell outta us, man," he said, grinning. "Don't ever do that again."

Jordan laughed.

"No promises," he said. "But I'll try."

The District Attorney's speech continued behind them, promising full investigations, transparency, and sweeping changes to how cases were handled. Cameras caught every moment. But Marcus barely heard any of it. This moment, this reunion, was all he cared about.

Tyson gave Jordan a wide grin and bumped fists with him. "Told you we'd get you outta there, bro."

Jordan shook his head, overwhelmed. "I still can't believe it. I woke up thinking it was just another day... then they tell me the DA's dropping everything, that they're clearing my name..." He trailed off, his throat working hard to keep the emotions down.

Marcus clapped him on the shoulder.

"You got a second chance. We all do."

They left the courthouse together, moving as a tight knot of family out into the bright afternoon. A few reporters shouted questions at them, cameras flashing, but Marcus just ignored them. His focus was on Jordan and shielding him from the chaos. Once they were safely by the truck, Jordan turned to him, his voice low and serious.

"How bad is it, man? I know... I know you didn't just stumble on all this by accident."

Marcus gave a grim smile. "Let's just say that it's bad. Real bad. And it ain't over yet."

Jordan nodded slowly, accepting that truth. "But we're together now," he said. "We'll face it together."

Marcus squeezed the back of his brother's neck. He was happy to have him there. Real, alive, home.

"Yeah," Marcus said. "Together."

He opened the truck door and Jordan climb in. Tyson hopped into the passenger seat, already arguing about who was buying dinner. Their mom stood there still dabbing at her eyes with a tissue but smiling now. A real, full smile that Marcus hadn't seen in a long time. As he pulled away from the courthouse, he allowed himself a rare moment to breathe. To believe.

Chapter 56

Marcus leaned back, resting his head against the worn fabric of the couch. The events of the past few months replayed in his mind like a broken record and the revelation of just how deep the corruption ran in Crest Ridge. Every move he'd made felt like a gamble with someone else's life on the line. And now, Jordan was free. He looked at the USB and wondered how that little thing could bring down a lot of people.

The sound of the front door opening jolted him from his thoughts. Tyson stepped in, kicking off his sneakers and tossing his keys onto the counter.

"You're still up?" Tyson asked, pulling a bottle of water from the fridge.

Marcus nodded, not looking up. "Couldn't sleep."

Tyson plopped down in the armchair across from him, cracking open the bottle. "You've been sitting here all night, haven't you?"

"Pretty much." Marcus set the USB down on the coffee table, watching it spin slightly before it came to rest.

Tyson took a sip of water, eyeing his cousin carefully. "What's on your mind?"

"Everything," Marcus admitted. He gestured toward the USB. "This little thing... it's done a lot. Exposed the truth. Got Jordan out. But it also cost me."

Tyson leaned forward, resting his elbows on his knees. "Jordan?"

"Yeah," Marcus said, his voice heavy. "He blames me. I get it. I pushed too hard. I put him and everyone else in danger. Now he wants space, and I don't know if we'll ever be the same."

Tyson was quiet for a moment. "You did what you had to do. If you hadn't, he'd still be locked up right now."

"I know," Marcus said. "But it doesn't change how it feels."

Tyson leaned back in the chair, crossing his arms. "You ever think about what would've happened if you hadn't done anything? If you'd just let it go?"

"All the time," he admitted. "I think about it every day. But then I remember what we were up against. If I hadn't fought back, they'd still be out there, running this town. More people would've been hurt, or worse. I couldn't live with that."

"So you did what you thought was right."

"Yeah," he said. "But doing the right thing doesn't always feel good. I keep asking myself... was it worth it?"

"It was. You saved me, Marcus. You got Jordan out. You exposed the people who were ruining this town. That has to count for something."

"It counts. But it came at a cost. I lost Jordan, at least for now. And Ma's still shaken up from what happened. She won't say it, but I know she's scared."

Tyson shifted uncomfortably. "We're all a little scared. But we're still here. And that's because of you."

Marcus looked at his younger cousin, seeing the determination in his eyes. Tyson had been through hell too. Kidnapped , threatened, and used as leverage. Yet here he was, strong and unwavering.

"You've grown up a lot through all this," Marcus said quietly.

Tyson shrugged. "Had to. You've been taking on the weight of the world by yourself. Someone had to have your back."

"I appreciate that. I really do."

"Look, I know this has been hard. But you can't keep carrying all of this by yourself. You're not Superman. You're just a guy trying to do the right thing. And that's enough."

Marcus stared at him for a moment. "You're smarter than I give you credit for, kid."

"Damn right I am," Tyson said with a grin.

After Tyson went to bed, Marcus stayed on the couch, staring at the USB drive again. He thought about all the people who had been hurt because of the corruption. Jordan. The delivery driver. Countless others whose lives had been torn apart.

He also thought about the people who had stood by him. Sam, Tyson, Elena Chavez, Mr. Miller. They had believed in him when he wasn't sure he believed in himself. Reaching for his phone, he scrolled through the messages he'd received since the live stream. Dozens of people had reached out. Some to thank him, others to share their own stories of injustice.

One message stood out. It was from a woman whose brother had been wrongfully convicted in a neighboring county. She thanked Marcus for giving her hope that the system could be challenged. He stared at the message for a long time before replying:

"Keep fighting. Don't give up. Change starts with us."

Marcus stood and walked to the window, looking out at the quiet street. The town was different now. People were talking about the corruption, demanding accountability. It wasn't the end, but it was a start.

He thought about Jordan, wondering where he was and if he was okay. Marcus hoped that one day, his brother would understand why he had done what he did. For now, all he could do was move forward.

"I can't fix everything," he said quietly to himself. "But I can be better. For them. For this town."

The weight of the past few months wasn't gone, but it felt lighter somehow. He wasn't alone in this fight anymore.

Chapter 57

The smell of frying chicken and sweet cornbread filled the small kitchen, warm and comforting. Laughter floated in the air, mingling with the clinking of plates and the low hum of music from a Bluetooth speaker perched on the counter.

Marcus leaned against the wall for a moment, taking it all in. His mom moved around the kitchen with a lightness he hadn't seen in a long time as she sung along to the music. Tyson lounged on the couch, balancing a plate on his knees, teasing Jordan about how he was "getting soft" after all that time locked up.

Jordan laughed. A real, deep laugh that made Marcus's chest ache in the best way.

The house was packed tighter than usual. Neighbors, family friends, even people Marcus barely knew had shown up to celebrate. They brought casseroles, sodas, pies, anything they could. Crest Ridge might've been battered, but today, it was standing together.

Marcus pushed off the wall and moved toward the door, needing a little air. He stepped out onto the small porch, breathing in the crisp evening breeze. He wasn't alone for long. Footsteps creaked behind him, and he turned to see Myia approaching, her arms crossed tightly over her chest. She looked different tonight. tired, guarded, but there was something softer in her eyes too.

"I owe you an apology," she said, her voice low but steady.

Marcus blinked. He hadn't expected that, not from her.

"You don't have to—" he started, but she cut him off with a small shake of her head.

"No. I do." She stepped closer, wrapping her arms around herself like she was bracing against the wind. "I didn't believe in you. Not really. I thought you were just... chasing something you couldn't catch. Stirring up trouble that was only going to make things worse for all of us."

Marcus didn't respond. He let her get it out.

"And when Ty got dragged into it..." She exhaled sharply, glancing back toward the house where his laughter echoed faintly. "I was furious. I'm still not happy about that part."

"I get it," he said quietly. And he did. Tyson had always been her soft spot. The one she worried about, the one she protected like a lioness. Seeing him caught up in all this had scared her, and scared people didn't always react kindly.

"But..." Myia looked up at him again, something raw and honest flickering across her face. "You were right. About all of it. You didn't just help Jordan. You helped the whole damn town."

Marcus swallowed hard against the lump rising in his throat.

"I didn't do it alone," he said. "Tyson helped. So did others. Even you, in your own way."

She gave a small, sad laugh. "Yeah, well. I wish I could say I helped more." She shifted. "You have every right to be mad at me."

"I'm not mad," Marcus said after a moment. "I'm just... tired. Tired of fighting with people I care about when there's already so much coming at us from outside."

They stood there for a long moment, the weight of everything that had happened hanging between them.

"I'm proud of you," Myia said finally, her voice thick with emotion. "I don't think I ever told you that before. But I am. I'm proud of what you did."

Marcus's throat tightened. He nodded once, afraid if he tried to speak, he might lose it. Inside the house, someone called Jordan's name, and a fresh wave of laughter broke out. The sound pulled Marcus and Myia back to the present.

"We should get back in there," Myia said, wiping at her eyes quickly. "Before Tyson eats all the food."

Marcus chuckled. "Yeah. That sounds about right."

They headed inside together.

The living room was even more crowded now, people squeezed in wherever they could find space. Jordan sat at the center of it all, accepting hugs, claps on the back, and good-natured teasing with a grin that didn't seem to leave his face. Their mom stood by the kitchen doorway, her eyes shining as she watched her sons, her family, become whole again.

Marcus made his way to the couch where Tyson was holding court with a group of younger guys from the neighborhood. He was telling an exaggerated version of the livestream that had exposed Haynes.

"...And then Marcus is ducking behind crates like some kind of action hero," he said, making the crowd laugh. "I'm over here trying not to breathe too loud!"

Marcus rolled his eyes but couldn't help smiling.

"Don't let him fool you," he said, cutting in. "Tyson almost tripped over a rat the size of a football."

The group roared with laughter, Tyson included, and the tension that had knotted inside Marcus for months finally loosened.

As the night wore on, the celebration mellowed into something softer — quieter conversations, old music playing low in the background, people trading stories about Jordan, about Crest Ridge, about the future. Marcus sat back, plate in hand, watching it all. He caught his mom's eye from across the room. She smiled and mouthed the words thank you.

Marcus nodded, his heart full. Tonight wasn't the end. He knew that. There were still people out there who would want revenge. There were still cracks in the system that needed to be exposed. But tonight was theirs. Tonight, they had won something real.

The house had finally gone quiet. Empty plates and crumpled napkins littered the tables. A few half-empty soda bottles sat forgotten on the counter. Marcus stood by the kitchen sink, rinsing a glass, when he heard soft footsteps behind him. He turned to see

Jordan standing there, looking a little awkward, like he didn't quite know what to do with himself now that the noise and celebration had faded.

Marcus set the glass down and grabbed a towel, drying his hands. "Couldn't sleep?" he asked.

Jordan shrugged, stuffing his hands into the pockets of the hoodie someone had given him earlier. It was a little too big, the sleeves swallowing his hands, but he didn't seem to care.

"Too quiet," Jordan said. "After being locked up for so long...quiet feels louder, you know?"

Marcus nodded, understanding more than he could say.

"Come on," he said, jerking his chin toward the porch. "Let's get some air."

They stepped outside into the cool night. Marcus dropped onto the porch steps, and he sat beside him. For a while, they didn't talk. They just sat, listening to the creak of the old house settling and the distant hum of a passing car. Finally, Jordan broke the silence.

"I thought I was never getting out," he said, voice low and raw. "After everything that happened...I thought that was it. That they'd leave me to rot."

Marcus swallowed hard. He had thought the same thing more times than he could admit.

"I wasn't gonna let that happen," Marcus said. "Not while I was still breathing."

Jordan glanced at him, studying his face like he was seeing him for the first time.

"You really went to war for me," he said quietly.

"Wasn't just for you. It was for all of us. You, Mom, Tyson...this whole damn town. They needed someone to pull the curtain back."

Jordan leaned forward, resting his elbows on his knees.

"I heard some of it, you know. In there. Guards talking. Other inmates whispering. People on the outside were saying your name. Saying you were stirring up trouble."

"Yeah," Marcus said dryly. "Stirred up a hell of a mess."

Jordan gave a small laugh, but it faded quickly. His hands fidgeted, picking at a loose thread on his sleeve.

"You ever scared?" he asked suddenly.

Marcus turned to look at him. "All the time," he said. "Every day. Especially when it started getting real. When people started disappearing, when Tyson was kidnapped and don't get me started on that. When Mom's house got watched. When they burned down the shop."

Jordan sucked in a breath, his eyes widening slightly. "They burned down the shop?"

"Yeah. Lost everything. But it's just stuff. Stuff can be replaced."

Jordan was quiet for a long time, wrestling with something. Finally, he said, "I feel guilty."

"Guilty? For what?"

"For all of it. You almost got yourself killed trying to save me." Jordan's voice cracked a little. "And Mom... she's been through enough. And Tyson...he shouldn't have had to—"

"Hey." Marcus interrupted. "Listen to me. None of this is your fault, Jordan. You didn't ask for any of it. You didn't deserve what happened to you."

Jordan shook his head, staring out into the dark. "I kept thinking...if I had just fought back harder... if I had just been smarter..."

"No. This system was built to crush you. To crush people like us. You surviving it doesn't make you weak. It makes you stronger than they'll ever be."

Jordan's throat worked as he tried to swallow the emotion rising in him.

"I'm scared, Marcus," he admitted in a hoarse whisper. "I don't know how to be...out here anymore. I don't know who I am now."

Marcus's heart broke a little at those words. He thought about all the nights he had lain awake, picturing his brother locked away, fading into someone he didn't recognize.

"You're still you," he said. "It's gonna take time, yeah. It's not gonna be easy. But you're not alone. We're here. Mom's here. Tyson's here. Hell, even Myia's coming around."

Jordan gave a weak chuckle. "She still look like she wants to kill you half the time."

Marcus laughed. "Yeah, but now she hugs me after she yells at me, so...progress."

Jordan sat back, looking up at the stars peeking through the thin clouds. "What now?" he asked.

Marcus thought about it. About everything they had lost, everything they had fought for. About the fight still ahead.

"Now we rebuild," he answered. "We help clean up the mess. We make sure they don't bury the truth again. And you... you get your life back."

Jordan shook his head slowly. "Feels like starting from nothing."

Marcus nudged him. "Starting from nothing just means you can build whatever you want."

They sat there a while longer, side by side, not saying anything more.

Finally, Jordan stood and stretched. "I should get some sleep. Big day tomorrow, right?"

Marcus rose too. "Yeah. Big day."

Jordan hesitated at the door.

"Thanks, bro," he said, voice thick with emotion.

Marcus clapped him on the back. "Always."

As they went back inside, Marcus caught a glimpse of his own reflection in the darkened window. Tired. Battered. Scarred. But alive.

Chapter 58

Jordan rubbed the sleep from his eyes, still adjusting to waking up somewhere that wasn't behind bars. He sat up slowly on his bed in his old room. The smell of bacon and coffee drifted from the kitchen. For a split second, he tensed, waiting for the sound of heavy boots or keys rattling against metal bars, but all he heard was laughter. Real laughter.

He exhaled shakily and ran a hand over his face. He remembered that he as home. Fresh clothes hugged his frame. A simple T-shirt and jeans that actually fit. No ill-sized prison uniforms, no cold concrete floors. Just warmth. Just family.

The door to his room swung open, and in walked Ellis. Jordan froze for a second, his brain struggling to catch up. He had shot up like a weed while he was away. He was nearly eye-level with Jordan now, his shoulders broader, his steps more confident.

"Dang, kid," he said, a grin breaking over his face. "You been eating magic beans or something?"

Ellis laughed and grabbed Jordan in a tight hug that knocked him back onto the bed. "You're finally home, bro!"

Jordan hugged him fiercely, feeling the way Ellis's frame had filled out. "Man, you're taller than me now. I'm supposed to be the big brother."

Ellis stepped back and puffed out his chest playfully. "You're still older. Just not bigger." He shot Marcus a smug look. "And guess who wins in one-on-one now?"

Marcus laughed as he leaned against the doorway. "He's been talking trash for weeks, waiting for you to come home."

Before Jordan could answer, he heard another voice from the kitchen.

"Well, if it ain't Sleeping Beauty finally awake."

Darren walked in, wiping his hands on a towel, his familiar easy smile making Jordan's chest tighten. He hadn't seen his dad in person in what felt like forever. Only quick, supervised visits behind glass, never like this.

"Dad," Jordan breathed.

His father crossed the room in two long strides and clapped a hand on Jordan's shoulder. "Proud of you, son. Proud you made it out." His voice cracked slightly at the end, and he cleared his throat.

Before Jordan could say anything else, a heavier, slower set of footsteps entered the room.

Granddad.

The old man shuffled in with his cane, but his eyes were sharp and full of life. He wore his usual faded jeans and a ball cap that read World's Best Dad. He didn't say much at first, just looked Jordan up and down like he was sizing him up for a fight. Then, without warning, he pulled him into a one-armed hug, nearly crushing him.

"Tougher than prison walls, huh?" Granddad said gruffly. "Good. You'll need to be."

Jordan smiled against his granddad's chest. "It's good to see you, Granddad."

"Better be good. We got work to do." He finally let him go and nodded toward the kitchen. "Come on. Your mom's got enough food in there to feed an army."

Jordan followed, the weight in his chest easing with every step. Marcus walked beside him, clapping him on the back.

At the table, plates were already stacked high. Pancakes, scrambled eggs, bacon, biscuits, and fresh fruit. Their mom, her brown locs pulled up into a bun, was bustling around. She stopped and beamed when she saw Jordan walking toward her.

"Sit down, baby," she said, wiping her hands. "You need a real meal."

Jordan slid into a chair, still feeling slightly surreal. Ellis plopped down next to him, already reaching for the bacon. Their dad poured coffee, humming to himself. Granddad settled in with a grunt, claiming the seat with the best view of the kitchen.

Jordan just sat there, taking it all in. No concrete walls. No bars. No chains. Just his family. Laughing, joking, talking over each other, arguing about who made the best pancakes.

His chest ached with gratitude and something harder, resolve. He wasn't just going to survive. He was going to live. Marcus slid a plate across the table to him, stacked high with food. He gave Jordan a smile that was equal parts pride and relief.

"Eat," he said. "You're gonna need your strength."

He picked up his fork, laughing quietly when Ellis bumped his shoulder trying to grab a biscuit.

Across the table, Granddad was already lecturing their dad about overcooking the bacon. Their mom rolled her eyes and poured another round of coffee. Marcus was texting someone, probably Myia, without even looking at his plate.

Jordan chuckled and took a bite, humming in appreciation. "I forgot how good real food tastes," he mumbled around a mouthful of biscuit.

Janelle watched him with misty eyes, her hand lightly resting over his on the table. She hadn't let him out of her sight since he got home. "So," she said gently, "what's next, baby?"

Jordan looked up, startled by the question. "I don't know," he admitted. "I hadn't thought that far ahead."

Tyson leaned back in his chair, tossing an apple up and catching it lazily. "Well, you got options now," he said. "You're not trapped anymore."

Marcus nodded. "Whatever you want to do, we'll back you."

Jordan put his biscuit down, suddenly serious. "I don't even know where to start. I mean...I don't have a job. Don't even know if anyone will hire me with everything that happened."

Janelle squeezed his hand. "We'll figure it out," she said. "Maybe go back to school if you want. Or get a trade. You're smart, Jordan. Smarter than you give yourself credit for."

"What about the shop?" he asked, glancing between Marcus and Tyson. "I know it burned down."

"We'll rebuild. Insurance might cover part of it. Even if it doesn't... we'll figure it out."

Tyson tossed the apple one more time and caught it with a grin. "Been thinking about starting something new anyway. Maybe a community garage. Teach kids how to fix up cars. Keep them outta trouble."

Jordan's eyes lit up a little at that. "For real?"

Tyson nodded. "For real. You'd be good at it too. Always were good with your hands."

Jordan smiled. "That sounds...cool," he said. "Really cool."

Janelle stood, moving around the table to kiss Jordan's forehead. "No matter what you decide, you're not alone," she said softly. "We're proud of you. You hear me? Proud."

Jordan blinked rapidly and nodded, unable to speak for a moment.

Marcus clapped him on the back. "And when you're ready...maybe you can help us hold Haynes and the rest of those bastards accountable. They're not done trying to cover their tracks."

Jordan's expression hardened, a glimmer of his old fire coming back. "Yeah," he said. "I'd like that.

The kitchen door creaked open, and Myia peeked in, a shy smile on her face "Am I late?" she asked.

Marcus stood and waved her inside. "Nah, just in time."

She crossed the kitchen, leaning down to hug Jordan tightly. "Welcome home," she whispered.

Jordan hugged her back, looking more at ease than he had all morning. Myia pulled away and gave Marcus a look that said we'll talk later, but there was no heat behind it this time. Jordan grinned, looking around the table at all of them. It was just breakfast. But it felt like the start of something bigger. Something better.

Marcus sat at the back of what remained of his shop. Yet despite the damage, Marcus could almost see the place as it had been before, alive with energy, filled with the hum of conversations, and the sound of tools in motion. He could picture it, but for now, it was a distant memory.

Tyson was pacing near the doorway dragging a pen across a notepad. He had been quiet for the past few minutes, but Marcus could tell his mind was racing. He had always been one to get straight to the point when something needed doing, but today, there was a certain weight to the silence between them.

"We can start with the basics," Tyson said, breaking the stillness. He was looking at a sketch he had quickly scribbled on his pad, a rough layout of what the shop could look like after it was rebuilt. "We'll need a contractor, supplies—probably a small loan to cover the costs. We can make this work, Marcus."

Marcus's gaze drifted to the charred remnants of his shop's back counter. His hand subconsciously traced the outline of the tools still scattered on the floor, as if the action could somehow restore the business that had once meant everything to him. The shop had been his life, but it had also been a place of safety, a place that kept him grounded. And now, it was a symbol of the battle he'd just fought, the fire that had destroyed so much but hadn't burned him out.

"We'll make it work, all right," Marcus said with determination. "But this time, we'll do it right."

Tyson shot him a sideways glance, clearly catching the edge in his voice. "What's that mean?"

Marcus paused. The sun was shining brightly now, but Marcus had seen enough darkness in the last few months to know that the light never lasted forever. He could rebuild the shop, sure. He could put everything back together. But what would that mean if the people of Crest Ridge were still trapped in a cycle of corruption and fear?

He looked at Tyson. "I'm not just thinking about the shop, Ty. I'm thinking about the people here. People who don't have a voice. People who need help, but don't know where to turn."

Tyson raised an eyebrow. "What do you mean?"

Marcus exhaled slowly. He crossed the room to the window. Outside, the city of Crest Ridge spread out before him. He saw dilapidated buildings, crumbling infrastructure, and a handful of people moving through the streets like ghosts. The very air felt heavy with unspoken problems, with a kind of silence that hung over the people who lived here. And in the distance, he could almost hear the echo of the unrest that had been brewing for years.

"I've been thinking about all the people who've been hurt," Marcus said, his voice taking on a deeper tone. "The ones who got caught up in the mess. People who don't have the resources or the connections to fight back. I've spent so much time looking for answers for Jordan, for my family. I don't want to stop there. There's so much more I can do."

"So, you're saying you want to keep going, be some kind of detective for the people in Crest Ridge?"

Marcus nodded. He turned to face Tyson, meeting his eyes. "Yeah. I've already done it once. Exposed the corruption. I'm good at this, Ty. And people need someone who knows how to dig deep, how to follow the trail to the truth. I've got the skills, the knowledge. I know I could do more."

"I get it. You want to make a real difference. But that's a hell of a commitment, Marcus. You know how dangerous it can get. It's not just about uncovering corruption. It's about being in the crosshairs once you've done it."

"I know," Marcus said. "I've been there. But I can't just walk away from this. It's not just about me anymore. It's about this city."

"Well, I can't argue with you there. You're right about one thing. This place needs someone who can stand up for it. But what are you thinking? How do you want to go about it?"

Marcus's mind began to race as he thought about how to structure his plan. He'd spent years working with law enforcement, learning the ropes, following cases, and understanding the system's weaknesses. The knowledge was there, but this time, it wouldn't be about the badge or the politics. This time, it would be about helping people who had no one else to turn to.

"We start small," Marcus said, a sense of purpose settling in his chest. "I'll take on cases as they come. Investigate when someone's been wronged, dig into the system and expose the people who are behind it. But I need to be careful this time. We can't go at it like we did before. We need to keep a low profile."

"And I'll help however I can. You know that, right? But I want to make sure we're on the same page. You're not just throwing yourself back into the fire, are you?"

"That's kind of what I do. But this time, we're doing it smart."

Marcus knew that this wasn't just about opening up a new chapter in his life. It was about giving others the opportunity to fight back and to seek justice when it seemed impossible. He had the skills, the experience, and now, a mission.

"I'm in," Tyson said, breaking the silence. "Whatever it takes, I'm in."

Marcus smiled, feeling a sense of resolve settle in him. The road ahead wouldn't be easy, and there would be setbacks along the way, but it felt like the right thing to do. Rebuilding the shop was only part of the bigger picture. The real work lay ahead. Helping those who had been forgotten by the system and giving them a fighting chance. This wasn't just the end of the past. It was the beginning of something new.

Chapter 59

Six months had passed since the fire. The days of uncertainty and destruction felt distant now, replaced by a sense of purpose that had taken root in Marcus's heart. The shop, once reduced to ash and memories, had been rebuilt, stronger, more vibrant, and even more connected to the community than before. Thanks to the help of friends, neighbors, and people who had once been customers, the space was alive with energy. Every corner of the shop was filled with laughter, tools clinking against metal, and the hum of busy hands.

The front of the shop gleamed under the midday sun. The windows were sparkled clean and the new sign hung proudly above the entrance: *Marcus's Auto & Community Garage*. It was a place where people didn't just bring their cars. They brought their stories, their struggles, and their dreams. The walls were adorned with photos of the people who had helped rebuild, a testament to what could be accomplished when a community came together.

Inside, the shop was bustling. People worked in pairs, heads bent over their cars, learning the tricks of the trade under Marcus's watchful eye. There were weekly classes, a mix of hands-on car repair lessons, and community-building workshops where he taught not just skills, but the importance of self-reliance and empowerment. It was exactly the kind of place he had always dreamed of; where knowledge was shared freely, and people walked away with a sense of pride and ownership.

Tyson stood beside him at the counter. He had become not just a business partner, but a trusted ally in all of Marcus's endeavors. His easygoing attitude balanced Marcus's seriousness, and together, they had created a solid foundation for the business. There had been a few bumps along the way, delays in deliveries, unforeseen repairs, but nothing had stopped them. The shop was growing, and business was better than it had been in years.

Marcus glanced around at the busy scene. A few of the regulars were gathering around the workbenches and exchanging tips on restoring old car models. A young woman was under a car, trying to figure out how to replace the brake pads, while a group of teenagers watched her, eager to learn. Laughter echoed in the back, where a group of kids were working with some of the older men to fix up an old van.

"Things are looking good," Tyson said, watching the activity around them. "I didn't think we'd be back on our feet this quickly."

Marcus nodded, but his mind wasn't fully on the conversation. His thoughts were drifting to the future. What next? The shop was running smoothly, the community was thriving, and he was making a real difference in the lives of the people here. But he couldn't shake the feeling that there was more work to be done. The city was still plagued by corruption, and even though Haynes had been brought down, the undercurrents of the system still ran deep.

Suddenly, the door opened, and a man stepped inside. He was tall, dressed in a dark jacket and wearing a wide-brimmed hat that obscured most of his features. His presence immediately caught Marcus's attention. There was something about the way he carried himself that hinted at secrecy, like a man who didn't want to be noticed but couldn't quite help but make an impression.

Tyson straightened up, his gaze flicking to Marcus. "You know him?"

He shook his head. "Never seen him before."

The man approached the counter. He gave a small nod of acknowledgment, and his voice was low but steady when he spoke. "Marcus Carter?"

"Who's asking?" Marcus replied, crossing his arms.

The man extended a hand. "Name's Victor Harris. I need your help."

Marcus didn't shake his hand. Instead, he studied him carefully. The name sounded vaguely familiar, but he couldn't place it. "Now is not the time. There are children here, if you didn't notice."

"I've been watching you, Carter. You've stirred up a lot of trouble lately."

Marcus stiffened. "If you're here to settle a score, you can turn around right now."

Victor held up his hands. "I'm not here to threaten you. I'm here because you're one of the few people in this town who's proven they have the guts to stand up to the corruption."

That caught Tyson off guard. "What do you mean by that?"

"You've exposed part of the rot in this town; the gang, the dirty cops. But you didn't get all of it. There's more. Much more."

Marcus frowned. "If you know something, spill it."

Victor shook his head. "Not yet. First, I need to know if you're serious about this. The people I'm talking about don't play games, and they don't leave loose ends. You step into this, and you'll be putting yourself, and your family, at risk again."

"I'll be the judge of that. And I'm not backing down from anyone. So either tell me what you know or get out."

For a moment, Victor just studied him, searching for any hint of hesitation. Whatever he saw must have satisfied him, because he gave a small nod and said, "Alright. But this stays between us for now."

He reached into his jacket and pulled out a manila folder, worn at the edges like it had been carried for a while. He placed it on the counter between them. Tyson, never one for patience, grabbed it first, flipping it open. Marcus leaned over his shoulder as they skimmed the contents.

Inside were a series of documents including financial records, complicated-looking ledgers, and property deeds for places all over Crest Ridge. Scattered between the paperwork were photographs. One showed a heavyset man stepping into a blacked-out SUV.

Another captured what looked like a handshake in a dim alley, both faces obscured by hats. And a third—a clear, crisp shot of a man Marcus didn't recognize. Mid-forties maybe, with slicked-back hair and a sharp suit, standing in front of what he recognized as one of the newer luxury buildings downtown.

"Who's this?" Marcus asked, tapping the photo.

Victor glanced around the open garage, then jerked his head toward the small office at the back. "Not here. Come on."

Without a word, they followed him. Marcus shut the office door behind them, closing out the noise of the shop. Tyson dropped into the battered leather chair by the desk, folder still open in his hands. Victor remained standing, his arms crossed tightly over his chest.

"Franklin Jackson," Victor said. "He's a developer. He came to Crest Ridge about five years ago and started buying up property all over town."

Marcus raised an eyebrow. "And?"

"And," he continued, "he's been working with people who don't want their names in the spotlight. People who've been quietly turning this town into their playground for drugs, money laundering, and worse."

Tyson leaned on the desk. "You're saying there's another gang running things here?"

"Not exactly," Victor said. "It's bigger than that. The gang you exposed? They were small-time players. The real power in Crest Ridge is hiding behind suits and business deals. Franklin Jones is one of them. And he's not working alone."

Marcus's mind raced. This was exactly what he had feared. The idea that even with Haynes gone, the rot in Crest Ridge wasn't finished. There were connections to city officials, law enforcement, even local businesses. It was a web of influence and corruption that seemed almost impossible to untangle.

Tyson, not buying the story, asked. "Why come to us? What's your angle?"

"Because I used to be one of them."

Marcus's eyes narrowed. "You're saying you were part of this?"

Victor nodded. "I was a fixer. A guy who made problems disappear. For years, I kept my head down, did what I was told. But then I saw what they were really doing. Families destroyed, lives ruined. I couldn't take it anymore."

"So you decided to grow a conscience," Tyson said, his voice laced with skepticism.

Victor's jaw tightened. "Believe me, I'm not proud of what I've done. But I want to make it right. That's why I'm here. I can't take these people down on my own. But you? You've already proven you're willing to fight."

Marcus studied him for a long moment. "If you're lying to me, I'll find out. And you won't like what happens."

Victor met his gaze, unflinching. "I'm not lying."

"This is a lot to take in. You're asking us to go up against some of the most powerful people in this town with nothing but a few papers and some pictures."

"It's more than that," Victor said. "I've got names, dates, records. Everything you need to expose them. But I need your help to get it out there and to make sure it sticks."

"Why us? Why not go to the authorities?"

Victor gave a bitter laugh. "Because the authorities are part of the problem. You know that better than anyone."

The folder sat on the counter like a ticking time bomb. The contents spoke of corruption that ran deeper than he'd imagined. Yet, as the minutes ticked by in silence, he couldn't shake the weight pressing on his chest.

"I know this is a lot," Victor said. "And I'm not asking you to dive in blind. Take your time. But we both know what's at stake here."

"What's at stake is my family. Every time I've gotten involved in something like this, they've paid the price. Jordan went to jail. He was kidnapped. My mom was put under surveillance like she was some criminal. I can't keep putting them in the crossfire."

"I get it. Believe me, I do. I've got people I care about too. That's why I walked away from all this in the first place. But walking away doesn't make it go away. The people we're dealing with don't stop just because you look the other way."

"I didn't say I'm looking the other way. But if I do this, I need to know what I'm walking into. No surprises."

Victor nodded slowly. "That's fair. Let me give you the short version. Franklin is the face of this operation; real estate developer, charming public persona, all that. But behind the scenes, he's laundering money for people who'd rather stay in the shadows. Drug money, mostly. The gang you exposed was just one cog in the machine. The rest of it? It's bigger. Smarter. And a hell of a lot more dangerous."

Tyson frowned. "And you think exposing him will be enough to bring it all down?"

"It's a start," Victor admitted. "But we have to be smart about it. These people have influence. They'll twist the narrative and discredit anyone who tries to take them down. That's why I came to you. You've got the community's trust and you're already in this deeper than you think."

Marcus looked away, his gaze falling on the folder again. "I don't know, man. Last time, I thought I was doing the right thing, and it almost got everyone I care about killed. I can't let that happen again."

"You don't have to decide right now. But think about this: if you don't do something, who will? How many more people are going to get hurt because these bastards think they're untouchable?"

Chapter 60

Marcus stared at the folder on the table.

Tyson shifted next to him, arms folded tight across his chest, a rare crease of worry between his brows. "You already know what he's saying is true," he said quietly. "You wouldn't be thinking this hard about it if you didn't."

Marcus dragged a hand down his face. "Yeah, I know." His voice was low, rough with the weight of the choice in front of him. "But knowing it and doing something about it are two different things. Last time... last time almost broke us. The shop, Mom, Jordan... even you. I don't want to gamble with people's lives again, Ty. Not unless I'm damn sure it's worth it."

Victor stayed silent, giving him the space to work through it, but Marcus could feel his eyes watching him, weighing his resolve. Tyson's fingers drummed a restless beat against his elbow.

"You're not wrong," Tyson said after a moment. "But you're not the same guy you were six months ago either. You learned. You got smarter. You built something. And we got your back, no matter what."

Marcus stared at the folder. In it was a list of names. Names he recognized. Names he didn't. Each one tied to the power structure that had ruled Crest Ridge from the shadows for years. Councilmen, business owners, even people in law enforcement. The very people sworn to protect and serve.

If he stepped back into this, there was no halfway. No standing on the sidelines. Either he would be all in, or he needed to walk away now and accept that someone else, maybe no one, would clean up the mess.

Victor added. "I get it. You're scared for the people you care about. You should be. Fear's not a weakness, it's a warning. But it can also be a chain, if you let it."

Marcus flexed his hands, feeling the tension in his muscles. He had spent so long fighting just to survive, to protect his family, to keep the small piece of peace he'd built here at the shop. But Victor was right about one thing. The corruption hadn't disappeared just because they had taken down Haynes. It had just gone quiet.

He thought about his family. About the kids who came to the shop for classes every week, laughing and learning in a place they finally felt safe. About the people who still whispered about injustice in the streets, too scared to say it out loud. If he stayed silent now, he was letting them down too.

Marcus let out a slow, hard breath. "Alright," he said finally, voice steady. "I'll look at the file. I'll dig. Quietly. If I find something that can't be ignored, something solid, we move. But I'm not making the same mistakes as before. No rushing in. No half-assed plans. We do it smart, and we do it together."

Tyson gave a small, relieved chuckle. "That's what I'm talking about."

Victor said. "Good. I knew you were the right man for this."

Marcus gave him a look. "Don't get it twisted. I'm doing this for Crest Ridge. Not for you."

"Understood."

Marcus picked up the folder, the weight of it heavier than it should have been, and tucked it under his arm. The decision had been made. The fear was still there, simmering beneath his skin, but it was joined by something else now. A slow, burning determination.

"One thing's for sure," Marcus said. "If they thought we were a problem before, they ain't seen nothing yet."

Tyson grinned wide, his old confidence returning. "Let's give 'em hell."

Victor's expression softened. "You're going to need that fire. Because the people we're up against? They've been in power for a long time. They won't go down easy."

Marcus opened the door to the garage, letting in the familiar sounds and smells of home. The shop was alive with the noise of tools, laughter, and community. It was everything he had fought for and everything he was willing to fight for again.

He turned back to Victor. "Then they better be ready. Because we're not backing down."

"Good. Because once we start this, there's no turning back."

Tyson stood, stretching his arms behind his head. "Guess we better stock up on coffee and patience. Sounds like it's gonna be a long few weeks."

Victor chuckled quietly. "I'll reach out when I have more. Until then, stay sharp. Watch your backs."

Marcus shook his hand firmly, then clapped Tyson on the shoulder as Victor headed out of the office and disappeared into the cooling evening air. The sound of the shop doors closing echoed through the space, leaving them alone with the heavy silence.

For a moment, neither spoke. Tyson shuffled through the folder again, shaking his head. "Man. It never ends, does it? Just when you think it's over, someone else crawls out the woodwork."

Marcus leaned against the desk, arms crossed, staring at the door Victor had just exited through. "That's how it works. People like Franklin think they're untouchable because no one's willing to fight back."

"Well," Tyson said with a grin, "they clearly haven't met us yet."

Marcus cracked a small smile but it didn't quite reach his eyes. His mind was already thinking about the risks, the people depending on him, the future he was trying to build. He thought about the shop they'd rebuilt with the community's help, the classes they taught every week now to young kids interested in mechanics. He thought about his family.

Especially Jordan.

In the six months since he'd come home, Jordan's life had started to slowly piece itself back together. He was different, quieter sometimes, more cautious, but there was light in him again. Jordan was hired at a local hardware store and was saving up to start community college in the fall. He was even coaching Ellis's varsity basketball team on weekends, something Marcus never would've imagined during those long months when he was locked away.

Jordan was rebuilding, just like all of them. And Marcus wasn't about to let someone like Franklin tear that down again.

Tyson folded the folder shut and tossed it onto the desk. "You sure about this, man?"

"I'm sure."

"Alright then. I'm with you."

They left it at that. No big speeches, no dramatic promises. Just the quiet, unshakable bond that had carried them through everything so far. Later that evening, after Tyson had left and the shop had gone still and dark, Marcus found himself back in his office. The rebuilt space smelled like fresh wood and motor oil. A new chapter, but still carrying the ghosts of the past. The manila folder sat where he'd left it, as if waiting for him to make up his mind one final time.

He sat down heavily in the chair. He flipped through the pages one more time. The property deeds, the shadowy photographs, the paper trail of corruption and greed. At the bottom of the stack was the picture of Franklin again, smirking in front of his luxury high-rise like he owned the whole damn city. Marcus stared at it for a long moment.

Then he reached into his pocket and pulled out his phone. He opened the camera app, switching it over to video mode. For a second, he just held it there, his reflection staring back at him in the darkened screen. He thought about Jordan. About his mom, who'd stood by him even when she was scared. About Tyson, who never once let him walk alone into a fight. About the community, tired of being pushed around and lied to. And about Crest Ridge—the city he loved, broken and battered but still standing.

With a deep breath, he hit record.

"My name is Marcus Carter," he began, his voice steady. "For the past year, I've been uncovering corruption in Crest Ridge. Corruption that runs deeper than most people realize. What started as a fight to clear my brother's name has turned into something much bigger. There are people in this town who are using their power to hurt others, and I can't sit by and let it happen."

He paused. "I'm just a mechanic from Crest Ridge. Nothing fancy. Not a politician, not a lawyer. Just someone who got tired of watching good people get hurt while the ones responsible walked free.

This city deserves better. My family deserves better. The kids who come into my shop every Saturday to learn how to fix an engine, they deserve better."

He gave a small, almost bitter smile.

"I don't have all the answers. And yeah, sometimes I'm scared. But I figure if you're not scared, you're not paying attention. Courage isn't about not feeling fear. It's about what you do anyway, even when your hands are shaking."

He took a breath, steadying himself for the words he knew he had to say next.

"To anyone out there watching this: if you're tired of being afraid, if you're tired of letting people like Franklin Jones write the rules while the rest of us pay the price, then stand with me. Because this time, we're not just exposing one man. We're tearing the whole rotten system out by the roots."

His gaze locked on the camera, fierce and unflinching.

"This is only the beginning."

He ended the recording, staring at the screen for a moment before uploading the video to his social media accounts. Not long after posting the video, his phone buzzed with a notification. It was a direct message from an unknown account.

"You've got guts, Carter. But this fight is bigger than you know. If you're serious about taking this on, meet me at the old mill tomorrow night. Midnight. Come alone."

Marcus stared at the message, his heart pounding. The path ahead was uncertain, but one thing was clear: there was no turning back now. As he locked the door to the shop that night, Marcus felt a strange sense of clarity. He wasn't sure what the future held, but he felt like he was exactly where he was supposed to be. The corruption in Crest Ridge would not end overnight. But with every step he took, he was determined to make a difference. Even if it meant becoming the reluctant hero the town needed.